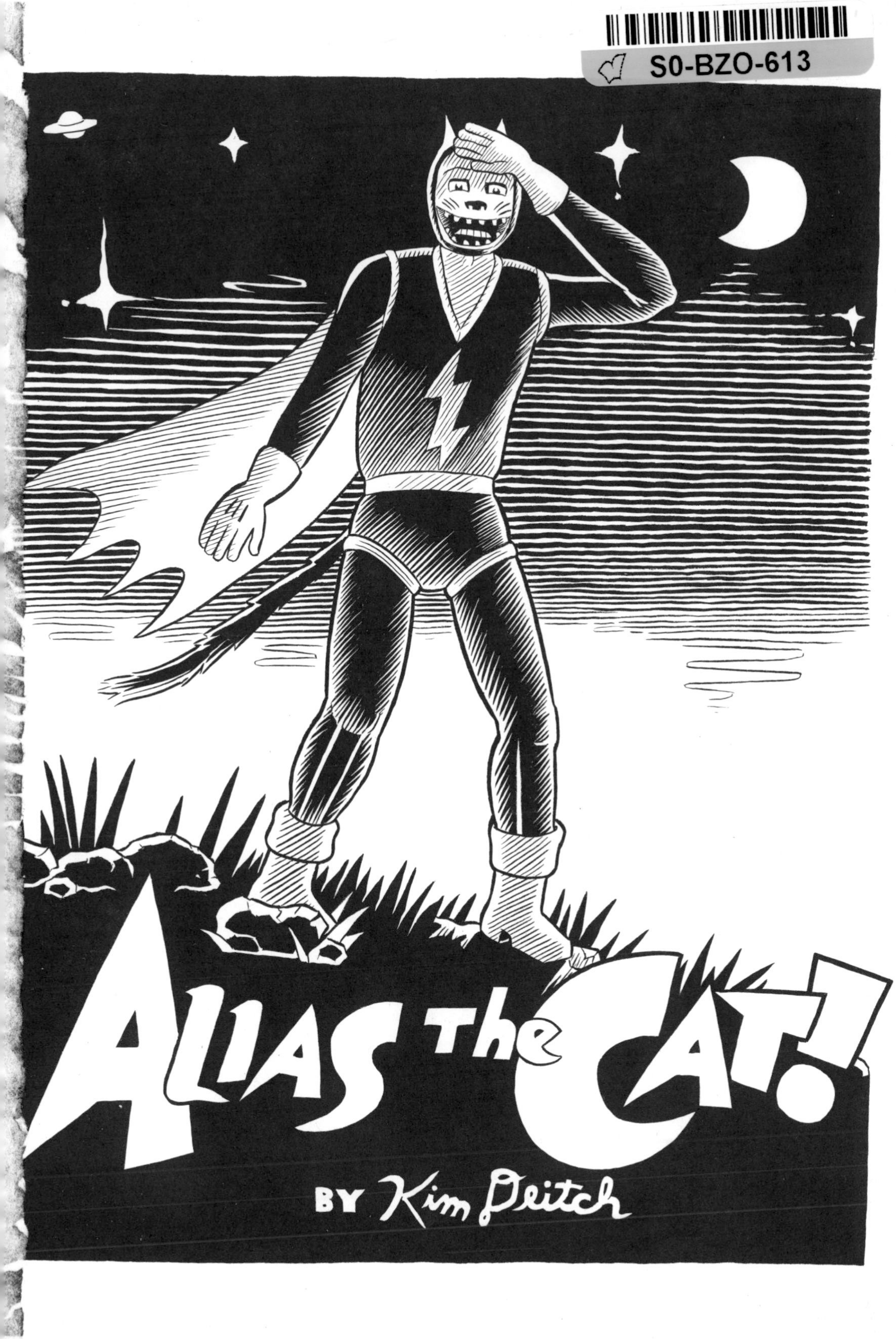
ALIAS the CAT!
BY Kim Deitch

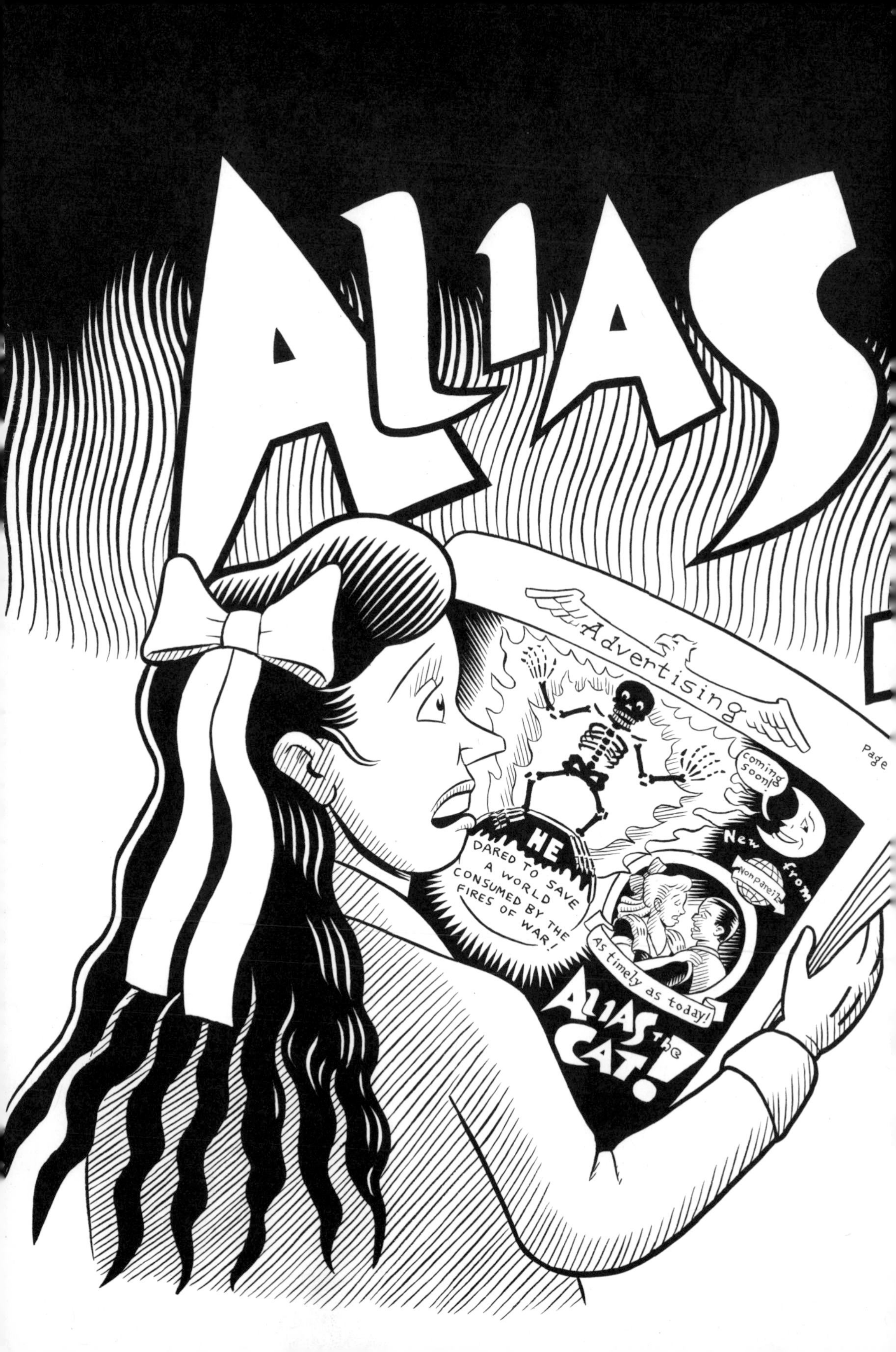
ALIAS
Advertising
Page
Coming Soon!
HE DARED TO SAVE A WORLD CONSUMED BY THE FIRES OF WAR!
New from Nonpareil
As timely as today!
ALIAS the CAT!

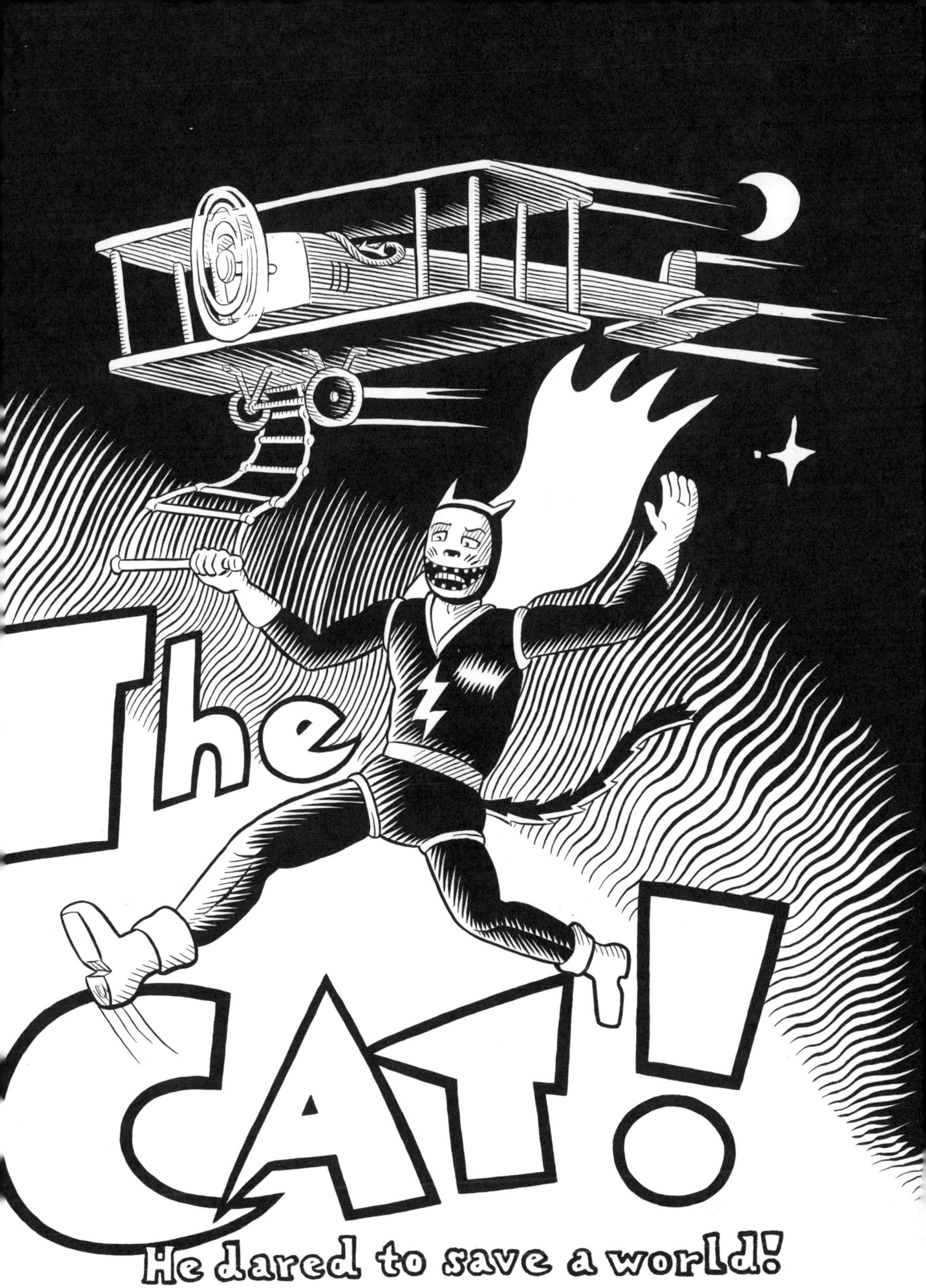
The CAT!

He dared to save a world!

Kim Deitch

PANTHEON BOOKS, NEW YORK

This is a work of fiction. Names, characters, places, and inci-
dents either are the product of the author's imagination or are
used fictitiously. Any resemblance to actual persons, living or
dead, events, or locales is entirely coincidental.
Copyright© 2002 Fantagraphics Books, Inc., and Kim Deitch.
Copyright© 2004 Kim Deitch. Copyright© 2005 Kim Deitch.
Copyright© 2007 Kim Deitch.
All rights reserved. Published in the United States by Pantheon
Books, a division of Random House, inc., New York, and in Can-
ada by Random House of Canada Limited, Toronto.
Pantheon Books and colophon are registered trademarks of Random House Inc.

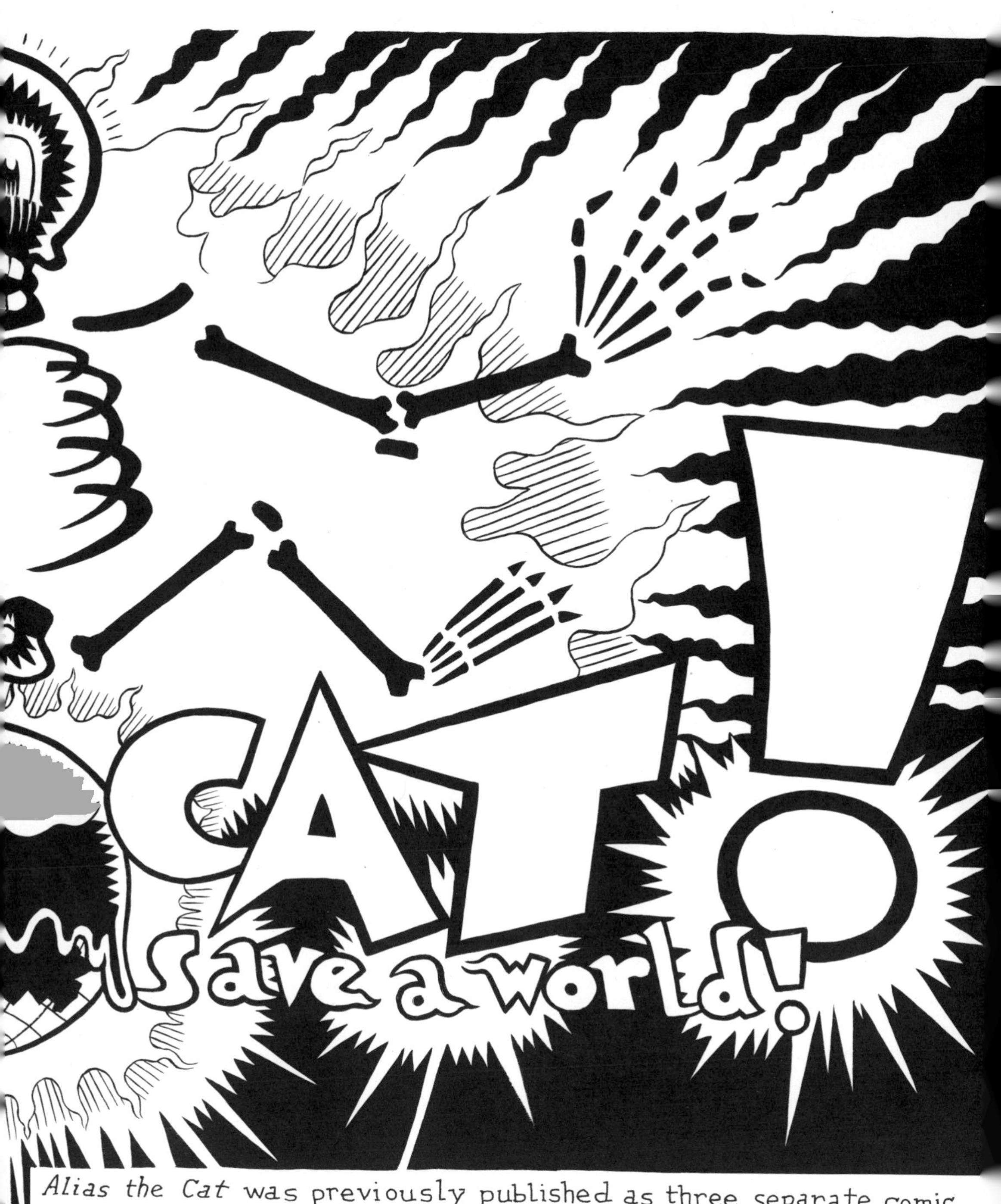
CAT!
save a world!

Alias the Cat was previously published as three separate comic books under the names *The Stuff of Dreams*, May 2002; *The Stuff of Dreams #2*, May 2004; and *The Stuff of Dreams #3*, August 2005, respectively.

Library of Congress Cataloguing-in-Publication Data Deitch, Kim, 1944
p. cm.
ISBN-13: 978-0-375-42431-1
ISBN-10: 0-375-42431-8
1. Graphic novels. I. Title
PN6727. D383A45 2007
741.5—dc22 2006048586

www.pantheonbooks.com
Book design by Chip Kidd and Kim Deitch
Printed in Canada
First Edition
9 8 7 6 5 4 3 2 1

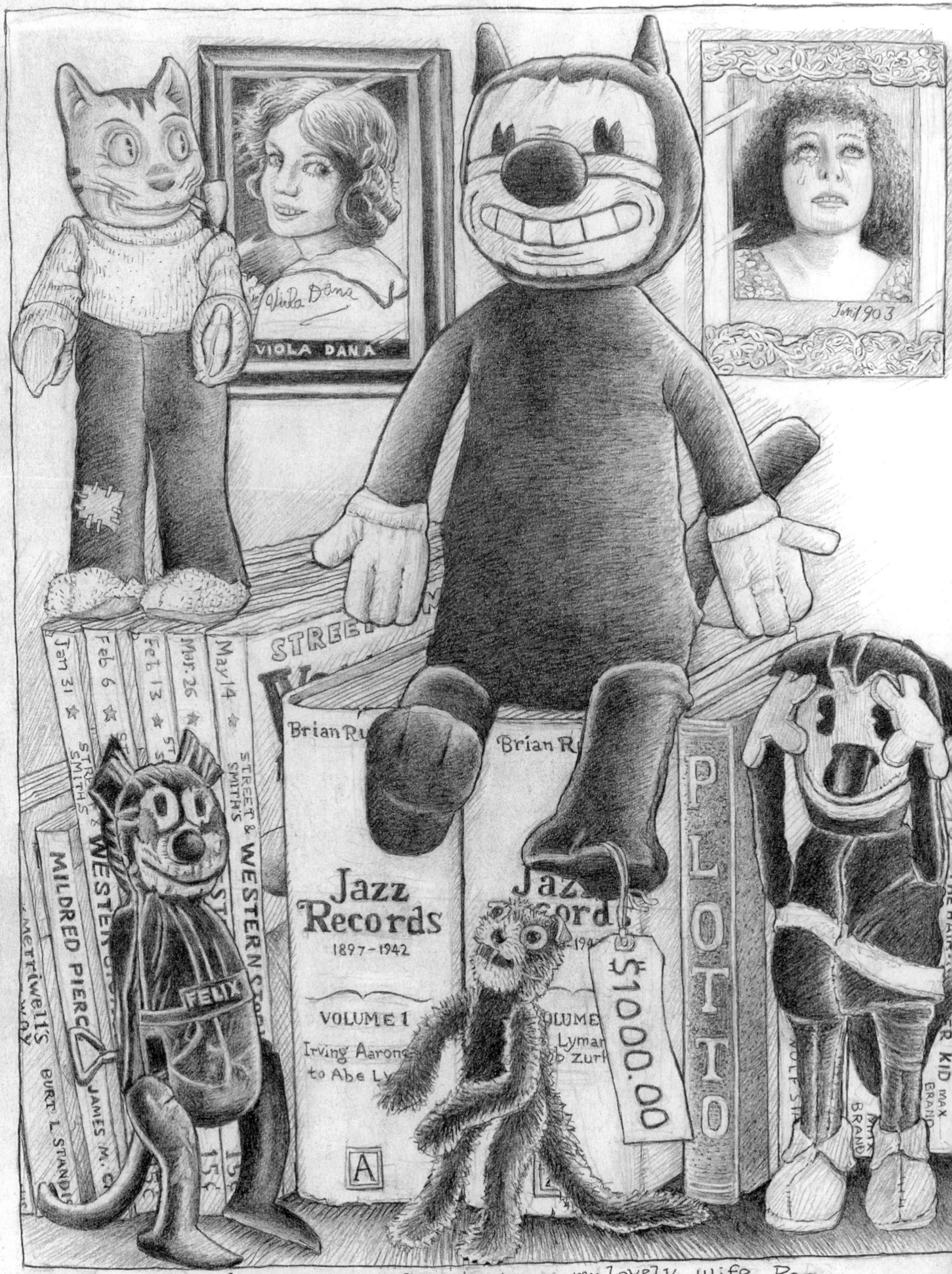

VIOLA DANA
Jan 31
Feb 6
Feb 13
Mar 26
May 14
STREET & SMITH'S
Jazz Records
1897 - 1942
VOLUME 1
FELIX
$1000.00
PLOTTO
MAX BRAND

This book is dedicated to my best pal and co-adventurer, my lovely wife, Pam.

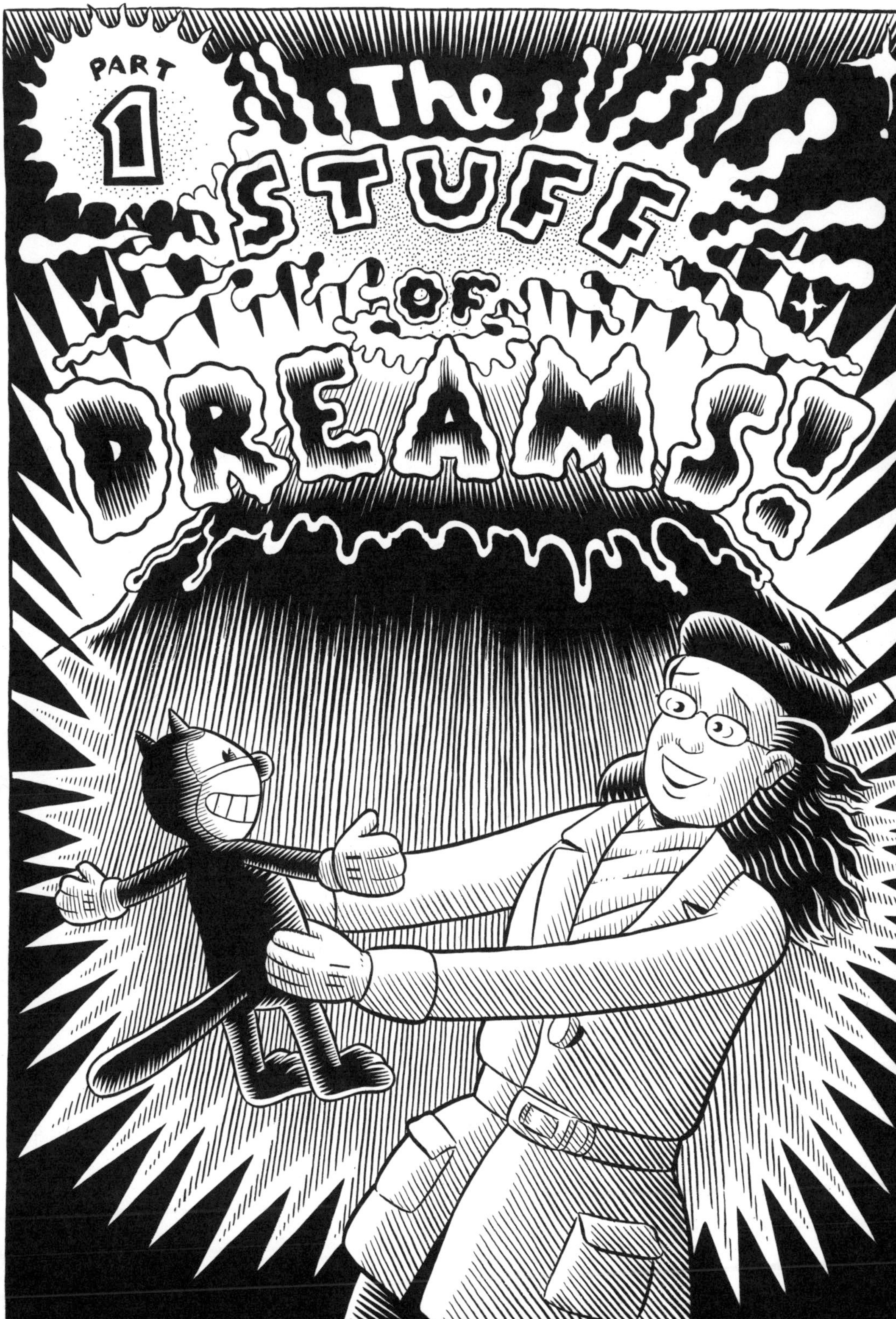
PART 1
The STUFF OF DREAMS!

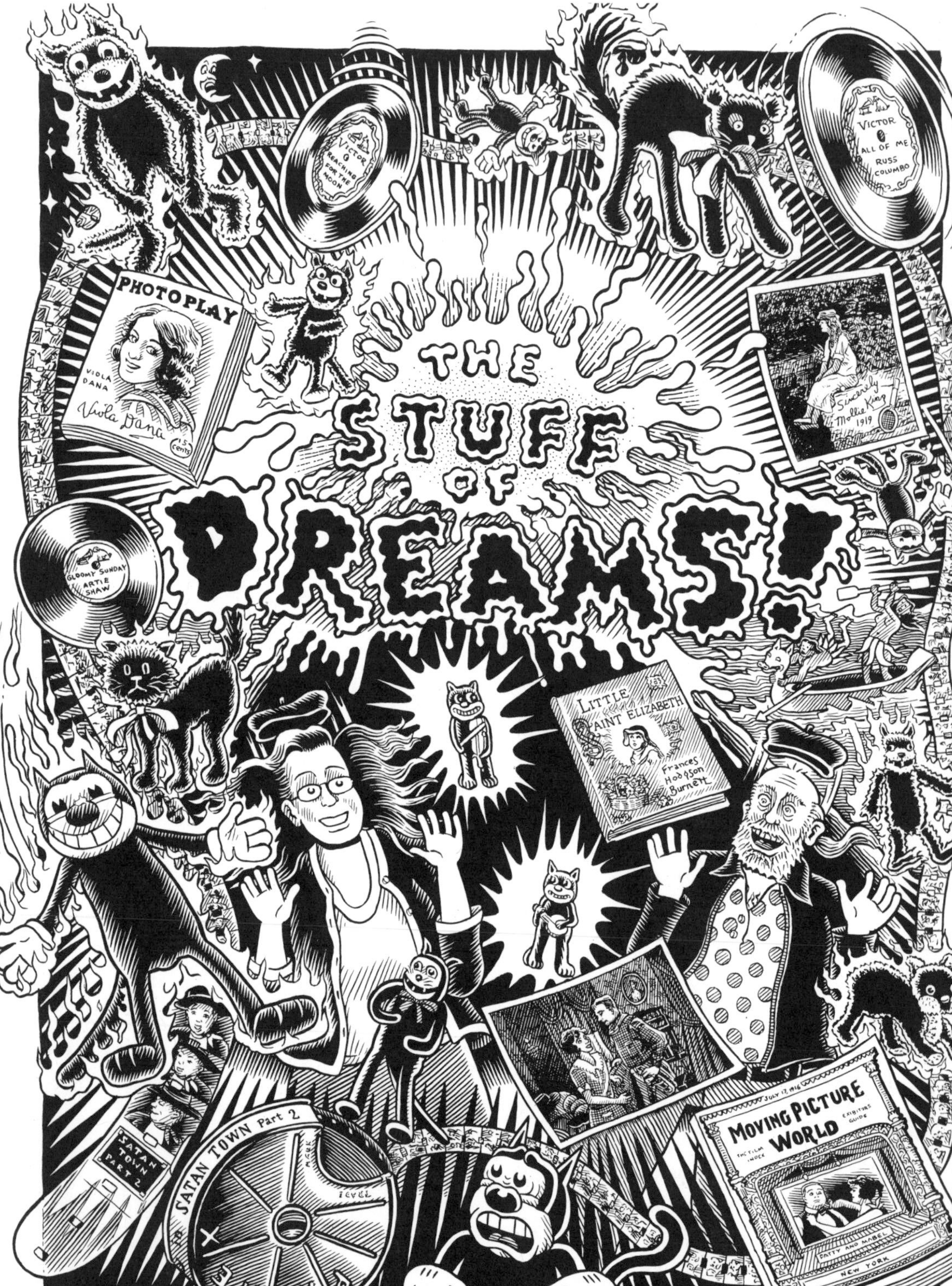
THE STUFF OF DREAMS!
VICTOR
REACHING FOR THE MOON
VICTOR
ALL OF ME
RUSS COLUMBO
PHOTOPLAY
VIOLA DANA
Viola Dana
15 cents
Sincerely Mollie King 1919
GLOOMY SUNDAY
ARTIE SHAW
LITTLE SAINT ELIZABETH
Frances Hodgson Burnett
SATAN TOWN PART 2
SATAN TOWN Part 2
PATHE
JULY 15, 1916
MOVING PICTURE WORLD
EXIBITORS GUIDE
THE FILM INDEX
FATTY AND MABEL
NEW YORK

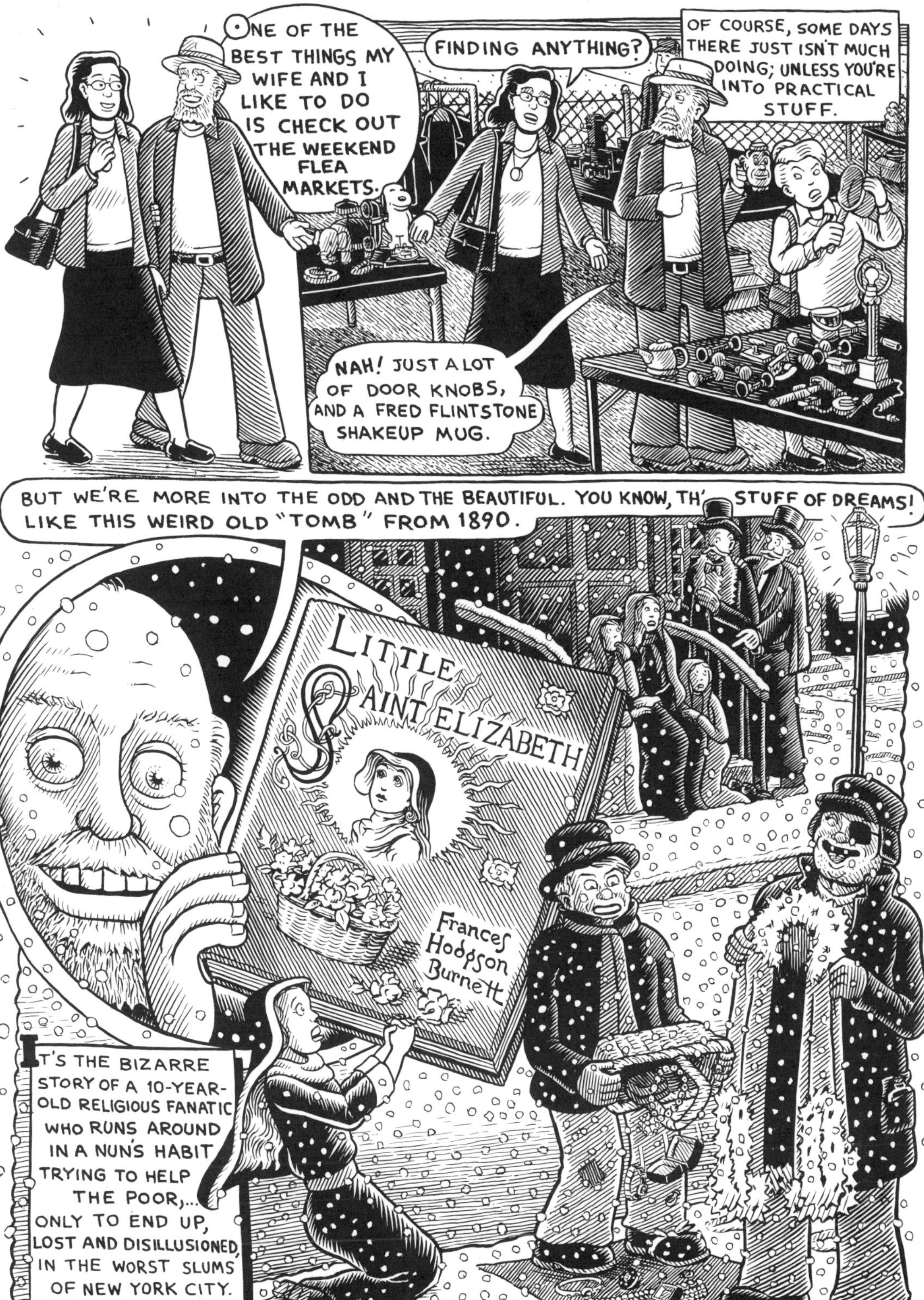
ONE OF THE BEST THINGS MY WIFE AND I LIKE TO DO IS CHECK OUT THE WEEKEND FLEA MARKETS.
FINDING ANYTHING?
OF COURSE, SOME DAYS THERE JUST ISN'T MUCH DOING; UNLESS YOU'RE INTO PRACTICAL STUFF.
NAH! JUST A LOT OF DOOR KNOBS, AND A FRED FLINTSTONE SHAKEUP MUG.
BUT WE'RE MORE INTO THE ODD AND THE BEAUTIFUL. YOU KNOW, TH' STUFF OF DREAMS! LIKE THIS WEIRD OLD "TOMB" FROM 1890.
LITTLE SAINT ELIZABETH
Frances Hodgson Burnett
IT'S THE BIZARRE STORY OF A 10-YEAR-OLD RELIGIOUS FANATIC WHO RUNS AROUND IN A NUN'S HABIT TRYING TO HELP THE POOR,... ONLY TO END UP, LOST AND DISILLUSIONED, IN THE WORST SLUMS OF NEW YORK CITY.

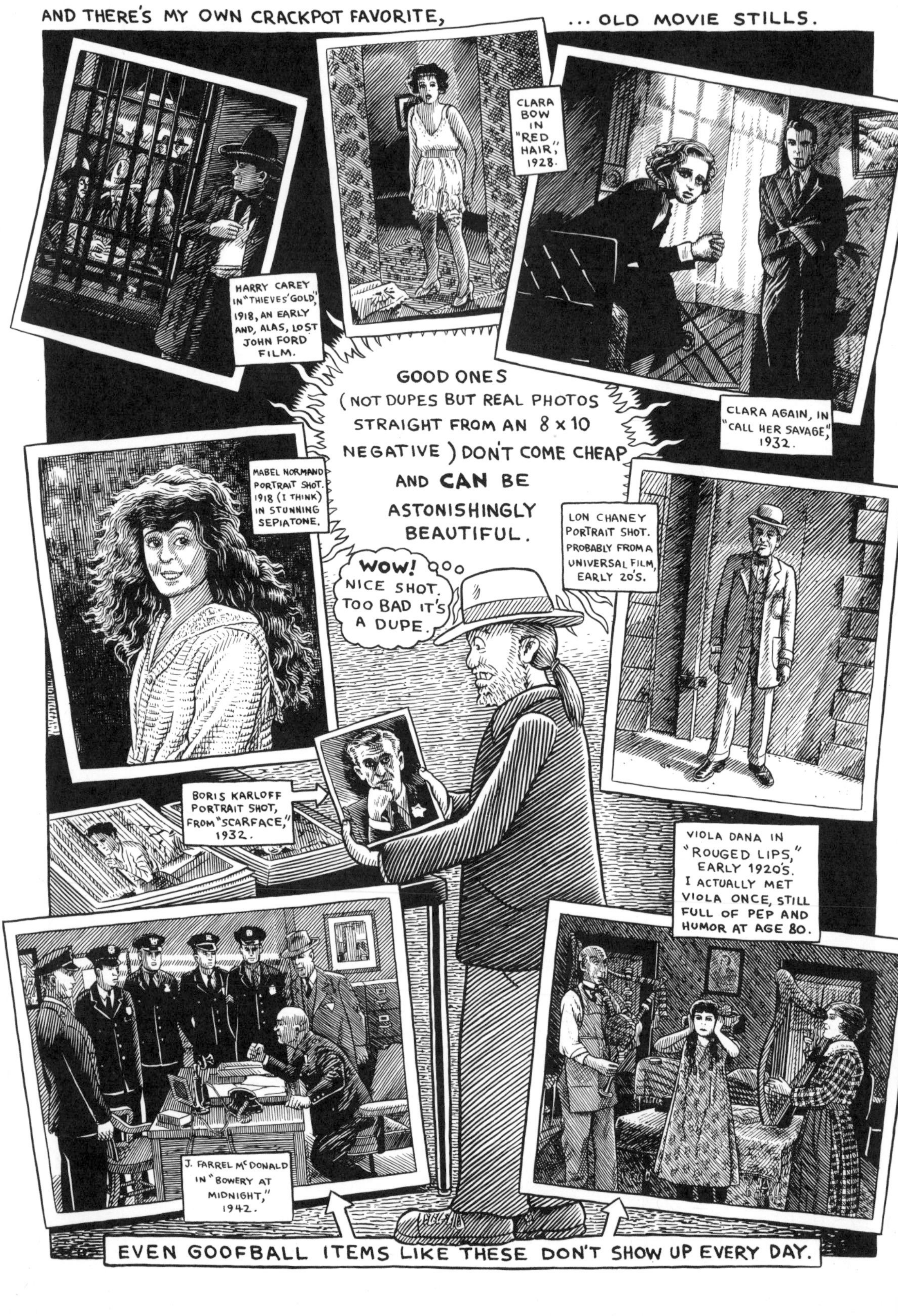
AND THERE'S MY OWN CRACKPOT FAVORITE, ... OLD MOVIE STILLS.
HARRY CAREY IN "THIEVES' GOLD," 1918, AN EARLY AND, ALAS, LOST JOHN FORD FILM.
CLARA BOW IN "RED HAIR," 1928.
CLARA AGAIN, IN "CALL HER SAVAGE," 1932.
GOOD ONES (NOT DUPES BUT REAL PHOTOS STRAIGHT FROM AN 8 x 10 NEGATIVE) DON'T COME CHEAP AND CAN BE ASTONISHINGLY BEAUTIFUL.
MABEL NORMAND PORTRAIT SHOT. 1918 (I THINK) IN STUNNING SEPIATONE.
LON CHANEY PORTRAIT SHOT. PROBABLY FROM A UNIVERSAL FILM, EARLY 20'S.
WOW! NICE SHOT. TOO BAD IT'S A DUPE.
BORIS KARLOFF PORTRAIT SHOT, FROM "SCARFACE," 1932.
VIOLA DANA IN "ROUGED LIPS," EARLY 1920'S. I ACTUALLY MET VIOLA ONCE, STILL FULL OF PEP AND HUMOR AT AGE 80.
J. FARREL McDONALD IN "BOWERY AT MIDNIGHT," 1942.
EVEN GOOFBALL ITEMS LIKE THESE DON'T SHOW UP EVERY DAY.

OR THERE'S THE FILMS THEMSELVES; LIKE "SATAN TOWN," STARRING HARRY CAREY, APPARENTLY LOST EXCEPT FOR A CONDENSED VERSION ON 9.5 MILLIMETER FILM. *

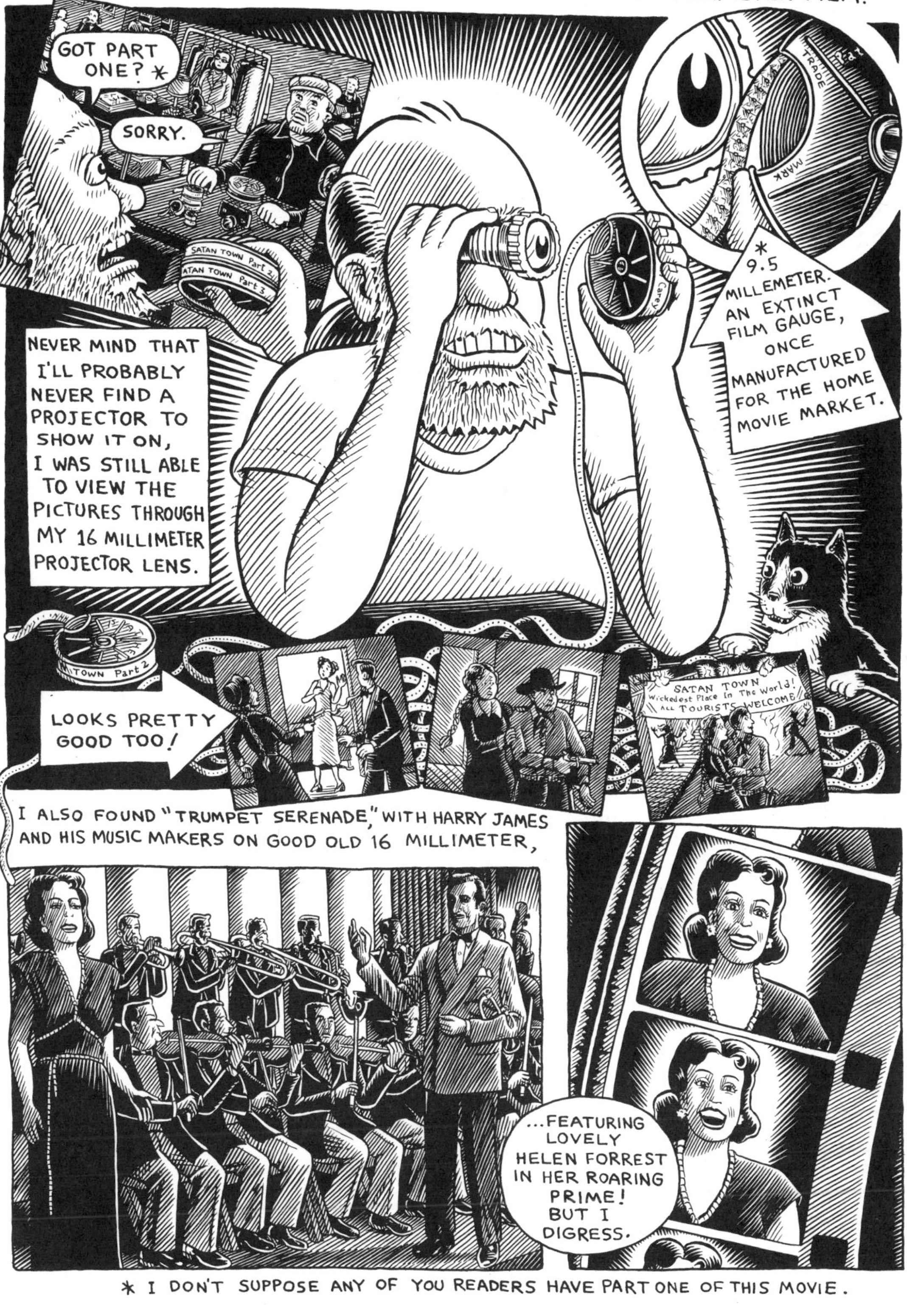

* I DON'T SUPPOSE ANY OF YOU READERS HAVE PART ONE OF THIS MOVIE.

BUT THIS STORY CONCERNS MY WIFE'S BIG FLEA MARKET PASSION, OLD STUFFED CAT TOYS.
AND I'M NOT TALKING ABOUT BEANIE BABIES EITHER.

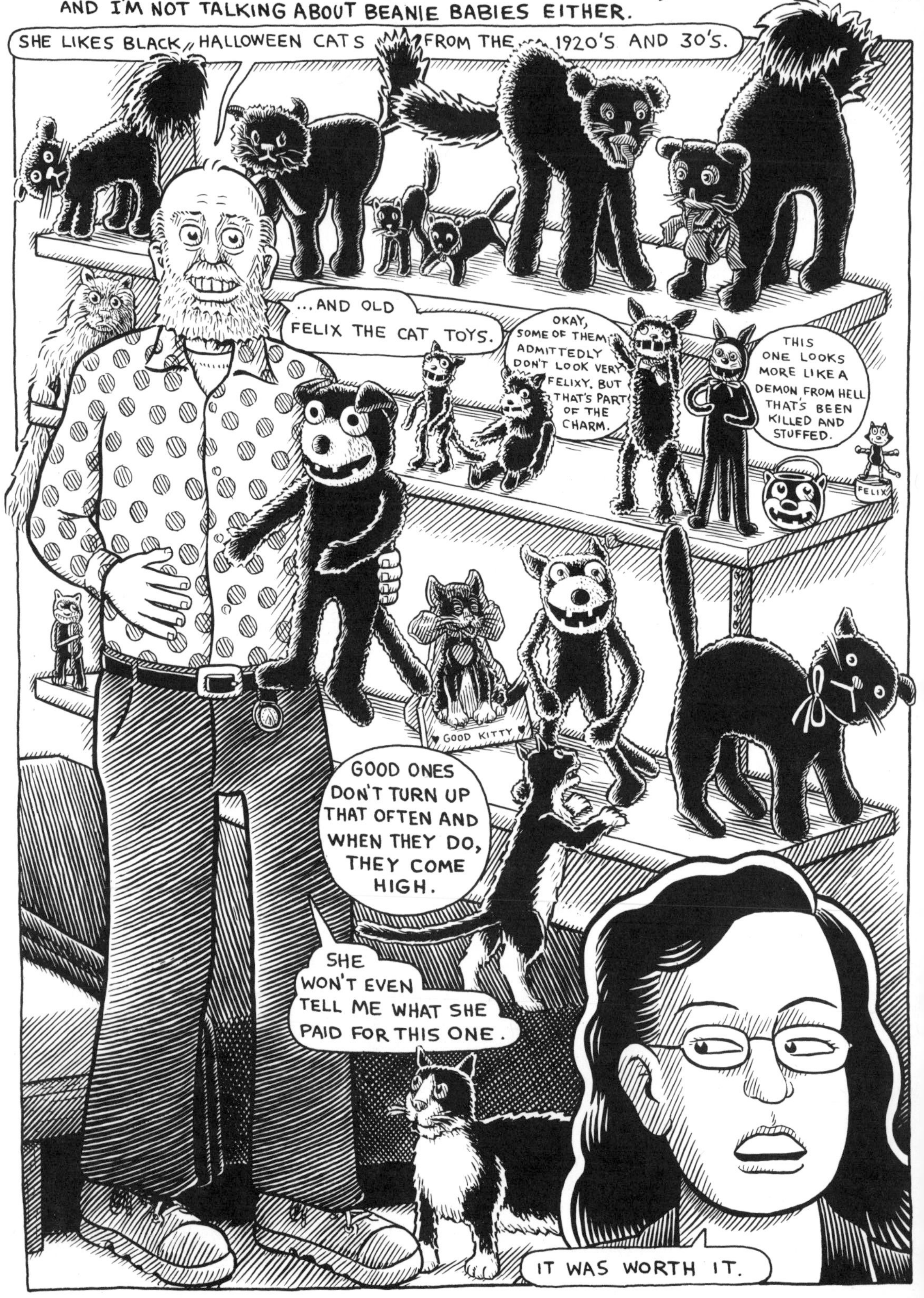
SHE LIKES BLACK HALLOWEEN CATS FROM THE 1920'S AND 30'S.
...AND OLD FELIX THE CAT TOYS.
OKAY, SOME OF THEM ADMITTEDLY DON'T LOOK VERY FELIXY. BUT THAT'S PART OF THE CHARM.
THIS ONE LOOKS MORE LIKE A DEMON FROM HELL THAT'S BEEN KILLED AND STUFFED.
FELIX
GOOD KITTY
GOOD ONES DON'T TURN UP THAT OFTEN AND WHEN THEY DO, THEY COME HIGH.
SHE WON'T EVEN TELL ME WHAT SHE PAID FOR THIS ONE.
IT WAS WORTH IT.

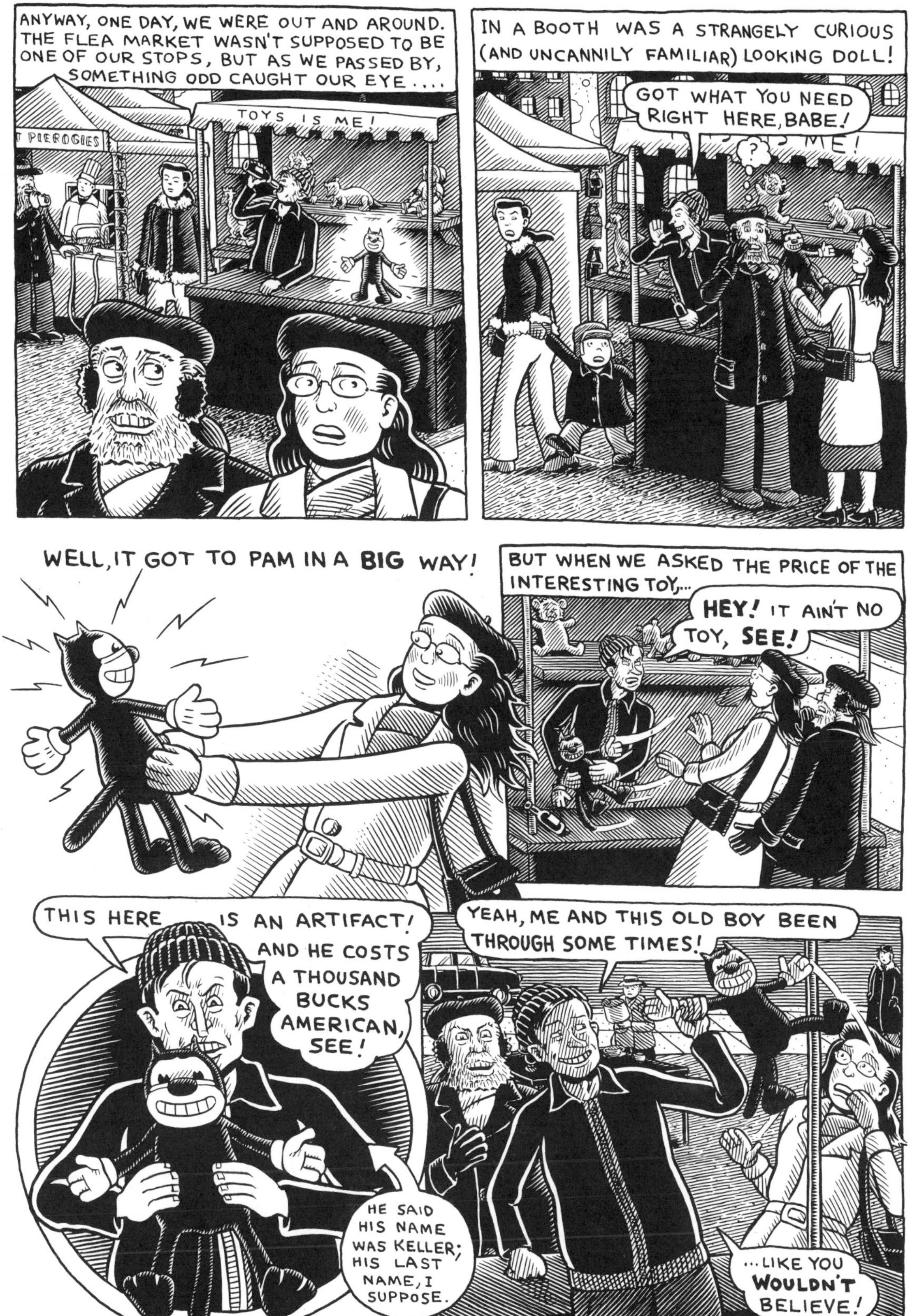

ANYWAY, ONE DAY, WE WERE OUT AND AROUND. THE FLEA MARKET WASN'T SUPPOSED TO BE ONE OF OUR STOPS, BUT AS WE PASSED BY, SOMETHING ODD CAUGHT OUR EYE....
PIEROGIES
TOYS IS ME!
IN A BOOTH WAS A STRANGELY CURIOUS (AND UNCANNILY FAMILIAR) LOOKING DOLL!
GOT WHAT YOU NEED RIGHT HERE, BABE!
?
WELL, IT GOT TO PAM IN A **BIG** WAY!
BUT WHEN WE ASKED THE PRICE OF THE INTERESTING TOY,...
HEY! IT AIN'T NO TOY, **SEE!**
THIS HERE IS AN ARTIFACT!
AND HE COSTS A THOUSAND BUCKS AMERICAN, SEE!
HE SAID HIS NAME WAS KELLER; HIS LAST NAME, I SUPPOSE.
YEAH, ME AND THIS OLD BOY BEEN THROUGH SOME TIMES!
...LIKE YOU **WOULDN'T** BELIEVE!

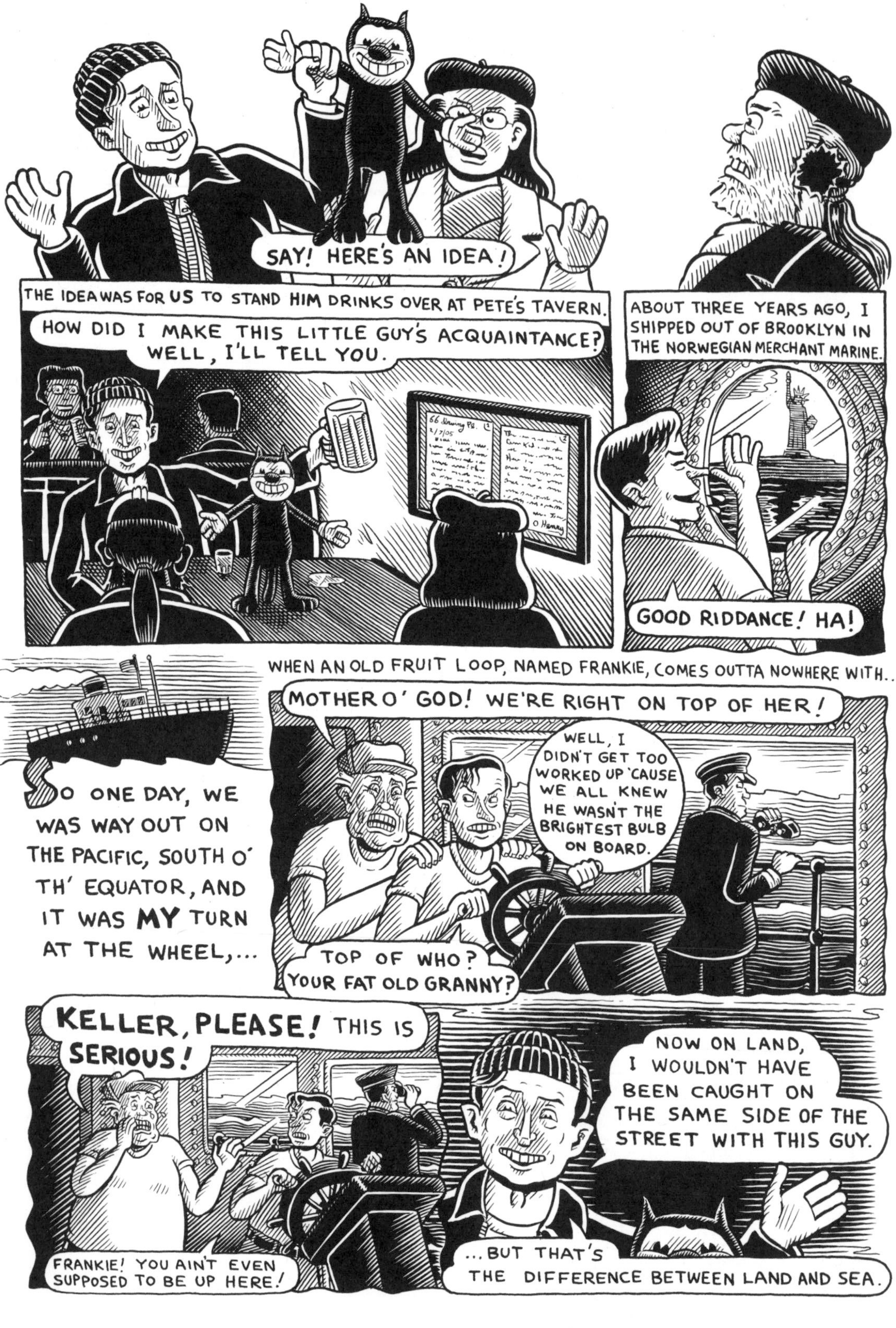
SAY! HERE'S AN IDEA!
THE IDEA WAS FOR US TO STAND HIM DRINKS OVER AT PETE'S TAVERN.
HOW DID I MAKE THIS LITTLE GUY'S ACQUAINTANCE? WELL, I'LL TELL YOU.
66 Irving Pl.
2/7/05
O Henry
ABOUT THREE YEARS AGO, I SHIPPED OUT OF BROOKLYN IN THE NORWEGIAN MERCHANT MARINE.
GOOD RIDDANCE! HA!
SO ONE DAY, WE WAS WAY OUT ON THE PACIFIC, SOUTH O' TH' EQUATOR, AND IT WAS MY TURN AT THE WHEEL,...
WHEN AN OLD FRUIT LOOP, NAMED FRANKIE, COMES OUTTA NOWHERE WITH...
MOTHER O' GOD! WE'RE RIGHT ON TOP OF HER!
WELL, I DIDN'T GET TOO WORKED UP 'CAUSE WE ALL KNEW HE WASN'T THE BRIGHTEST BULB ON BOARD.
TOP OF WHO? YOUR FAT OLD GRANNY?
KELLER, PLEASE! THIS IS SERIOUS!
FRANKIE! YOU AIN'T EVEN SUPPOSED TO BE UP HERE!
NOW ON LAND, I WOULDN'T HAVE BEEN CAUGHT ON THE SAME SIDE OF THE STREET WITH THIS GUY.
...BUT THAT'S THE DIFFERENCE BETWEEN LAND AND SEA.

BESIDES, HE WAS THE ONLY OTHER YANK ON THAT NORWEGIAN TRAMP, OUTSIDE OF ME!

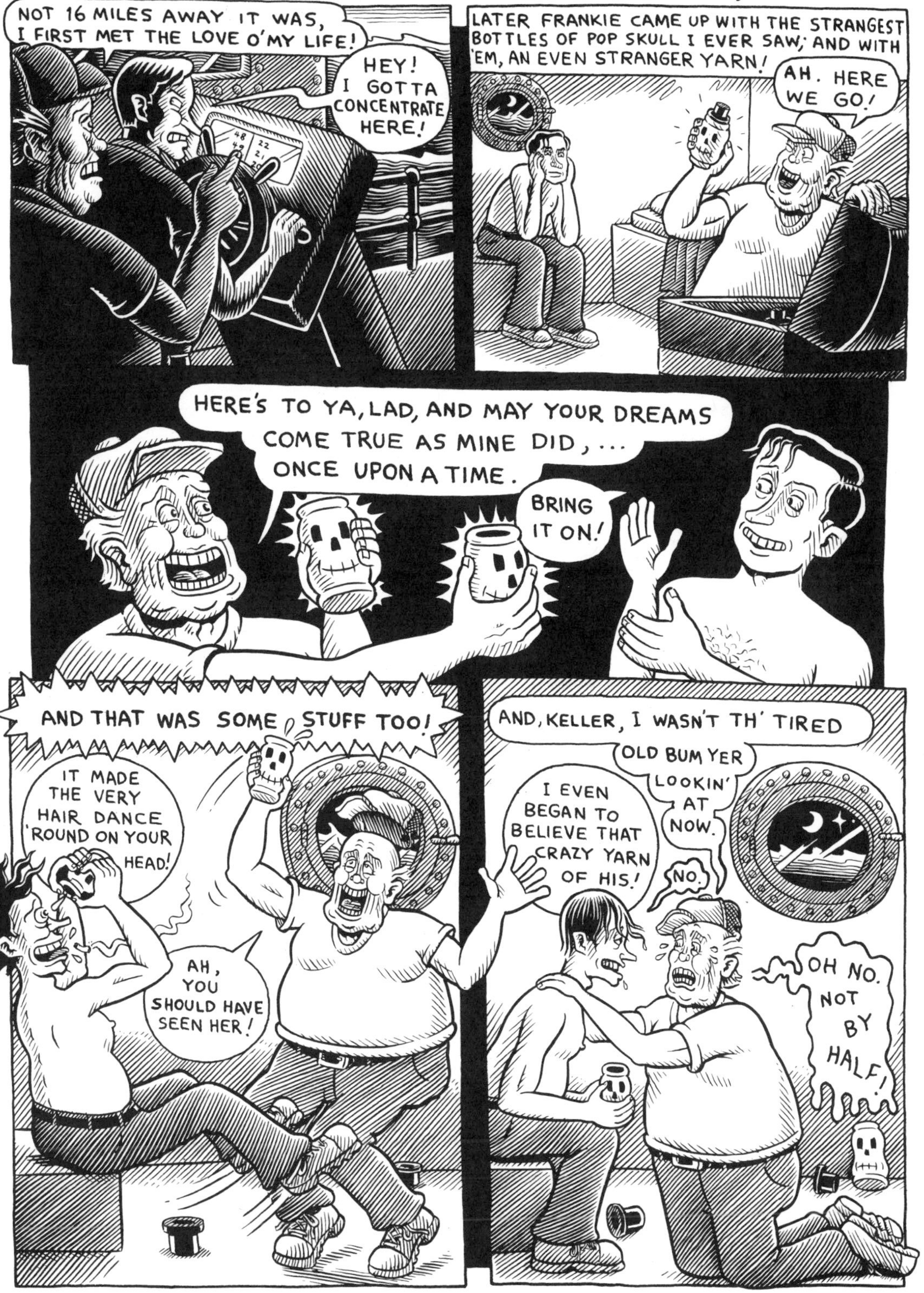
NOT 16 MILES AWAY IT WAS, I FIRST MET THE LOVE O'MY LIFE!
HEY! I GOTTA CONCENTRATE HERE!
LATER FRANKIE CAME UP WITH THE STRANGEST BOTTLES OF POP SKULL I EVER SAW; AND WITH 'EM, AN EVEN STRANGER YARN!
AH. HERE WE GO!
HERE'S TO YA, LAD, AND MAY YOUR DREAMS COME TRUE AS MINE DID, ... ONCE UPON A TIME.
BRING IT ON!
AND THAT WAS SOME STUFF TOO!
IT MADE THE VERY HAIR DANCE 'ROUND ON YOUR HEAD!
AH, YOU SHOULD HAVE SEEN HER!
AND, KELLER, I WASN'T TH' TIRED
OLD BUM YER LOOKIN' AT NOW.
I EVEN BEGAN TO BELIEVE THAT CRAZY YARN OF HIS!
NO.
OH NO. NOT BY HALF!

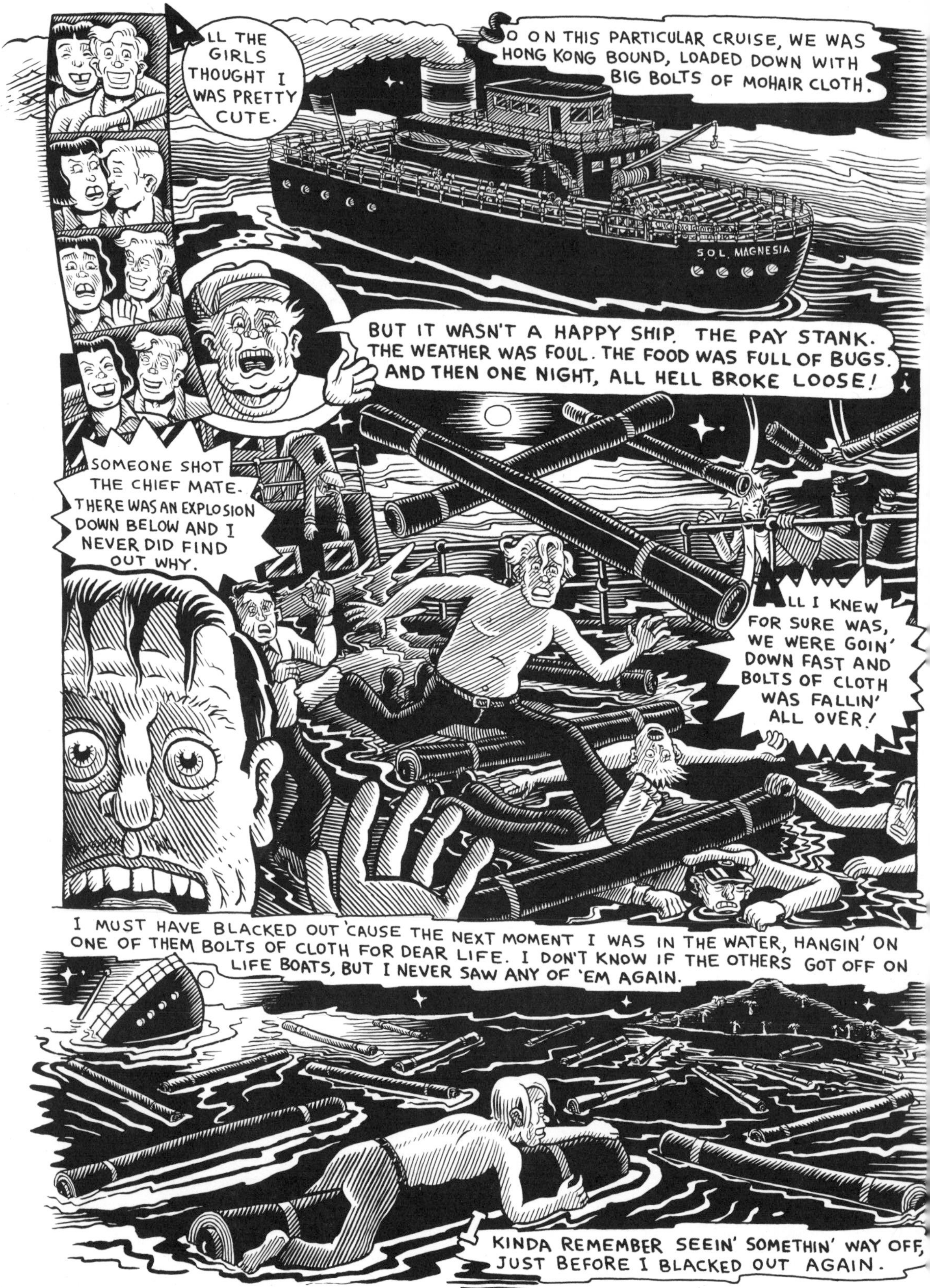
ALL THE GIRLS THOUGHT I WAS PRETTY CUTE.
SO ON THIS PARTICULAR CRUISE, WE WAS HONG KONG BOUND, LOADED DOWN WITH BIG BOLTS OF MOHAIR CLOTH.
S.O.L. MAGNESIA
BUT IT WASN'T A HAPPY SHIP. THE PAY STANK. THE WEATHER WAS FOUL. THE FOOD WAS FULL OF BUGS. AND THEN ONE NIGHT, ALL HELL BROKE LOOSE!
SOMEONE SHOT THE CHIEF MATE. THERE WAS AN EXPLOSION DOWN BELOW AND I NEVER DID FIND OUT WHY.
ALL I KNEW FOR SURE WAS, WE WERE GOIN' DOWN FAST AND BOLTS OF CLOTH WAS FALLIN' ALL OVER!
I MUST HAVE BLACKED OUT 'CAUSE THE NEXT MOMENT I WAS IN THE WATER, HANGIN' ON ONE OF THEM BOLTS OF CLOTH FOR DEAR LIFE. I DON'T KNOW IF THE OTHERS GOT OFF ON LIFE BOATS, BUT I NEVER SAW ANY OF 'EM AGAIN.
I KINDA REMEMBER SEEIN' SOMETHIN' WAY OFF, JUST BEFORE I BLACKED OUT AGAIN.

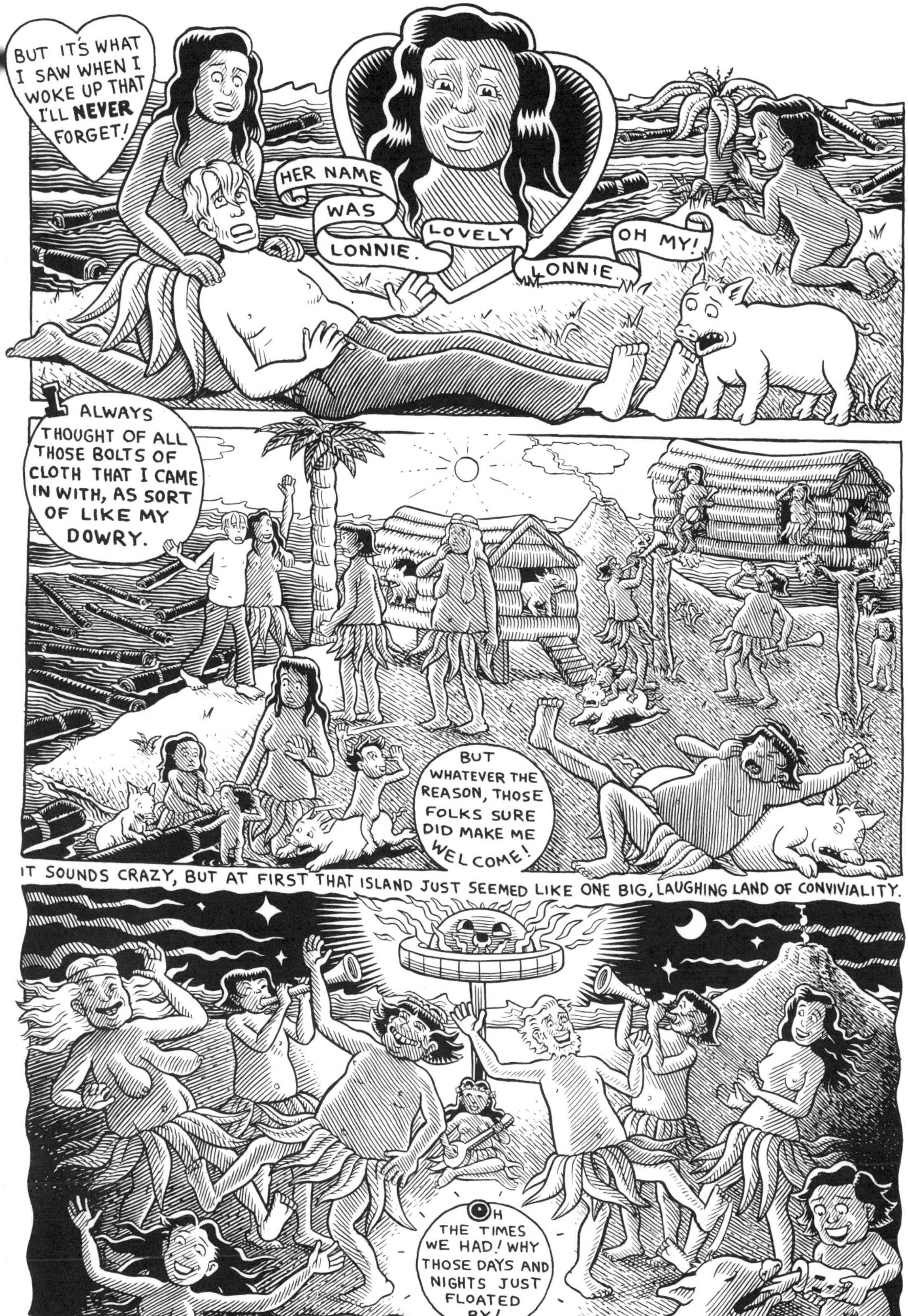

BUT IT'S WHAT I SAW WHEN I WOKE UP THAT I'LL NEVER FORGET!
HER NAME WAS LONNIE.
LOVELY LONNIE.
OH MY!
I ALWAYS THOUGHT OF ALL THOSE BOLTS OF CLOTH THAT I CAME IN WITH, AS SORT OF LIKE MY DOWRY.
BUT WHATEVER THE REASON, THOSE FOLKS SURE DID MAKE ME WELCOME!
IT SOUNDS CRAZY, BUT AT FIRST THAT ISLAND JUST SEEMED LIKE ONE BIG, LAUGHING LAND OF CONVIVIALITY.
OH THE TIMES WE HAD! WHY THOSE DAYS AND NIGHTS JUST FLOATED BY!

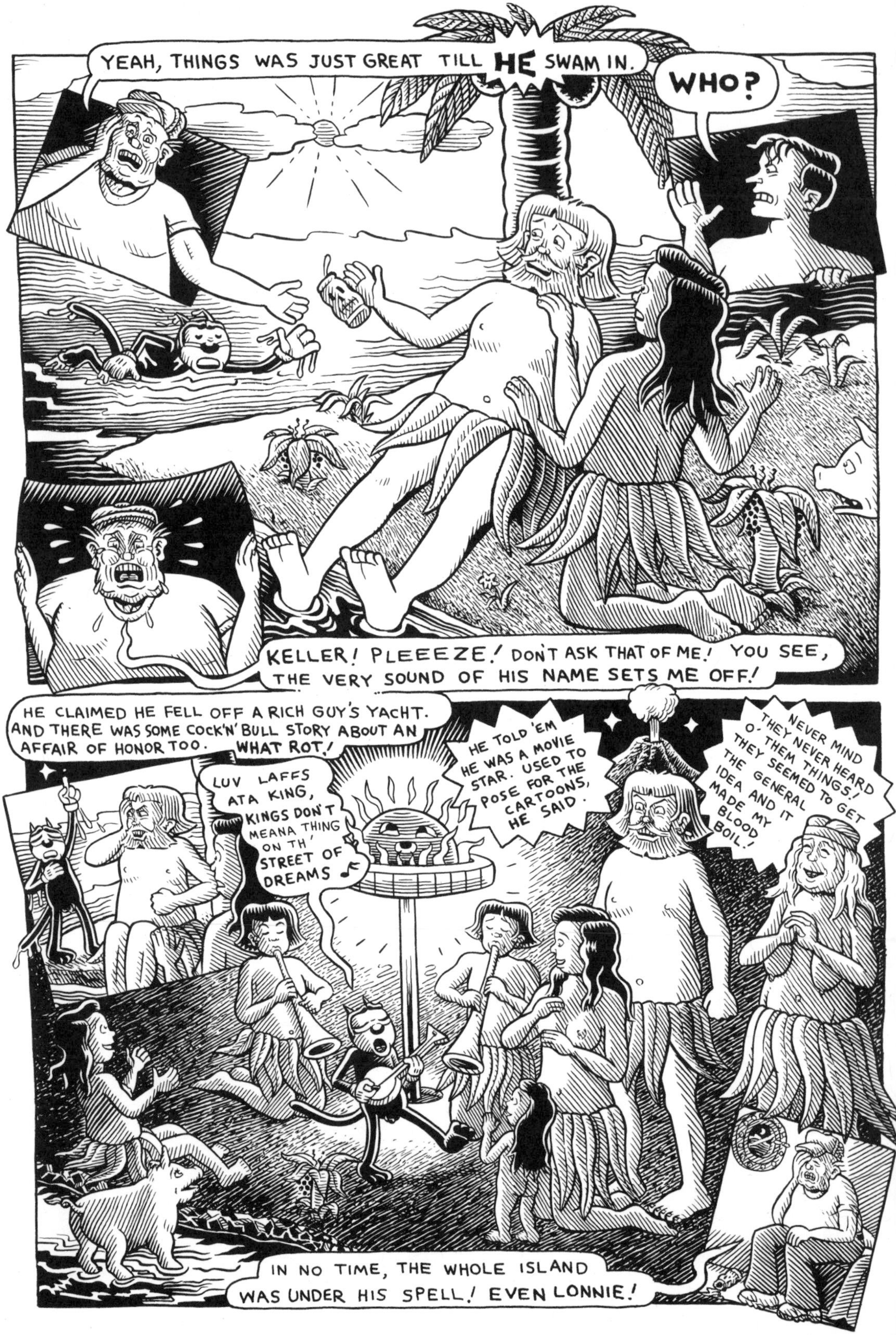
YEAH, THINGS WAS JUST GREAT TILL HE SWAM IN.
WHO?
KELLER! PLEEEZE! DON'T ASK THAT OF ME! YOU SEE, THE VERY SOUND OF HIS NAME SETS ME OFF!
HE CLAIMED HE FELL OFF A RICH GUY'S YACHT. AND THERE WAS SOME COCK'N' BULL STORY ABOUT AN AFFAIR OF HONOR TOO. WHAT ROT!
LUV LAFFS ATA KING, KINGS DON'T MEANA THING ON TH' STREET OF DREAMS
HE TOLD 'EM HE WAS A MOVIE STAR. USED TO POSE FOR THE CARTOONS, HE SAID.
NEVER MIND THEY NEVER HEARD O' THEM THINGS! THEY SEEMED TO GET THE GENERAL IDEA AND IT MADE MY BLOOD BOIL!
IN NO TIME, THE WHOLE ISLAND WAS UNDER HIS SPELL! EVEN LONNIE!

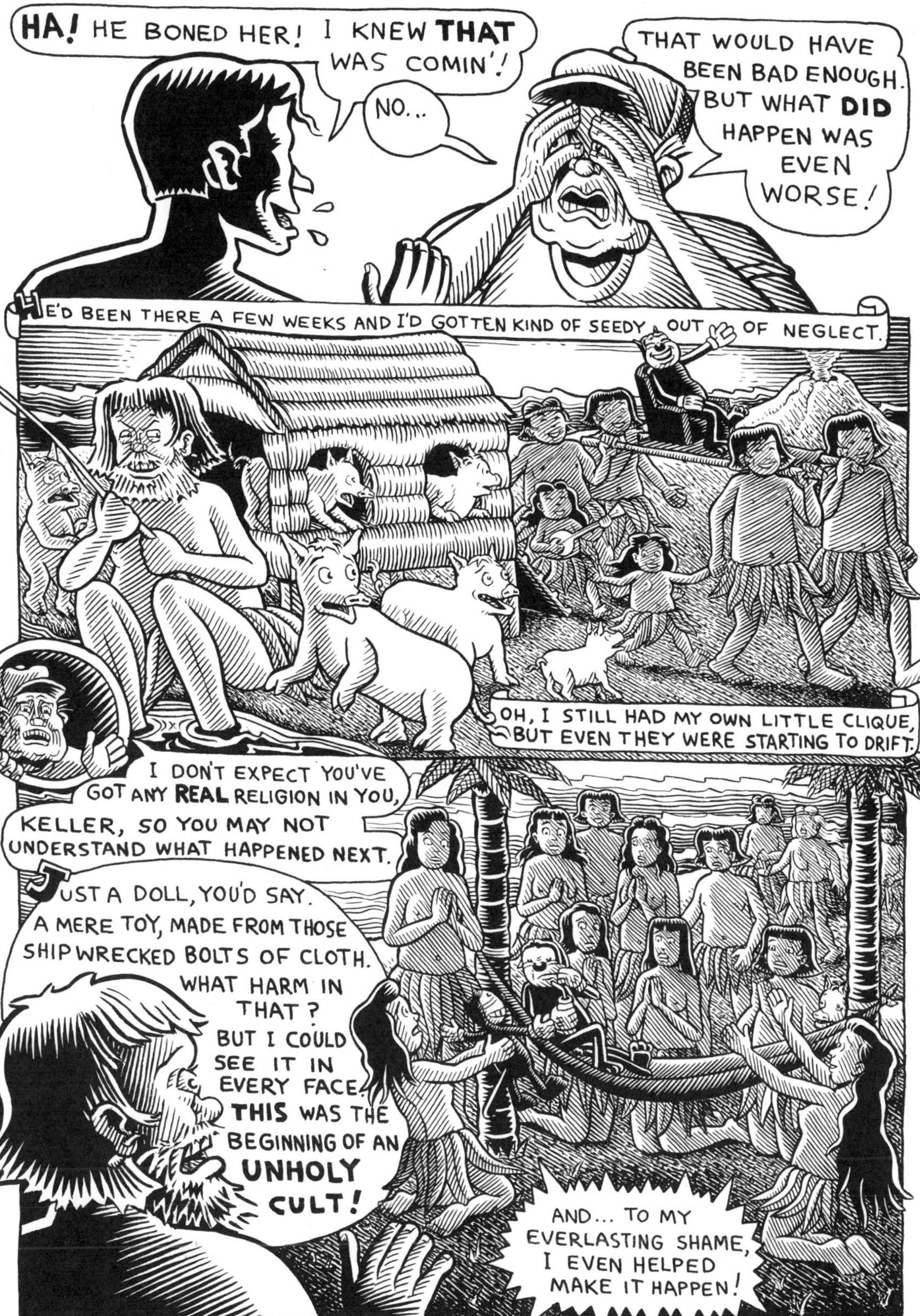
HA! HE BONED HER! I KNEW THAT WAS COMIN'!
NO...
THAT WOULD HAVE BEEN BAD ENOUGH. BUT WHAT DID HAPPEN WAS EVEN WORSE!
HE'D BEEN THERE A FEW WEEKS AND I'D GOTTEN KIND OF SEEDY OUT OF NEGLECT.
OH, I STILL HAD MY OWN LITTLE CLIQUE, BUT EVEN THEY WERE STARTING TO DRIFT.
I DON'T EXPECT YOU'VE GOT ANY REAL RELIGION IN YOU, KELLER, SO YOU MAY NOT UNDERSTAND WHAT HAPPENED NEXT.
JUST A DOLL, YOU'D SAY. A MERE TOY, MADE FROM THOSE SHIPWRECKED BOLTS OF CLOTH. WHAT HARM IN THAT? BUT I COULD SEE IT IN EVERY FACE. THIS WAS THE BEGINNING OF AN UNHOLY CULT!
AND... TO MY EVERLASTING SHAME, I EVEN HELPED MAKE IT HAPPEN!

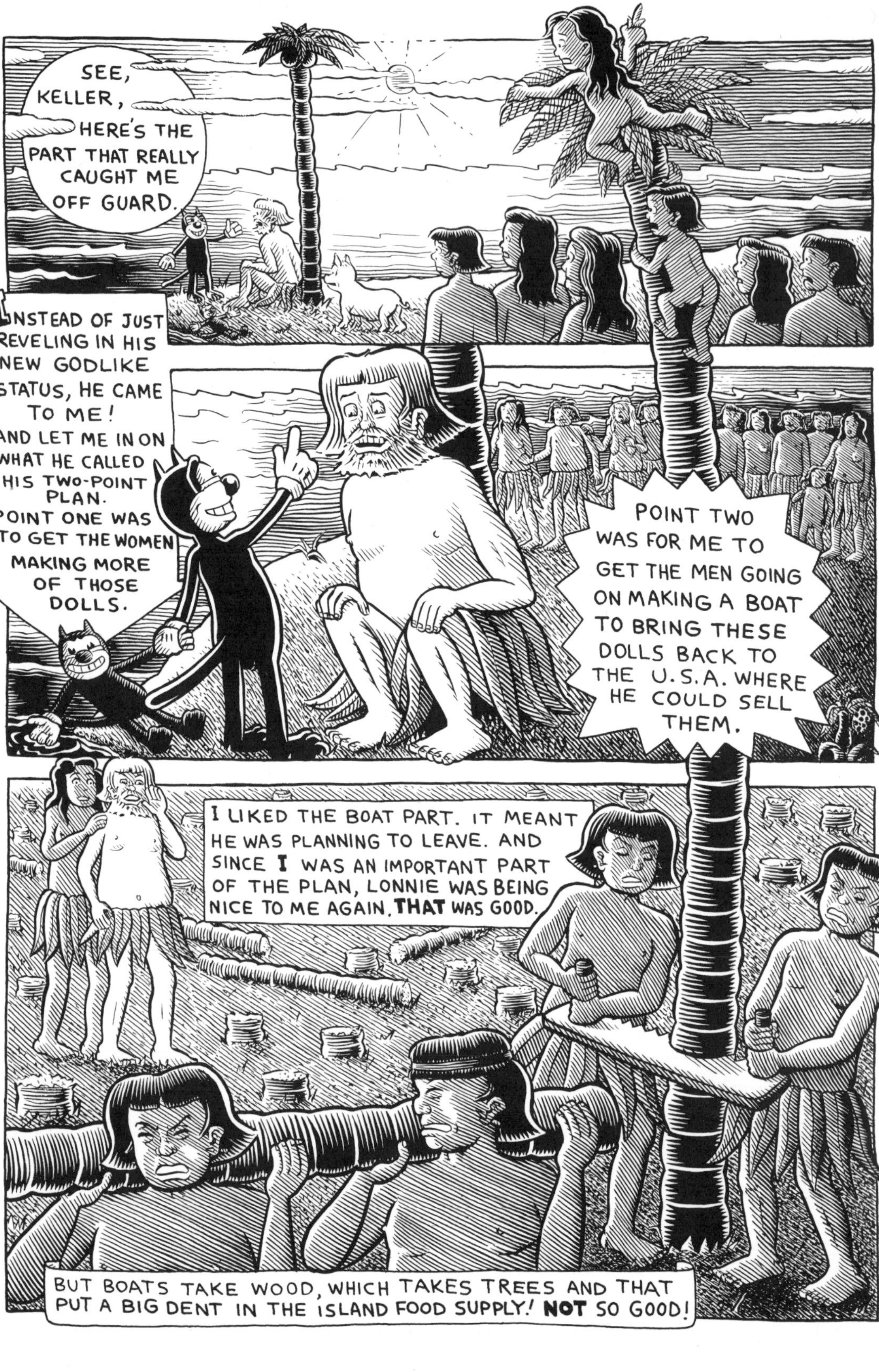
SEE, KELLER, HERE'S THE PART THAT REALLY CAUGHT ME OFF GUARD.
INSTEAD OF JUST REVELING IN HIS NEW GODLIKE STATUS, HE CAME TO ME! AND LET ME IN ON WHAT HE CALLED HIS TWO-POINT PLAN. POINT ONE WAS TO GET THE WOMEN MAKING MORE OF THOSE DOLLS.
POINT TWO WAS FOR ME TO GET THE MEN GOING ON MAKING A BOAT TO BRING THESE DOLLS BACK TO THE U.S.A. WHERE HE COULD SELL THEM.
I LIKED THE BOAT PART. IT MEANT HE WAS PLANNING TO LEAVE. AND SINCE I WAS AN IMPORTANT PART OF THE PLAN, LONNIE WAS BEING NICE TO ME AGAIN, THAT WAS GOOD.
BUT BOATS TAKE WOOD, WHICH TAKES TREES AND THAT PUT A BIG DENT IN THE ISLAND FOOD SUPPLY! NOT SO GOOD!

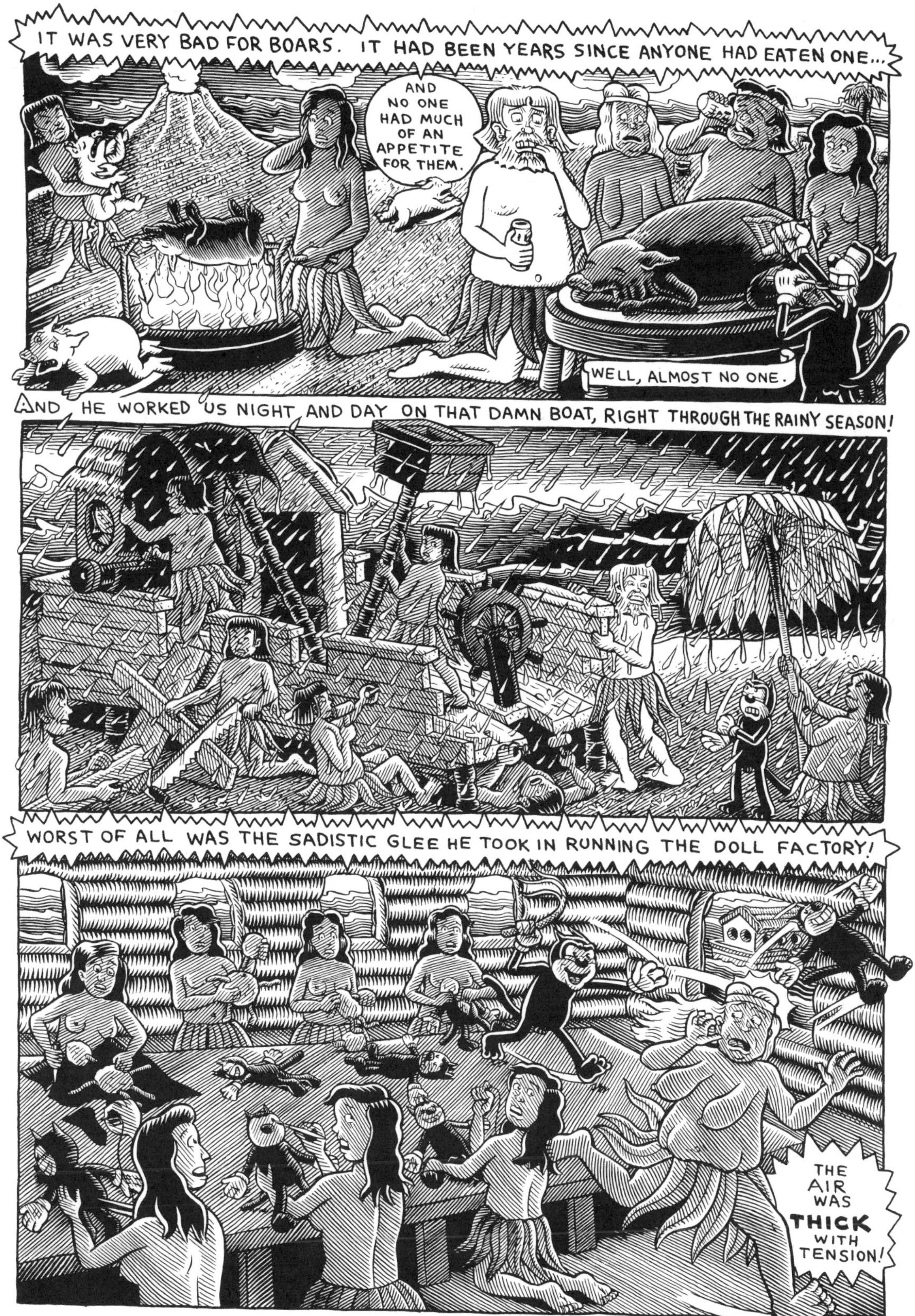
IT WAS VERY BAD FOR BOARS. IT HAD BEEN YEARS SINCE ANYONE HAD EATEN ONE...
AND NO ONE HAD MUCH OF AN APPETITE FOR THEM.
WELL, ALMOST NO ONE.
AND HE WORKED US NIGHT AND DAY ON THAT DAMN BOAT, RIGHT THROUGH THE RAINY SEASON!
WORST OF ALL WAS THE SADISTIC GLEE HE TOOK IN RUNNING THE DOLL FACTORY!
THE AIR WAS THICK WITH TENSION!

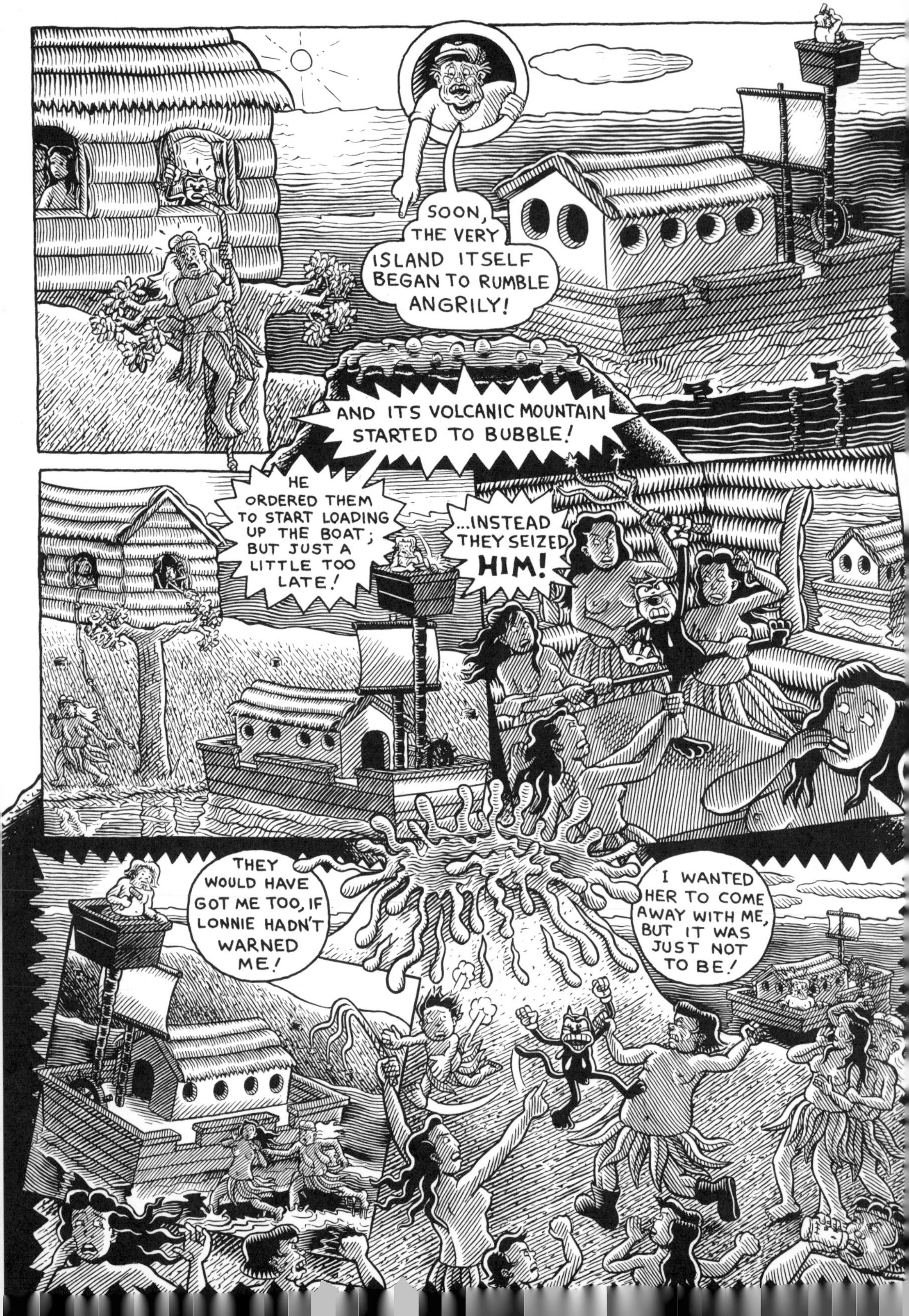
SOON, THE VERY ISLAND ITSELF BEGAN TO RUMBLE ANGRILY!
AND ITS VOLCANIC MOUNTAIN STARTED TO BUBBLE!
HE ORDERED THEM TO START LOADING UP THE BOAT; BUT JUST A LITTLE TOO LATE!
...INSTEAD THEY SEIZED HIM!
THEY WOULD HAVE GOT ME TOO, IF LONNIE HADN'T WARNED ME!
I WANTED HER TO COME AWAY WITH ME, BUT IT WAS JUST NOT TO BE!

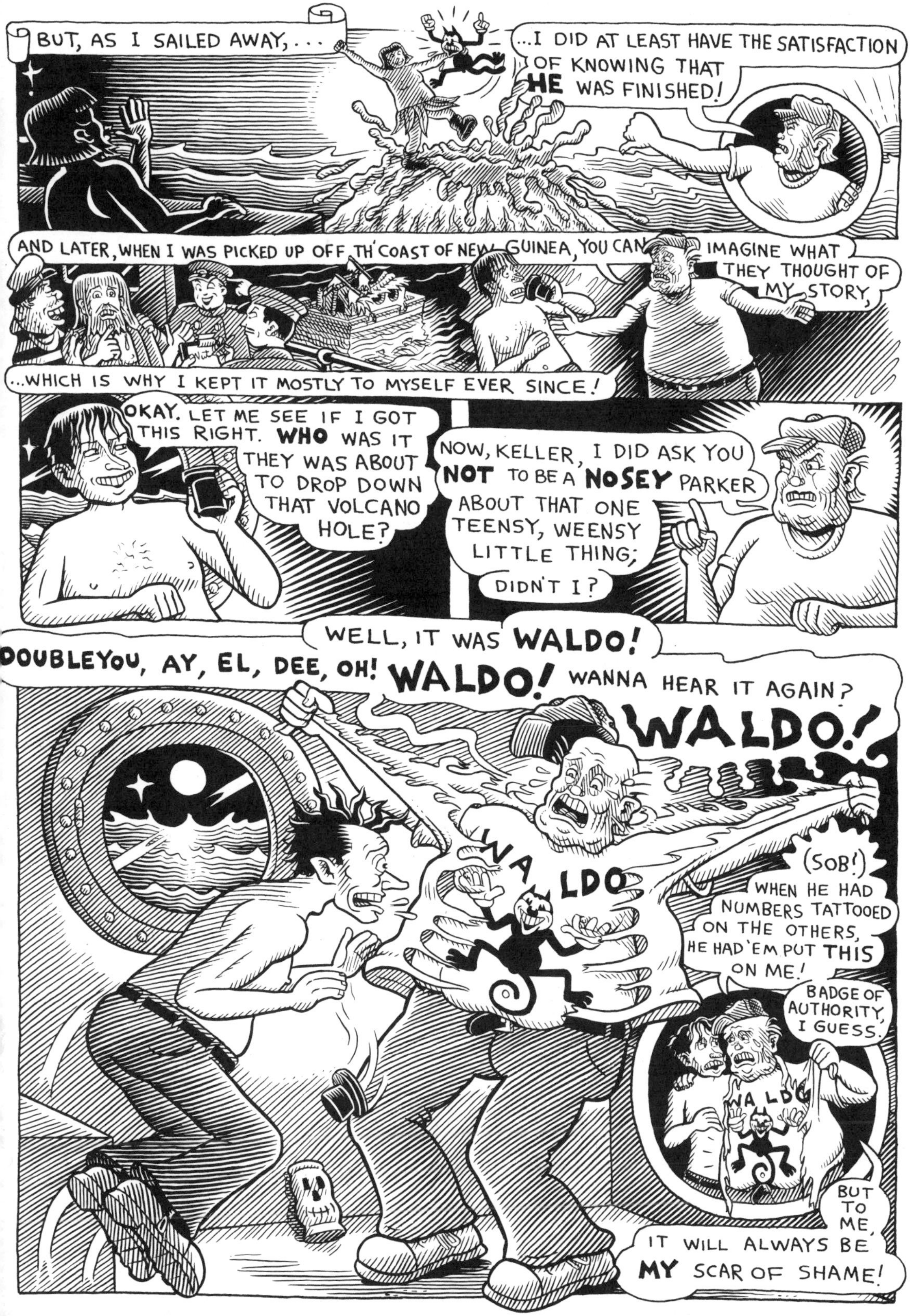
BUT, AS I SAILED AWAY, . . .
...I DID AT LEAST HAVE THE SATISFACTION OF KNOWING THAT HE WAS FINISHED!
AND LATER, WHEN I WAS PICKED UP OFF TH' COAST OF NEW GUINEA, YOU CAN IMAGINE WHAT THEY THOUGHT OF MY STORY,
...WHICH IS WHY I KEPT IT MOSTLY TO MYSELF EVER SINCE!
OKAY. LET ME SEE IF I GOT THIS RIGHT. WHO WAS IT THEY WAS ABOUT TO DROP DOWN THAT VOLCANO HOLE?
NOW, KELLER, I DID ASK YOU NOT TO BE A NOSEY PARKER ABOUT THAT ONE TEENSY, WEENSY LITTLE THING;
DIDN'T I?
WELL, IT WAS WALDO!
DOUBLEYOU, AY, EL, DEE, OH! WALDO! WANNA HEAR IT AGAIN?
WALDO!
WALDO
(SOB!)
WHEN HE HAD NUMBERS TATTOOED ON THE OTHERS, HE HAD 'EM PUT THIS ON ME!
BADGE OF AUTHORITY, I GUESS.
WALDO
BUT TO ME,
IT WILL ALWAYS BE MY SCAR OF SHAME!

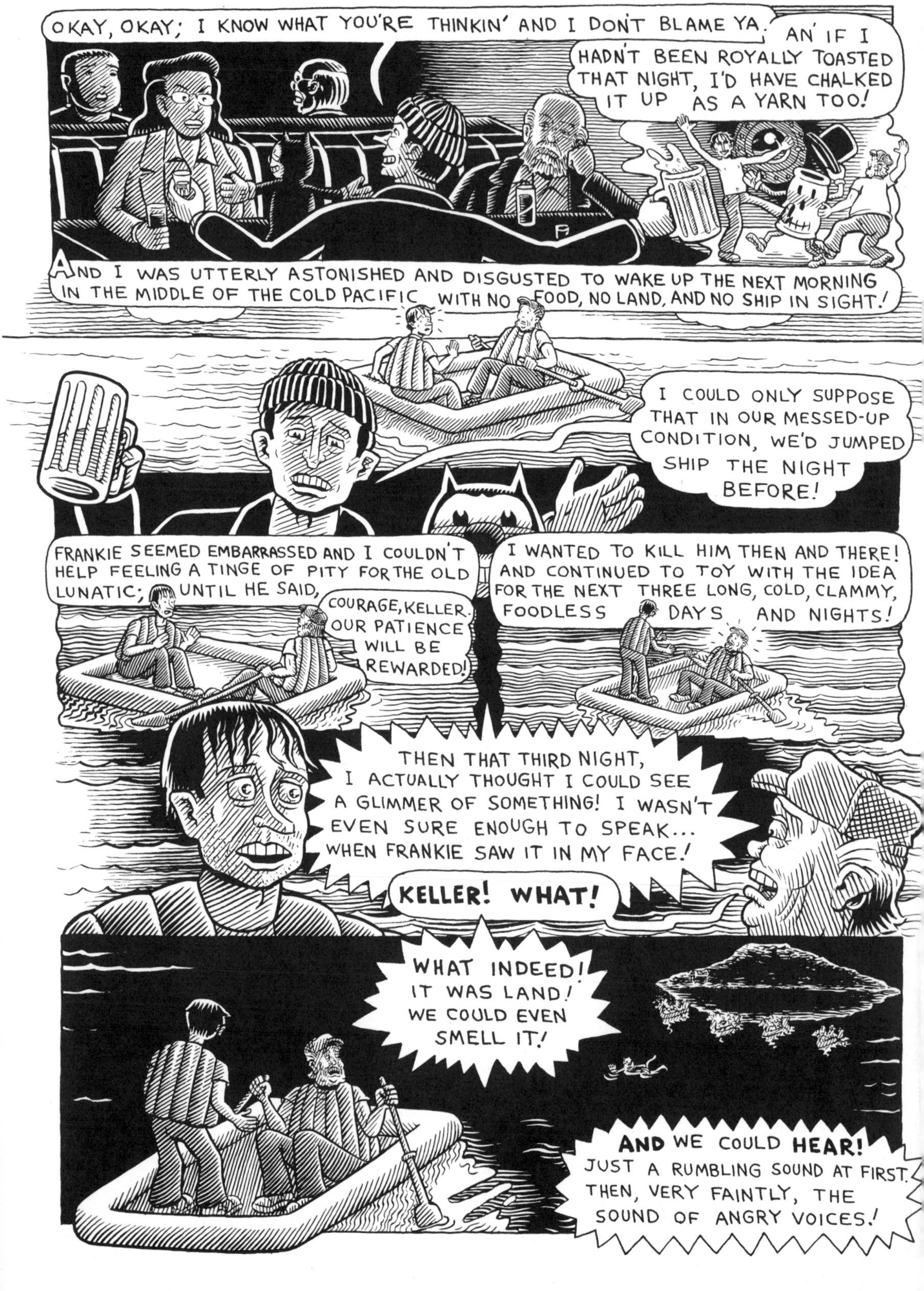
OKAY, OKAY; I KNOW WHAT YOU'RE THINKIN' AND I DON'T BLAME YA.
AN' IF I HADN'T BEEN ROYALLY TOASTED THAT NIGHT, I'D HAVE CHALKED IT UP AS A YARN TOO!
AND I WAS UTTERLY ASTONISHED AND DISGUSTED TO WAKE UP THE NEXT MORNING IN THE MIDDLE OF THE COLD PACIFIC WITH NO FOOD, NO LAND, AND NO SHIP IN SIGHT!
I COULD ONLY SUPPOSE THAT IN OUR MESSED-UP CONDITION, WE'D JUMPED SHIP THE NIGHT BEFORE!
FRANKIE SEEMED EMBARRASSED AND I COULDN'T HELP FEELING A TINGE OF PITY FOR THE OLD LUNATIC; UNTIL HE SAID,
COURAGE, KELLER. OUR PATIENCE WILL BE REWARDED!
I WANTED TO KILL HIM THEN AND THERE! AND CONTINUED TO TOY WITH THE IDEA FOR THE NEXT THREE LONG, COLD, CLAMMY, FOODLESS DAYS AND NIGHTS!
THEN THAT THIRD NIGHT, I ACTUALLY THOUGHT I COULD SEE A GLIMMER OF SOMETHING! I WASN'T EVEN SURE ENOUGH TO SPEAK... WHEN FRANKIE SAW IT IN MY FACE!
KELLER! WHAT!
WHAT INDEED! IT WAS LAND! WE COULD EVEN SMELL IT!
AND WE COULD HEAR! JUST A RUMBLING SOUND AT FIRST. THEN, VERY FAINTLY, THE SOUND OF ANGRY VOICES!

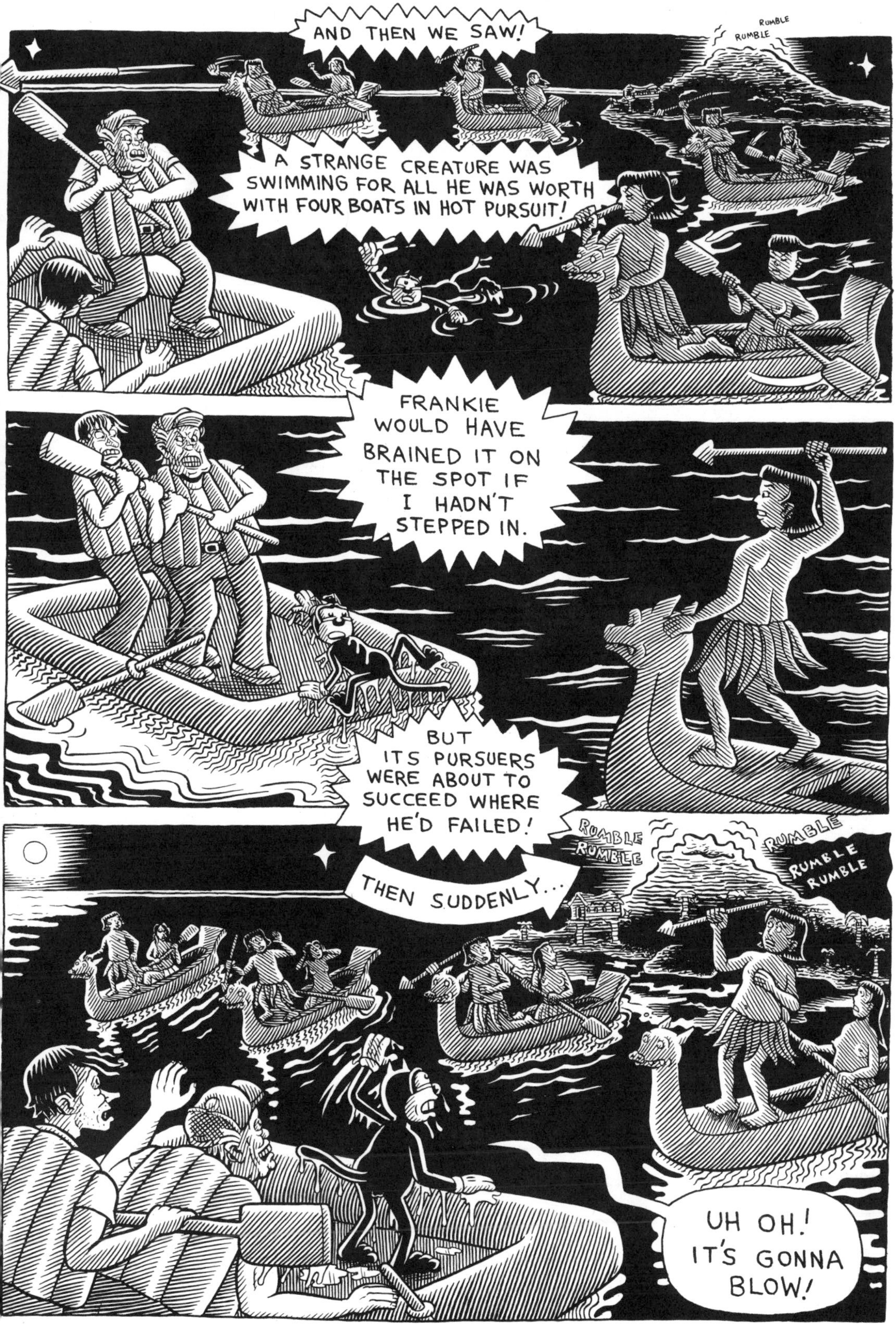

AND THEN WE SAW!
RUMBLE RUMBLE
A STRANGE CREATURE WAS SWIMMING FOR ALL HE WAS WORTH WITH FOUR BOATS IN HOT PURSUIT!
FRANKIE WOULD HAVE BRAINED IT ON THE SPOT IF I HADN'T STEPPED IN.
BUT ITS PURSUERS WERE ABOUT TO SUCCEED WHERE HE'D FAILED!
RUMBLE RUMBLE
RUMBLE
RUMBLE RUMBLE
THEN SUDDENLY...
UH OH! IT'S GONNA BLOW!

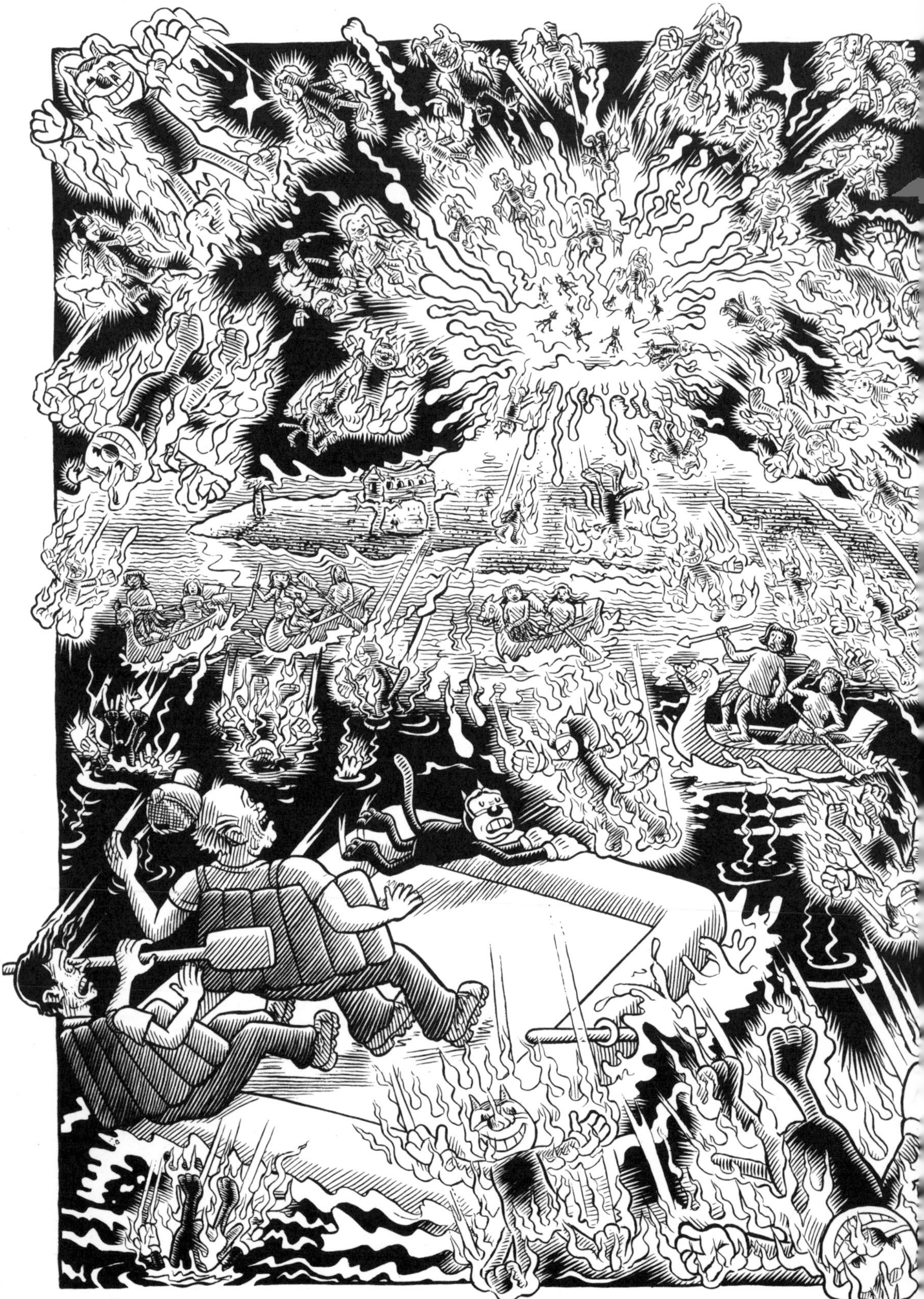

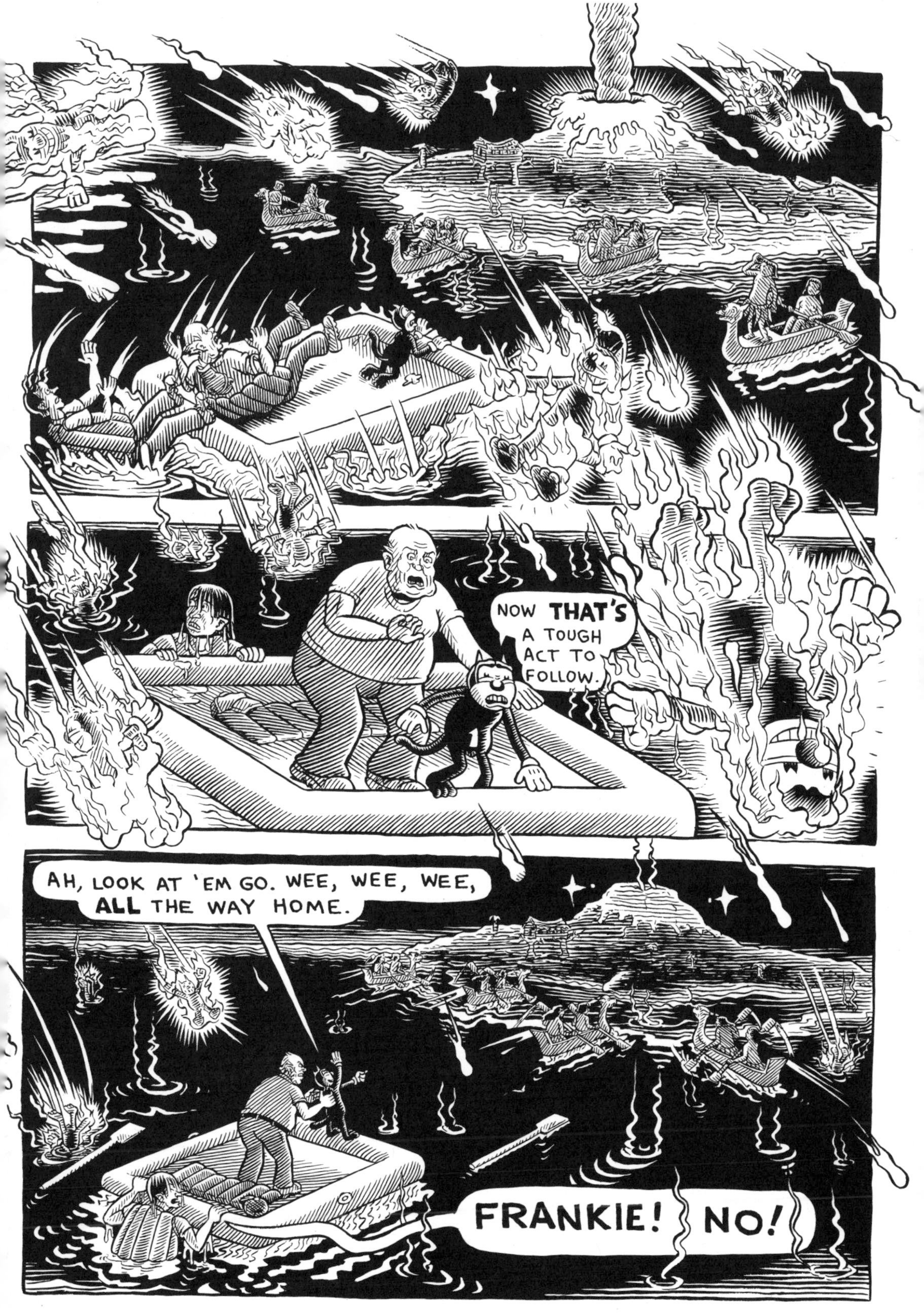
NOW THAT'S A TOUGH ACT TO FOLLOW.
AH, LOOK AT 'EM GO. WEE, WEE, WEE, ALL THE WAY HOME.
FRANKIE! NO!

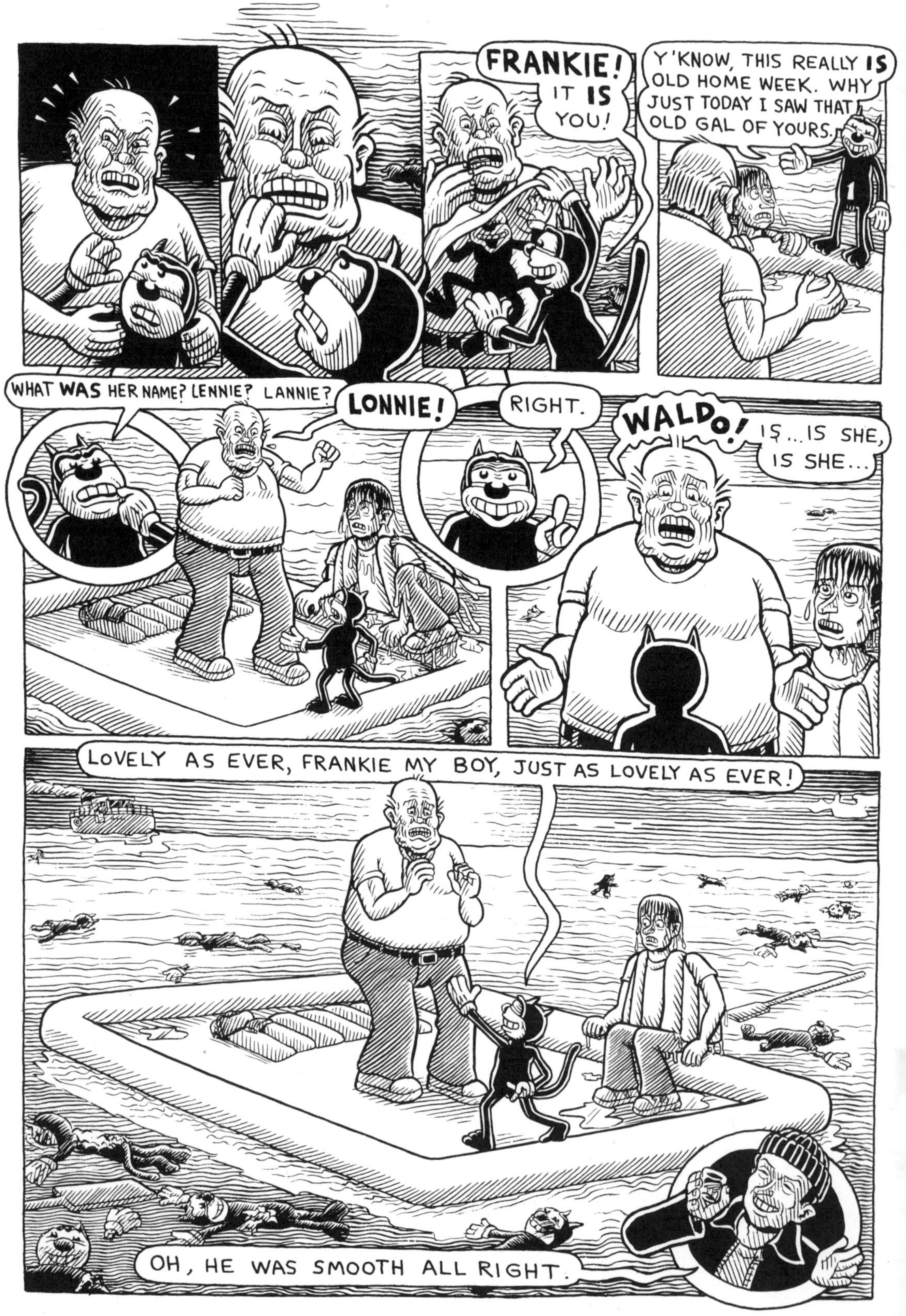
FRANKIE! IT IS YOU!
Y'KNOW, THIS REALLY IS OLD HOME WEEK. WHY JUST TODAY I SAW THAT OLD GAL OF YOURS.
WHAT WAS HER NAME? LENNIE? LANNIE?
LONNIE!
RIGHT.
WALDO!
IS...IS SHE, IS SHE...
LOVELY AS EVER, FRANKIE MY BOY, JUST AS LOVELY AS EVER!
OH, HE WAS SMOOTH ALL RIGHT.

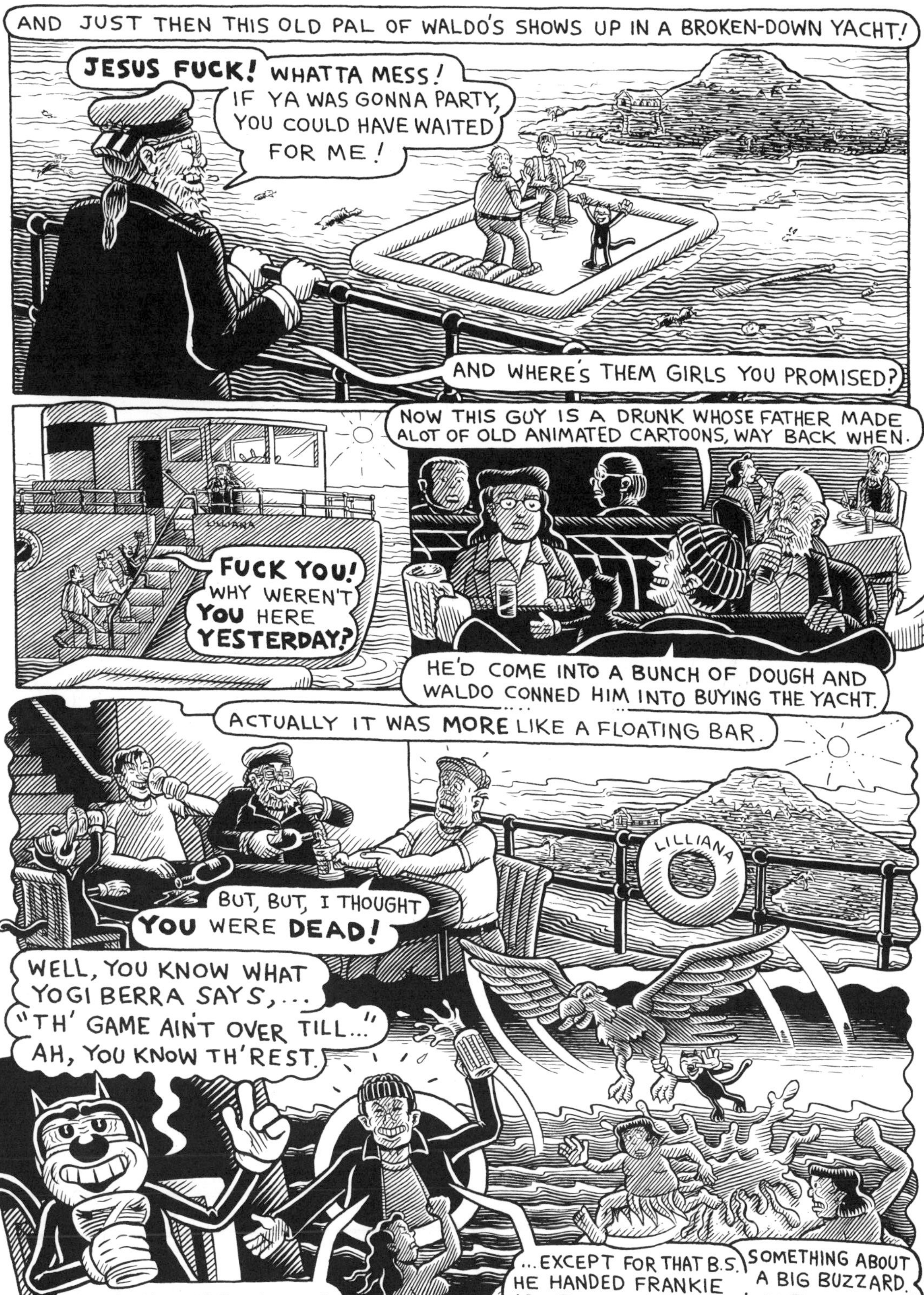

AND JUST THEN THIS OLD PAL OF WALDO'S SHOWS UP IN A BROKEN-DOWN YACHT!
JESUS FUCK! WHATTA MESS! IF YA WAS GONNA PARTY, YOU COULD HAVE WAITED FOR ME!
AND WHERE'S THEM GIRLS YOU PROMISED?
LILLIANA
FUCK YOU! WHY WEREN'T YOU HERE YESTERDAY?
NOW THIS GUY IS A DRUNK WHOSE FATHER MADE ALOT OF OLD ANIMATED CARTOONS, WAY BACK WHEN.
HE'D COME INTO A BUNCH OF DOUGH AND WALDO CONNED HIM INTO BUYING THE YACHT.
ACTUALLY IT WAS MORE LIKE A FLOATING BAR.
BUT, BUT, I THOUGHT YOU WERE DEAD!
LILLIANA
WELL, YOU KNOW WHAT YOGI BERRA SAYS, ... "TH' GAME AIN'T OVER TILL..." AH, YOU KNOW TH' REST.
YEAH, HE WAS SMOOTH;
...EXCEPT FOR THAT B.S. HE HANDED FRANKIE ABOUT HIS GREAT ESCAPE;
SOMETHING ABOUT A BIG BUZZARD. WHAT A CROCK!

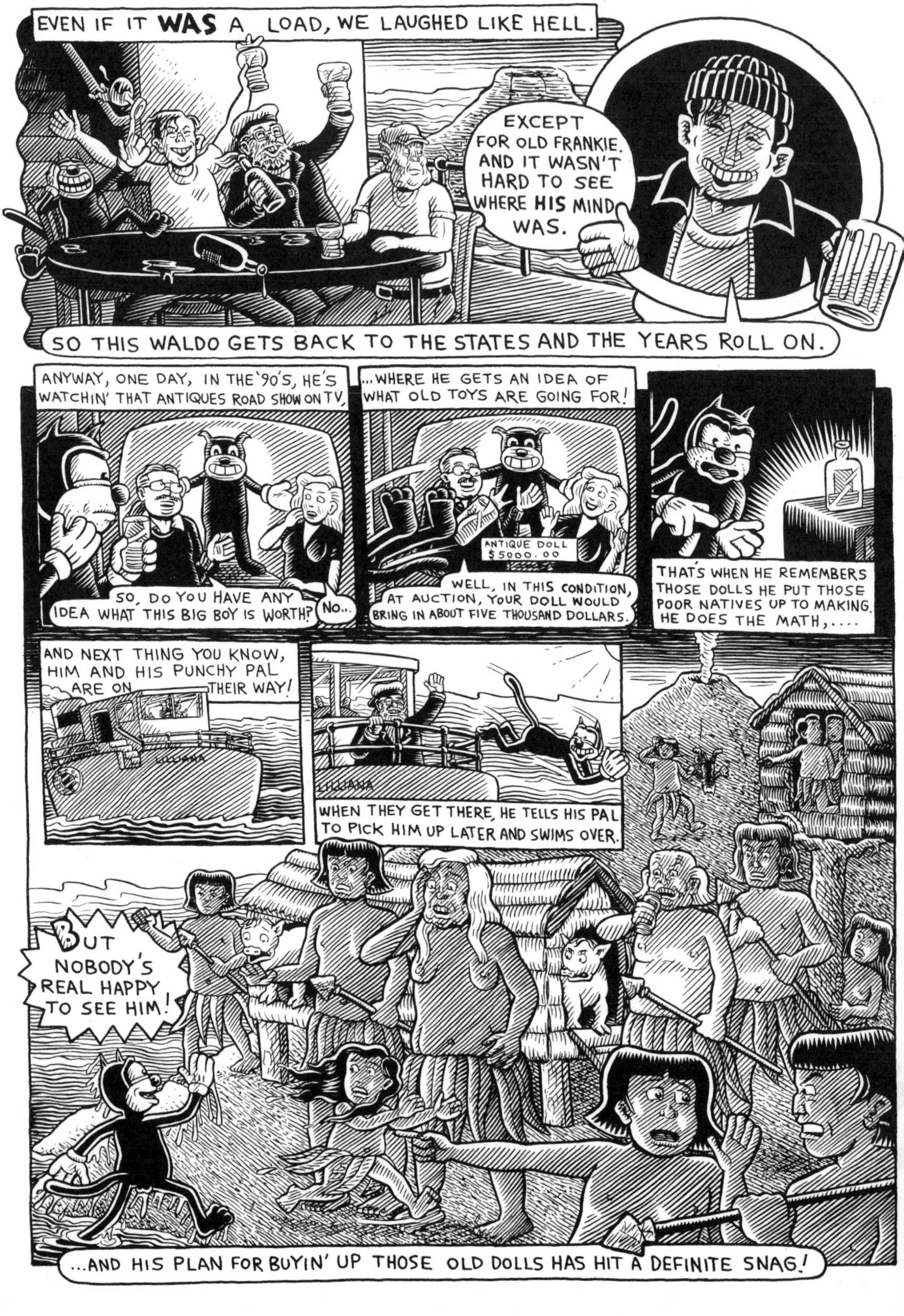
EVEN IF IT **WAS** A LOAD, WE LAUGHED LIKE HELL.
EXCEPT FOR OLD FRANKIE. AND IT WASN'T HARD TO SEE WHERE **HIS** MIND WAS.
SO THIS WALDO GETS BACK TO THE STATES AND THE YEARS ROLL ON.
ANYWAY, ONE DAY, IN THE '90'S, HE'S WATCHIN' THAT ANTIQUES ROAD SHOW ON TV,
SO, DO YOU HAVE ANY IDEA WHAT THIS BIG BOY IS WORTH?
NO..
...WHERE HE GETS AN IDEA OF WHAT OLD TOYS ARE GOING FOR!
ANTIQUE DOLL $5000.00
WELL, IN THIS CONDITION, AT AUCTION, YOUR DOLL WOULD BRING IN ABOUT FIVE THOUSAND DOLLARS.
THAT'S WHEN HE REMEMBERS THOSE DOLLS HE PUT THOSE POOR NATIVES UP TO MAKING. HE DOES THE MATH,....
AND NEXT THING YOU KNOW, HIM AND HIS PUNCHY PAL ARE ON THEIR WAY!
LILLIANA
LILLIANA
WHEN THEY GET THERE, HE TELLS HIS PAL TO PICK HIM UP LATER AND SWIMS OVER.
BUT NOBODY'S REAL HAPPY TO SEE HIM!
...AND HIS PLAN FOR BUYIN' UP THOSE OLD DOLLS HAS HIT A DEFINITE SNAG!

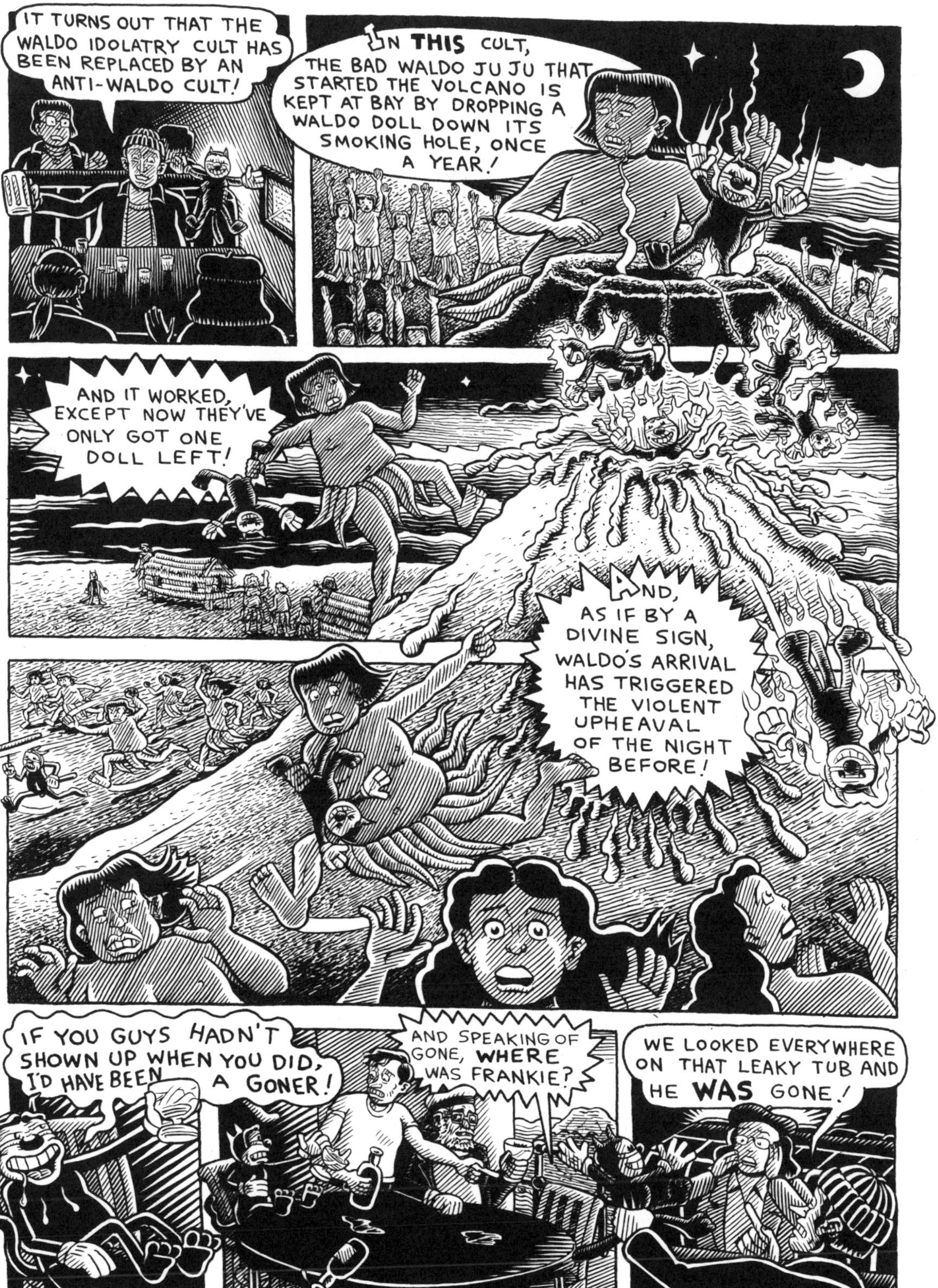
IT TURNS OUT THAT THE WALDO IDOLATRY CULT HAS BEEN REPLACED BY AN ANTI-WALDO CULT!
IN THIS CULT, THE BAD WALDO JU JU THAT STARTED THE VOLCANO IS KEPT AT BAY BY DROPPING A WALDO DOLL DOWN ITS SMOKING HOLE, ONCE A YEAR!
AND IT WORKED, EXCEPT NOW THEY'VE ONLY GOT ONE DOLL LEFT!
AND, AS IF BY A DIVINE SIGN, WALDO'S ARRIVAL HAS TRIGGERED THE VIOLENT UPHEAVAL OF THE NIGHT BEFORE!
IF YOU GUYS HADN'T SHOWN UP WHEN YOU DID, I'D HAVE BEEN A GONER!
AND SPEAKING OF GONE, WHERE WAS FRANKIE?
WE LOOKED EVERYWHERE ON THAT LEAKY TUB AND HE WAS GONE!

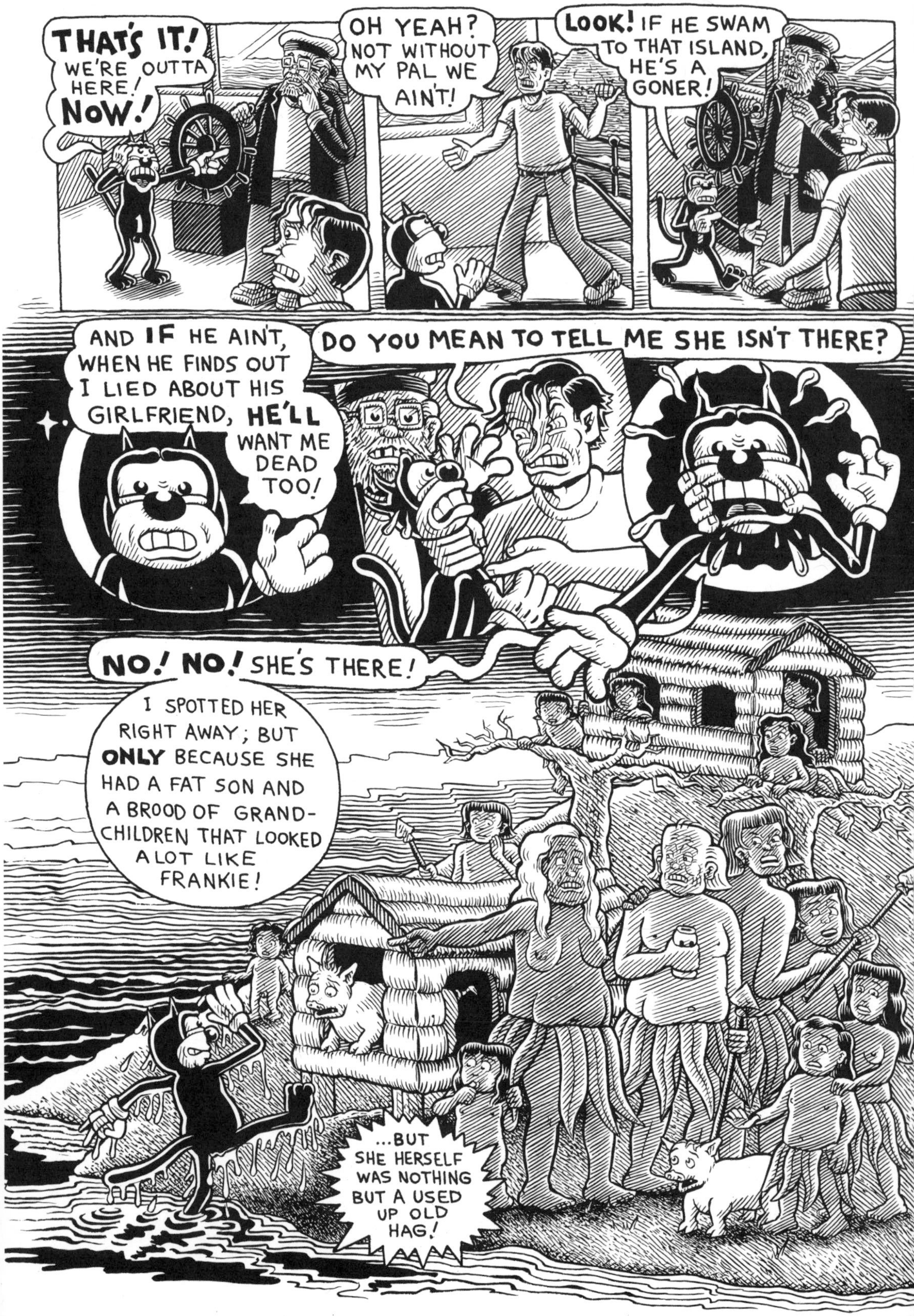

THAT'S IT! WE'RE OUTTA HERE! NOW!
OH YEAH? NOT WITHOUT MY PAL WE AIN'T!
LOOK! IF HE SWAM TO THAT ISLAND, HE'S A GONER!
AND IF HE AIN'T, WHEN HE FINDS OUT I LIED ABOUT HIS GIRLFRIEND, HE'LL WANT ME DEAD TOO!
DO YOU MEAN TO TELL ME SHE ISN'T THERE?
NO! NO! SHE'S THERE!
I SPOTTED HER RIGHT AWAY; BUT ONLY BECAUSE SHE HAD A FAT SON AND A BROOD OF GRAND-CHILDREN THAT LOOKED A LOT LIKE FRANKIE!
...BUT SHE HERSELF WAS NOTHING BUT A USED UP OLD HAG!

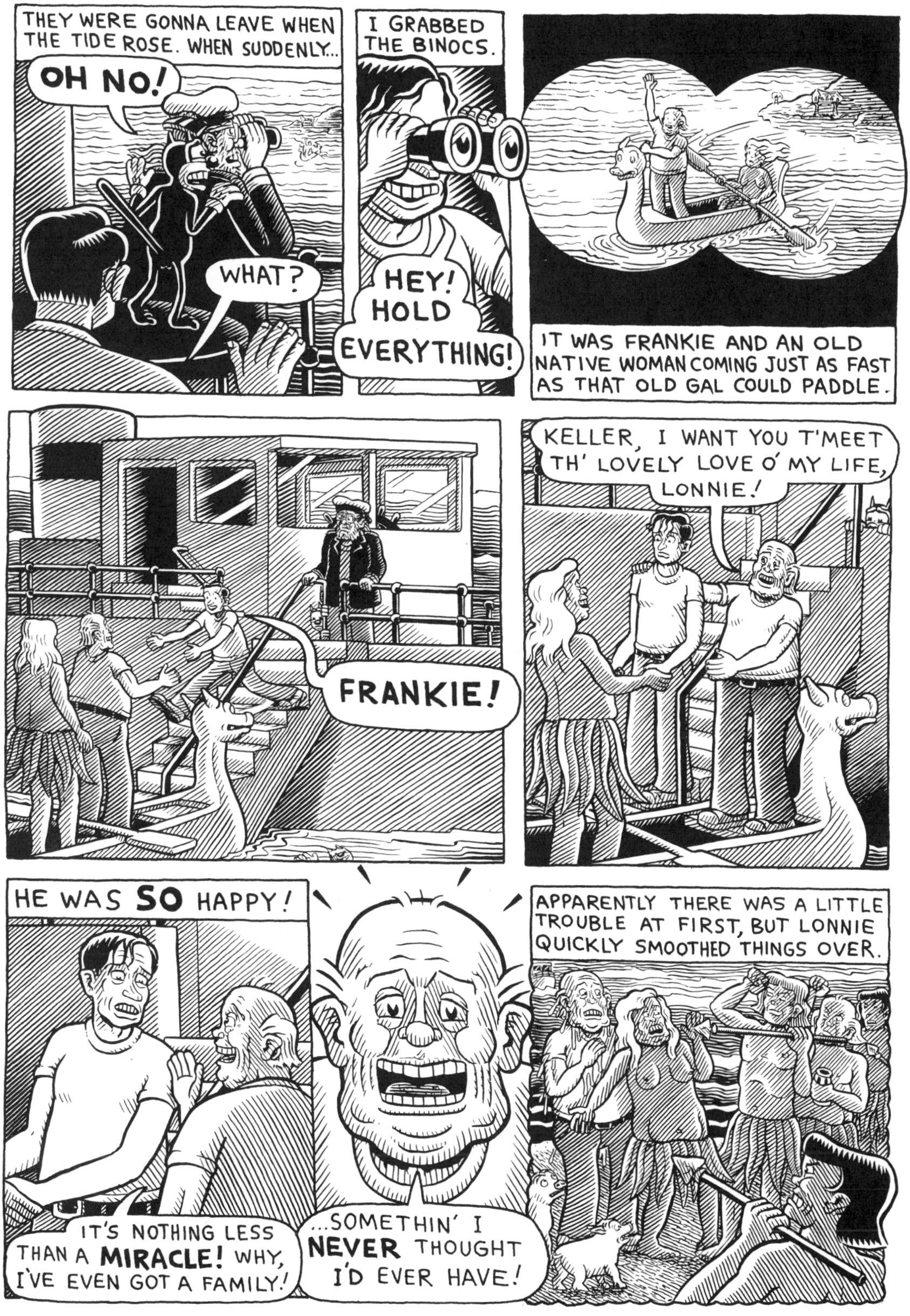
THEY WERE GONNA LEAVE WHEN THE TIDE ROSE. WHEN SUDDENLY...
OH NO!
WHAT?
I GRABBED THE BINOCS.
HEY! HOLD EVERYTHING!
IT WAS FRANKIE AND AN OLD NATIVE WOMAN COMING JUST AS FAST AS THAT OLD GAL COULD PADDLE.
FRANKIE!
KELLER, I WANT YOU T'MEET TH' LOVELY LOVE O' MY LIFE, LONNIE!
HE WAS SO HAPPY!
IT'S NOTHING LESS THAN A MIRACLE! WHY, I'VE EVEN GOT A FAMILY!
...SOMETHIN' I NEVER THOUGHT I'D EVER HAVE!
APPARENTLY THERE WAS A LITTLE TROUBLE AT FIRST, BUT LONNIE QUICKLY SMOOTHED THINGS OVER.

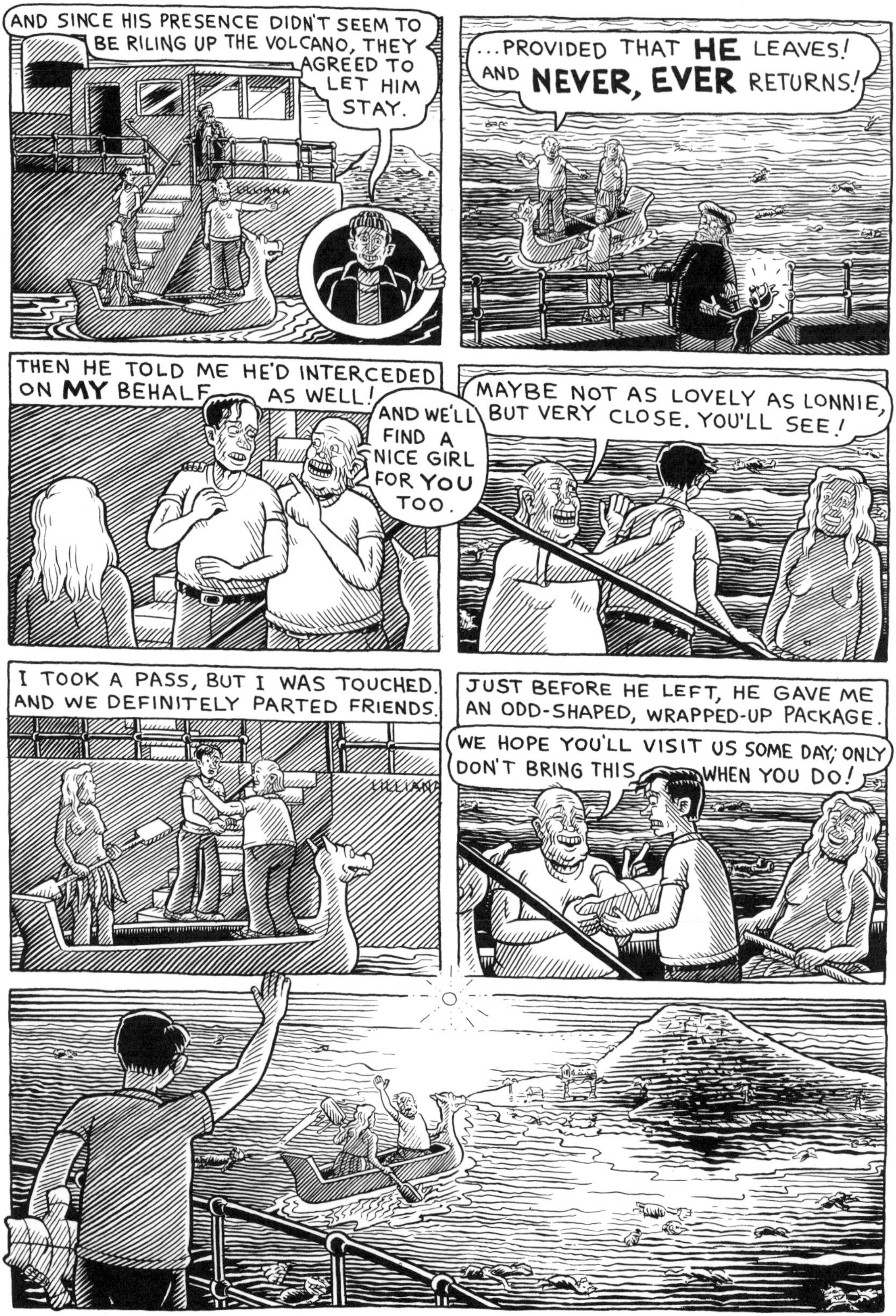
AND SINCE HIS PRESENCE DIDN'T SEEM TO BE RILING UP THE VOLCANO, THEY AGREED TO LET HIM STAY.
LILLIANA
...PROVIDED THAT **HE** LEAVES! AND **NEVER, EVER** RETURNS!
THEN HE TOLD ME HE'D INTERCEDED ON **MY** BEHALF AS WELL!
AND WE'LL FIND A NICE GIRL FOR **YOU** TOO.
MAYBE NOT AS LOVELY AS LONNIE, BUT VERY CLOSE. YOU'LL SEE!
I TOOK A PASS, BUT I WAS TOUCHED. AND WE DEFINITELY PARTED FRIENDS.
LILLIANA
JUST BEFORE HE LEFT, HE GAVE ME AN ODD-SHAPED, WRAPPED-UP PACKAGE.
WE HOPE YOU'LL VISIT US SOME DAY; ONLY DON'T BRING THIS WHEN YOU DO!

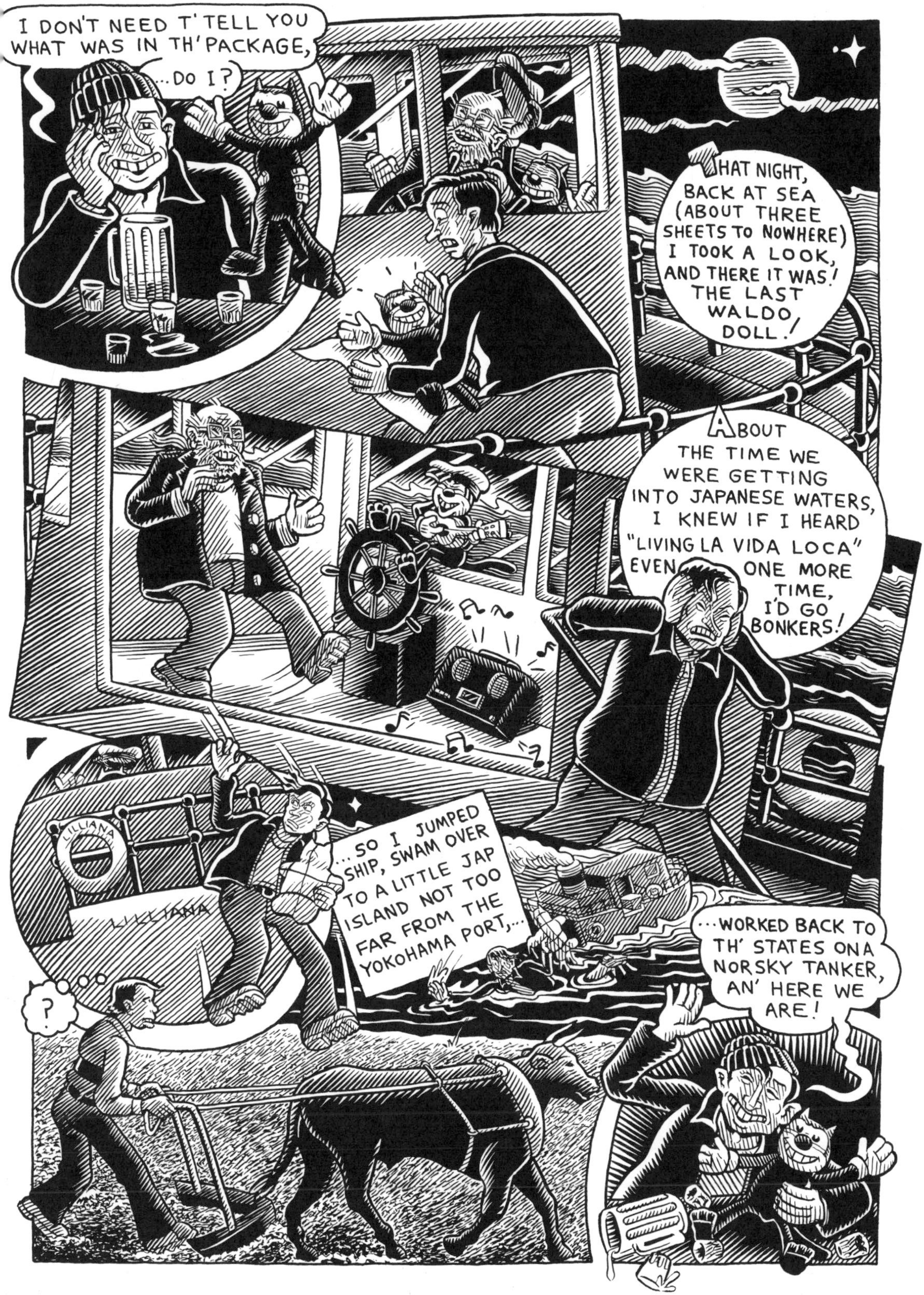
I DON'T NEED T' TELL YOU WHAT WAS IN TH' PACKAGE,
...DO I?
THAT NIGHT, BACK AT SEA (ABOUT THREE SHEETS TO NOWHERE) I TOOK A LOOK, AND THERE IT WAS! THE LAST WALDO DOLL!
ABOUT THE TIME WE WERE GETTING INTO JAPANESE WATERS, I KNEW IF I HEARD "LIVING LA VIDA LOCA" EVEN ONE MORE TIME, I'D GO BONKERS!
LILLIANA
LILLIANA
...SO I JUMPED SHIP, SWAM OVER TO A LITTLE JAP ISLAND NOT TOO FAR FROM THE YOKOHAMA PORT,...
?
...WORKED BACK TO TH' STATES ON A NORSKY TANKER, AN' HERE WE ARE!

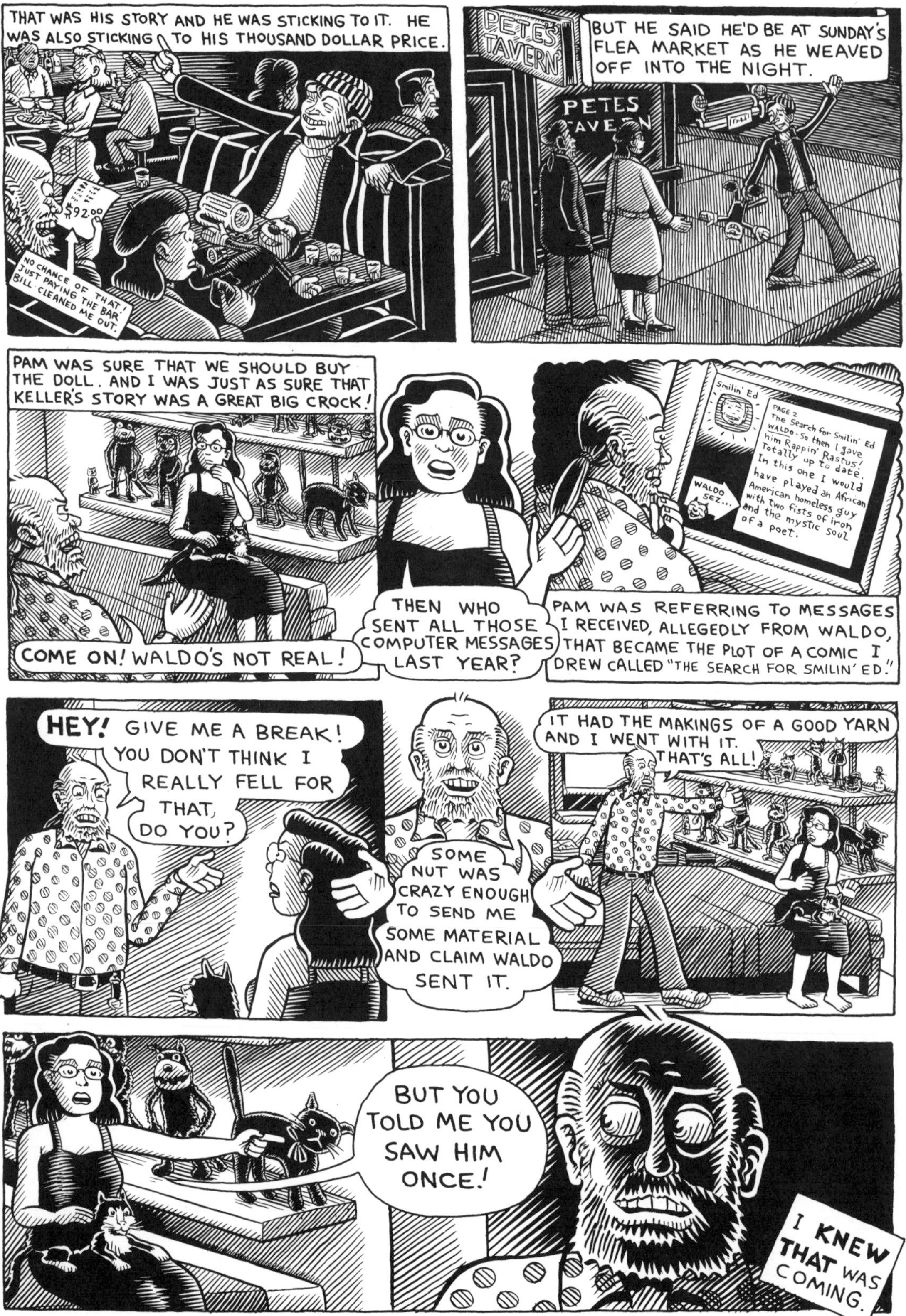
THAT WAS HIS STORY AND HE WAS STICKING TO IT. HE WAS ALSO STICKING TO HIS THOUSAND DOLLAR PRICE.
$92.00
NO CHANCE OF THAT! JUST PAYING THE BAR BILL CLEANED ME OUT.
PETE'S TAVERN
BUT HE SAID HE'D BE AT SUNDAY'S FLEA MARKET AS HE WEAVED OFF INTO THE NIGHT.
PETES TAVERN
PAM WAS SURE THAT WE SHOULD BUY THE DOLL. AND I WAS JUST AS SURE THAT KELLER'S STORY WAS A GREAT BIG CROCK!
COME ON! WALDO'S NOT REAL!
THEN WHO SENT ALL THOSE COMPUTER MESSAGES LAST YEAR?
Smilin' Ed
PAGE 2
The Search for Smilin' Ed
WALDO - So then I gave him Rappin' Rastus! Totally up to date. In this one I would have played an African American homeless guy with two fists of iron and the mystic soul of a poet.
WALDO SEZ...
PAM WAS REFERRING TO MESSAGES I RECEIVED, ALLEGEDLY FROM WALDO, THAT BECAME THE PLOT OF A COMIC I DREW CALLED "THE SEARCH FOR SMILIN' ED."
HEY! GIVE ME A BREAK! YOU DON'T THINK I REALLY FELL FOR THAT, DO YOU?
SOME NUT WAS CRAZY ENOUGH TO SEND ME SOME MATERIAL AND CLAIM WALDO SENT IT.
IT HAD THE MAKINGS OF A GOOD YARN AND I WENT WITH IT. THAT'S ALL!
BUT YOU TOLD ME YOU SAW HIM ONCE!
I KNEW THAT WAS COMING.

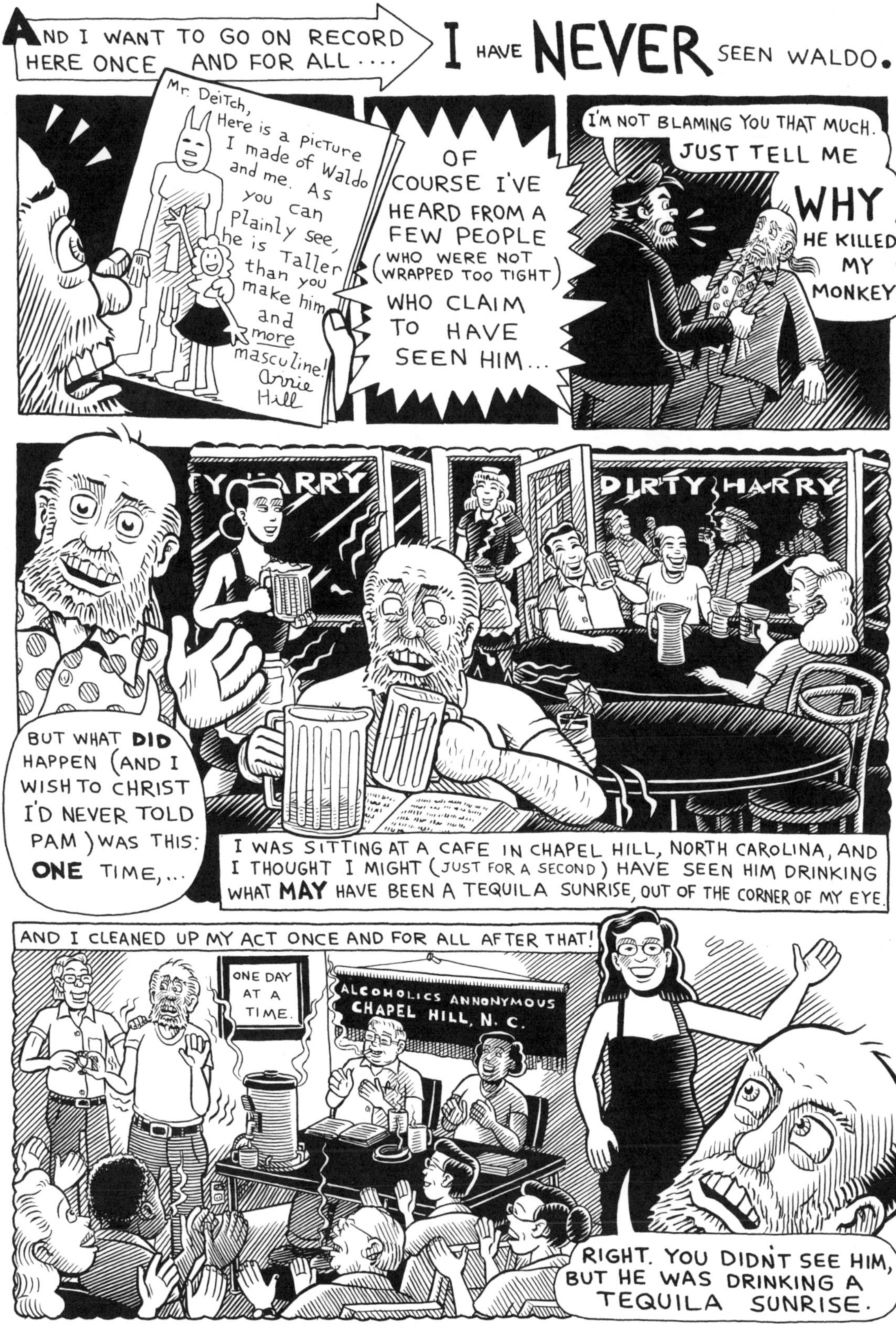
AND I WANT TO GO ON RECORD HERE ONCE AND FOR ALL....
I HAVE NEVER SEEN WALDO.
Mr. DeiTch, Here is a picture I made of Waldo and me. As you can plainly see, he is Taller than you make him and more masculine! Annie Hill
OF COURSE I'VE HEARD FROM A FEW PEOPLE (WHO WERE NOT WRAPPED TOO TIGHT) WHO CLAIM TO HAVE SEEN HIM...
I'M NOT BLAMING YOU THAT MUCH. JUST TELL ME WHY HE KILLED MY MONKEY!
DIRTY HARRY
BUT WHAT DID HAPPEN (AND I WISH TO CHRIST I'D NEVER TOLD PAM) WAS THIS: ONE TIME,...
I WAS SITTING AT A CAFE IN CHAPEL HILL, NORTH CAROLINA, AND I THOUGHT I MIGHT (JUST FOR A SECOND) HAVE SEEN HIM DRINKING WHAT MAY HAVE BEEN A TEQUILA SUNRISE, OUT OF THE CORNER OF MY EYE.
AND I CLEANED UP MY ACT ONCE AND FOR ALL AFTER THAT!
ONE DAY AT A TIME.
ALCOHOLICS ANNONYMOUS CHAPEL HILL, N.C.
RIGHT. YOU DIDN'T SEE HIM, BUT HE WAS DRINKING A TEQUILA SUNRISE.

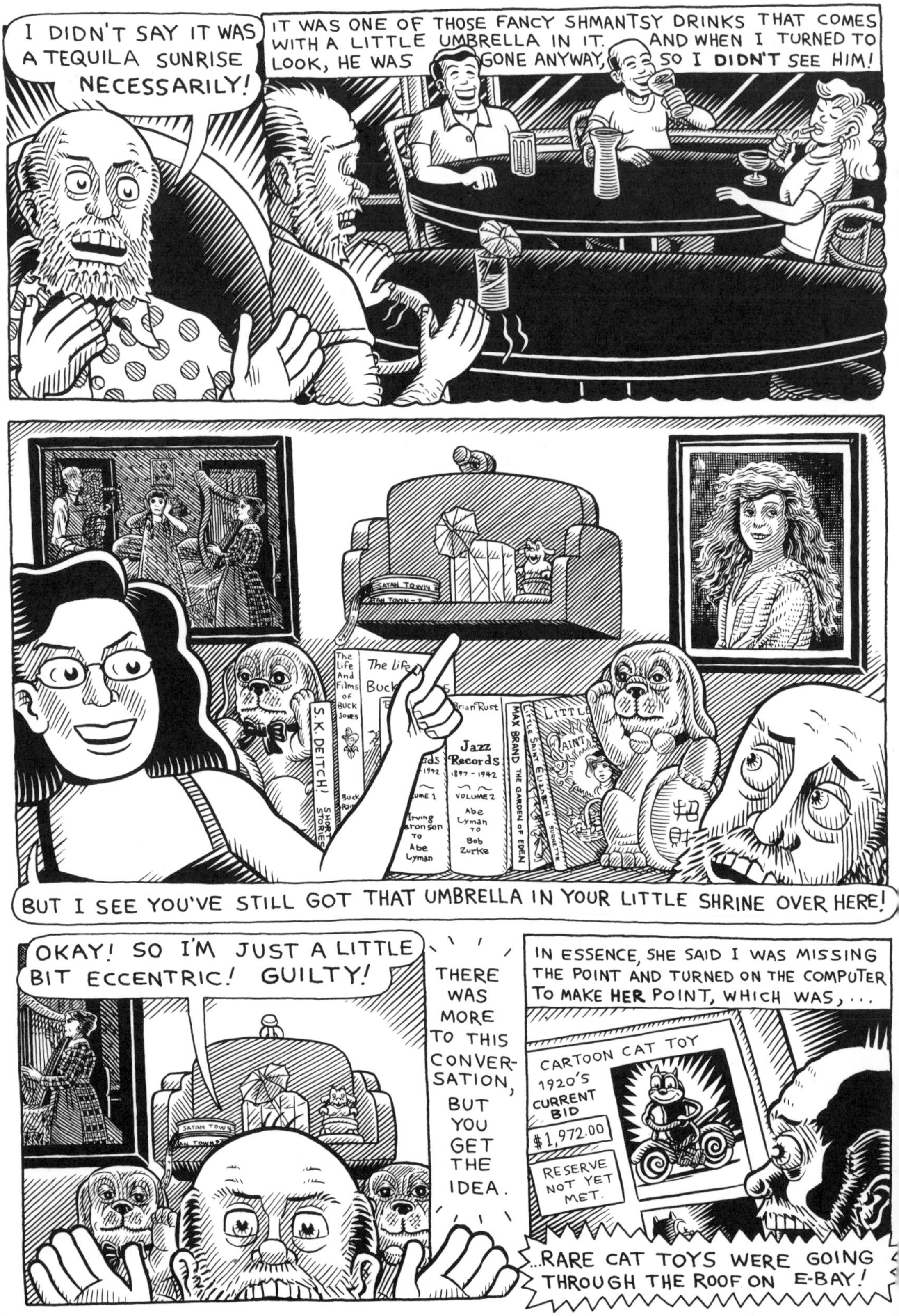
I DIDN'T SAY IT WAS A TEQUILA SUNRISE NECESSARILY!
IT WAS ONE OF THOSE FANCY SHMANTSY DRINKS THAT COMES WITH A LITTLE UMBRELLA IN IT.
AND WHEN I TURNED TO LOOK, HE WAS GONE ANYWAY, SO I DIDN'T SEE HIM!
SATAN TOWN
SATAN TOWN - 2
The Life And Films of BUCK JONES
The Life Buck
S.K. DEITCH! SHORT STORIES
Brian Rust
Jazz Records 1897 - 1942
VOLUME 1 Irving Aronson TO Abe Lyman
VOLUME 2 Abe Lyman TO Bob Zurke
MAX BRAND THE GARDEN OF EDEN
LITTLE SAINT ELIZABETH
BUT I SEE YOU'VE STILL GOT THAT UMBRELLA IN YOUR LITTLE SHRINE OVER HERE!
OKAY! SO I'M JUST A LITTLE BIT ECCENTRIC! GUILTY!
SATAN TOWN
THERE WAS MORE TO THIS CONVER-SATION, BUT YOU GET THE IDEA.
IN ESSENCE, SHE SAID I WAS MISSING THE POINT AND TURNED ON THE COMPUTER TO MAKE HER POINT, WHICH WAS, . . .
CARTOON CAT TOY
1920'S
CURRENT BID
$1,972.00
RESERVE NOT YET MET.
...RARE CAT TOYS WERE GOING THROUGH THE ROOF ON E-BAY!

SO I FIGURED **HELL!** LET'S GO FOR IT! WE GOT THE CASH TOGETHER, WENT BACK ON SUNDAY AND GUESS WHAT? **NO KELLER!** AND FEATURE THIS!........

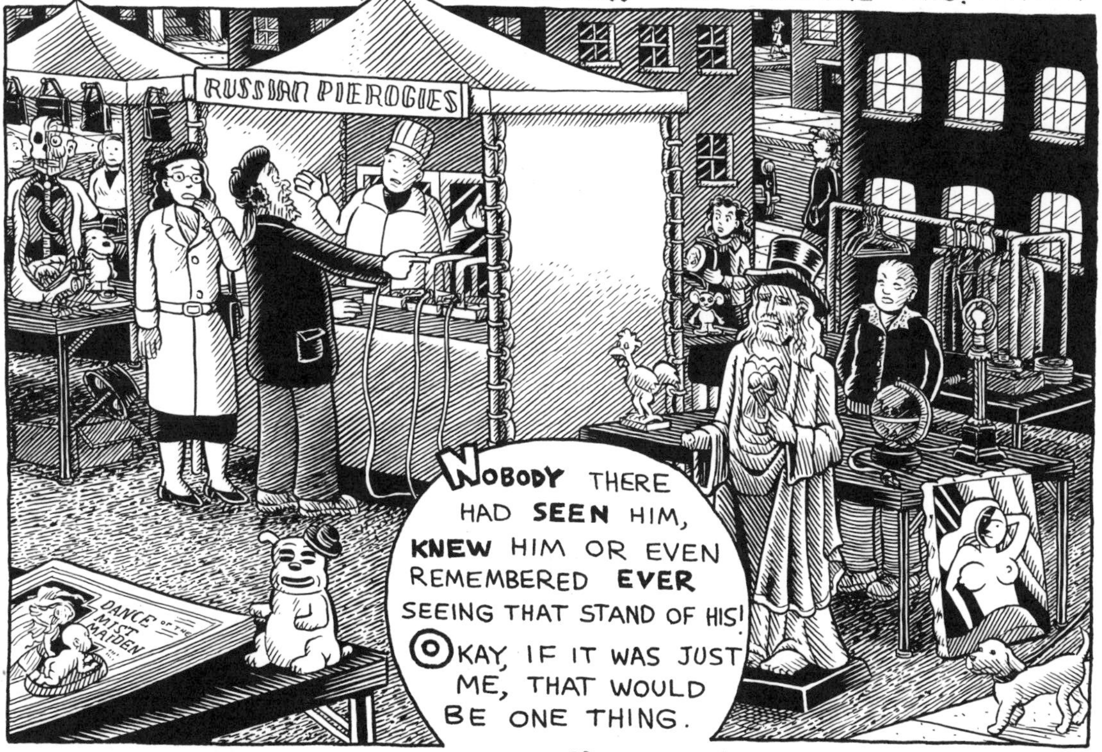
RUSSIAN PIEROGIES
DANCE OF THE MIST MAIDEN
NOBODY THERE HAD SEEN HIM, KNEW HIM OR EVEN REMEMBERED EVER SEEING THAT STAND OF HIS! OKAY, IF IT WAS JUST ME, THAT WOULD BE ONE THING.

BUT PAM SAW IT TOO, AND I **KNOW** SHE'S NOT NUTS!

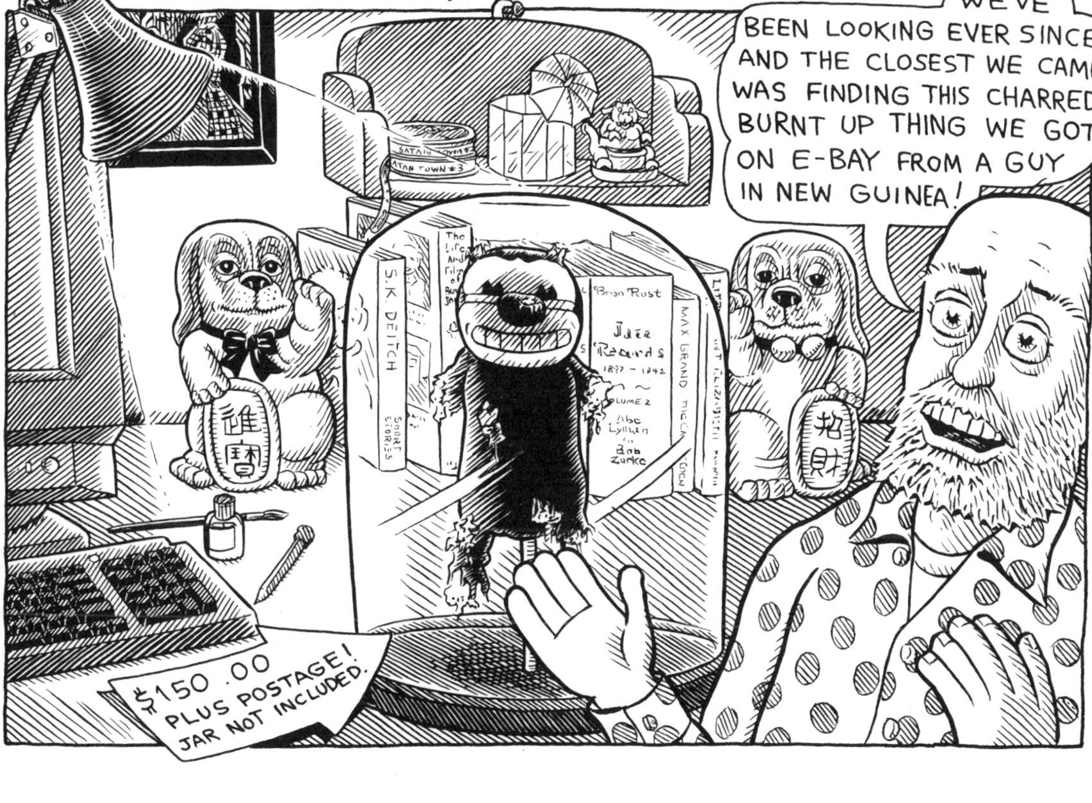
WE'VE BEEN LOOKING EVER SINCE; AND THE CLOSEST WE CAME WAS FINDING THIS CHARRED, BURNT UP THING WE GOT ON E-BAY FROM A GUY IN NEW GUINEA!
S.K. DEITCH SHORT STORIES
Brian Rust Jazz Records 1897 - 1942
MAX GRAND
$150.00 PLUS POSTAGE! JAR NOT INCLUDED.

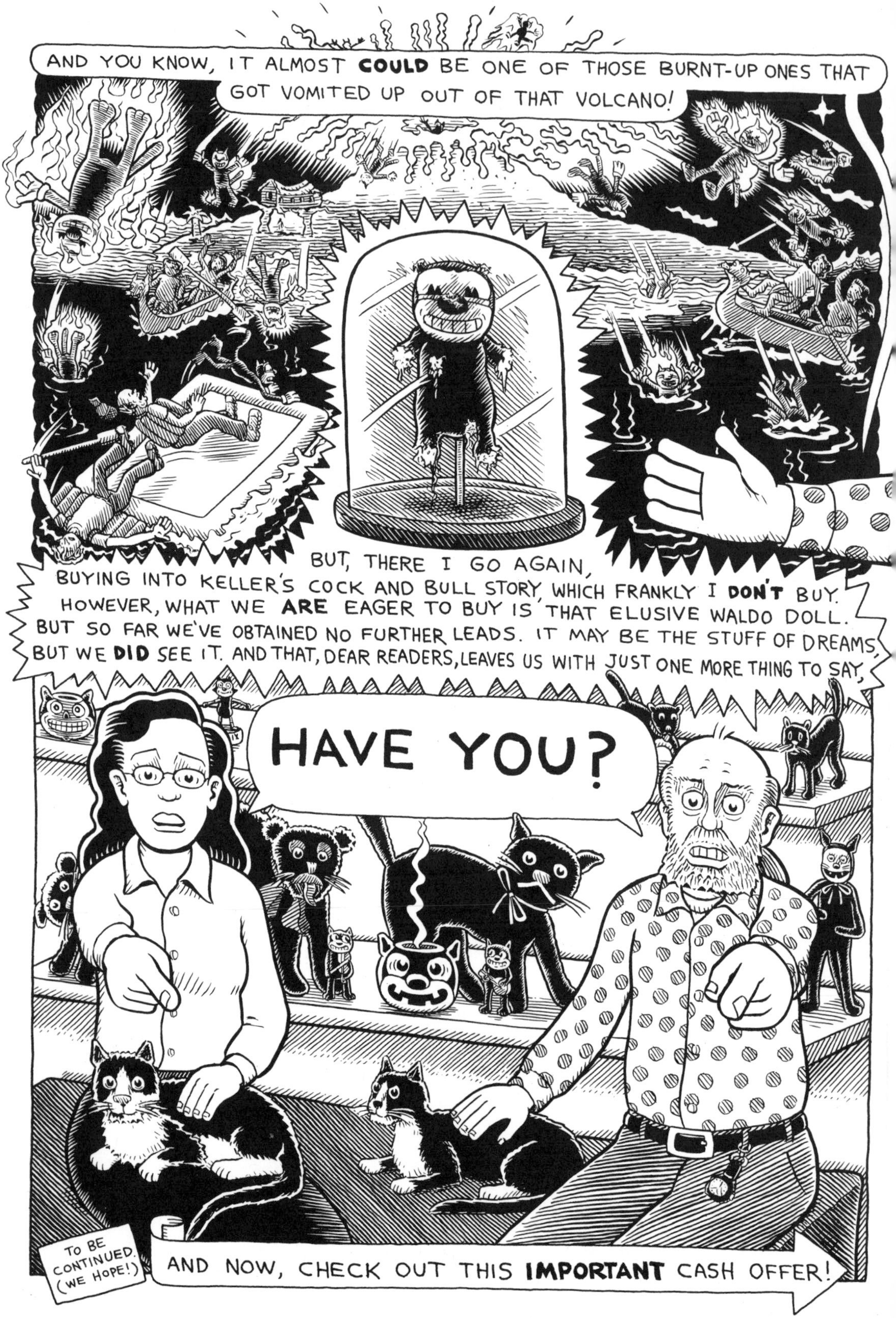

AND YOU KNOW, IT ALMOST **COULD** BE ONE OF THOSE BURNT-UP ONES THAT GOT VOMITED UP OUT OF THAT VOLCANO!
BUT, THERE I GO AGAIN, BUYING INTO KELLER'S COCK AND BULL STORY, WHICH FRANKLY I **DON'T** BUY. HOWEVER, WHAT WE **ARE** EAGER TO BUY IS THAT ELUSIVE WALDO DOLL. BUT SO FAR WE'VE OBTAINED NO FURTHER LEADS. IT MAY BE THE STUFF OF DREAMS, BUT WE **DID** SEE IT. AND THAT, DEAR READERS, LEAVES US WITH JUST ONE MORE THING TO SAY,
HAVE YOU?
TO BE CONTINUED. (WE HOPE!)
AND NOW, CHECK OUT THIS **IMPORTANT** CASH OFFER!

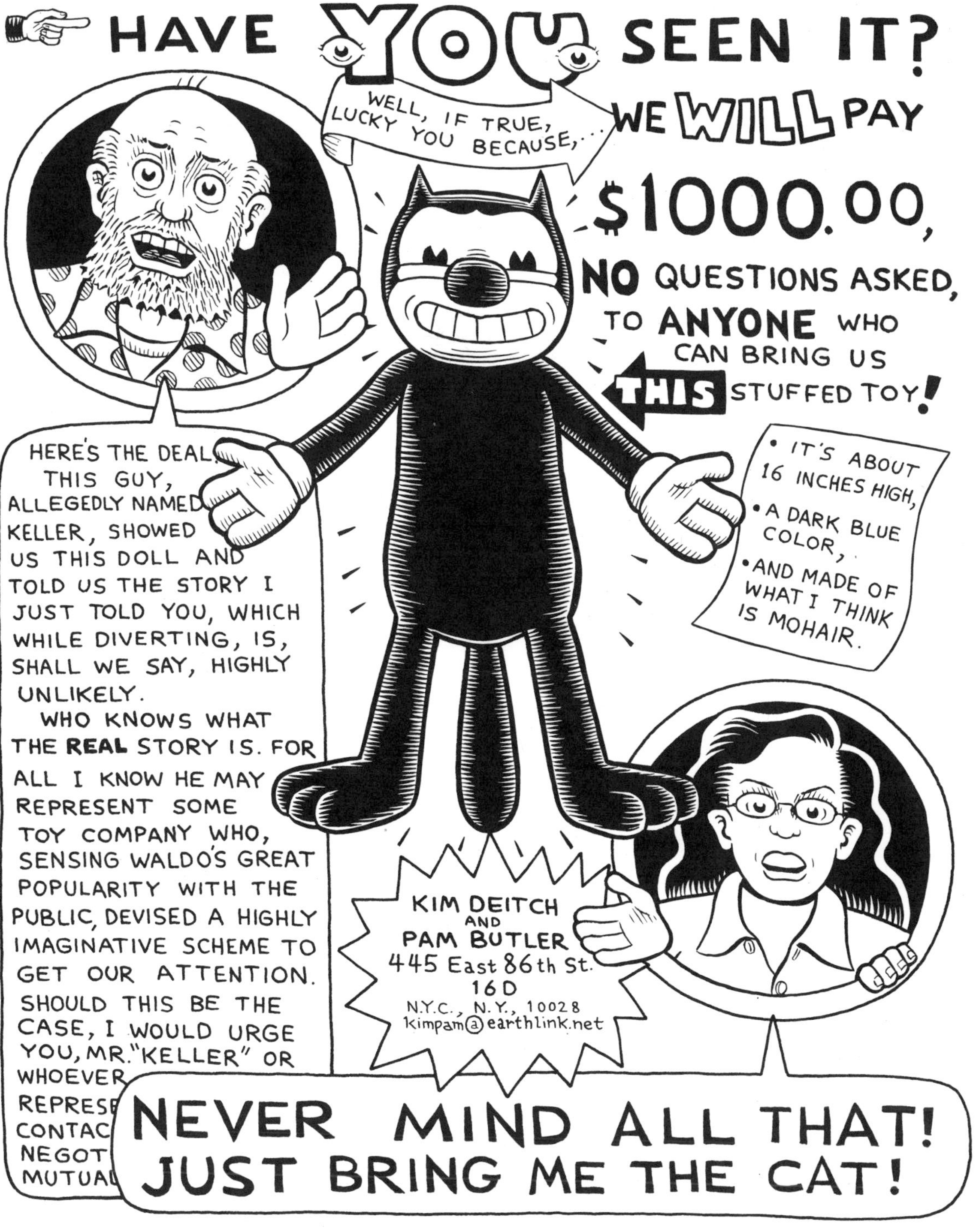
HAVE YOU SEEN IT?
WELL, IF TRUE, LUCKY YOU BECAUSE,...
WE WILL PAY $1000.00, NO QUESTIONS ASKED, TO ANYONE WHO CAN BRING US THIS STUFFED TOY!
• IT'S ABOUT 16 INCHES HIGH, • A DARK BLUE COLOR, • AND MADE OF WHAT I THINK IS MOHAIR.
HERE'S THE DEAL. THIS GUY, ALLEGEDLY NAMED KELLER, SHOWED US THIS DOLL AND TOLD US THE STORY I JUST TOLD YOU, WHICH WHILE DIVERTING, IS, SHALL WE SAY, HIGHLY UNLIKELY. WHO KNOWS WHAT THE REAL STORY IS. FOR ALL I KNOW HE MAY REPRESENT SOME TOY COMPANY WHO, SENSING WALDO'S GREAT POPULARITY WITH THE PUBLIC, DEVISED A HIGHLY IMAGINATIVE SCHEME TO GET OUR ATTENTION. SHOULD THIS BE THE CASE, I WOULD URGE YOU, MR. "KELLER" OR WHOEVER
KIM DEITCH AND PAM BUTLER 445 East 86th St. 16D N.Y.C., N.Y., 10028 kimpam@earthlink.net
NEVER MIND ALL THAT! JUST BRING ME THE CAT!

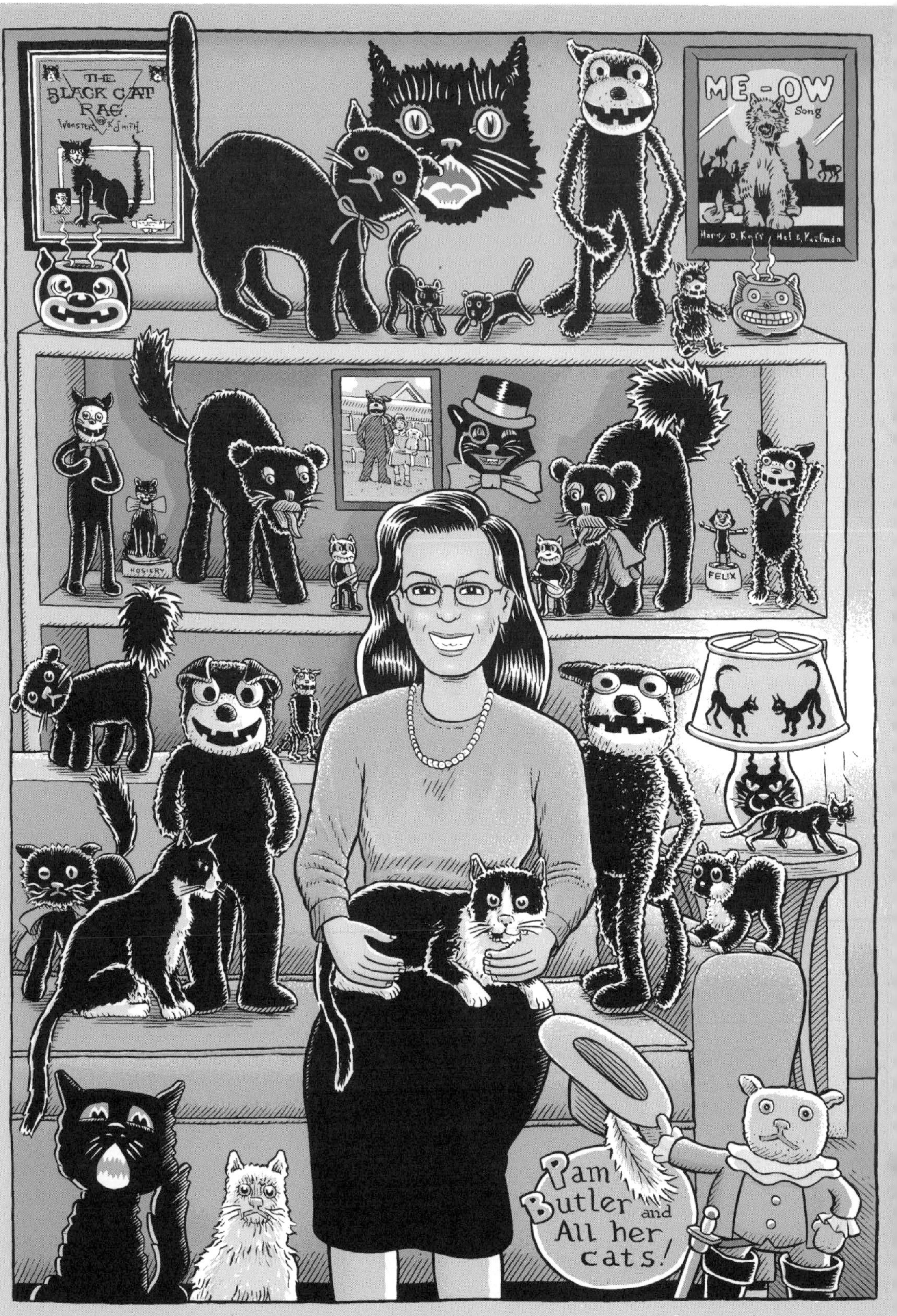
THE BLACK CAT RAG
ME-OW
Song
HOSIERY
FELIX
Pam Butler and All her cats!

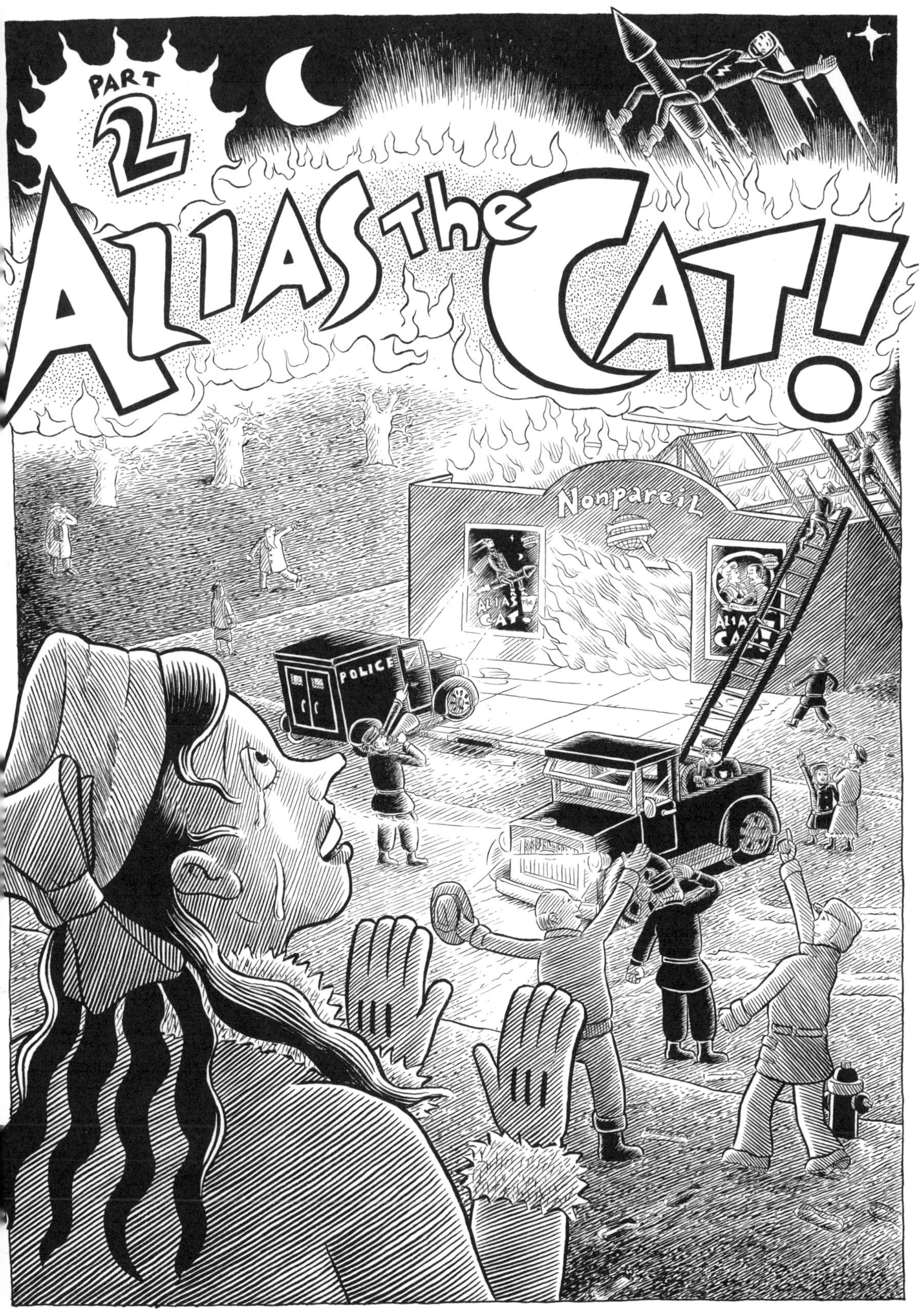
PART 2
ALIAS the CAT!
Nonpareil
ALIAS the CAT
ALIAS CAT
POLICE

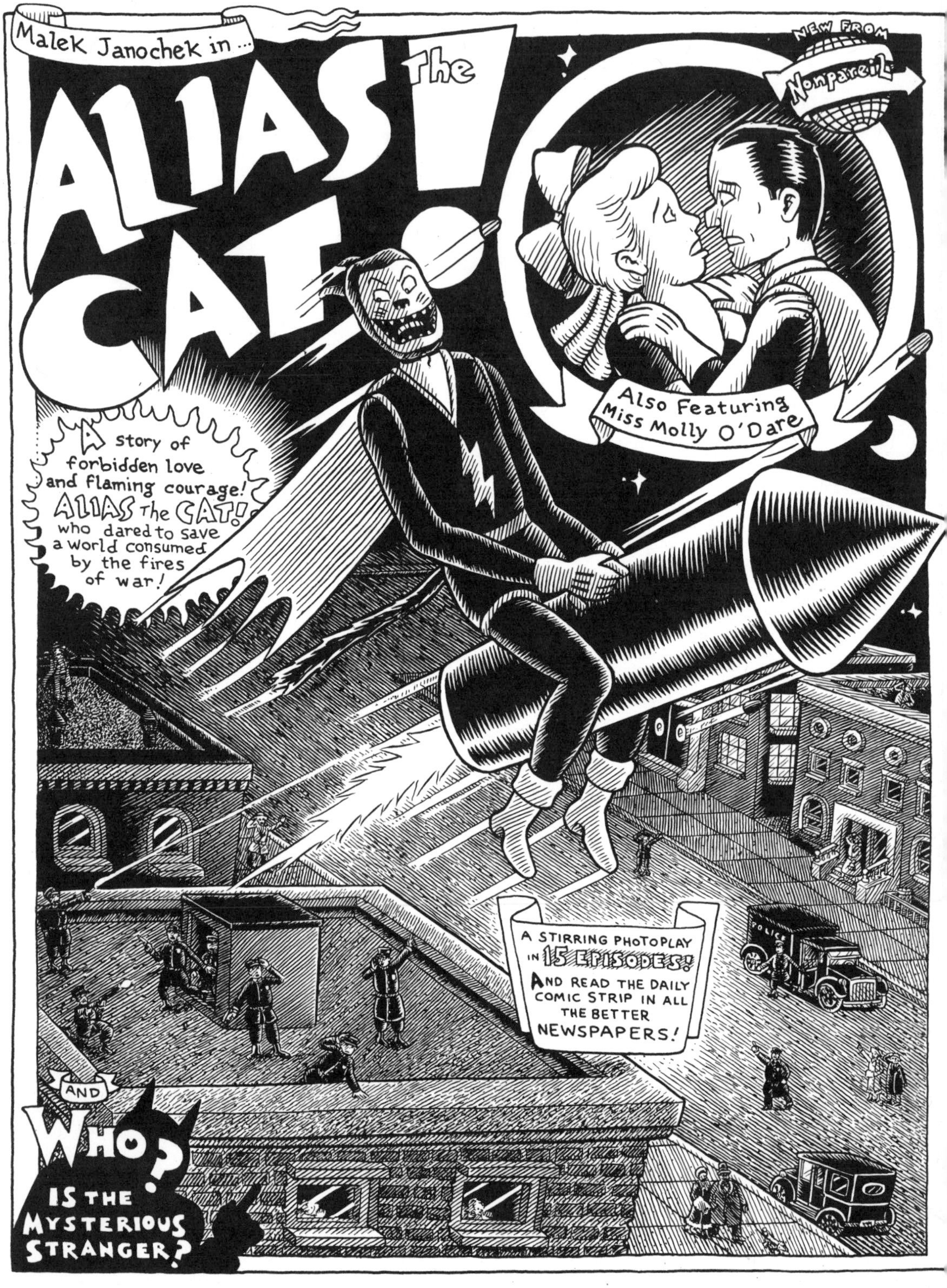

Malek Janochek in...
ALIAS the CAT!
NEW FROM Nonpareil
Also Featuring Miss Molly O'Dare
A story of forbidden love and flaming courage! ALIAS the CAT! who dared to save a world consumed by the fires of war!
A STIRRING PHOTOPLAY IN 15 EPISODES!
AND READ THE DAILY COMIC STRIP IN ALL THE BETTER NEWSPAPERS!
POLICE
AND
WHO? IS THE MYSTERIOUS STRANGER?

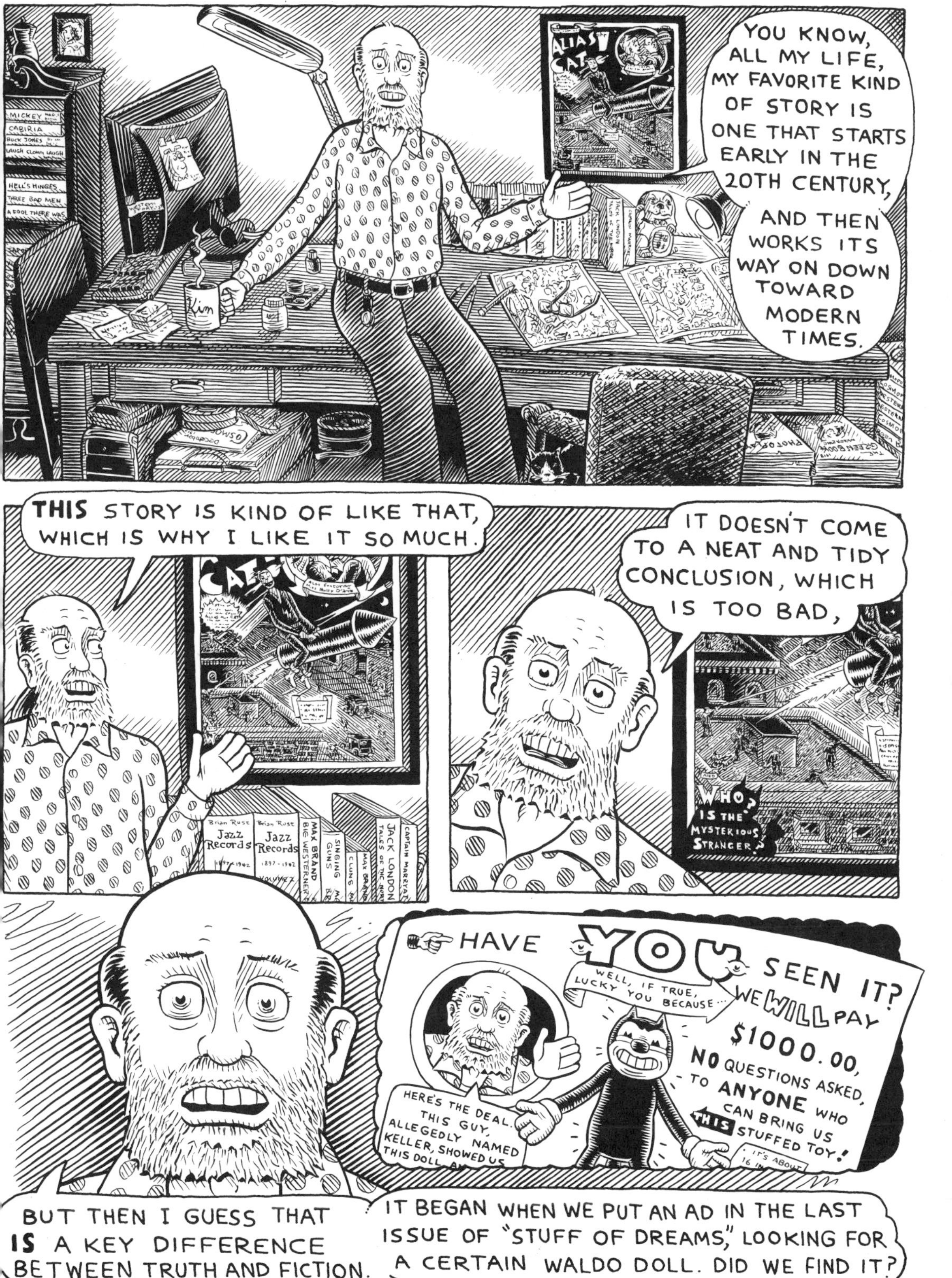

YOU KNOW, ALL MY LIFE, MY FAVORITE KIND OF STORY IS ONE THAT STARTS EARLY IN THE 20TH CENTURY,
AND THEN WORKS ITS WAY ON DOWN TOWARD MODERN TIMES.
THIS STORY IS KIND OF LIKE THAT, WHICH IS WHY I LIKE IT SO MUCH.
IT DOESN'T COME TO A NEAT AND TIDY CONCLUSION, WHICH IS TOO BAD,
WHO? IS THE MYSTERIOUS STRANGER?
Brian Rust Jazz Records
MAX BRAND BIG WESTERNER
JACK LONDON
CAPTAIN MARRYAT
HAVE YOU SEEN IT?
WELL, IF TRUE, LUCKY YOU BECAUSE...
WE WILL PAY $1000.00, NO QUESTIONS ASKED, TO ANYONE WHO CAN BRING US THIS STUFFED TOY!
HERE'S THE DEAL. THIS GUY, ALLEGEDLY NAMED KELLER, SHOWED US THIS DOLL
BUT THEN I GUESS THAT IS A KEY DIFFERENCE BETWEEN TRUTH AND FICTION.
IT BEGAN WHEN WE PUT AN AD IN THE LAST ISSUE OF "STUFF OF DREAMS," LOOKING FOR A CERTAIN WALDO DOLL. DID WE FIND IT?

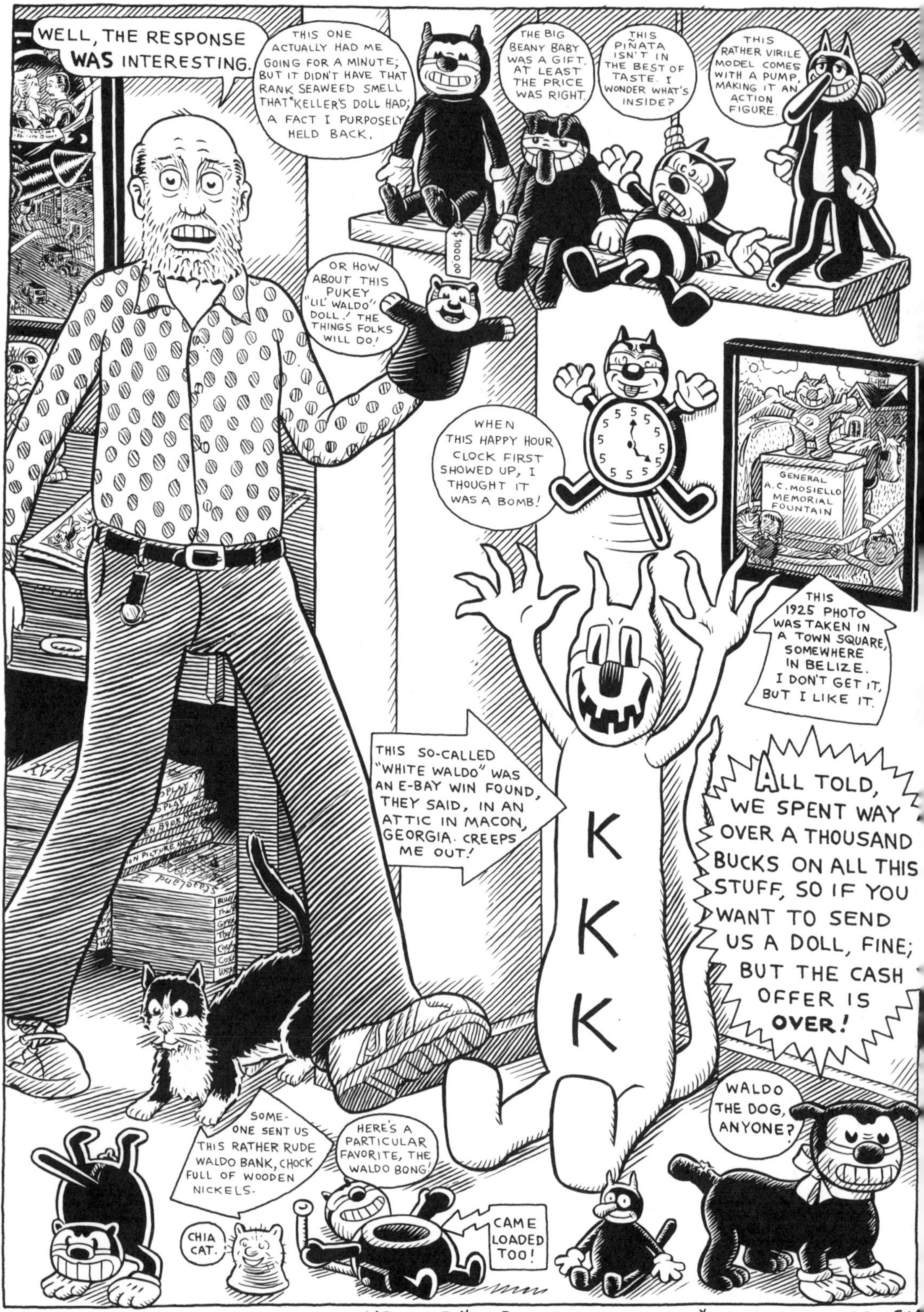
WELL, THE RESPONSE WAS INTERESTING.
THIS ONE ACTUALLY HAD ME GOING FOR A MINUTE; BUT IT DIDN'T HAVE THAT RANK SEAWEED SMELL THAT*KELLER'S DOLL HAD; A FACT I PURPOSELY HELD BACK.
THE BIG BEANY BABY WAS A GIFT. AT LEAST THE PRICE WAS RIGHT.
THIS PIÑATA ISN'T IN THE BEST OF TASTE. I WONDER WHAT'S INSIDE?
THIS RATHER VIRILE MODEL COMES WITH A PUMP, MAKING IT AN ACTION FIGURE.
$1000.00
OR HOW ABOUT THIS PUKEY "LIL' WALDO" DOLL! THE THINGS FOLKS WILL DO!
WHEN THIS HAPPY HOUR CLOCK FIRST SHOWED UP, I THOUGHT IT WAS A BOMB!
GENERAL A.C. MOSIELLO MEMORIAL FOUNTAIN
THIS 1925 PHOTO WAS TAKEN IN A TOWN SQUARE, SOMEWHERE IN BELIZE. I DON'T GET IT, BUT I LIKE IT.
THIS SO-CALLED "WHITE WALDO" WAS AN E-BAY WIN FOUND, THEY SAID, IN AN ATTIC IN MACON, GEORGIA. CREEPS ME OUT!
KKK
ALL TOLD, WE SPENT WAY OVER A THOUSAND BUCKS ON ALL THIS STUFF, SO IF YOU WANT TO SEND US A DOLL, FINE; BUT THE CASH OFFER IS OVER!
SOME-ONE SENT US THIS RATHER RUDE WALDO BANK, CHOCK FULL OF WOODEN NICKELS.
HERE'S A PARTICULAR FAVORITE, THE WALDO BONG!
CHIA CAT.
CAME LOADED TOO!
WALDO THE DOG, ANYONE?

BOTTOM LINE: WE NEVER SAW KELLER* OR HIS CAT AGAIN *SEE STUFF OF DREAMS#1

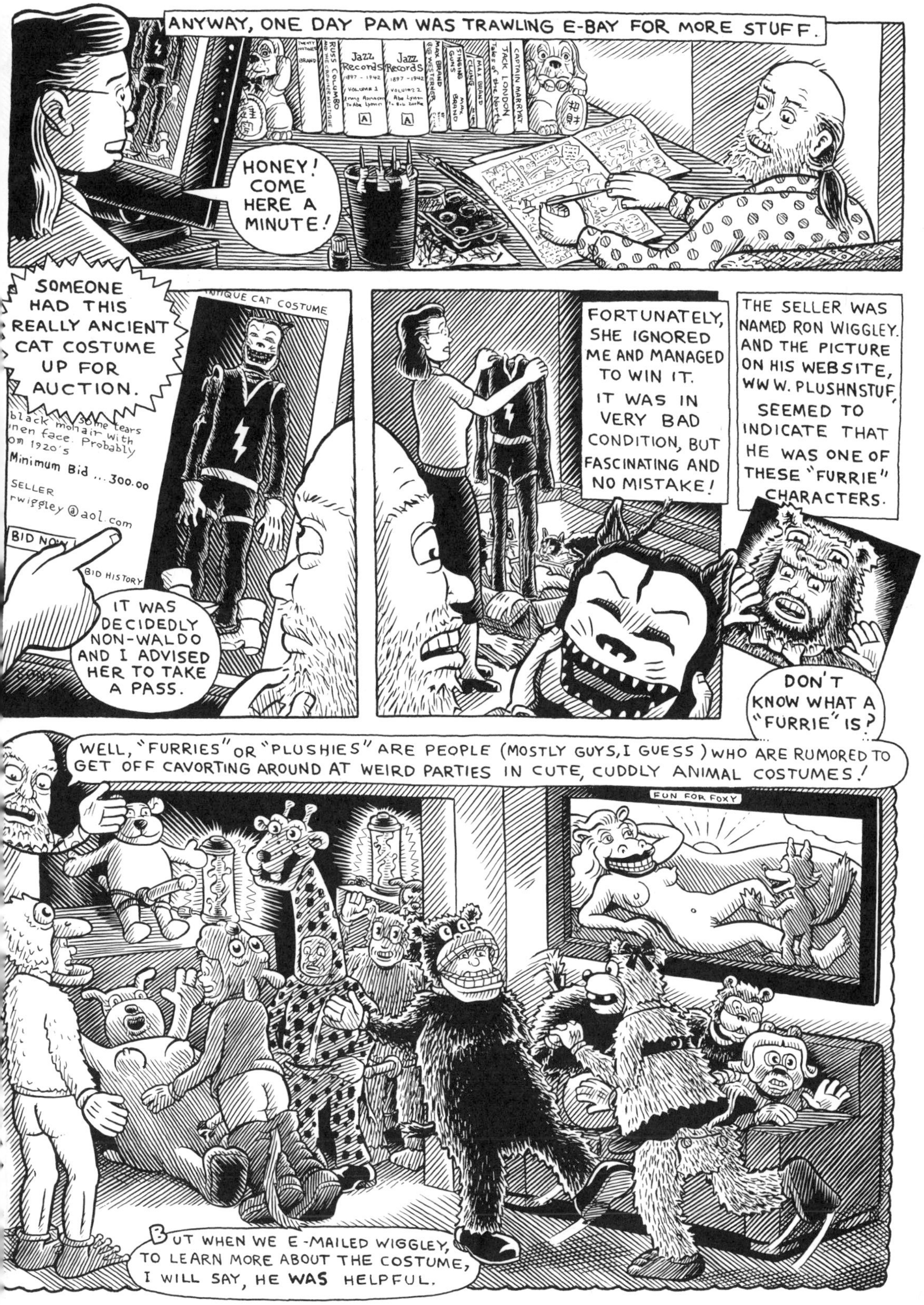

ANYWAY, ONE DAY PAM WAS TRAWLING E-BAY FOR MORE STUFF.
RUSS COLUMBO AND THE CROONER MYSTIQUE
Jazz Records 1897 - 1942 VOLUME 1
Jazz Records 1897 - 1942 VOLUME 2
MAX BRAND
JACK LONDON Tales of the North
CAPTAIN MARRYAT
HONEY! COME HERE A MINUTE!
SOMEONE HAD THIS REALLY ANCIENT CAT COSTUME UP FOR AUCTION.
NTIQUE CAT COSTUME
black mohair some tears
inen face. Probably
om 1920's
Minimum Bid ... 300.00
SELLER
rwiggley @ aol.com
BID NOW
BID HISTORY
IT WAS DECIDEDLY NON-WALDO AND I ADVISED HER TO TAKE A PASS.
FORTUNATELY, SHE IGNORED ME AND MANAGED TO WIN IT.
IT WAS IN VERY BAD CONDITION, BUT FASCINATING AND NO MISTAKE!
THE SELLER WAS NAMED RON WIGGLEY. AND THE PICTURE ON HIS WEBSITE, WWW. PLUSHNSTUF, SEEMED TO INDICATE THAT HE WAS ONE OF THESE "FURRIE" CHARACTERS.
DON'T KNOW WHAT A "FURRIE" IS?
WELL, "FURRIES" OR "PLUSHIES" ARE PEOPLE (MOSTLY GUYS, I GUESS) WHO ARE RUMORED TO GET OFF CAVORTING AROUND AT WEIRD PARTIES IN CUTE, CUDDLY ANIMAL COSTUMES!
FUN FOR FOXY
BUT WHEN WE E-MAILED WIGGLEY, TO LEARN MORE ABOUT THE COSTUME, I WILL SAY, HE WAS HELPFUL.

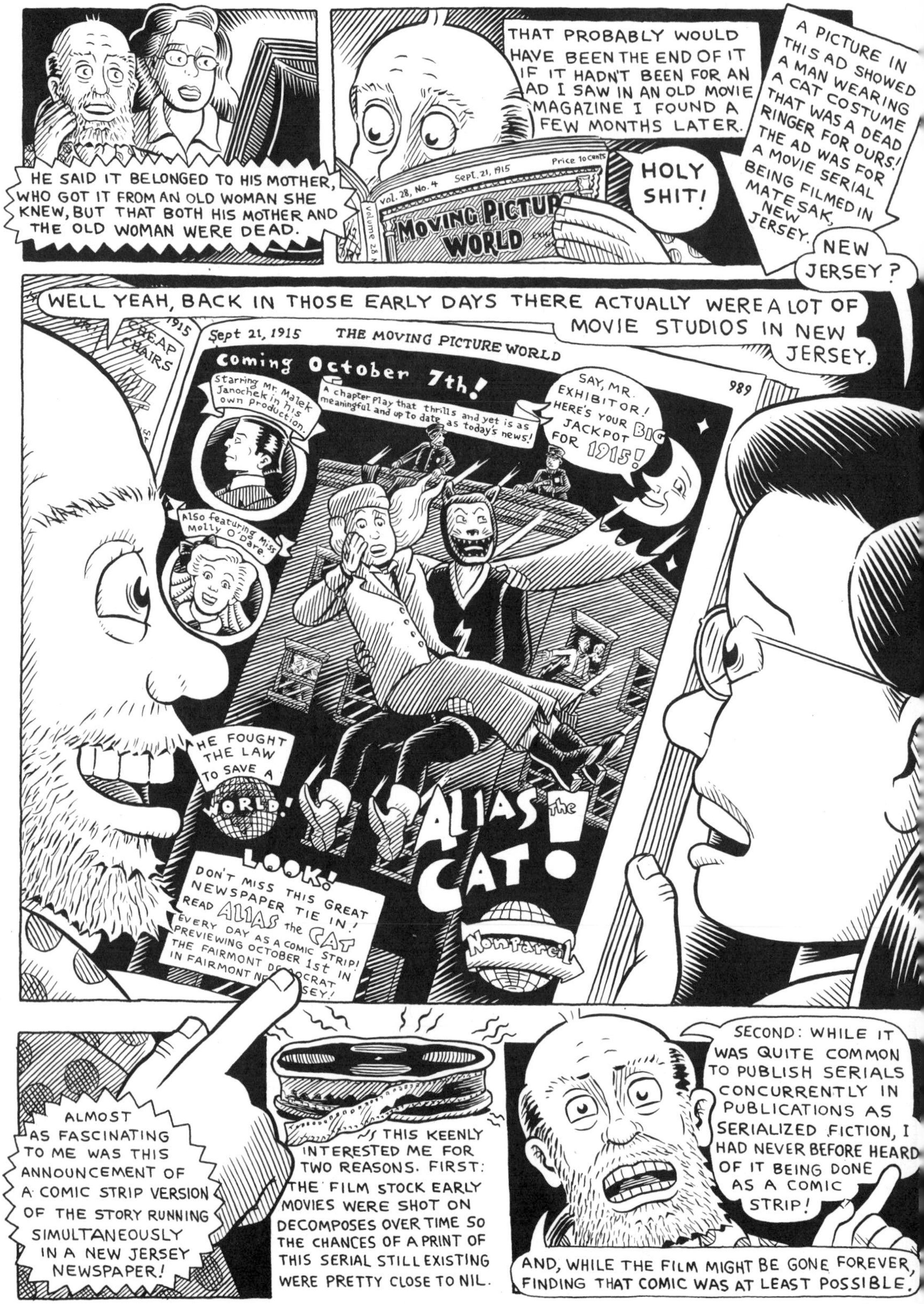
HE SAID IT BELONGED TO HIS MOTHER, WHO GOT IT FROM AN OLD WOMAN SHE KNEW, BUT THAT BOTH HIS MOTHER AND THE OLD WOMAN WERE DEAD.
THAT PROBABLY WOULD HAVE BEEN THE END OF IT IF IT HADN'T BEEN FOR AN AD I SAW IN AN OLD MOVIE MAGAZINE I FOUND A FEW MONTHS LATER.
Vol. 28, No. 4 Sept. 21, 1915 Price 10 cents
MOVING PICTURE WORLD
HOLY SHIT!
A PICTURE IN THIS AD SHOWED A MAN WEARING A CAT COSTUME THAT WAS A DEAD RINGER FOR OURS! THE AD WAS FOR A MOVIE SERIAL BEING FILMED IN MATESAK, NEW JERSEY.
NEW JERSEY?
WELL YEAH, BACK IN THOSE EARLY DAYS THERE ACTUALLY WERE A LOT OF MOVIE STUDIOS IN NEW JERSEY.
1915
CHEAP CHAIRS
Sept 21, 1915 THE MOVING PICTURE WORLD
989
Coming October 7th!
Starring Mr. Malek Janochek in his own production.
A chapter play that thrills and yet is as meaningful and up to date as today's news!
SAY, MR. EXHIBITOR! HERE'S YOUR BIG JACKPOT FOR 1915!
Also featuring Miss Molly O'Dare.
HE FOUGHT THE LAW TO SAVE A WORLD!
ALIAS the CAT!
LOOK! DON'T MISS THIS GREAT NEWSPAPER TIE IN! READ ALIAS the CAT EVERY DAY AS A COMIC STRIP! PREVIEWING OCTOBER 1st IN THE FAIRMONT DEMOCRAT IN FAIRMONT NEW JERSEY!
Nonpareil
ALMOST AS FASCINATING TO ME WAS THIS ANNOUNCEMENT OF A COMIC STRIP VERSION OF THE STORY RUNNING SIMULTANEOUSLY IN A NEW JERSEY NEWSPAPER!
THIS KEENLY INTERESTED ME FOR TWO REASONS. FIRST: THE FILM STOCK EARLY MOVIES WERE SHOT ON DECOMPOSES OVER TIME SO THE CHANCES OF A PRINT OF THIS SERIAL STILL EXISTING WERE PRETTY CLOSE TO NIL.
SECOND: WHILE IT WAS QUITE COMMON TO PUBLISH SERIALS CONCURRENTLY IN PUBLICATIONS AS SERIALIZED FICTION, I HAD NEVER BEFORE HEARD OF IT BEING DONE AS A COMIC STRIP!
AND, WHILE THE FILM MIGHT BE GONE FOREVER, FINDING THAT COMIC WAS AT LEAST POSSIBLE.

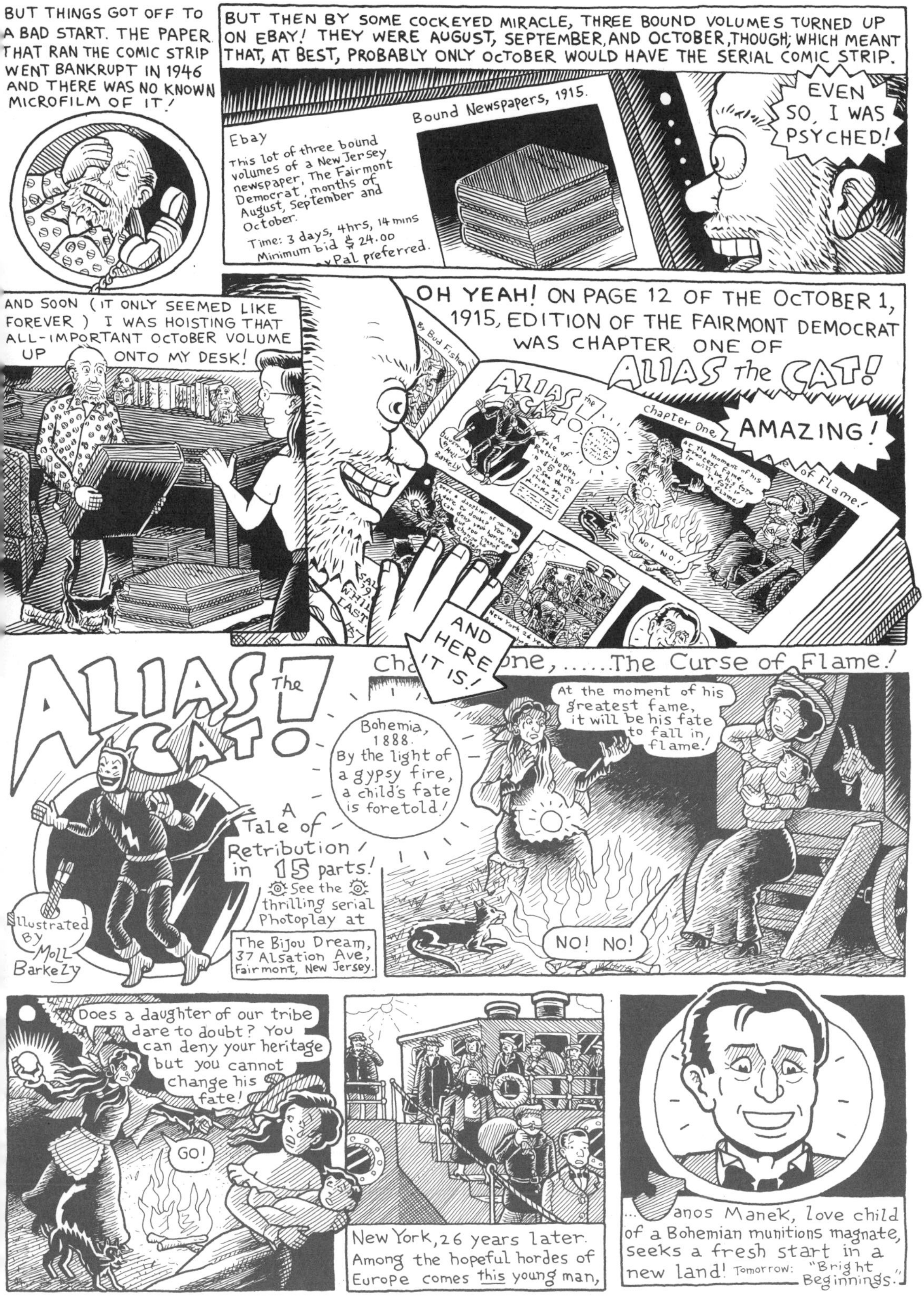
BUT THINGS GOT OFF TO A BAD START. THE PAPER THAT RAN THE COMIC STRIP WENT BANKRUPT IN 1946 AND THERE WAS NO KNOWN MICROFILM OF IT!
BUT THEN BY SOME COCKEYED MIRACLE, THREE BOUND VOLUMES TURNED UP ON EBAY! THEY WERE AUGUST, SEPTEMBER, AND OCTOBER, THOUGH; WHICH MEANT THAT, AT BEST, PROBABLY ONLY OCTOBER WOULD HAVE THE SERIAL COMIC STRIP.
Ebay
This lot of three bound volumes of a New Jersey newspaper, The Fairmont Democrat, months of August, September and October.
Time: 3 days, 4hrs, 14 mins
Minimum bid $24.00
Bound Newspapers, 1915.
EVEN SO, I WAS PSYCHED!
AND SOON (IT ONLY SEEMED LIKE FOREVER) I WAS HOISTING THAT ALL-IMPORTANT OCTOBER VOLUME UP ONTO MY DESK!
OH YEAH! ON PAGE 12 OF THE OCTOBER 1, 1915, EDITION OF THE FAIRMONT DEMOCRAT WAS CHAPTER ONE OF ALIAS the CAT!
AMAZING!
AND HERE IT IS!
ALIAS The CAT!
A Tale of Retribution in 15 parts!
See the thrilling serial Photoplay at
The Bijou Dream, 37 Alsation Ave, Fairmont, New Jersey.
Illustrated By Moll Barkezy
Chapter One, ...The Curse of Flame!
Bohemia, 1888. By the light of a gypsy fire, a child's fate is foretold!
At the moment of his greatest fame, it will be his fate to fall in flame!
NO! NO!
Does a daughter of our tribe dare to doubt? You can deny your heritage but you cannot change his fate!
GO!
New York, 26 years later. Among the hopeful hordes of Europe comes this young man,
...anos Manek, love child of a Bohemian munitions magnate, seeks a fresh start in a new land! Tomorrow: "Bright Beginnings."

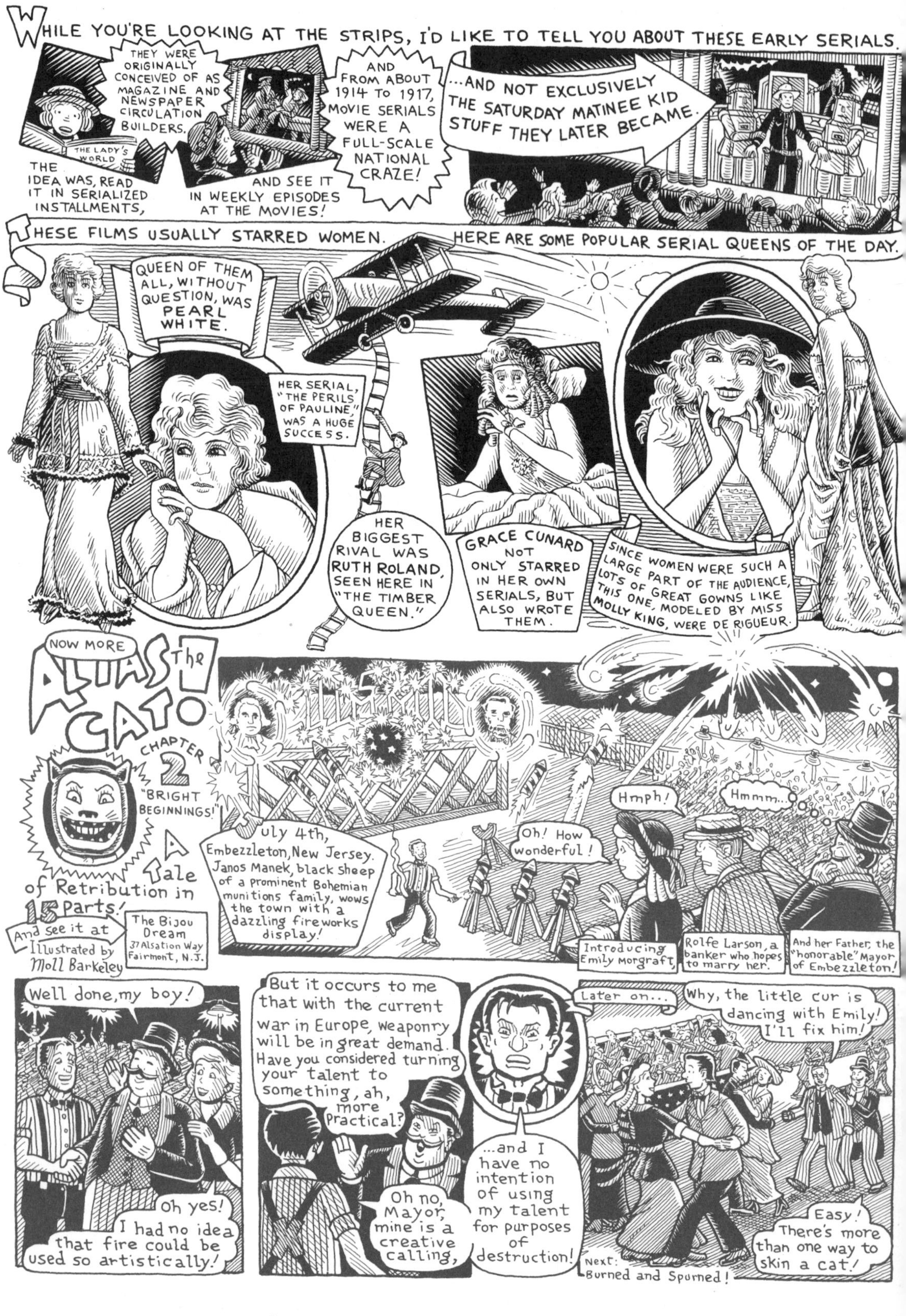
WHILE YOU'RE LOOKING AT THE STRIPS, I'D LIKE TO TELL YOU ABOUT THESE EARLY SERIALS.
THEY WERE ORIGINALLY CONCEIVED OF AS MAGAZINE AND NEWSPAPER CIRCULATION BUILDERS.
THE LADY'S WORLD
THE IDEA WAS, READ IT IN SERIALIZED INSTALLMENTS,
AND SEE IT IN WEEKLY EPISODES AT THE MOVIES!
AND FROM ABOUT 1914 TO 1917, MOVIE SERIALS WERE A FULL-SCALE NATIONAL CRAZE!
...AND NOT EXCLUSIVELY THE SATURDAY MATINEE KID STUFF THEY LATER BECAME.
THESE FILMS USUALLY STARRED WOMEN.
HERE ARE SOME POPULAR SERIAL QUEENS OF THE DAY.
QUEEN OF THEM ALL, WITHOUT QUESTION, WAS PEARL WHITE.
HER SERIAL, "THE PERILS OF PAULINE," WAS A HUGE SUCCESS.
HER BIGGEST RIVAL WAS RUTH ROLAND, SEEN HERE IN "THE TIMBER QUEEN."
GRACE CUNARD NOT ONLY STARRED IN HER OWN SERIALS, BUT ALSO WROTE THEM.
SINCE WOMEN WERE SUCH A LARGE PART OF THE AUDIENCE, LOTS OF GREAT GOWNS LIKE THIS ONE, MODELED BY MISS MOLLY KING, WERE DE RIGUEUR.
NOW MORE
ALIAS THE CAT!
CHAPTER 2
"BRIGHT BEGINNINGS!"
A Tale of Retribution in 15 Parts!
And see it at
The Bijou Dream 37 Alsation Way Fairmont, N.J.
Illustrated by Moll Barkeley
July 4th, Embezzleton, New Jersey. Janos Manek, black sheep of a prominent Bohemian munitions family, wows the town with a dazzling fireworks display!
Oh! How wonderful!
Hmph!
Hmmm...
Introducing Emily Morgraft
Rolfe Larson, a banker who hopes to marry her.
And her Father, the "honorable" Mayor of Embezzleton!
Well done, my boy!
Oh yes! I had no idea that fire could be used so artistically!
But it occurs to me that with the current war in Europe, weaponry will be in great demand. Have you considered turning your talent to something, ah, more practical?
Oh no, Mayor, mine is a creative calling,
...and I have no intention of using my talent for purposes of destruction!
Later on...
Why, the little cur is dancing with Emily! I'll fix him!
Easy! There's more than one way to skin a cat!
Next: Burned and Spurned!

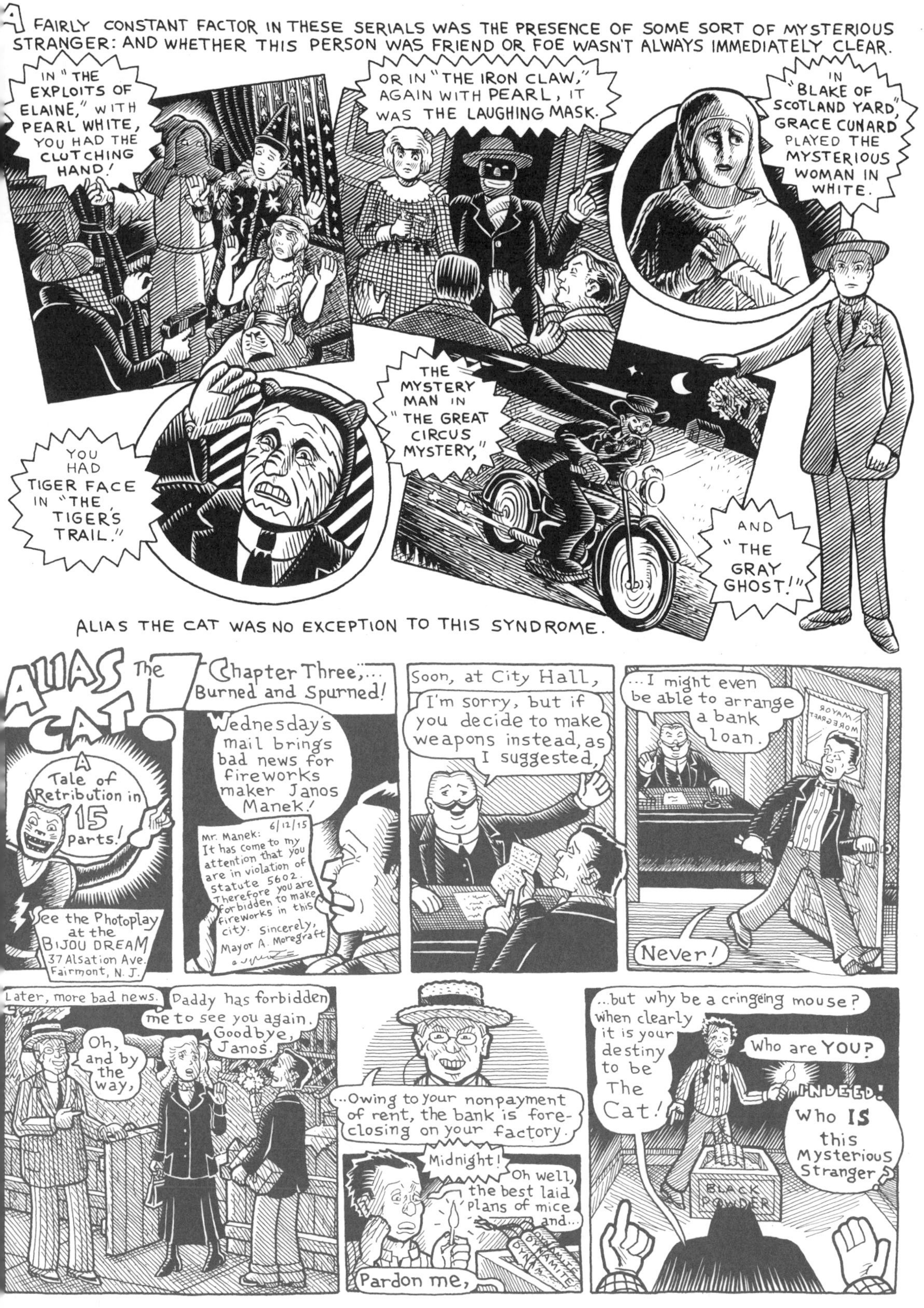

A FAIRLY CONSTANT FACTOR IN THESE SERIALS WAS THE PRESENCE OF SOME SORT OF MYSTERIOUS STRANGER: AND WHETHER THIS PERSON WAS FRIEND OR FOE WASN'T ALWAYS IMMEDIATELY CLEAR.
IN "THE EXPLOITS OF ELAINE," WITH PEARL WHITE, YOU HAD THE CLUTCHING HAND!
OR IN "THE IRON CLAW," AGAIN WITH PEARL, IT WAS THE LAUGHING MASK.
IN "BLAKE OF SCOTLAND YARD," GRACE CUNARD PLAYED THE MYSTERIOUS WOMAN IN WHITE.
YOU HAD TIGER FACE IN "THE TIGER'S TRAIL."
THE MYSTERY MAN IN "THE GREAT CIRCUS MYSTERY,"
AND "THE GRAY GHOST!"
ALIAS THE CAT WAS NO EXCEPTION TO THIS SYNDROME.
ALIAS The CAT! 7
A Tale of Retribution in 15 parts!
See the Photoplay at the BIJOU DREAM 37 Alsation Ave. Fairmont, N. J.
Chapter Three;... Burned and Spurned!
Wednesday's mail brings bad news for fireworks maker Janos Manek!
Mr. Manek: 6/12/15 It has come to my attention that you are in violation of statute 5602. Therefore you are forbidden to make fireworks in this city. Sincerely, Mayor A. Moregraft
Soon, at City Hall,
I'm sorry, but if you decide to make weapons instead, as I suggested,
...I might even be able to arrange a bank loan.
MAYOR MOREGRAFT
Never!
Later, more bad news.
Daddy has forbidden me to see you again. Goodbye, Janos.
Oh, and by the way,
...Owing to your nonpayment of rent, the bank is fore-closing on your factory.
Midnight!
Oh well, the best laid plans of mice and...
DYNAMITE
Pardon me,
...but why be a cringeing mouse? when clearly it is your destiny to be The Cat!
Who are YOU?
INDEED! Who IS this Mysterious Stranger?
BLACK POWDER

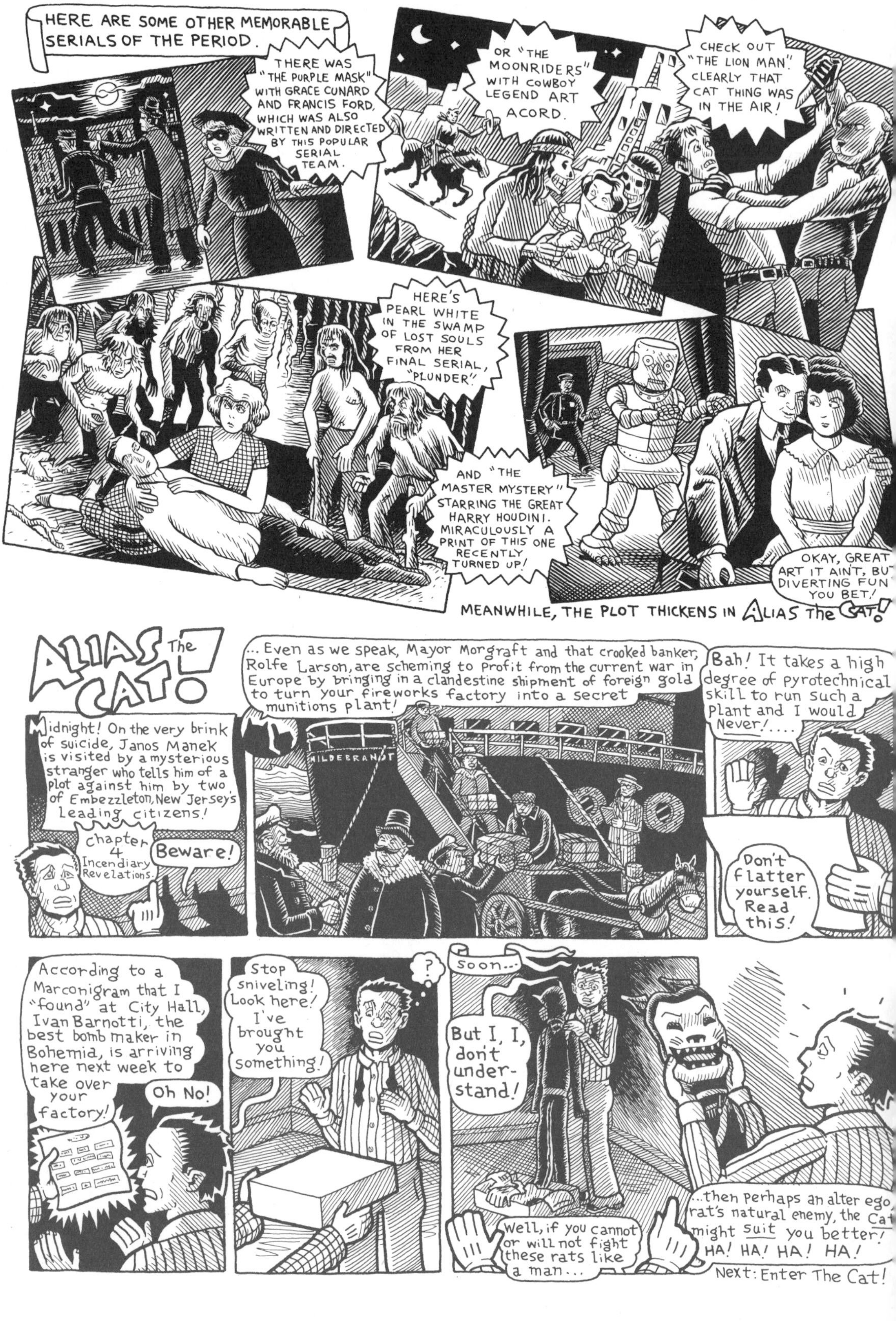
HERE ARE SOME OTHER MEMORABLE SERIALS OF THE PERIOD.
THERE WAS "THE PURPLE MASK" WITH GRACE CUNARD AND FRANCIS FORD, WHICH WAS ALSO WRITTEN AND DIRECTED BY THIS POPULAR SERIAL TEAM.
OR "THE MOONRIDERS" WITH COWBOY LEGEND ART ACORD.
CHECK OUT "THE LION MAN". CLEARLY THAT CAT THING WAS IN THE AIR!
HERE'S PEARL WHITE IN THE SWAMP OF LOST SOULS FROM HER FINAL SERIAL, "PLUNDER".
AND "THE MASTER MYSTERY" STARRING THE GREAT HARRY HOUDINI. MIRACULOUSLY A PRINT OF THIS ONE RECENTLY TURNED UP!
OKAY, GREAT ART IT AIN'T, BUT DIVERTING FUN YOU BET!
MEANWHILE, THE PLOT THICKENS IN ALIAS THE CAT!
ALIAS THE CAT!
Midnight! On the very brink of suicide, Janos Manek is visited by a mysterious stranger who tells him of a plot against him by two of Embezzleton, New Jersey's leading citizens!
Chapter 4 Incendiary Revelations.
Beware!
... Even as we speak, Mayor Morgraft and that crooked banker, Rolfe Larson, are scheming to profit from the current war in Europe by bringing in a clandestine shipment of foreign gold to turn your fireworks factory into a secret munitions plant!
HILDEBRANDT
Bah! It takes a high degree of pyrotechnical skill to run such a plant and I would Never!....
Don't flatter yourself. Read this!
According to a Marconigram that I "found" at City Hall, Ivan Barnotti, the best bomb maker in Bohemia, is arriving here next week to take over your factory!
Oh No!
Stop sniveling! Look here! I've brought you something!
?
Soon...
But I, I, don't under-stand!
Well, if you cannot or will not fight these rats like a man...
...then perhaps an alter ego rat's natural enemy, the Cat might suit you better! HA! HA! HA! HA!
Next: Enter The Cat!

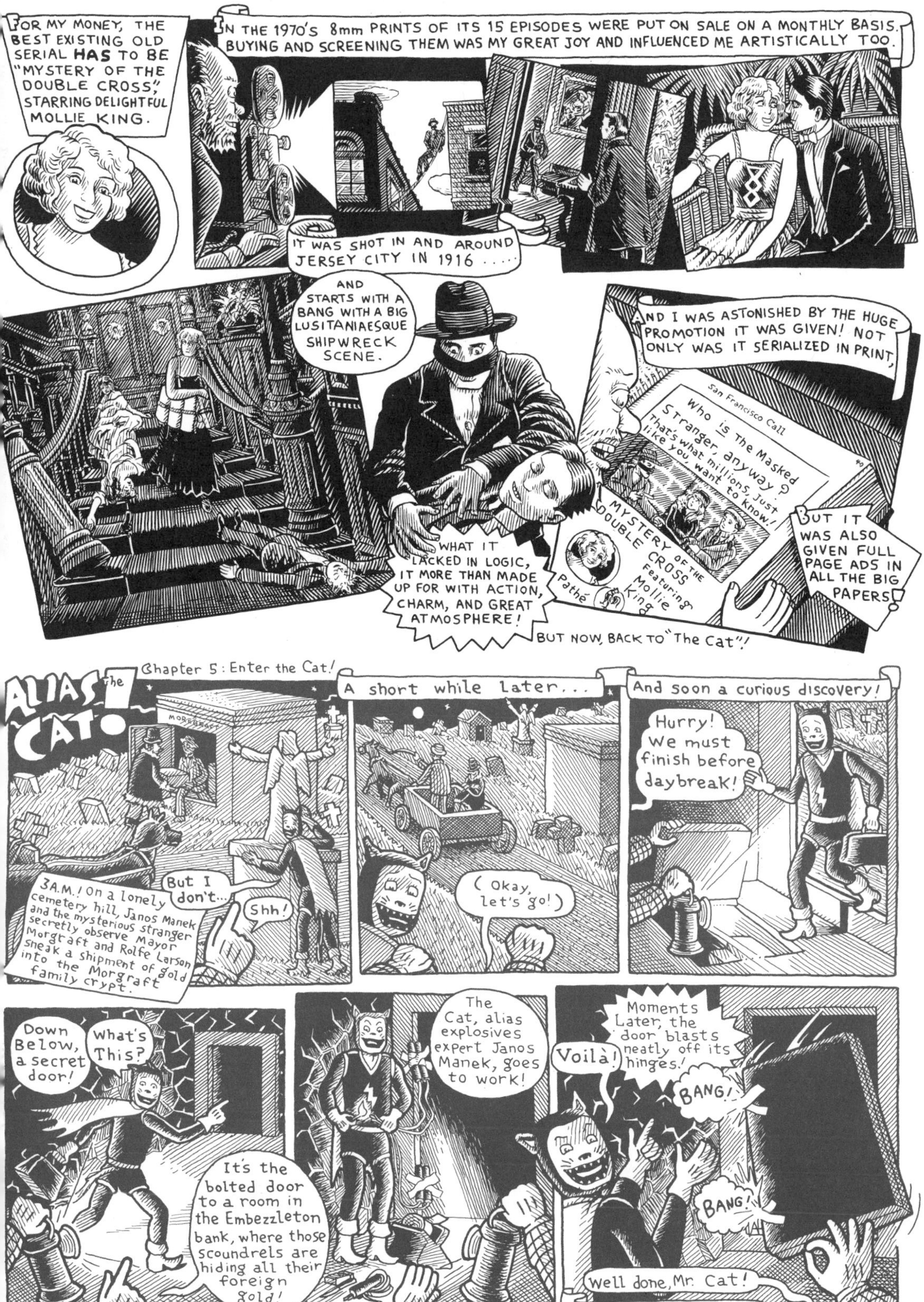
FOR MY MONEY, THE BEST EXISTING OLD SERIAL HAS TO BE "MYSTERY OF THE DOUBLE CROSS," STARRING DELIGHTFUL MOLLIE KING.
IN THE 1970'S 8mm PRINTS OF ITS 15 EPISODES WERE PUT ON SALE ON A MONTHLY BASIS. BUYING AND SCREENING THEM WAS MY GREAT JOY AND INFLUENCED ME ARTISTICALLY TOO.
IT WAS SHOT IN AND AROUND JERSEY CITY IN 1916 .....
AND STARTS WITH A BANG WITH A BIG LUSITANIAESQUE SHIPWRECK SCENE.
AND I WAS ASTONISHED BY THE HUGE PROMOTION IT WAS GIVEN! NOT ONLY WAS IT SERIALIZED IN PRINT,
San Francisco Call
Who is The Masked Stranger, anyway? That's what millions, just like you, want to know!
MYSTERY OF THE DOUBLE CROSS Featuring Mollie King
Pathé
BUT IT WAS ALSO GIVEN FULL PAGE ADS IN ALL THE BIG PAPERS!
WHAT IT LACKED IN LOGIC, IT MORE THAN MADE UP FOR WITH ACTION, CHARM, AND GREAT ATMOSPHERE!
BUT NOW, BACK TO "The Cat"!
ALIAS the CAT!
Chapter 5: Enter the Cat!
MORGRAFT
3A.M.! On a lonely cemetery hill, Janos Manek and the mysterious stranger secretly observe Mayor Morgraft and Rolfe Larson sneak a shipment of gold into the Morgraft family crypt.
But I don't...
Shh!
A short while later...
(Okay, let's go!)
And soon a curious discovery!
Hurry! We must finish before daybreak!
Down Below, a secret door!
What's This?
It's the bolted door to a room in the Embezzleton bank, where those scoundrels are hiding all their foreign gold!
The Cat, alias explosives expert Janos Manek, goes to work!
Moments Later, the door blasts neatly off its hinges!
Voilà!
BANG!
BANG!
Well done, Mr. Cat!
NEXT: flowing Gold!

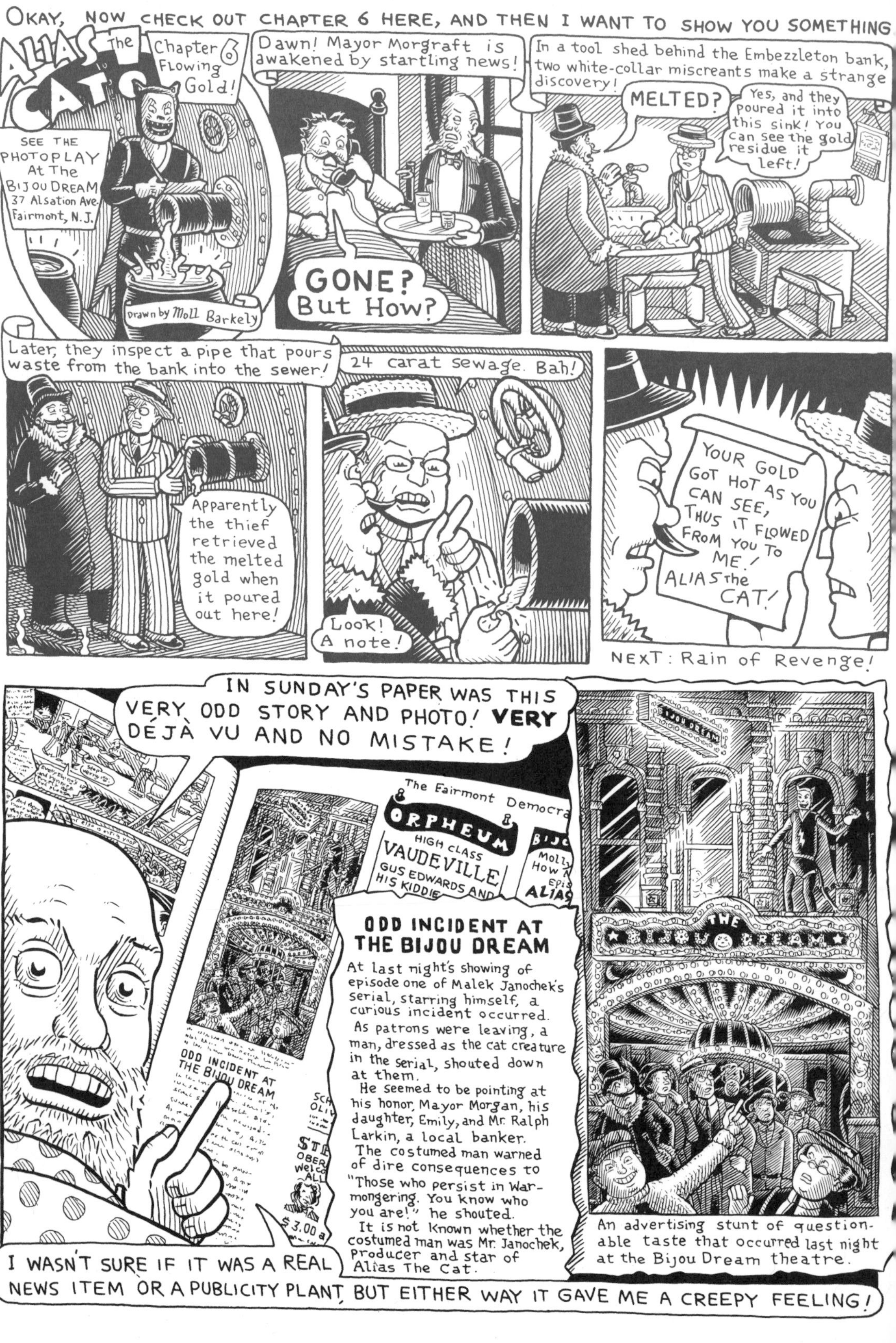
OKAY, NOW CHECK OUT CHAPTER 6 HERE, AND THEN I WANT TO SHOW YOU SOMETHING
ALIAS The CAT
Chapter 6 Flowing Gold!
SEE THE PHOTOPLAY At The BIJOU DREAM 37 Alsation Ave. Fairmont, N.J.
Drawn by Moll Barkely
Dawn! Mayor Morgraft is awakened by startling news!
GONE? But How?
In a tool shed behind the Embezzleton bank, two white-collar miscreants make a strange discovery!
MELTED?
Yes, and they poured it into this sink! You can see the gold residue it left!
Later, they inspect a pipe that pours waste from the bank into the sewer!
Apparently the thief retrieved the melted gold when it poured out here!
24 carat sewage. Bah!
Look! A note!
YOUR GOLD GOT HOT AS YOU CAN SEE, THUS IT FLOWED FROM YOU TO ME! ALIAS the CAT!
NEXT: Rain of Revenge!
IN SUNDAY'S PAPER WAS THIS VERY ODD STORY AND PHOTO! VERY DÉJÀ VU AND NO MISTAKE!
The Fairmont Democra
ORPHEUM
HIGH CLASS VAUDEVILLE
GUS EDWARDS AND HIS KIDDIE
ODD INCIDENT AT THE BIJOU DREAM
ODD INCIDENT AT THE BIJOU DREAM
At last night's showing of episode one of Malek Janochek's serial, starring himself, a curious incident occurred.
As patrons were leaving, a man, dressed as the cat creature in the serial, shouted down at them.
He seemed to be pointing at his honor, Mayor Morgan, his daughter, Emily, and Mr. Ralph Larkin, a local banker.
The costumed man warned of dire consequences to "Those who persist in War-mongering. You know who you are!" he shouted.
It is not known whether the costumed man was Mr. Janochek, Producer and star of Alias The Cat.
THE BIJOU DREAM
An advertising stunt of questionable taste that occurred last night at the Bijou Dream theatre.
I WASN'T SURE IF IT WAS A REAL NEWS ITEM OR A PUBLICITY PLANT, BUT EITHER WAY IT GAVE ME A CREEPY FEELING!

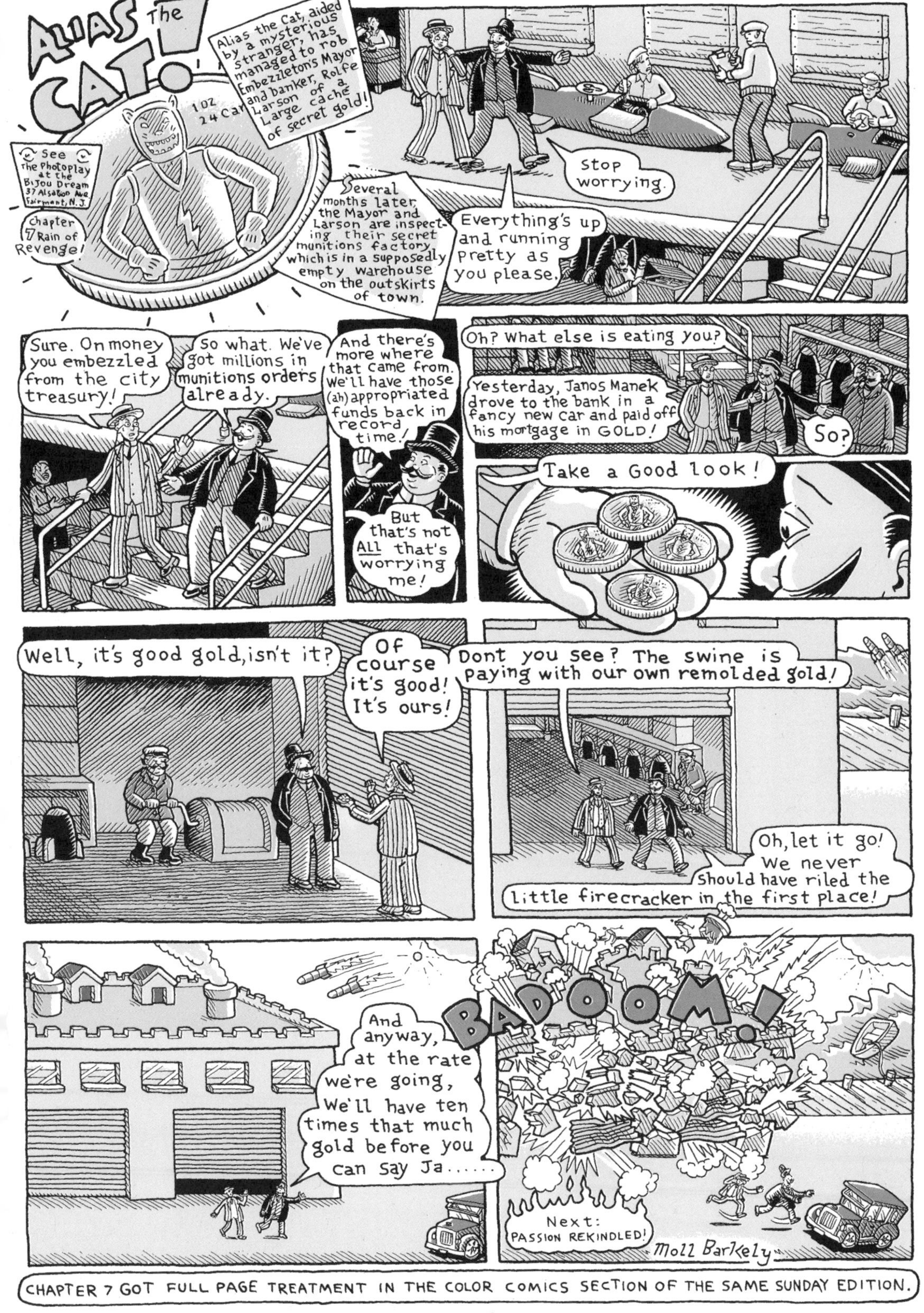

ALIAS the CAT!
1 OZ
24 Car
Alias the Cat, aided by a mysterious stranger, has managed to rob Embezzleton's Mayor and banker, Rolfe Larson of a Large caché of secret gold!
See The Photoplay at the BiJou Dream 37 Alsation Ave. Fairmont, N.J.
Chapter 7 Rain of Revenge!
Several months later, the Mayor and Larson are inspecting their secret munitions factory which is in a supposedly empty warehouse on the outskirts of town.
Stop worrying.
Everything's up and running pretty as you please.
Sure. On money you embezzled from the city treasury!
So what. We've got millions in munitions orders already.
And there's more where that came from. We'll have those (ah) appropriated funds back in record time.
But that's not ALL that's worrying me!
Oh? What else is eating you?
Yesterday, Janos Manek drove to the bank in a fancy new car and paid off his mortgage in GOLD!
So?
Take a Good look!
Well, it's good gold, isn't it?
Of course it's good! It's ours!
Dont you see? The swine is paying with our own remolded gold!
Oh, let it go! We never should have riled the little firecracker in the first place!
And anyway, at the rate we're going, we'll have ten times that much gold before you can say Ja......
BADOOOM!
Next: PASSION REKINDLED!
Moll Barkely

CHAPTER 7 GOT FULL PAGE TREATMENT IN THE COLOR COMICS SECTION OF THE SAME SUNDAY EDITION.

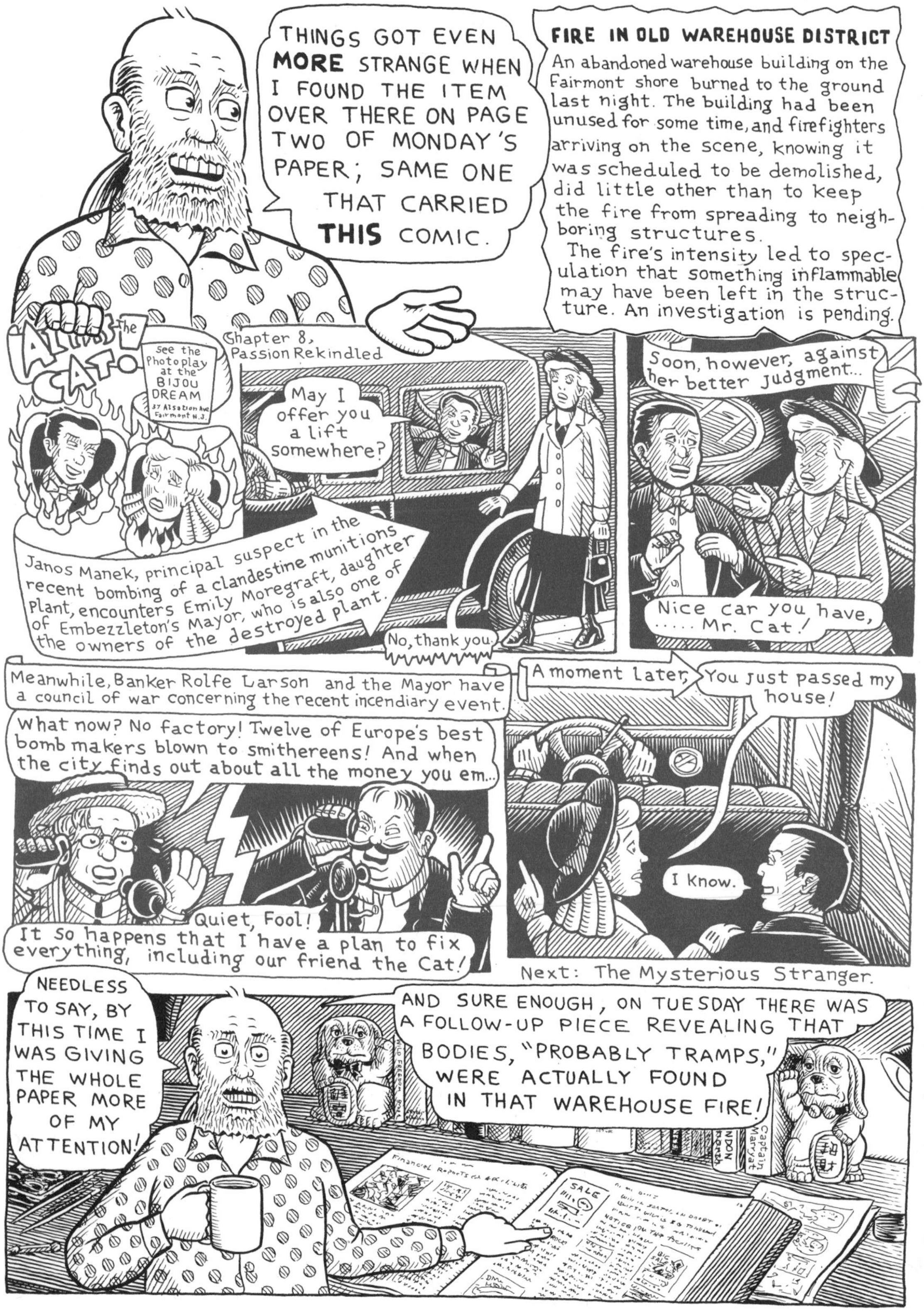

THINGS GOT EVEN **MORE** STRANGE WHEN I FOUND THE ITEM OVER THERE ON PAGE TWO OF MONDAY'S PAPER; SAME ONE THAT CARRIED **THIS** COMIC.
FIRE IN OLD WAREHOUSE DISTRICT
An abandoned warehouse building on the Fairmont shore burned to the ground last night. The building had been unused for some time, and firefighters arriving on the scene, knowing it was scheduled to be demolished, did little other than to keep the fire from spreading to neighboring structures.
The fire's intensity led to speculation that something inflammable may have been left in the structure. An investigation is pending.
ALIAS the CAT!
See the Photoplay at the BIJOU DREAM 37 Alsation Ave. Fairmont N.J.
Chapter 8, Passion Rekindled
May I offer you a lift somewhere?
Janos Manek, principal suspect in the recent bombing of a clandestine munitions Plant, encounters Emily Moregraft, daughter of Embezzleton's Mayor, who is also one of the owners of the destroyed plant.
No, thank you.
Soon, however, against her better judgment...
Nice car you have, ... Mr. Cat!
Meanwhile, Banker Rolfe Larson and the Mayor have a council of war concerning the recent incendiary event.
What now? No factory! Twelve of Europe's best bomb makers blown to smithereens! And when the city finds out about all the money you em...
Quiet, Fool!
It so happens that I have a plan to fix everything, including our friend the Cat!
A moment later,
You just passed my house!
I know.
Next: The Mysterious Stranger.
NEEDLESS TO SAY, BY THIS TIME I WAS GIVING THE WHOLE PAPER MORE OF MY ATTENTION!
AND SURE ENOUGH, ON TUESDAY THERE WAS A FOLLOW-UP PIECE REVEALING THAT BODIES, "PROBABLY TRAMPS," WERE ACTUALLY FOUND IN THAT WAREHOUSE FIRE!
Captain Marryat
SALE

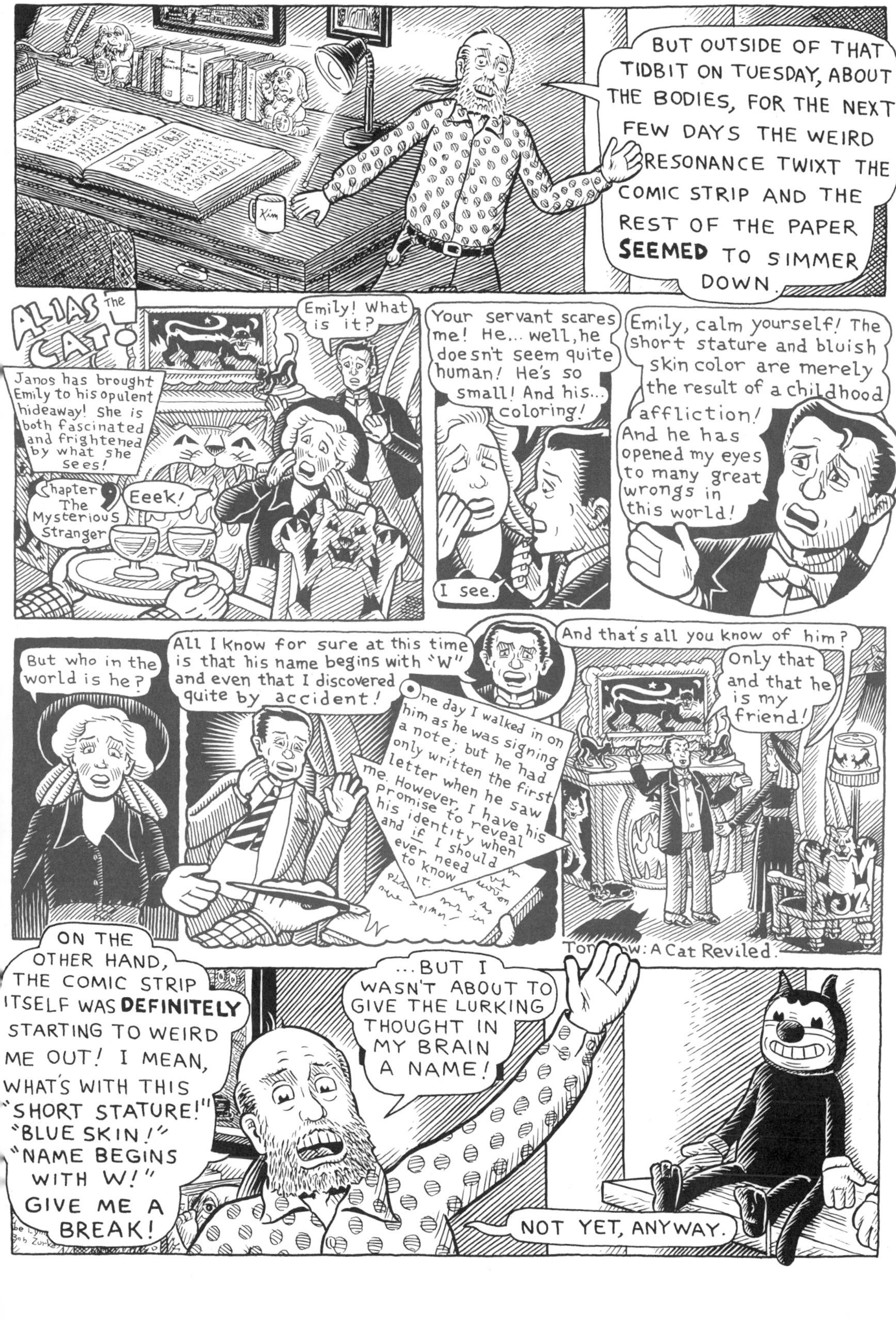

BUT OUTSIDE OF THAT TIDBIT ON TUESDAY, ABOUT THE BODIES, FOR THE NEXT FEW DAYS THE WEIRD RESONANCE TWIXT THE COMIC STRIP AND THE REST OF THE PAPER **SEEMED** TO SIMMER DOWN.
Kim
ALIAS the CAT!
Janos has brought Emily to his opulent hideaway! She is both fascinated and frightened by what she sees!
Chapter 9 The Mysterious Stranger
Eeek!
Emily! What is it?
Your servant scares me! He... well, he doesn't seem quite human! He's so small! And his... coloring!
I see.
Emily, calm yourself! The short stature and bluish skin color are merely the result of a childhood affliction! And he has opened my eyes to many great wrongs in this world!
But who in the world is he?
All I know for sure at this time is that his name begins with "W" and even that I discovered quite by accident!
One day I walked in on him as he was signing a note; but he had only written the first letter when he saw me. However, I have his promise to reveal his identity when and if I should ever need to know it.
W
And that's all you know of him?
Only that and that he is my friend!
A Cat Reviled.
ON THE OTHER HAND, THE COMIC STRIP ITSELF WAS **DEFINITELY** STARTING TO WEIRD ME OUT! I MEAN, WHAT'S WITH THIS "SHORT STATURE!" "BLUE SKIN!" "NAME BEGINS WITH W!" GIVE ME A BREAK!
...BUT I WASN'T ABOUT TO GIVE THE LURKING THOUGHT IN MY BRAIN A NAME!
NOT YET, ANYWAY.

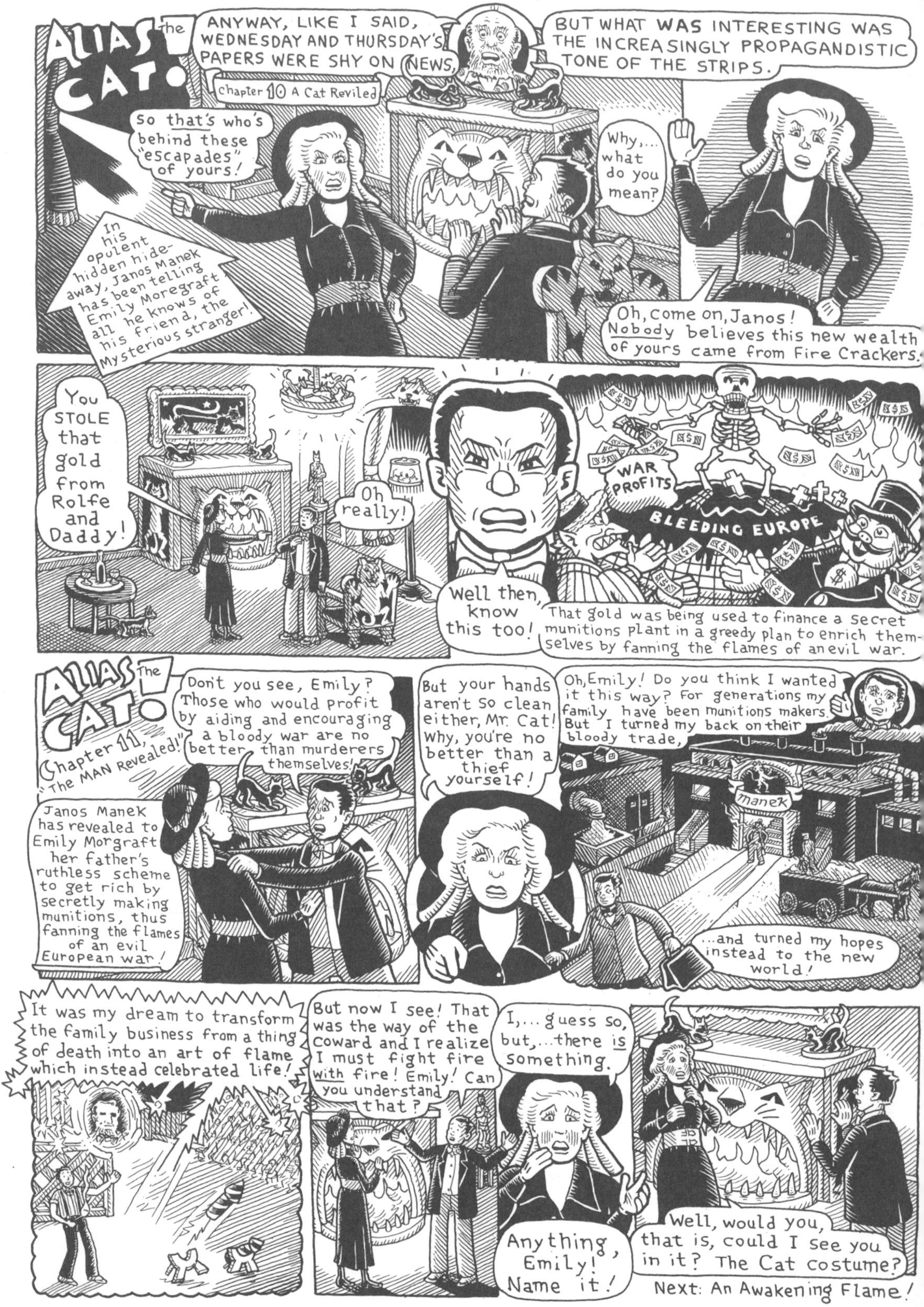
ALIAS the CAT!
ANYWAY, LIKE I SAID, WEDNESDAY AND THURSDAY'S PAPERS WERE SHY ON NEWS,
BUT WHAT WAS INTERESTING WAS THE INCREASINGLY PROPAGANDISTIC TONE OF THE STRIPS.
Chapter 10 A Cat Reviled
So that's who's behind these "escapades" of yours!
In his opulent hidden hide-away, Janos Manek has been telling Emily Moregraft all he knows of his friend, the Mysterious stranger!
Why,... what do you mean?
Oh, come on, Janos! Nobody believes this new wealth of yours came from Fire Crackers.
You STOLE that gold from Rolfe and Daddy!
Oh really!
Well then, know this too!
WAR PROFITS
BLEEDING EUROPE
That gold was being used to finance a secret munitions plant in a greedy plan to enrich themselves by fanning the flames of an evil war.
ALIAS The CAT!
Chapter 11, "The MAN Revealed!"
Don't you see, Emily? Those who would profit by aiding and encouraging a bloody war are no better than murderers themselves!
Janos Manek has revealed to Emily Morgraft her father's ruthless scheme to get rich by secretly making munitions, thus fanning the flames of an evil European war!
But your hands aren't so clean either, Mr. Cat! Why, you're no better than a thief yourself!
Oh, Emily! Do you think I wanted it this way? For generations my family have been munitions makers. But I turned my back on their bloody trade,
manek
...and turned my hopes instead to the new world!
It was my dream to transform the family business from a thing of death into an art of flame which instead celebrated life!
But now I see! That was the way of the coward and I realize I must fight fire with fire! Emily! Can you understand that?
I,... guess so, but,...there is something.
Anything, Emily! Name it!
Well, would you, that is, could I see you in it? The Cat costume?
Next: An Awakening Flame!

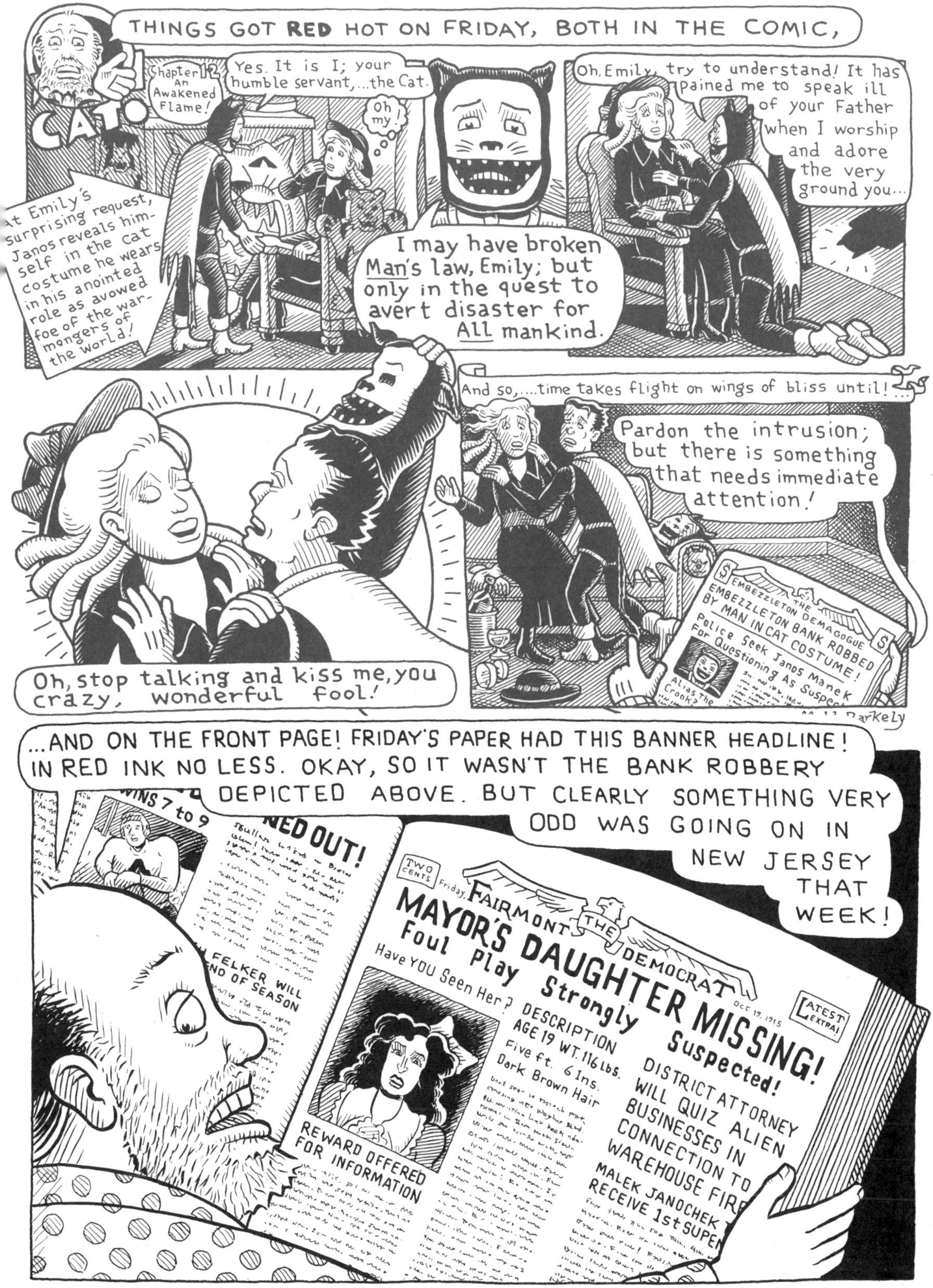

THINGS GOT RED HOT ON FRIDAY, BOTH IN THE COMIC,
CAT
Chapter 12 An Awakened Flame!
Yes. It is I; your humble servant, ...the Cat.
Oh my!
At Emily's surprising request, Janos reveals himself in the cat costume he wears in his anointed role as avowed foe of the war-mongers of the world!
I may have broken Man's law, Emily; but only in the quest to avert disaster for All mankind.
Oh, Emily, try to understand! It has pained me to speak ill of your Father when I worship and adore the very ground you...
Oh, stop talking and kiss me, you crazy, wonderful fool!
And so, ...time takes flight on wings of bliss until!...
Pardon the intrusion; but there is something that needs immediate attention!
THE EMBEZZLETON DEMAGOGUE
EMBEZZLETON BANK ROBBED BY MAN IN CAT COSTUME!
Police Seek Janos Manek For Questioning As Suspect
Alias The Crook?
...AND ON THE FRONT PAGE! FRIDAY'S PAPER HAD THIS BANNER HEADLINE! IN RED INK NO LESS. OKAY, SO IT WASN'T THE BANK ROBBERY DEPICTED ABOVE. BUT CLEARLY SOMETHING VERY ODD WAS GOING ON IN NEW JERSEY THAT WEEK!
WINS 7 to 9
NED OUT!
FELKER WILL END OF SEASON
TWO CENTS
Friday
THE FAIRMONT DEMOCRAT
OCT 19, 1915
LATEST EXTRA!
MAYOR'S DAUGHTER MISSING!
Foul Play Strongly Suspected!
Have YOU Seen Her?
DESCRIPTION AGE 19 WT. 116 lbs. Five ft. 6 Ins. Dark Brown Hair
REWARD OFFERED FOR INFORMATION
DISTRICT ATTORNEY WILL QUIZ ALIEN BUSINESSES IN CONNECTION TO WAREHOUSE FIRE
MALEK JANOCHEK RECEIVE 1st SUPEN

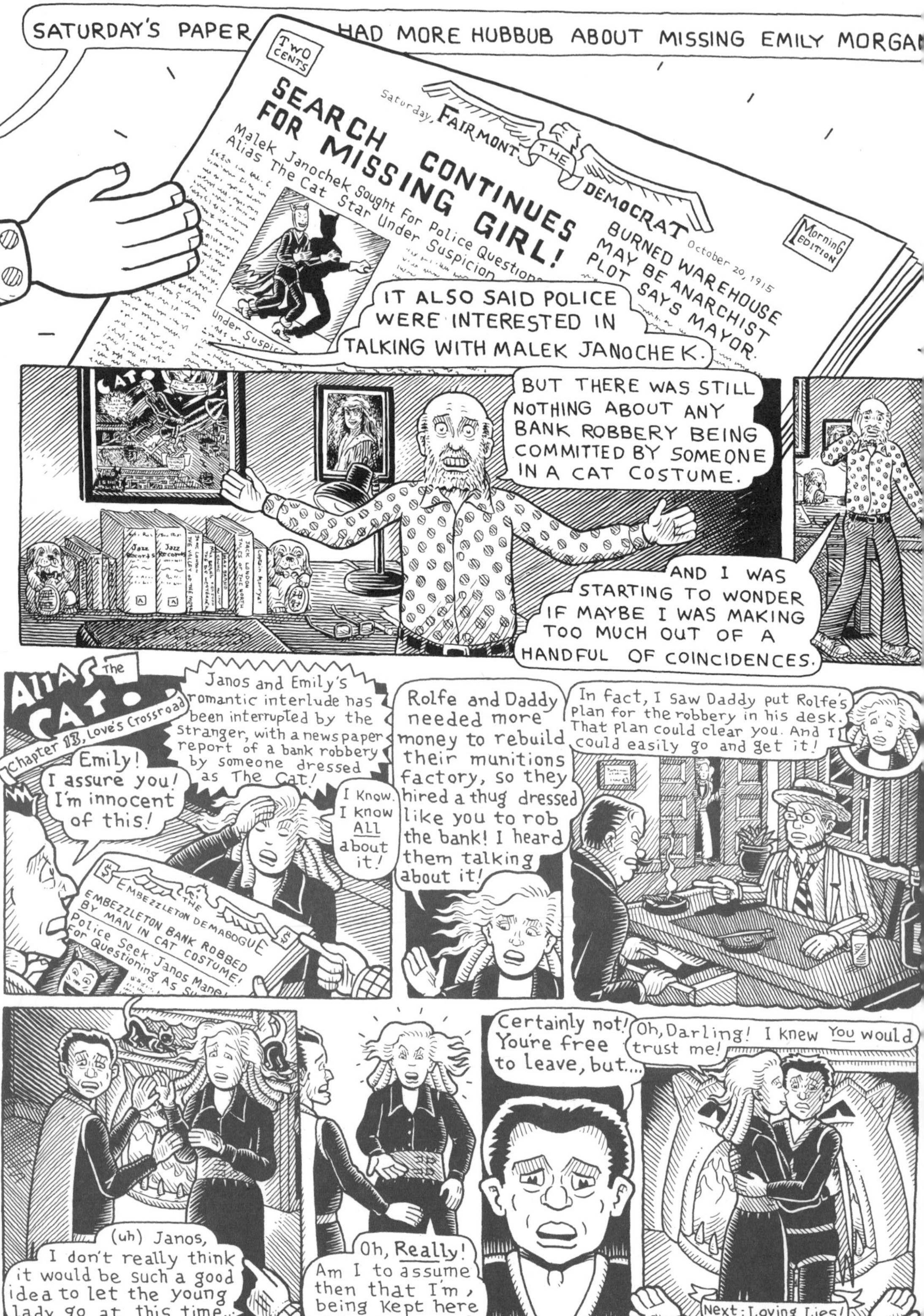

SATURDAY'S PAPER HAD MORE HUBBUB ABOUT MISSING EMILY MORGAN
TWO CENTS
Saturday, FAIRMONT THE DEMOCRAT October 20, 1915
MORNING EDITION
SEARCH CONTINUES FOR MISSING GIRL!
Malek Janochek Sought For Police Questioning
Alias The Cat Star Under Suspicion
BURNED WAREHOUSE MAY BE ANARCHIST PLOT SAYS MAYOR
IT ALSO SAID POLICE WERE INTERESTED IN TALKING WITH MALEK JANOCHEK.
BUT THERE WAS STILL NOTHING ABOUT ANY BANK ROBBERY BEING COMMITTED BY SOMEONE IN A CAT COSTUME.
AND I WAS STARTING TO WONDER IF MAYBE I WAS MAKING TOO MUCH OUT OF A HANDFUL OF COINCIDENCES.
ALIAS THE CAT
Chapter 13, Love's Crossroad
Janos and Emily's romantic interlude has been interrupted by the Stranger, with a newspaper report of a bank robbery by someone dressed as The Cat!
Emily! I assure you! I'm innocent of this!
THE EMBEZZLETON DEMABOGUE
EMBEZZLETON BANK ROBBED BY MAN IN CAT COSTUME!
Police Seek Janos Mane For Questioning As S
I Know. I know ALL about it!
Rolfe and Daddy needed more money to rebuild their munitions factory, so they hired a thug dressed like you to rob the bank! I heard them talking about it!
In fact, I saw Daddy put Rolfe's plan for the robbery in his desk. That plan could clear you. And I could easily go and get it!
(uh) Janos, I don't really think it would be such a good idea to let the young lady go at this time...
Oh, Really! Am I to assume then that I'm being Kept here as a prisoner?
Certainly not! You're free to leave, but....
Oh, Darling! I knew You would trust me!
Next: Loving Lies!

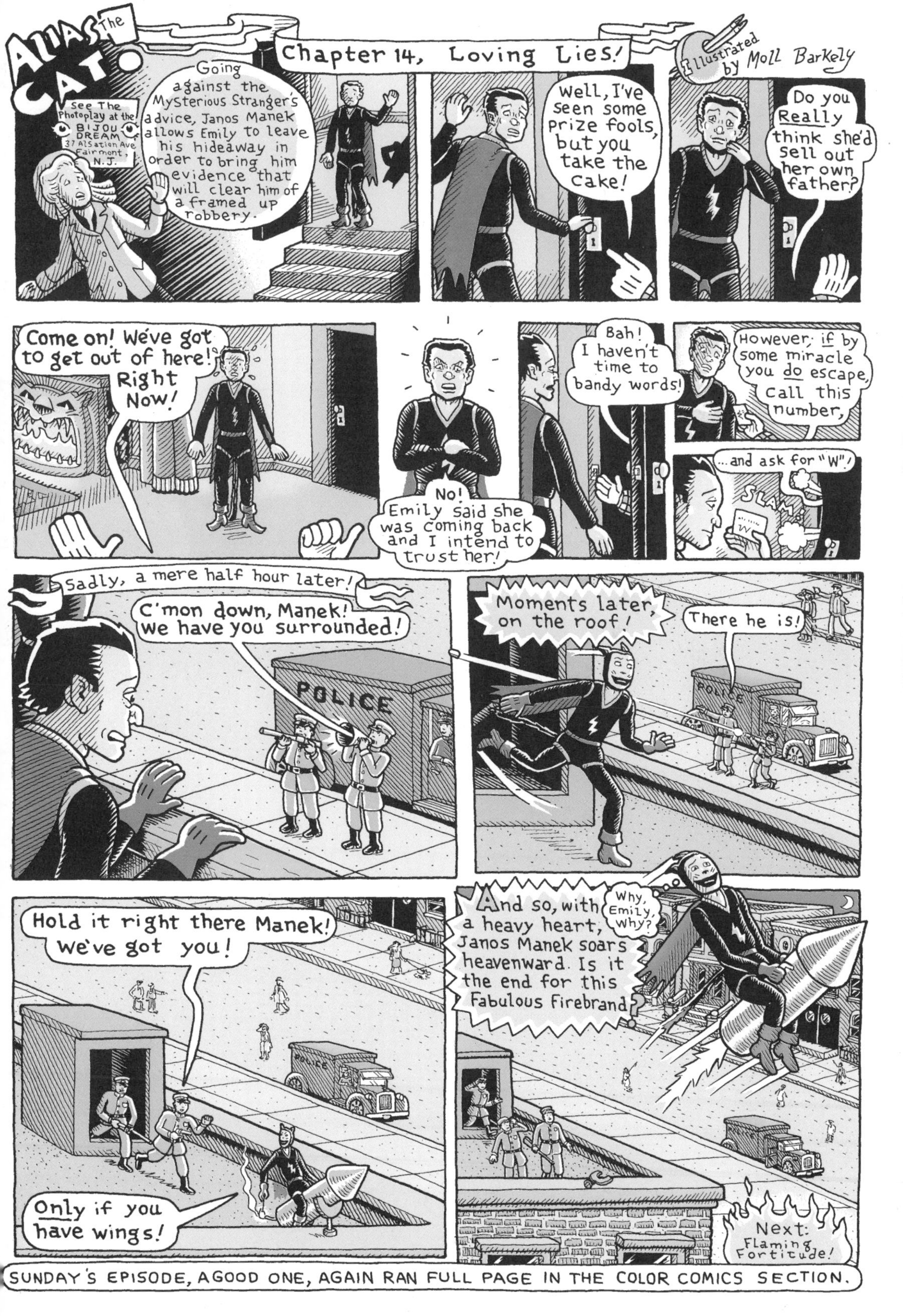
Alias The Cat
See The Photoplay at the BIJOU DREAM 37 Alsation Ave Fairmont, N.J.
Chapter 14, Loving Lies!
Illustrated by Moll Barkely
Going against the Mysterious Stranger's advice, Janos Manek allows Emily to leave his hideaway in order to bring him evidence that will clear him of a framed up robbery.
Well, I've seen some Prize fools, but you take the Cake!
Do you Really think she'd sell out her own father?
Come on! We've got to get out of here! Right Now!
No! Emily said she was coming back and I intend to trust her!
Bah! I haven't time to bandy words!
However, if by some miracle you do escape, call this number,
...and ask for "W"!
SLAM
W
Sadly, a mere half hour later!
C'mon down, Manek! We have you surrounded!
POLICE
Moments later, on the roof!
There he is!
Hold it right there Manek! We've got you!
Only if you have wings!
And so, with a heavy heart, Janos Manek soars heavenward. Is it the end for this Fabulous Firebrand?
Why, Emily, why?
Next: Flaming Fortitude!
SUNDAY'S EPISODE, A GOOD ONE, AGAIN RAN FULL PAGE IN THE COLOR COMICS SECTION.

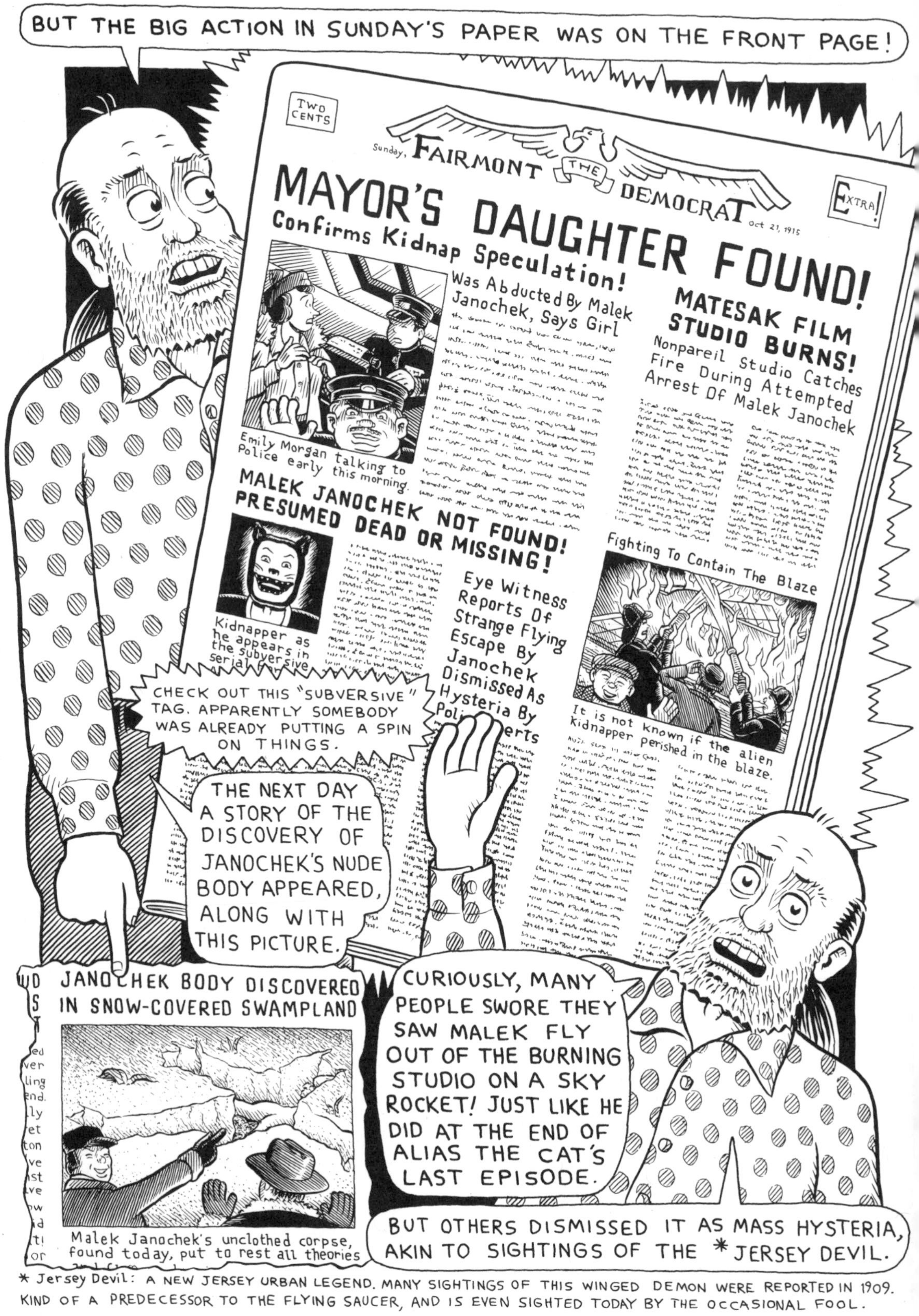
BUT THE BIG ACTION IN SUNDAY'S PAPER WAS ON THE FRONT PAGE!
TWO CENTS
Sunday, FAIRMONT THE DEMOCRAT
Oct 21, 1915
EXTRA!
MAYOR'S DAUGHTER FOUND!
Confirms Kidnap Speculation!
Was Abducted By Malek Janochek, Says Girl
Emily Morgan talking to Police early this morning.
MATESAK FILM STUDIO BURNS!
Nonpareil Studio Catches Fire During Attempted Arrest Of Malek Janochek
MALEK JANOCHEK NOT FOUND! PRESUMED DEAD OR MISSING!
Kidnapper as he appears in the subversive
Eye Witness Reports Of Strange Flying Escape By Janochek Dismissed As Hysteria By
Fighting To Contain The Blaze
It is not known if the alien kidnapper perished in the blaze.
CHECK OUT THIS "SUBVERSIVE" TAG. APPARENTLY SOMEBODY WAS ALREADY PUTTING A SPIN ON THINGS.
THE NEXT DAY A STORY OF THE DISCOVERY OF JANOCHEK'S NUDE BODY APPEARED, ALONG WITH THIS PICTURE.
JANOCHEK BODY DISCOVERED IN SNOW-COVERED SWAMPLAND
Malek Janochek's unclothed corpse, found today, put to rest all theories
CURIOUSLY, MANY PEOPLE SWORE THEY SAW MALEK FLY OUT OF THE BURNING STUDIO ON A SKY ROCKET! JUST LIKE HE DID AT THE END OF ALIAS THE CAT'S LAST EPISODE.
BUT OTHERS DISMISSED IT AS MASS HYSTERIA, AKIN TO SIGHTINGS OF THE * JERSEY DEVIL.

* Jersey Devil: A NEW JERSEY URBAN LEGEND. MANY SIGHTINGS OF THIS WINGED DEMON WERE REPORTED IN 1909. KIND OF A PREDECESSOR TO THE FLYING SAUCER, AND IS EVEN SIGHTED TODAY BY THE OCCASIONAL FOOL.

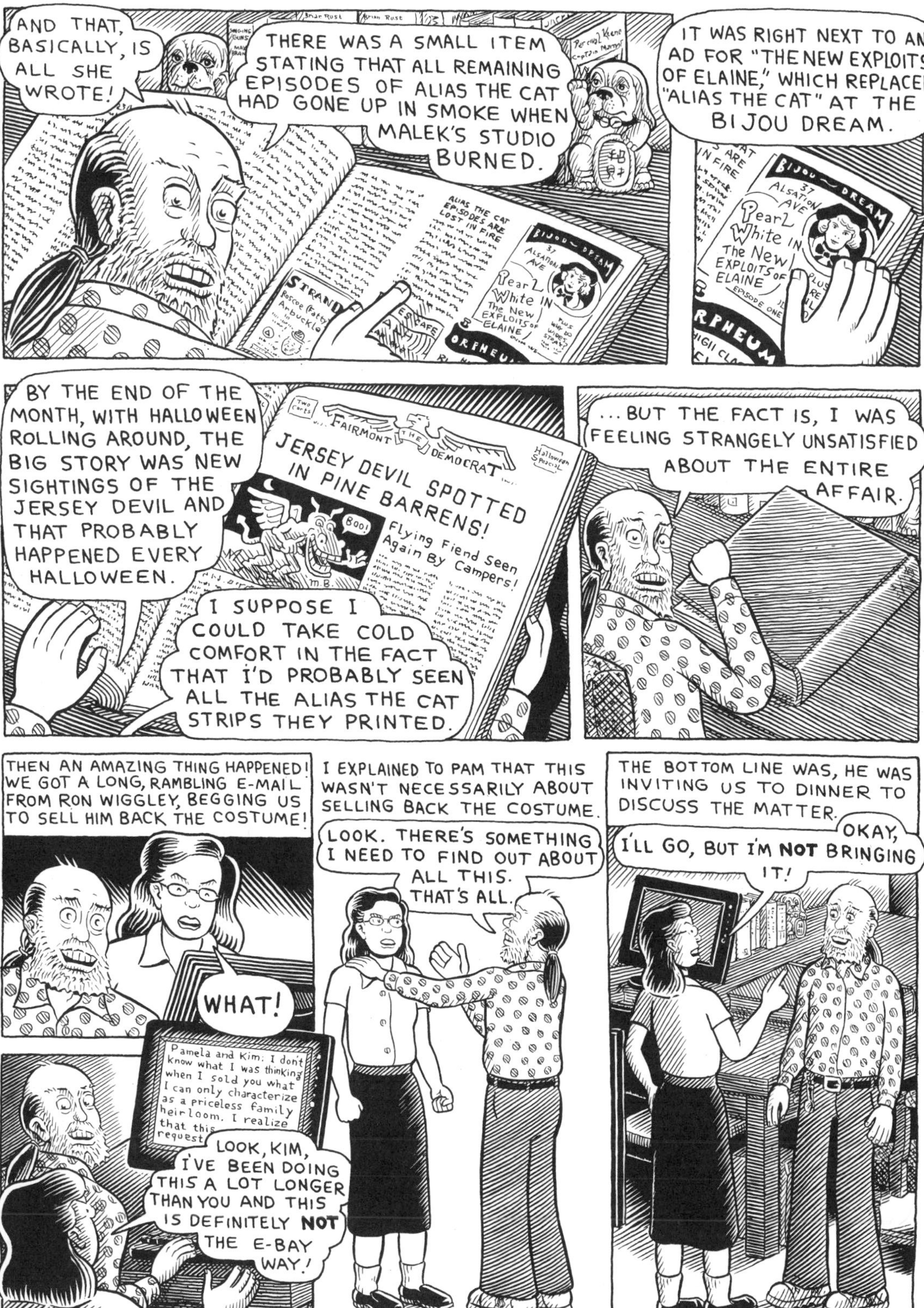
AND THAT, BASICALLY, IS ALL SHE WROTE!
THERE WAS A SMALL ITEM STATING THAT ALL REMAINING EPISODES OF ALIAS THE CAT HAD GONE UP IN SMOKE WHEN MALEK'S STUDIO BURNED.
ALIAS THE CAT EPISODES ARE LOST IN FIRE
IT WAS RIGHT NEXT TO AN AD FOR "THE NEW EXPLOITS OF ELAINE," WHICH REPLACED "ALIAS THE CAT" AT THE BIJOU DREAM.
BIJOU DREAM 37 ALSATION AVE
Pearl White IN The New EXPLOITS OF ELAINE
EPISODE ONE
BY THE END OF THE MONTH, WITH HALLOWEEN ROLLING AROUND, THE BIG STORY WAS NEW SIGHTINGS OF THE JERSEY DEVIL AND THAT PROBABLY HAPPENED EVERY HALLOWEEN.
FAIRMONT THE DEMOCRAT
Two Cents
Halloween Special
JERSEY DEVIL SPOTTED IN PINE BARRENS!
Flying Fiend Seen Again By Campers!
Boo!
I SUPPOSE I COULD TAKE COLD COMFORT IN THE FACT THAT I'D PROBABLY SEEN ALL THE ALIAS THE CAT STRIPS THEY PRINTED.
...BUT THE FACT IS, I WAS FEELING STRANGELY UNSATISFIED ABOUT THE ENTIRE AFFAIR.
THEN AN AMAZING THING HAPPENED! WE GOT A LONG, RAMBLING E-MAIL FROM RON WIGGLEY, BEGGING US TO SELL HIM BACK THE COSTUME!
WHAT!
Pamela and Kim: I don't know what I was thinking when I sold you what I can only characterize as a priceless family heirloom. I realize that this request
LOOK, KIM, I'VE BEEN DOING THIS A LOT LONGER THAN YOU AND THIS IS DEFINITELY NOT THE E-BAY WAY!
I EXPLAINED TO PAM THAT THIS WASN'T NECESSARILY ABOUT SELLING BACK THE COSTUME.
LOOK. THERE'S SOMETHING I NEED TO FIND OUT ABOUT ALL THIS. THAT'S ALL.
THE BOTTOM LINE WAS, HE WAS INVITING US TO DINNER TO DISCUSS THE MATTER.
OKAY, I'LL GO, BUT I'M NOT BRINGING IT!

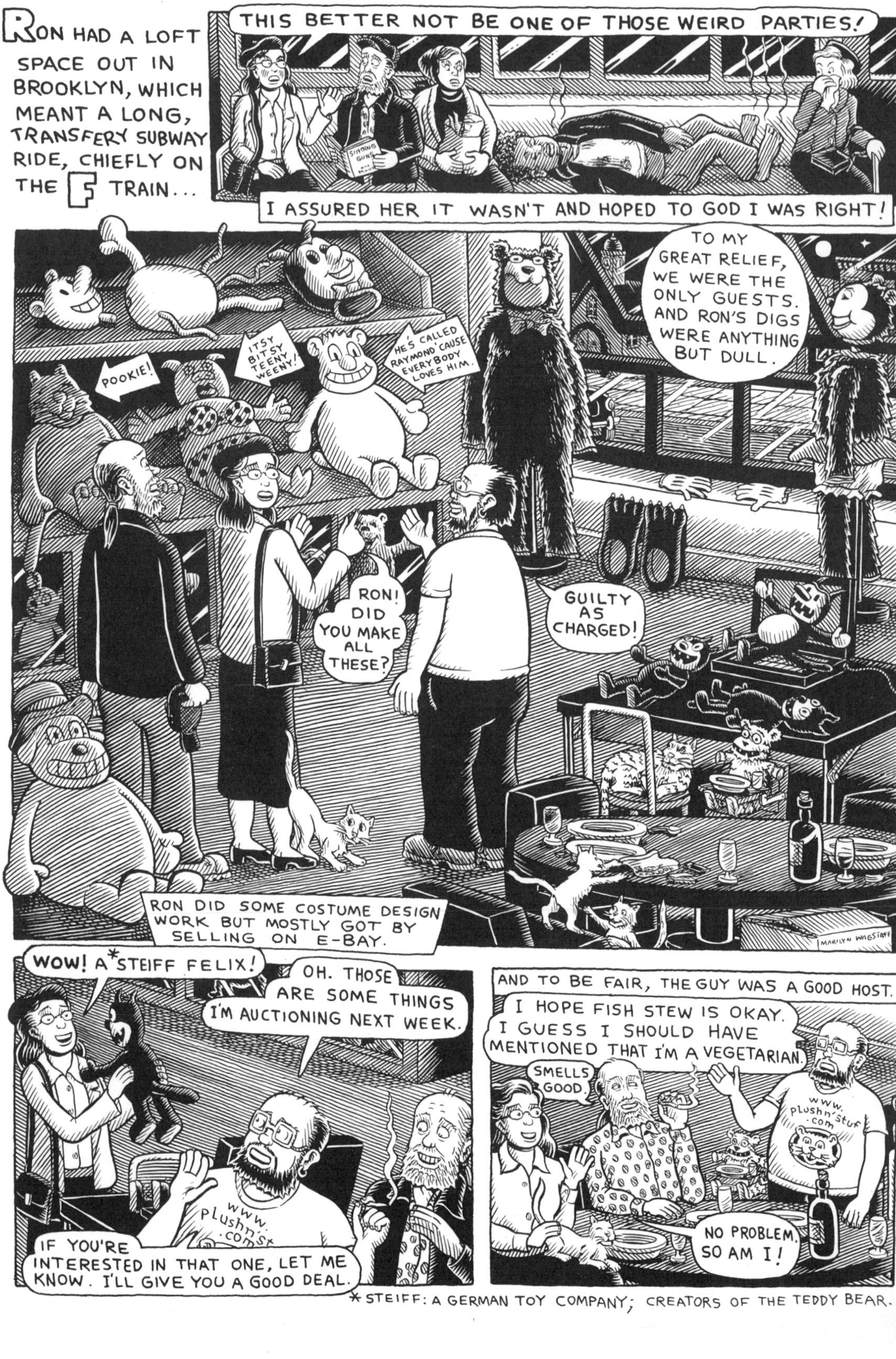
RON HAD A LOFT SPACE OUT IN BROOKLYN, WHICH MEANT A LONG, TRANSFERY SUBWAY RIDE, CHIEFLY ON THE F TRAIN...
THIS BETTER NOT BE ONE OF THOSE WEIRD PARTIES!
SINGING GUNS
I ASSURED HER IT WASN'T AND HOPED TO GOD I WAS RIGHT!
TO MY GREAT RELIEF, WE WERE THE ONLY GUESTS. AND RON'S DIGS WERE ANYTHING BUT DULL.
POOKIE!
ITSY BITSY TEENY WEENY!
HE'S CALLED RAYMOND 'CAUSE EVERYBODY LOVES HIM.
RON! DID YOU MAKE ALL THESE?
GUILTY AS CHARGED!
RON DID SOME COSTUME DESIGN WORK BUT MOSTLY GOT BY SELLING ON E-BAY.
WOW! A *STEIFF FELIX!
OH. THOSE ARE SOME THINGS I'M AUCTIONING NEXT WEEK.
IF YOU'RE INTERESTED IN THAT ONE, LET ME KNOW. I'LL GIVE YOU A GOOD DEAL.
AND TO BE FAIR, THE GUY WAS A GOOD HOST.
I HOPE FISH STEW IS OKAY. I GUESS I SHOULD HAVE MENTIONED THAT I'M A VEGETARIAN.
SMELLS GOOD.
www. plushn'stuf .com
NO PROBLEM. SO AM I!
* STEIFF: A GERMAN TOY COMPANY; CREATORS OF THE TEDDY BEAR.

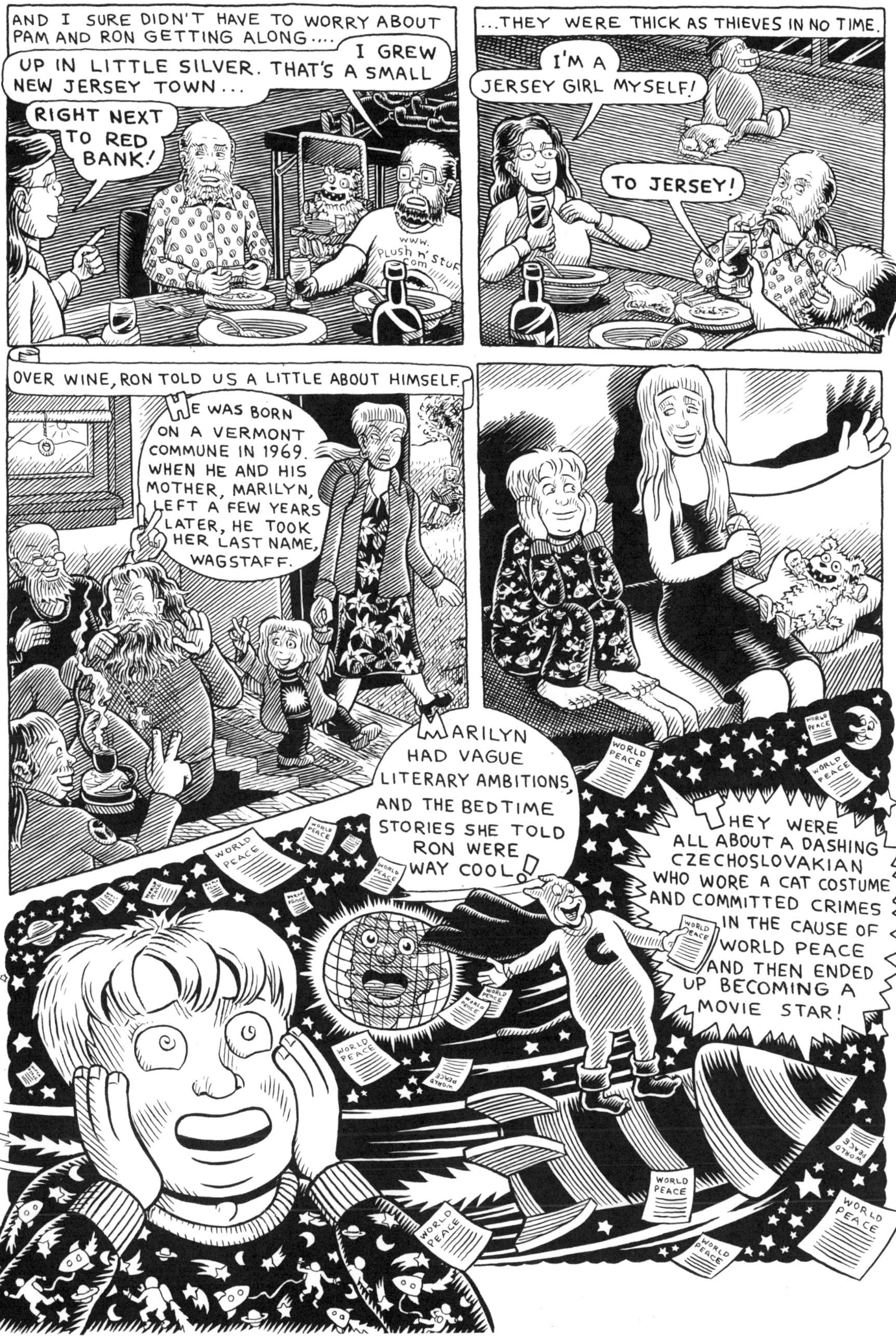
AND I SURE DIDN'T HAVE TO WORRY ABOUT PAM AND RON GETTING ALONG....
I GREW UP IN LITTLE SILVER. THAT'S A SMALL NEW JERSEY TOWN...
RIGHT NEXT TO RED BANK!
WWW. PLUSH N' STUFF .COM
...THEY WERE THICK AS THIEVES IN NO TIME.
I'M A JERSEY GIRL MYSELF!
TO JERSEY!
OVER WINE, RON TOLD US A LITTLE ABOUT HIMSELF.
HE WAS BORN ON A VERMONT COMMUNE IN 1969. WHEN HE AND HIS MOTHER, MARILYN, LEFT A FEW YEARS LATER, HE TOOK HER LAST NAME, WAGSTAFF.
MARILYN HAD VAGUE LITERARY AMBITIONS, AND THE BEDTIME STORIES SHE TOLD RON WERE WAY COOL!
THEY WERE ALL ABOUT A DASHING CZECHOSLOVAKIAN WHO WORE A CAT COSTUME AND COMMITTED CRIMES IN THE CAUSE OF WORLD PEACE AND THEN ENDED UP BECOMING A MOVIE STAR!
WORLD PEACE

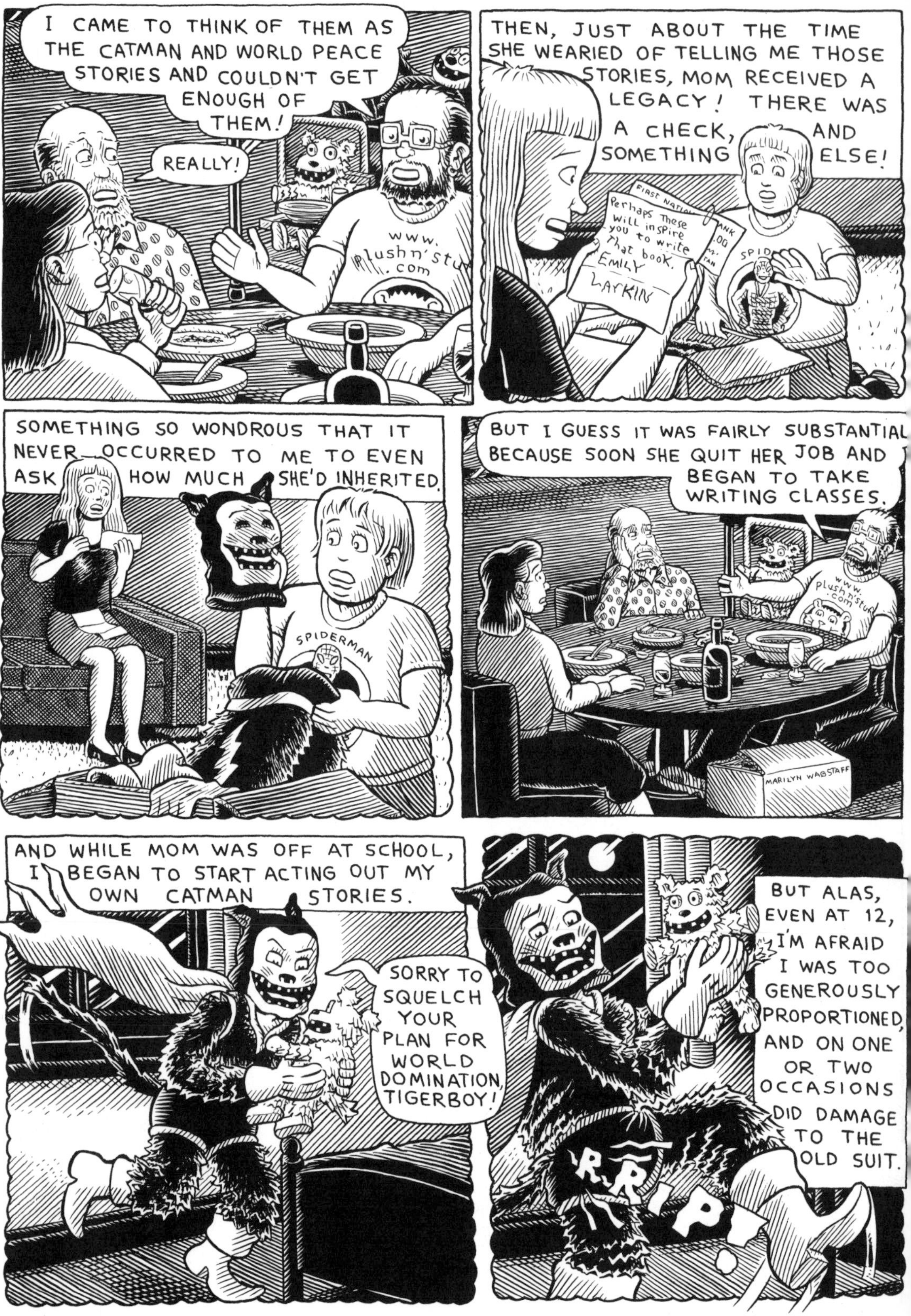
I CAME TO THINK OF THEM AS THE CATMAN AND WORLD PEACE STORIES AND COULDN'T GET ENOUGH OF THEM!
REALLY!
THEN, JUST ABOUT THE TIME SHE WEARIED OF TELLING ME THOSE STORIES, MOM RECEIVED A LEGACY! THERE WAS A CHECK, AND SOMETHING ELSE!
Perhaps These will inspire you to write That book.
EMILY
LARKIN
SOMETHING SO WONDROUS THAT IT NEVER OCCURRED TO ME TO EVEN ASK HOW MUCH SHE'D INHERITED.
SPIDERMAN
BUT I GUESS IT WAS FAIRLY SUBSTANTIAL BECAUSE SOON SHE QUIT HER JOB AND BEGAN TO TAKE WRITING CLASSES.
MARILYN WABSTAFF
AND WHILE MOM WAS OFF AT SCHOOL, I BEGAN TO START ACTING OUT MY OWN CATMAN STORIES.
SORRY TO SQUELCH YOUR PLAN FOR WORLD DOMINATION, TIGERBOY!
BUT ALAS, EVEN AT 12, I'M AFRAID I WAS TOO GENEROUSLY PROPORTIONED, AND ON ONE OR TWO OCCASIONS DID DAMAGE TO THE OLD SUIT.
R-RIP!

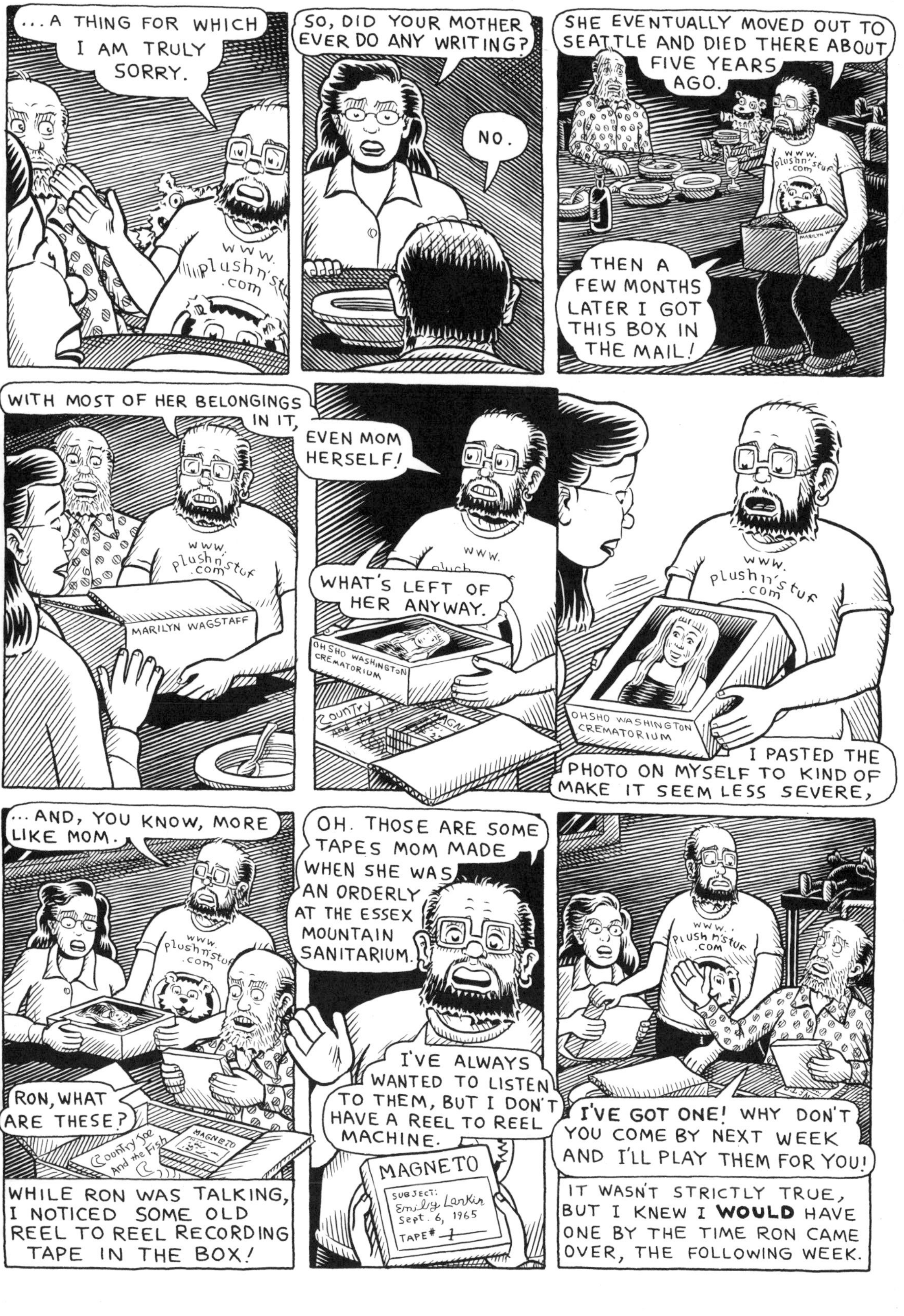
...A THING FOR WHICH I AM TRULY SORRY.
www.plushn'stuf.com
SO, DID YOUR MOTHER EVER DO ANY WRITING?
NO.
SHE EVENTUALLY MOVED OUT TO SEATTLE AND DIED THERE ABOUT FIVE YEARS AGO.
www.plushn'stuf.com
THEN A FEW MONTHS LATER I GOT THIS BOX IN THE MAIL!
WITH MOST OF HER BELONGINGS IN IT,
www.plushn'stuf.com
MARILYN WAGSTAFF
EVEN MOM HERSELF!
WHAT'S LEFT OF HER ANYWAY.
OHSHO WASHINGTON CREMATORIUM
www.plushn'stuf.com
OHSHO WASHINGTON CREMATORIUM
I PASTED THE PHOTO ON MYSELF TO KIND OF MAKE IT SEEM LESS SEVERE,
...AND, YOU KNOW, MORE LIKE MOM.
www.plushn'stuf.com
RON, WHAT ARE THESE?
Country Joe And the Fish
MAGNETO
WHILE RON WAS TALKING, I NOTICED SOME OLD REEL TO REEL RECORDING TAPE IN THE BOX!
OH. THOSE ARE SOME TAPES MOM MADE WHEN SHE WAS AN ORDERLY AT THE ESSEX MOUNTAIN SANITARIUM.
I'VE ALWAYS WANTED TO LISTEN TO THEM, BUT I DON'T HAVE A REEL TO REEL MACHINE.
MAGNETO
SUBJECT: Emily Larkin
Sept. 6, 1965
TAPE# 1
www.plushn'stuf.com
I'VE GOT ONE! WHY DON'T YOU COME BY NEXT WEEK AND I'LL PLAY THEM FOR YOU!
IT WASN'T STRICTLY TRUE, BUT I KNEW I WOULD HAVE ONE BY THE TIME RON CAME OVER, THE FOLLOWING WEEK.

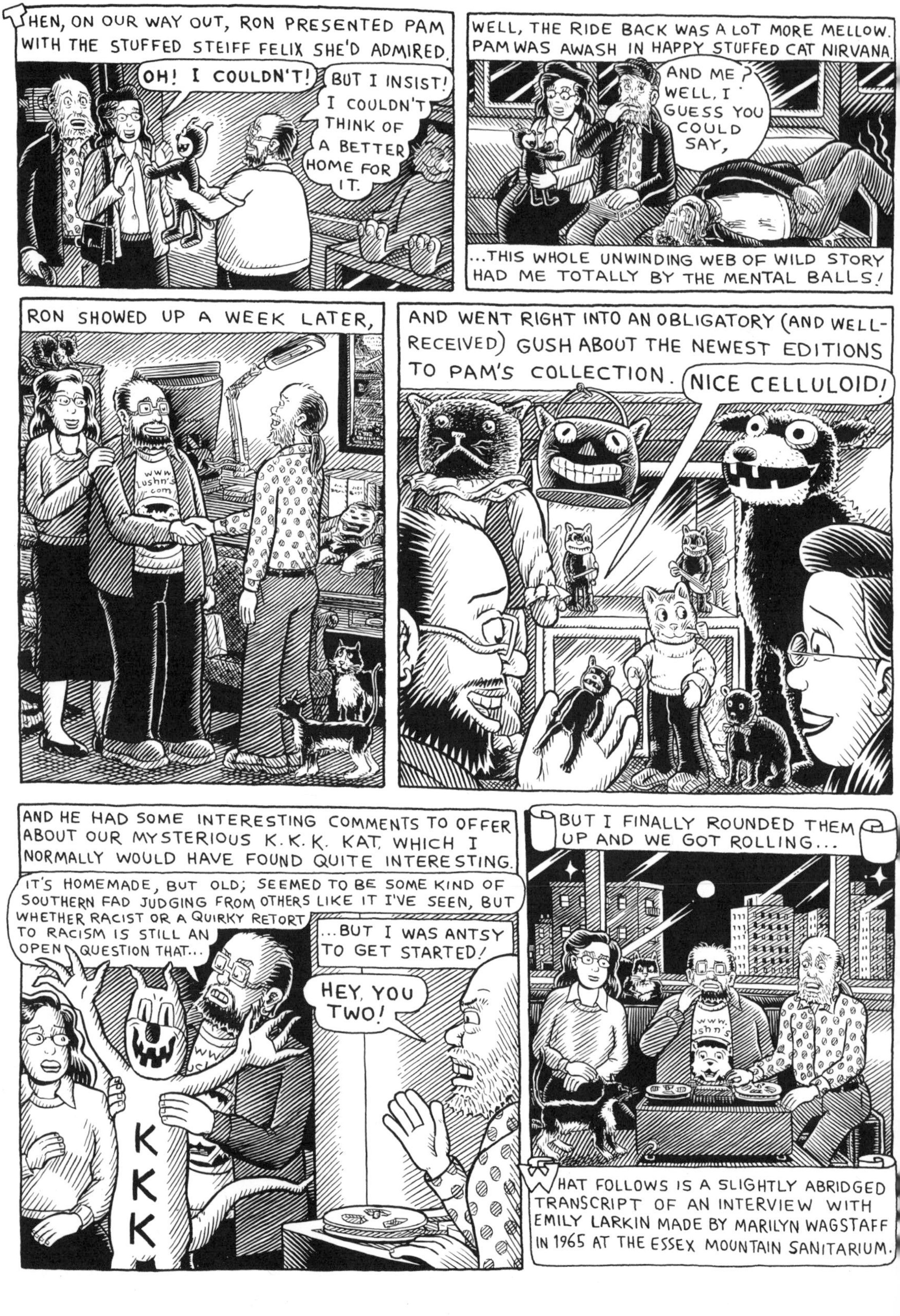
THEN, ON OUR WAY OUT, RON PRESENTED PAM WITH THE STUFFED STEIFF FELIX SHE'D ADMIRED.
OH! I COULDN'T!
BUT I INSIST! I COULDN'T THINK OF A BETTER HOME FOR IT.
WELL, THE RIDE BACK WAS A LOT MORE MELLOW. PAM WAS AWASH IN HAPPY STUFFED CAT NIRVANA.
AND ME? WELL, I GUESS YOU COULD SAY,
...THIS WHOLE UNWINDING WEB OF WILD STORY HAD ME TOTALLY BY THE MENTAL BALLS!
RON SHOWED UP A WEEK LATER,
AND WENT RIGHT INTO AN OBLIGATORY (AND WELL-RECEIVED) GUSH ABOUT THE NEWEST EDITIONS TO PAM'S COLLECTION.
NICE CELLULOID!
AND HE HAD SOME INTERESTING COMMENTS TO OFFER ABOUT OUR MYSTERIOUS K.K.K. KAT, WHICH I NORMALLY WOULD HAVE FOUND QUITE INTERESTING.
IT'S HOMEMADE, BUT OLD; SEEMED TO BE SOME KIND OF SOUTHERN FAD JUDGING FROM OTHERS LIKE IT I'VE SEEN, BUT WHETHER RACIST OR A QUIRKY RETORT TO RACISM IS STILL AN OPEN QUESTION THAT...
...BUT I WAS ANTSY TO GET STARTED!
HEY, YOU TWO!
KKK
BUT I FINALLY ROUNDED THEM UP AND WE GOT ROLLING...
WHAT FOLLOWS IS A SLIGHTLY ABRIDGED TRANSCRIPT OF AN INTERVIEW WITH EMILY LARKIN MADE BY MARILYN WAGSTAFF IN 1965 AT THE ESSEX MOUNTAIN SANITARIUM.

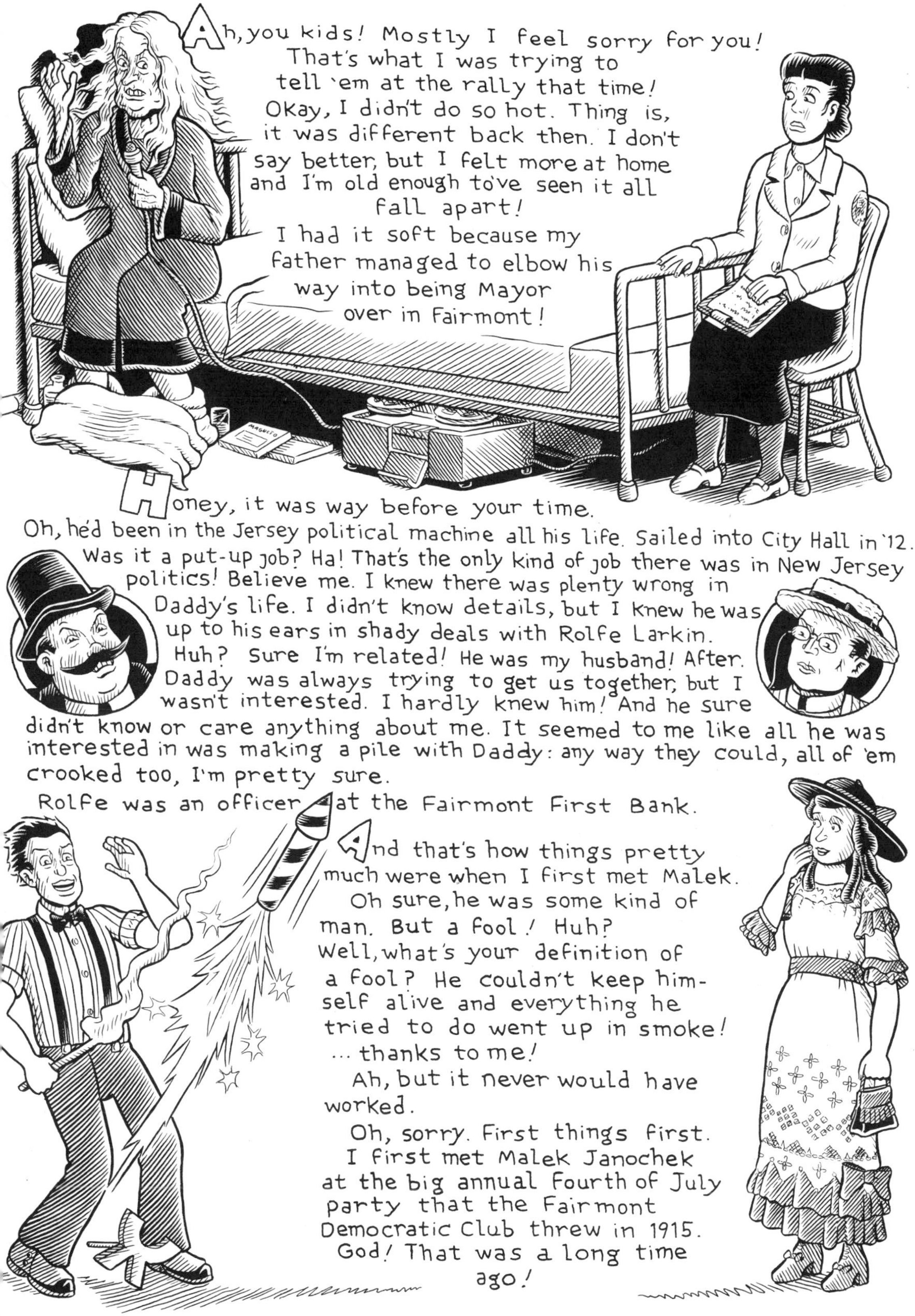
Ah, you kids! Mostly I feel sorry for you! That's what I was trying to tell 'em at the rally that time! Okay, I didn't do so hot. Thing is, it was different back then. I don't say better, but I felt more at home and I'm old enough to've seen it all fall apart!
I had it soft because my father managed to elbow his way into being Mayor over in Fairmont!
Honey, it was way before your time.
Oh, he'd been in the Jersey political machine all his life. Sailed into City Hall in '12. Was it a put-up job? Ha! That's the only kind of job there was in New Jersey politics! Believe me. I knew there was plenty wrong in Daddy's life. I didn't know details, but I knew he was up to his ears in shady deals with Rolfe Larkin.
Huh? Sure I'm related! He was my husband! After. Daddy was always trying to get us together, but I wasn't interested. I hardly knew him! And he sure didn't know or care anything about me. It seemed to me like all he was interested in was making a pile with Daddy: any way they could, all of 'em crooked too, I'm pretty sure.
Rolfe was an officer at the Fairmont First Bank.
And that's how things pretty much were when I first met Malek.
Oh sure, he was some kind of man. But a fool! Huh? Well, what's your definition of a fool? He couldn't keep him-self alive and everything he tried to do went up in smoke! ... thanks to me!
Ah, but it never would have worked.
Oh, sorry. First things first. I first met Malek Janochek at the big annual Fourth of July party that the Fairmont Democratic Club threw in 1915. God! That was a long time ago!

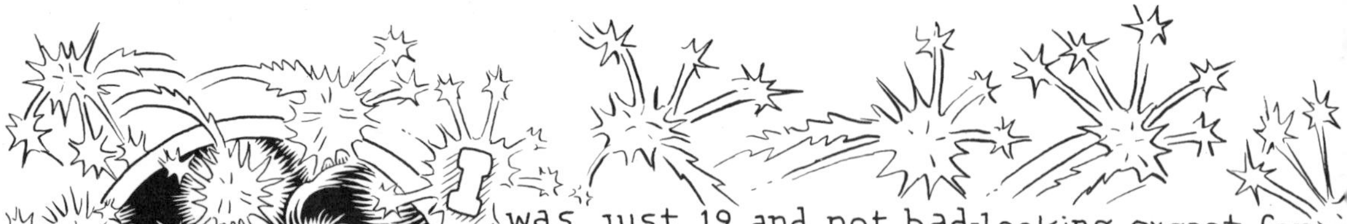

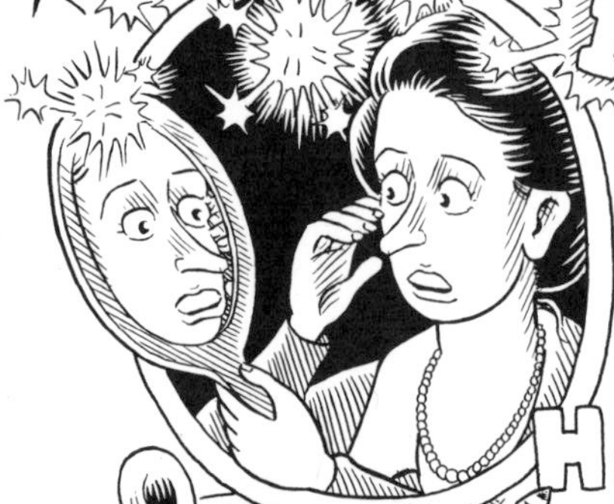

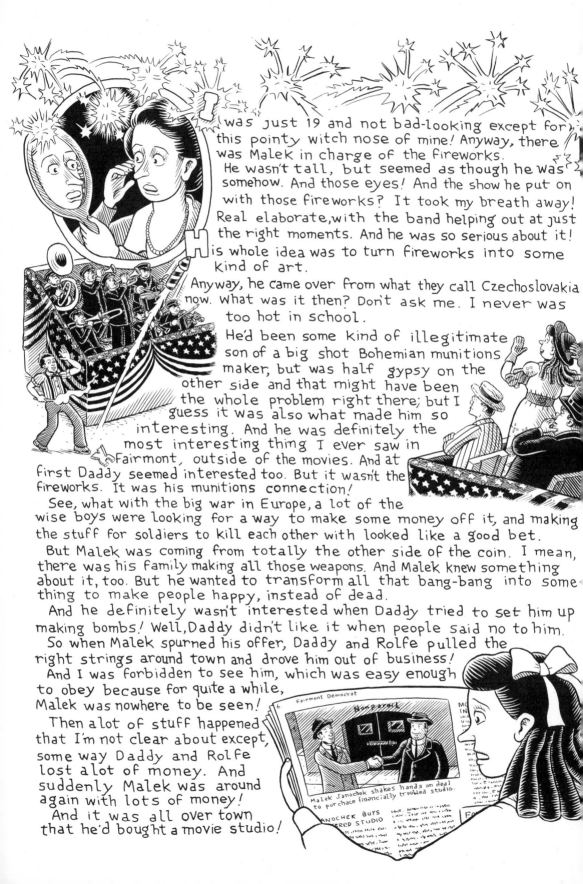

I was just 19 and not bad-looking except for this pointy witch nose of mine! Anyway, there was Malek in charge of the fireworks.

He wasn't tall, but seemed as though he was somehow. And those eyes! And the show he put on with those fireworks? It took my breath away! Real elaborate, with the band helping out at just the right moments. And he was so serious about it!

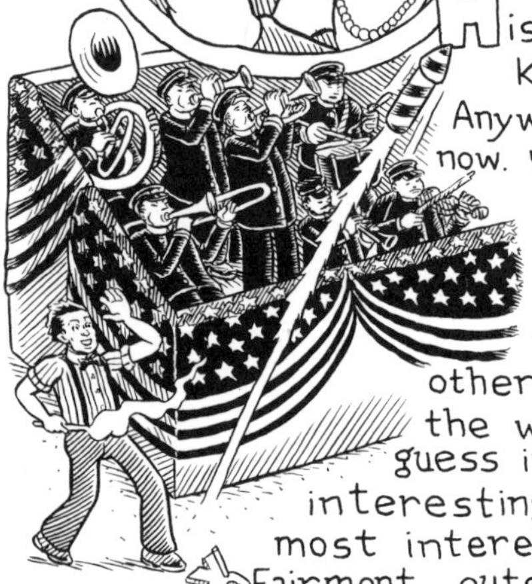

His whole idea was to turn fireworks into some kind of art.

Anyway, he came over from what they call Czechoslovakia now. What was it then? Don't ask me. I never was too hot in school.

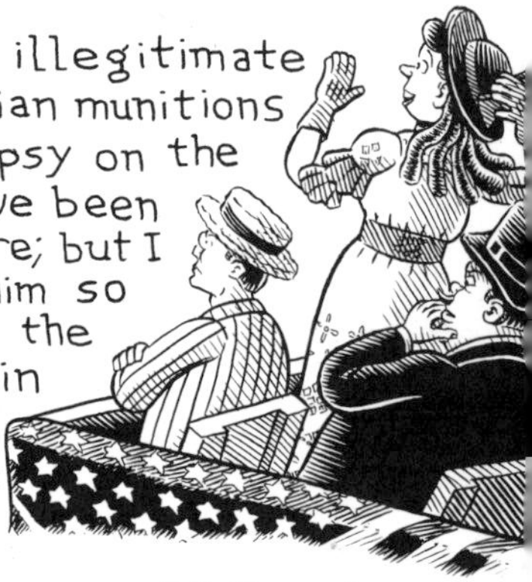

He'd been some kind of illegitimate son of a big shot Bohemian munitions maker, but was half gypsy on the other side and that might have been the whole problem right there; but I guess it was also what made him so interesting. And he was definitely the most interesting thing I ever saw in Fairmont, outside of the movies. And at first Daddy seemed interested too. But it wasn't the fireworks. It was his munitions connection!

See, what with the big war in Europe, a lot of the wise boys were looking for a way to make some money off it, and making the stuff for soldiers to kill each other with looked like a good bet.

But Malek was coming from totally the other side of the coin. I mean, there was his family making all those weapons. And Malek knew something about it, too. But he wanted to transform all that bang-bang into something to make people happy, instead of dead.

And he definitely wasn't interested when Daddy tried to set him up making bombs! Well, Daddy didn't like it when people said no to him.

So when Malek spurned his offer, Daddy and Rolfe pulled the right strings around town and drove him out of business!

And I was forbidden to see him, which was easy enough to obey because for quite a while, Malek was nowhere to be seen!

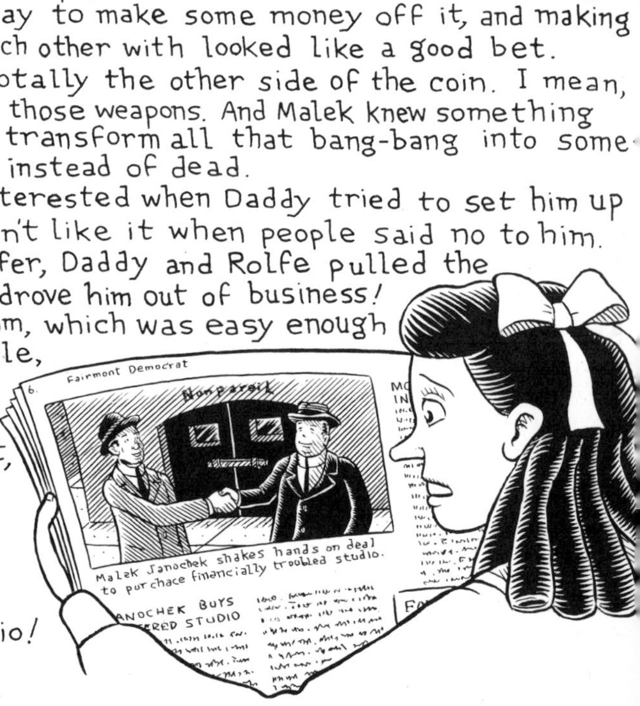

Fairmont Democrat
6.
Nonpareil
Malek Janochek shakes hands on deal to purchase financially troubled studio.
ANOCHEK BUYS
ERED STUDIO

Then alot of stuff happened that I'm not clear about except, some way Daddy and Rolfe lost alot of money. And suddenly Malek was around again with lots of money!

And it was all over town that he'd bought a movie studio!

Nonpareil Pictures over in Matesak. Anyway, it was all over town that Malek bought it and was gonna make a movie, a serial called (we later found out) Alias the Cat!

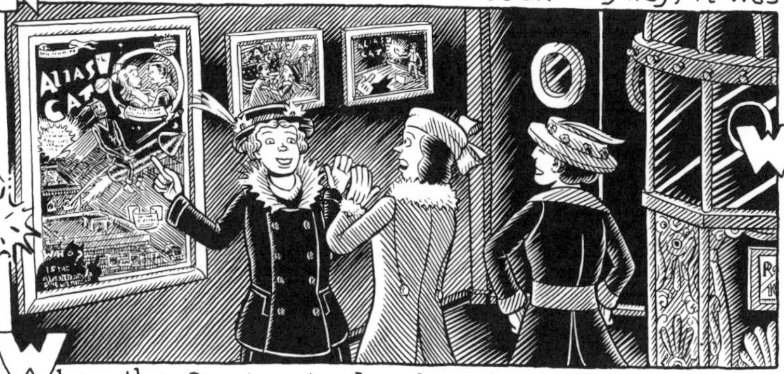
ALIAS CAT

What did I think? Are you kidding? I was thrilled and only prayed that he still liked me. Anyway, everyone was talking about the movie he was planning to star in.

When the first episode showed at the Bijou Dream, the whole town was there! To say that it caused a sensation is putting it mildly. People were furious! Why? Because it was all about us! And how Rolfe and Daddy drove Malek out of business. That's why!

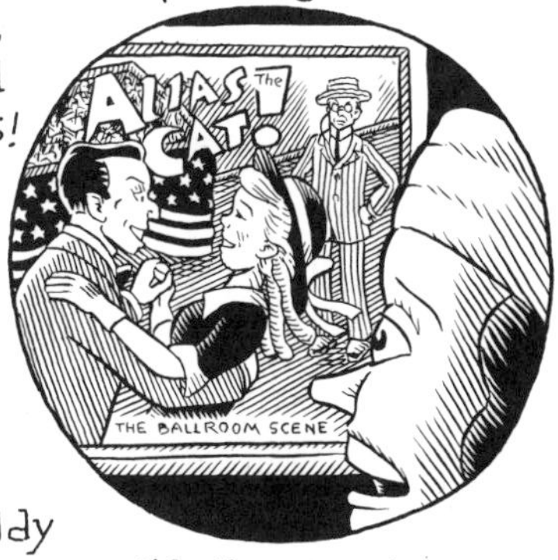
ALIAS The CAT!
THE BALLROOM SCENE

Oh sure, he changed the names but it was so obvious! Although I will say I was flattered to see Molly O'Dare playing what was supposed to be me. She wasn't as big as she later got to be, but you could tell she was gonna be.

But it was strange. In the serial, after Daddy and Rolfe run Malek out of business, he meets up with this mysterious stranger; only you never see him on-screen, just his shadow.

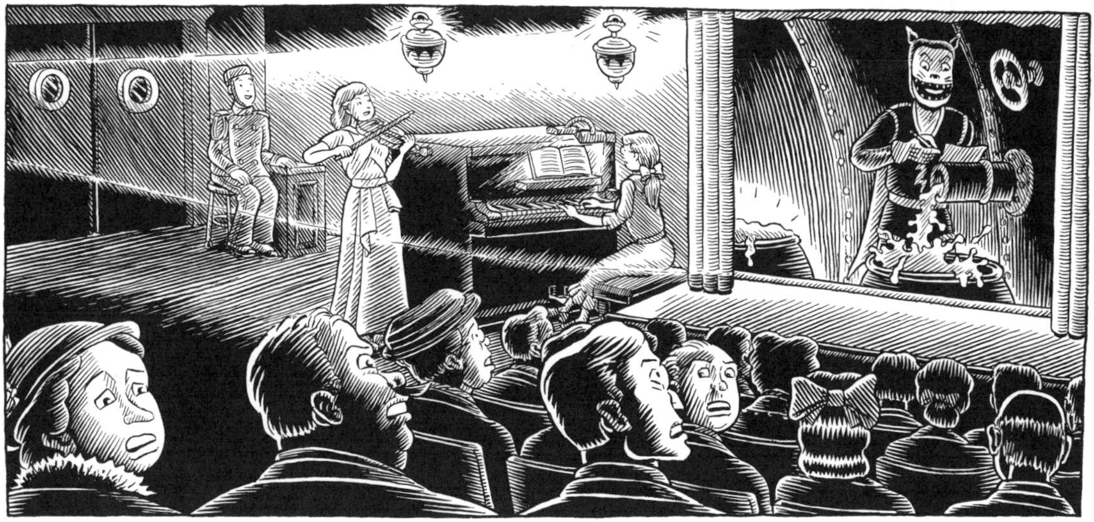

Anyway, this stranger shows Malek how Rolfe and Daddy fixed his wagon and helps him steal a fortune in gold from Rolfe's bank. Well, that part seemed pretty far-fetched, but I noticed that Rolfe and Daddy looked Godalmighty uncomfortable while we watched it!

Of course, we weren't as surprised as we might have been, since Malek also had the story running as a daily comic strip in the local paper. All the serials had their stories running in a magazine or a paper back then.

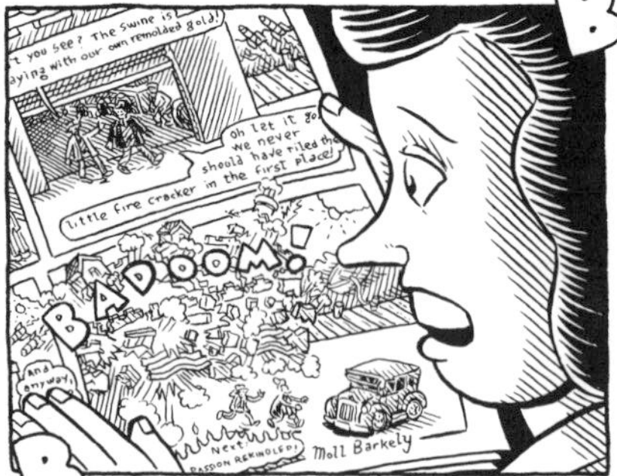
The swine is
with our own remolded gold!
Oh let it go
We never should have riled th
little fire cracker in the first place!
BADOOM!
And anyway!
Moll Barkely

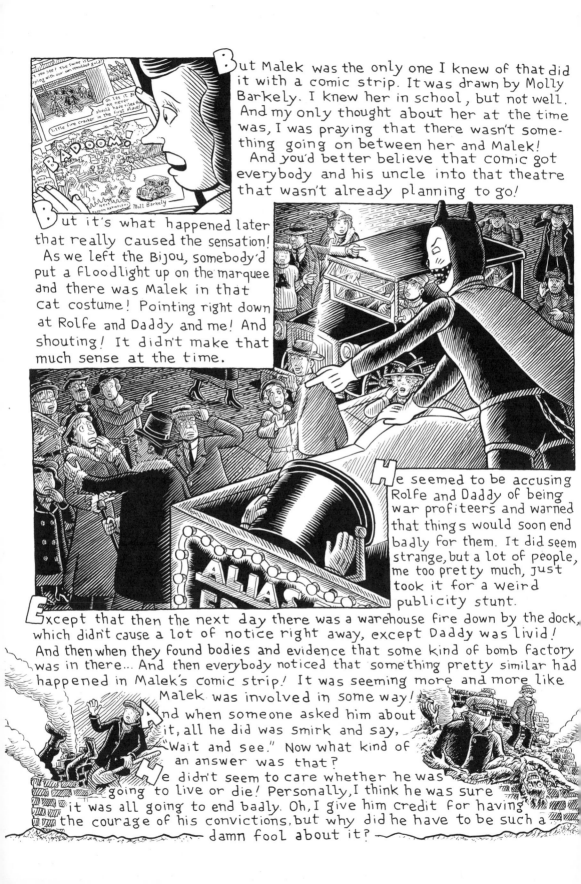

But Malek was the only one I knew of that did it with a comic strip. It was drawn by Molly Barkely. I knew her in school, but not well. And my only thought about her at the time was, I was praying that there wasn't something going on between her and Malek!

And you'd better believe that comic got everybody and his uncle into that theatre that wasn't already planning to go!

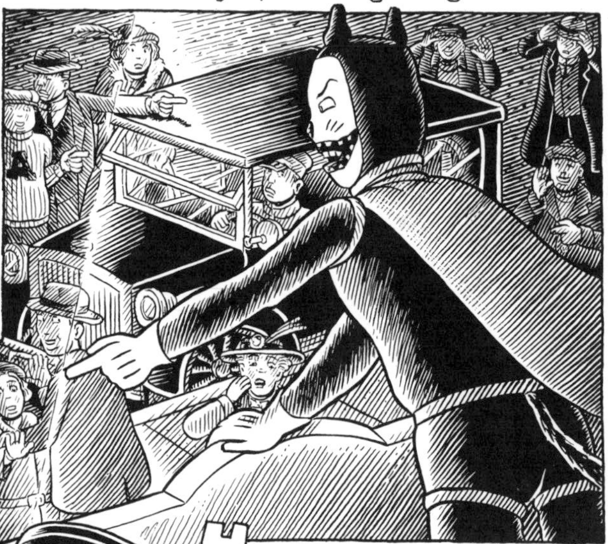

But it's what happened later that really caused the sensation! As we left the Bijou, somebody'd put a floodlight up on the marquee and there was Malek in that cat costume! Pointing right down at Rolfe and Daddy and me! And shouting! It didn't make that much sense at the time.

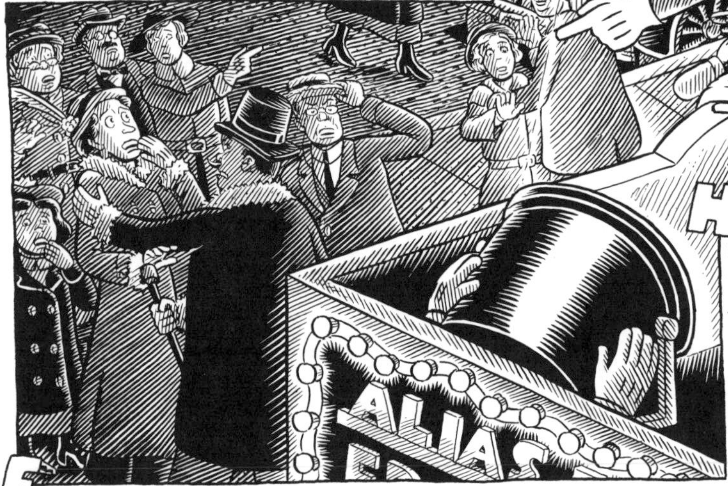
ALIAS

He seemed to be accusing Rolfe and Daddy of being war profiteers and warned that things would soon end badly for them. It did seem strange, but a lot of people, me too pretty much, just took it for a weird publicity stunt.

Except that then the next day there was a warehouse fire down by the dock, which didn't cause a lot of notice right away, except Daddy was livid! And then when they found bodies and evidence that some kind of bomb factory was in there... And then everybody noticed that something pretty similar had happened in Malek's comic strip! It was seeming more and more like Malek was involved in some way!

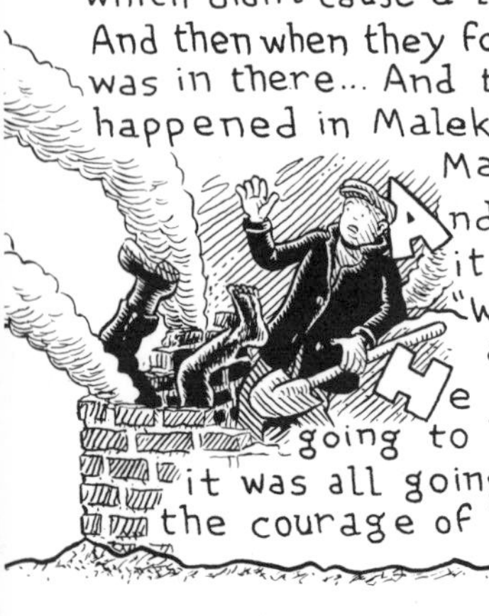

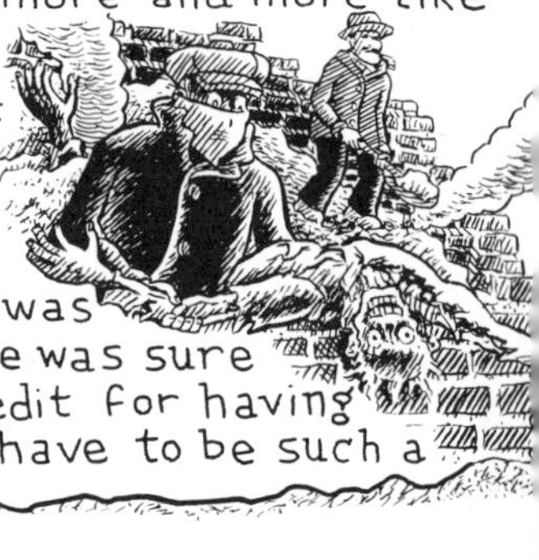

And when someone asked him about it, all he did was smirk and say, "Wait and see." Now what kind of an answer was that?

He didn't seem to care whether he was going to live or die! Personally, I think he was sure it was all going to end badly. Oh, I give him credit for having the courage of his convictions, but why did he have to be such a damn fool about it?

I've been asking myself that question for 50 years and I still can't figure it out! The thing is, every time I get my mind settled on all this and tell myself that what I did was all for the best, I look on the television and see what a mess the world is in and start wondering about it all over again!

They said he kidnapped me. Hell! I said he kidnapped me and what a bloomer of a lie that was! Okay, okay. I'm getting ahead of myself.

You see, after that warehouse burned down, rumors were flying that Malek was involved. But I found out that it was a secret munitions plant run by Rolfe and Daddy! And to cover their hides, they were noising it around that the place had actually been an anarchist bomb factory that Malek had been running!

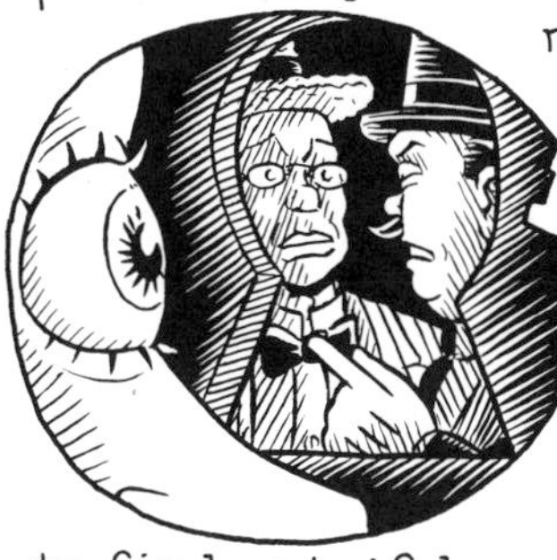

I heard them plotting over it in Daddy's study! How? By listening in at the door, that's how! I wanted to know what was going on just like everyone else in town! Except I was in a position to find out, and did! Besides, now I had a good excuse to go see Malek: to warn him and to find out if he still liked me!

So I drove over to Matesak where Malek's studio was. Getting in

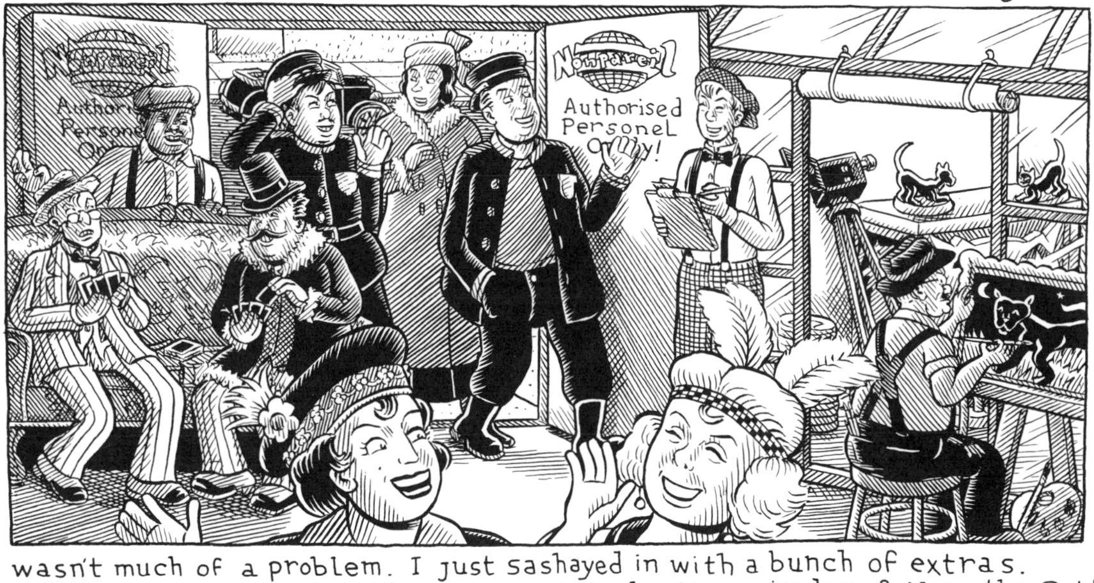
Nonpareil
Authorised Personel Only!

wasn't much of a problem. I just sashayed in with a bunch of extras. To my great surprise they were still shooting episodes of Alias the Cat!

I found Malek going over the next day's Alias the Cat comic with Molly Barkely. That didn't set too well with me except that the second he saw me I had the answer to my big question. He was thrilled to see me.

Before I knew it, I was getting the grand tour. Not that it was much to see. Just a couple of glassed-in sets that looked like greenhouses, to get the sun.

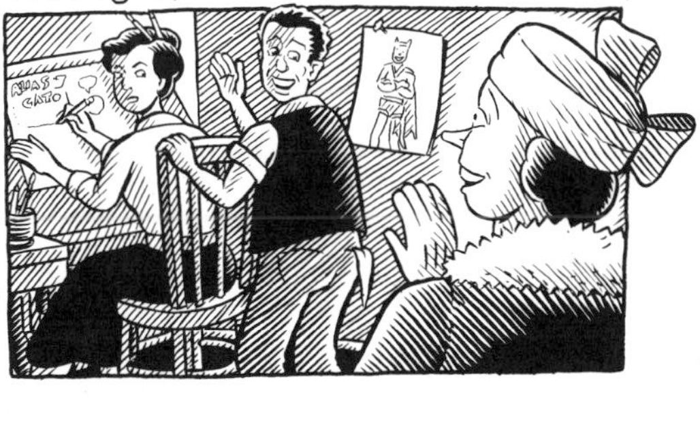

I did get to meet Molly O'Dare. She was wearing bright yellow makeup!

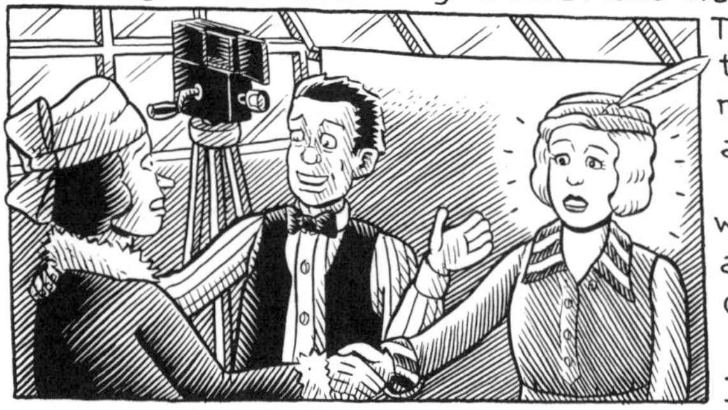

That was a surprise. They all did then to make 'em photograph normal. I have no idea why. But Malek seemed to be all business with her too.

I tried to warn him about what people were saying, but he seemed to know all about it and seemed pretty sure of himself.

When he invited me to dinner later, I accepted, figuring we'd go to some restaurant, but instead we drove to his place.

That was a surprise, but not the way you'd think. You see, in "Alias the Cat," Malek had his character living in this elegant hideaway, lots of beautiful things, and all the while Malek's place was pretty much of a mess!

It was quite clear he wasn't putting his money into that kind of thing. No. It was a big jumble of old fireworks and what-have-you!

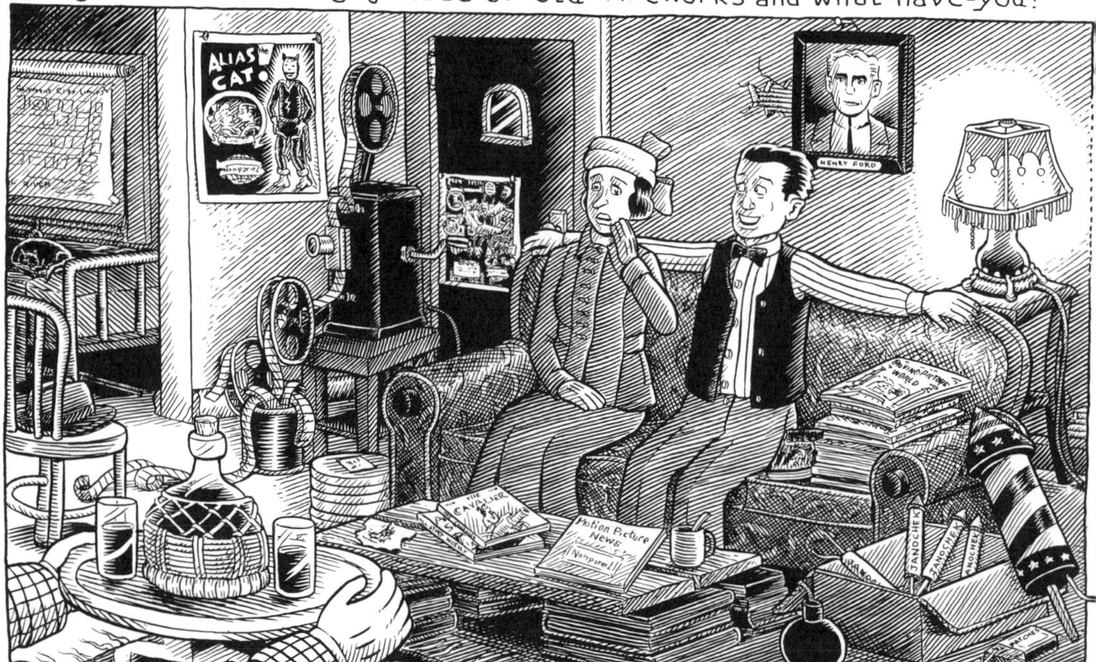
ALIAS the CAT
HENRY FORD
Motion Picture News
Nonpareil
JANOSCHEK

But that wasn't the biggest surprise. Oh no. The really weird part was his valet or manservant, Walden or Walter. I never did get the name right. But he was the weirdest thing I ever laid eyes on! Now I know this is going to sound strange, but I wasn't even altogether sure he was human! What did he look like?

Well, he was very, very, short and,... well, just kind of icky! It made me all nervous being around him. Malek saw it. He couldn't miss it because I started making excuses to leave. But he wouldn't hear of it. "I invited you to dinner and you shall have it," he said. And sure enough, I could smell something good cooking in the other room.

Okay, I'll give Walden that much credit. He could cook. No, it wasn't very romantic because as soon as we started eating, Malek started ranting about war mongers, war profiteers, and soon was making some pretty serious innuendos about what Daddy and Rolfe were up to in that department.

And then he started going on and on about Henry Ford and what a great man he was; with that peace ship thing he set up to end the war?

Oh, you never heard about that? Well, that doesn't really surprise me. The main thing about it is, it didn't work. Henry Ford may have known how to make cars, but I'm not so sure he was so bright otherwise. He got some ship, filled it with a lot of big brains and sailed off to Europe to try and patch up the war

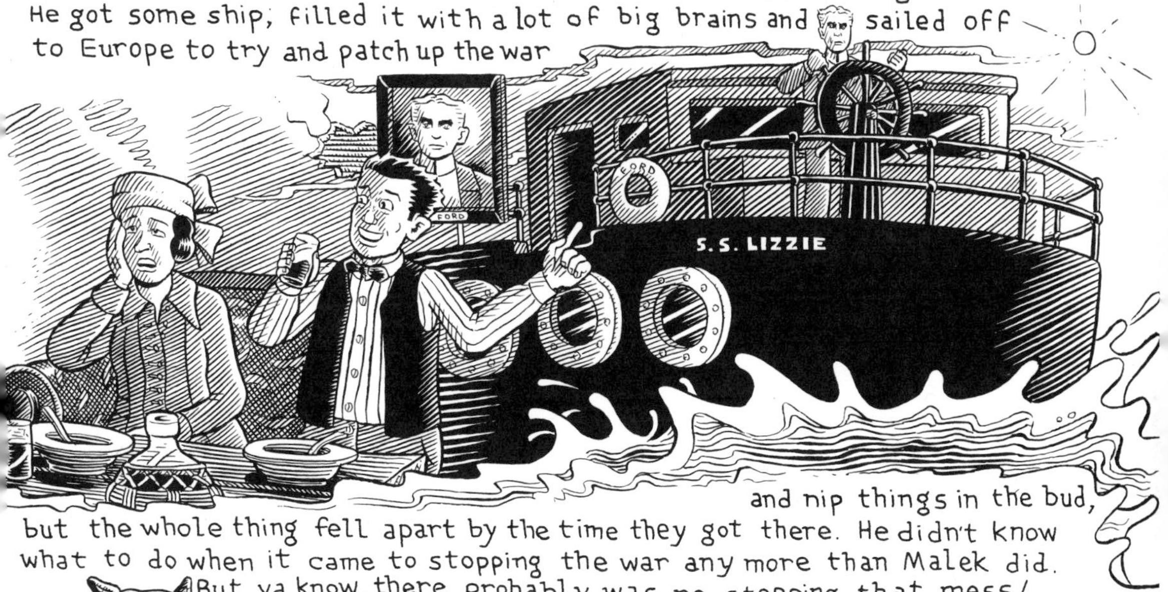
FORD
FORD
S. S. LIZZIE

and nip things in the bud, but the whole thing fell apart by the time they got there. He didn't know what to do when it came to stopping the war any more than Malek did.

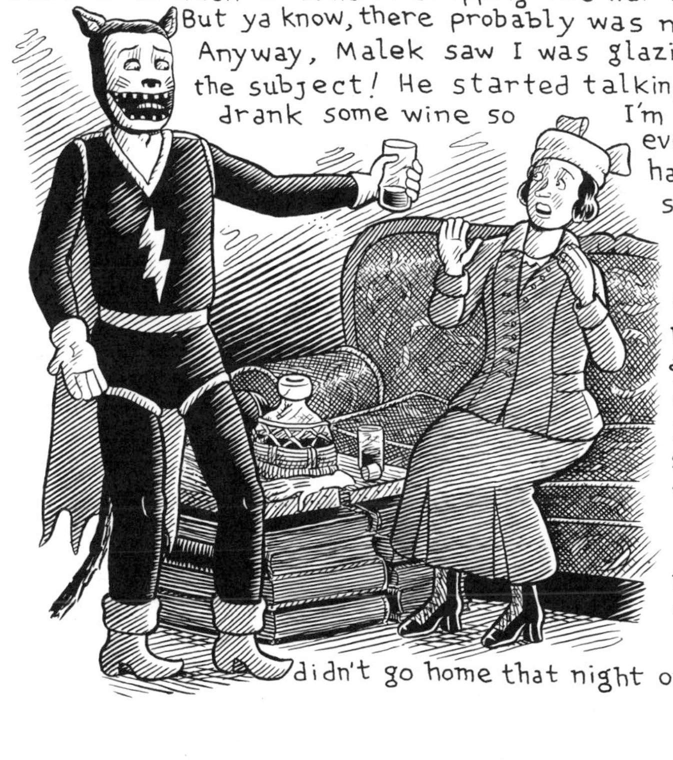

But ya know, there probably was no stopping that mess! Anyway, Malek saw I was glazing over and finally got off the subject! He started talking about the movie while we drank some wine so I'm a little fuzzy about every little detail of what happened next except that at some point he got into that costume!

What can I say? I mean, clearly I was already attracted to him and things had already gone further than I'd planned, but something just happened when I saw him standing in front of me in that suit! And before I knew it, we were, well, doing it!

The first time was a little rough. Yes, I did say the first time. But I must have been out of my mind because I didn't go home that night or the night after that either!

That's where the kidnapping thing started. And later, like a coward, I put the tin hat on it.

But the actual truth is those next two days were the greatest and most thrilling of my entire life. It was like something out of a book. And not the kind they wrote in those days, but more up to date with, well, you know. But don't get me wrong. Malek wouldn't have gotten anywhere with me if he hadn't been just about the most romantic person I ever knew! And so exciting!

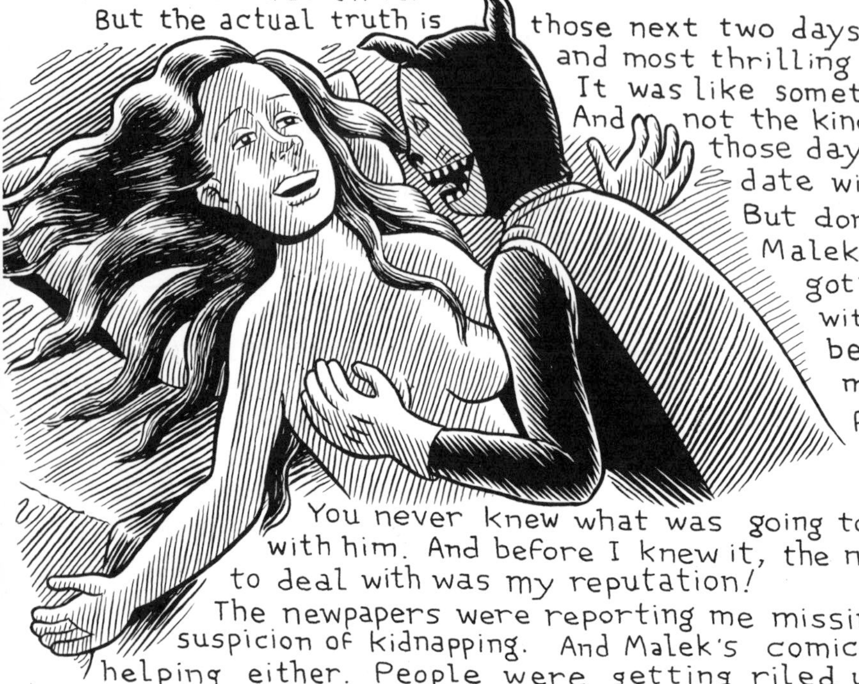

You never knew what was going to happen next with him. And before I knew it, the next thing I had to deal with was my reputation!

The newpapers were reporting me missing, with a strong suspicion of kidnapping. And Malek's comic strip wasn't helping either. People were getting riled up.

I knew I had to get out of there and besides, Okay, Daddy was a crook. Well, that was nothing new in New Jersey politics.

In those days it was an unspoken truth that you needed a good crook to make things work in politics. And I'm not altogether sure things have changed so much. I don't know. The fact is, when I left, I had no intention of betraying Malek.

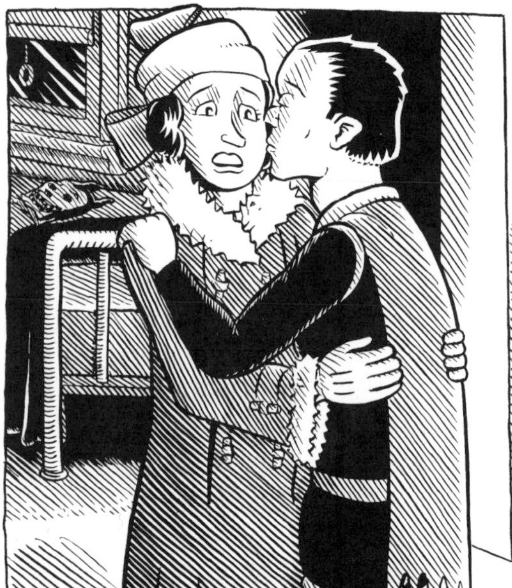

Except, when I was kissing him goodbye, I caught Walden watching us from the other room and it gave me the willies!

I'm not sure it wasn't him, whatever he was, that was actually calling the tune!

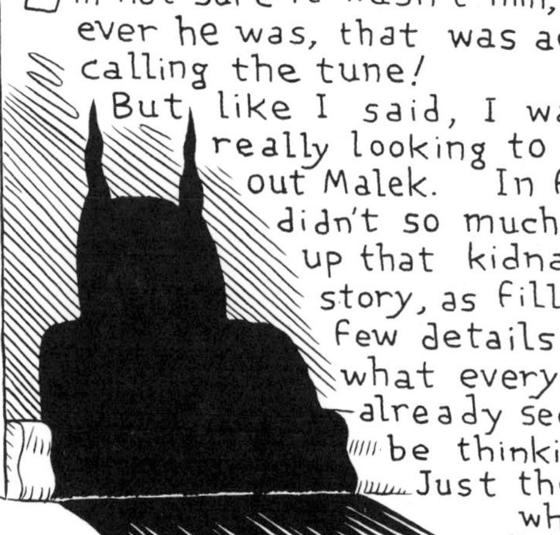

But like I said, I wasn't really looking to sell out Malek. In fact, I didn't so much make up that kidnapping story, as fill in a few details for what everyone already seemed to be thinking.

Just the same, what happened next

still makes me sick and really ashamed too. Oh yeah, I went along.

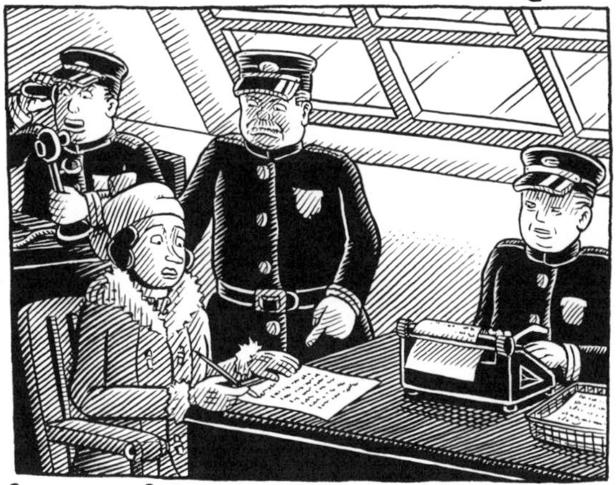

I was kidnapped by Malek Janochek, anarchist bomb maker, 'cause that's how they were working it. That big fire where they found all the burned bodies? Well, that's how they were covering it up; Rolfe and Daddy's secret munitions factory.

Did Malek blow it up? Probably. But Malek never actually told me that. It wouldn't have been such a good idea, little Quisling that I was.

Even so. If I'd thought it out, if I could have known that what happened next was going to happen. Well, of course that's easy to say now.

Anyway, the long arm of the law was out for Malek. In an amazingly short time, police had Malek's Nonpareil studio surrounded. They were demanding that Malek surrender himself, but he wasn't coming out and he wasn't letting anybody in either!

I drove over and was watching it all away from the mob.

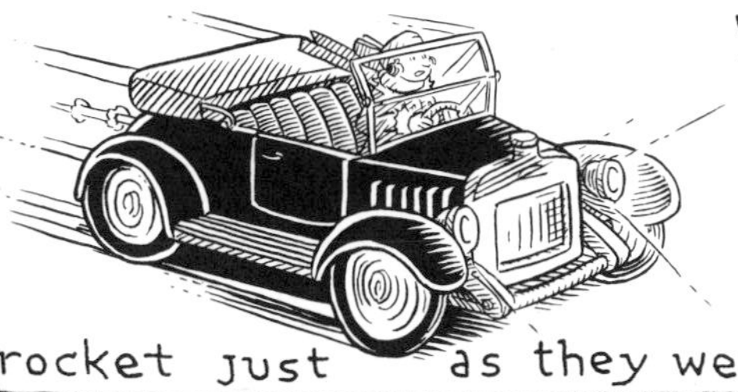

Well, it was only a matter of time before they got in there. I don't know how the fire started, whether Malek decided to burn the place or the Police started it, but the studio was burning. I was sick. And then it happened. Later, they said he lit a giant sky rocket just as they were about to take him.

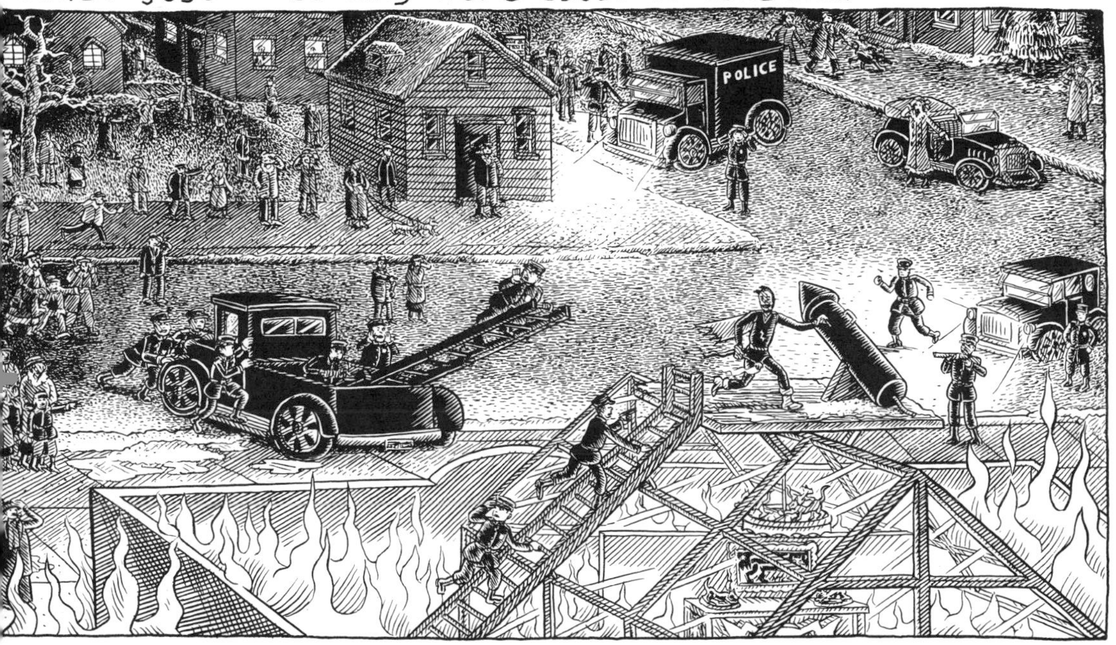
POLICE

And that was uncanny because that's exactly how the second and last episode anyone in the world ever saw of Alias the Cat ended! With Malek soaring up into the sky, riding that sky rocket!

It would have come out all right in episode 3, only for Malek there was no episode 3!

What? You're not sure you believe me? Hmph. Well, what of it? You probably won't believe the rest of it either. But it happened, and it was unbelievable. When I saw Malek launched into the sky, riding that sky rocket like a horse, I, well, I wanted with everything in me to beleive! To believe that somehow he'd pull out of this; that somehow, like a movie, that it was going to be alright.

And in spite of myself, I was actually thrilled watching him as he soared higher into the sky! And it wasn't just me because I heard cheering from the mob around the burning studio!

Only then, when he started falling, the cheering got louder and I was just sick!

What I did next. Why I did what I did next, well, I still can't understand it. It wasn't planned but even as he started falling, I started driving to the swampland he was falling toward.

The swamps were all frozen over or I never would have risked going there. Anyway, it was easy to find where he'd fallen, even at night, because there

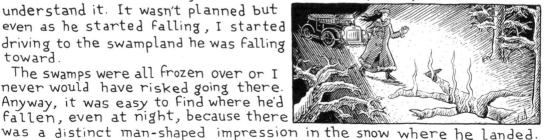

was a distinct man-shaped impression in the snow where he landed.

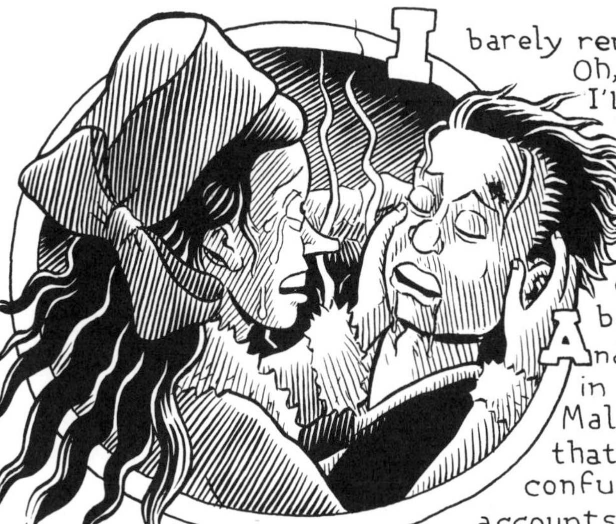

I barely remember doing what I did next. Oh, that's not completely true. I'll never forget looking into his dead face and how peaceful it looked. But the next part, I'm really not proud of this, but somehow I got that cat costume off his mangled body and took it away with me.

And that was the big mystery in the papers the next day: Malek's naked body. And I think that's why there was so much confusion about all the eye witness accounts of Malek's last ride and why even with all those witnesses, none of them were taken very seriously.

In fact, it was really kind of amazing how the whole thing got brushed under the rug. And I guess a lot of me kind of got brushed under too 'cause I was never the same.

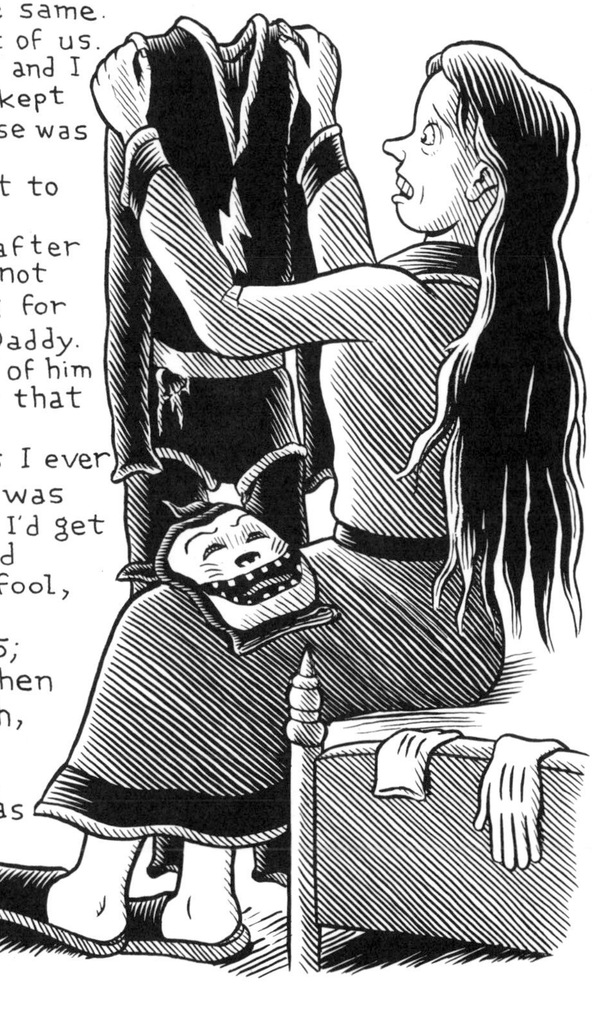

Oh sure, life went on for the rest of us. Daddy got re-elected the next year and I got married to Rolfe. And the war kept going till America and everyone else was up to their ears in it.

I got to hate it though I kept it to myself, like most things ... after.

See, I never did feel much alive after that. I never let Rolfe near me, not that he cared. All he was looking for was a way to cement things with Daddy.

But, boy oh boy, he sure got loose of him fast when Daddy went to jail over that school scandal, later.

And me, well, about the only times I ever even felt half alive after that was when no one else was around and I'd get out Malek's tattered costume and remember that crazy wonderful fool, Malek Janochek.

Other men? Well, once in 1925; anyway it had to be before '29, when Rolfe lost his shirt in the crash, because we still had the house.

I'd hired this Italian gardener. He wasn't too bright. In fact he was probably what they call retarded now.

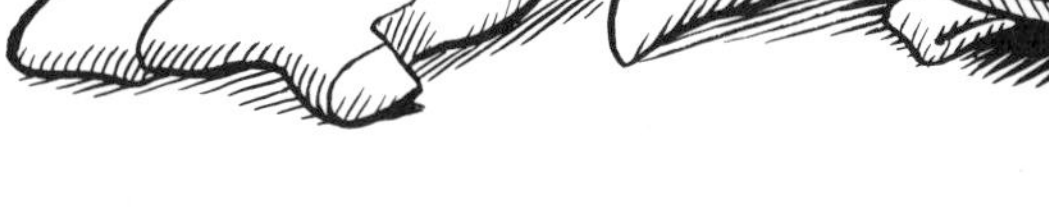

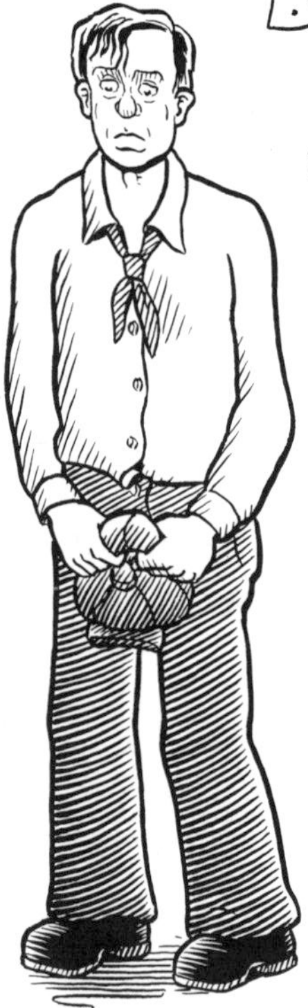

But there was something striking about him. And I think, in fact I know, the reason I hired him was because he reminded me of Malek, with that same kind of compact build that Malek had. Maybe in some way, the retarded part played into it too.

Anyway, one day, when no one was paying too much attention, I got the poor fool up into my bedroom and got him to put on Malek's old costume.

I'd patched it up as well as I could, except for the burnt parts; but it was a big disaster.

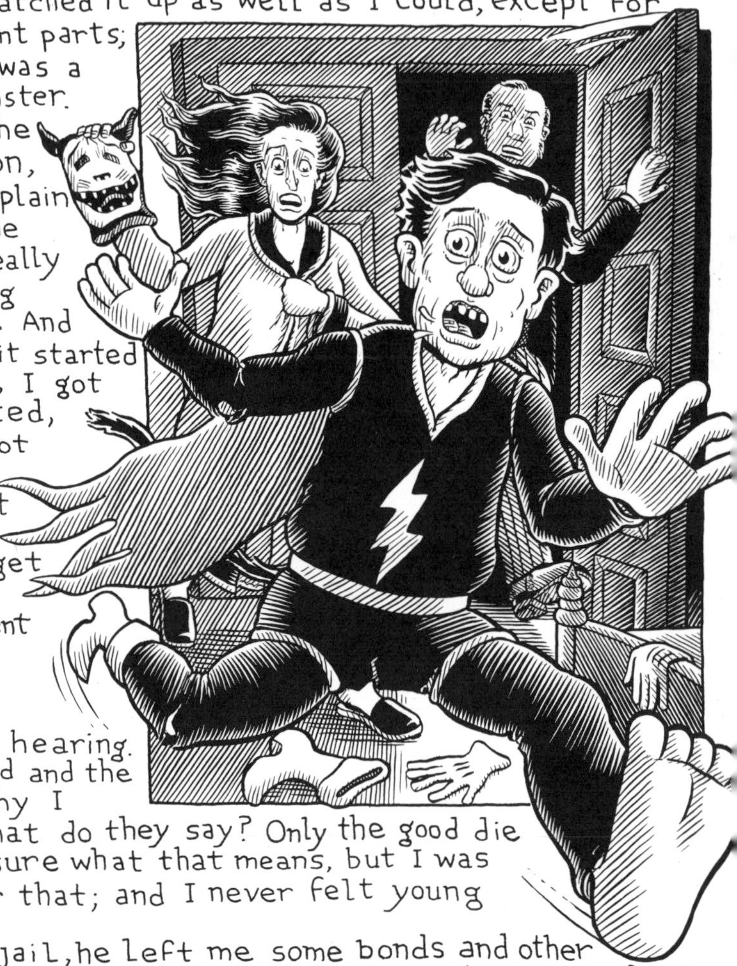

When he put it on, it was plain that he was really too big for it. And when it started to rip, I got agitated, that got this lummox agitated and it wasn't very pretty.

Of course I had to get rid of him after that and that's one experiment I never repeated.

What happened next? Honey, you've already heard all that's worth hearing. After that came the bad and the boring. I don't know why I didn't just die. But what do they say? Only the good die young? I'm not even sure what that means, but I was never much good after that; and I never felt young again, after Malek.

After Daddy died, in jail, he left me some bonds and other stuff. It wasn't a fortune, but I didn't really have to work after Rolfe divorced me. He was always scrambling after another pile after he lost it all. Later he got a job with his old bank, which kind of amazed me, but I guess he knew where too many bodies were buried for them to risk **not** hiring him!

Of course when World War II came along, I thought of Malek a lot. There it was all over again! And all those atomic bombs! What a world!

Oh yeah, Malek had the right idea, or at least part of it. But it was just too much like that old story they made us read in school.

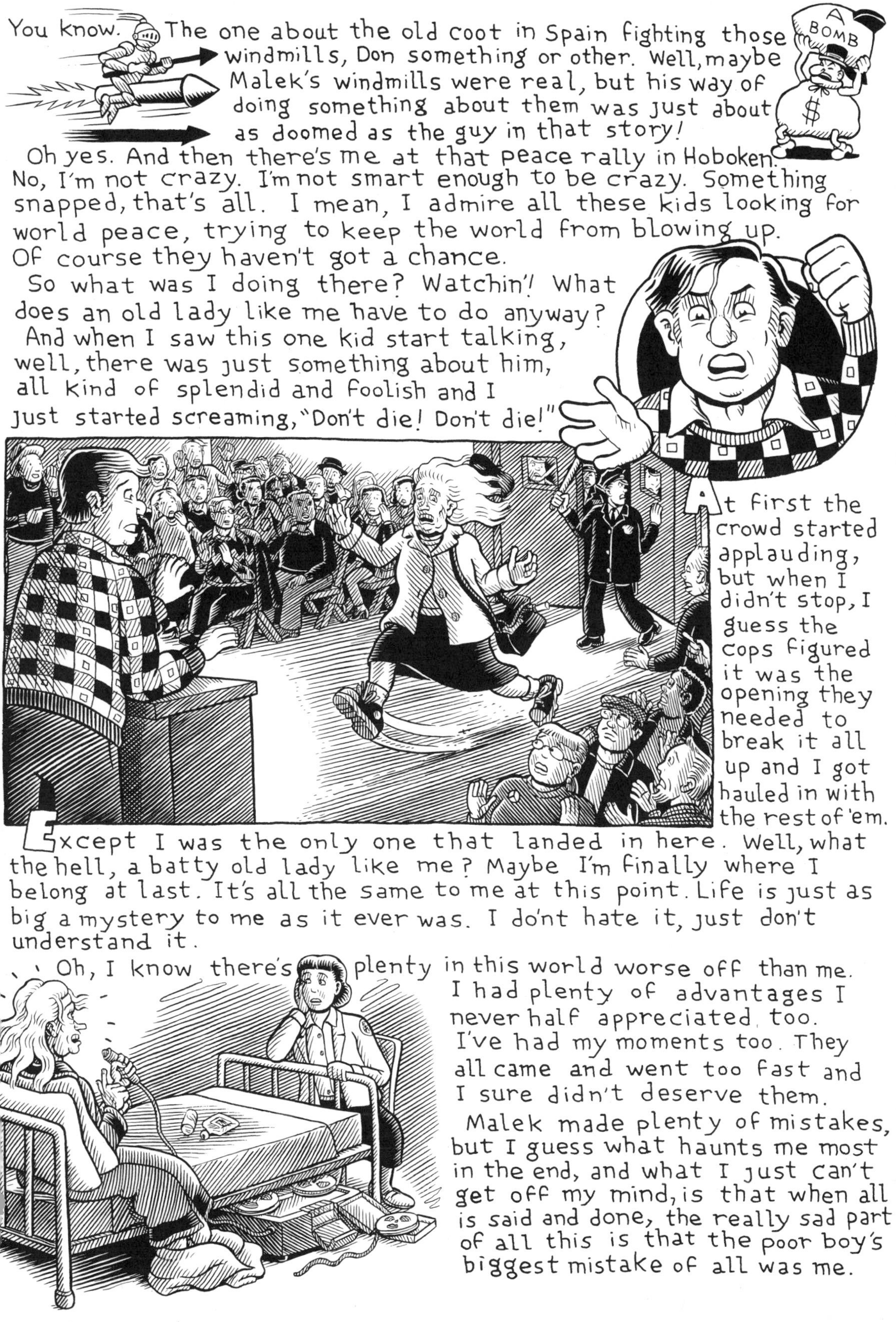

You know. The one about the old coot in Spain fighting those windmills, Don something or other. Well, maybe Malek's windmills were real, but his way of doing something about them was just about as doomed as the guy in that story!
A BOMB
$
Oh yes. And then there's me at that peace rally in Hoboken. No, I'm not crazy. I'm not smart enough to be crazy. Something snapped, that's all. I mean, I admire all these kids looking for world peace, trying to keep the world from blowing up. Of course they haven't got a chance.
So what was I doing there? Watchin'! What does an old lady like me have to do anyway?
And when I saw this one kid start talking, well, there was just something about him, all kind of splendid and foolish and I just started screaming, "Don't die! Don't die!"
At first the crowd started applauding, but when I didn't stop, I guess the cops figured it was the opening they needed to break it all up and I got hauled in with the rest of 'em.
Except I was the only one that landed in here. Well, what the hell, a batty old lady like me? Maybe I'm finally where I belong at last. It's all the same to me at this point. Life is just as big a mystery to me as it ever was. I don't hate it, just don't understand it.
. . . Oh, I know there's plenty in this world worse off than me. I had plenty of advantages I never half appreciated, too. I've had my moments too. They all came and went too fast and I sure didn't deserve them.
Malek made plenty of mistakes, but I guess what haunts me most in the end, and what I just can't get off my mind, is that when all is said and done, the really sad part of all this is that the poor boy's biggest mistake of all was me.

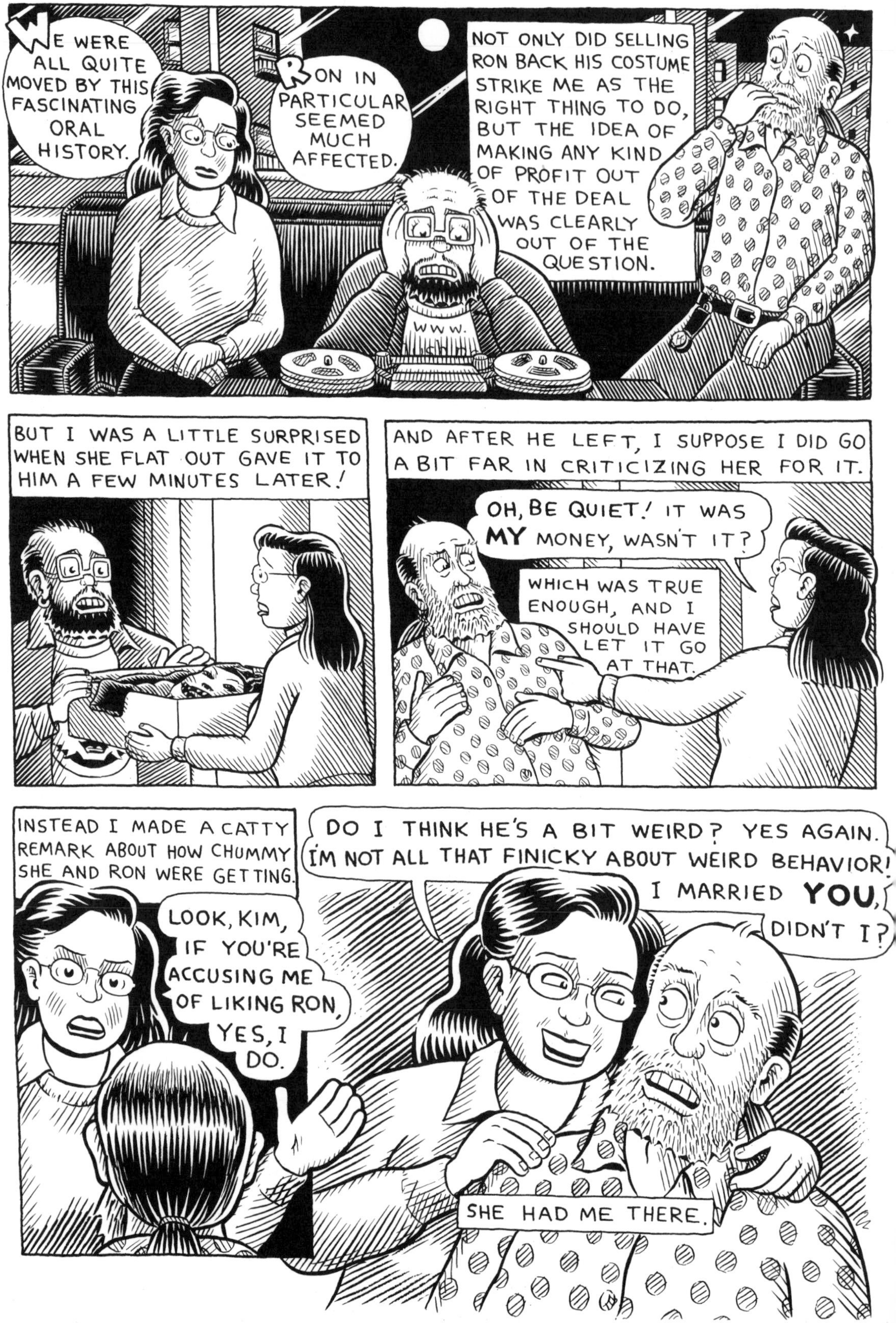
WE WERE ALL QUITE MOVED BY THIS FASCINATING ORAL HISTORY.
RON IN PARTICULAR SEEMED MUCH AFFECTED.
NOT ONLY DID SELLING RON BACK HIS COSTUME STRIKE ME AS THE RIGHT THING TO DO, BUT THE IDEA OF MAKING ANY KIND OF PROFIT OUT OF THE DEAL WAS CLEARLY OUT OF THE QUESTION.
WWW.
BUT I WAS A LITTLE SURPRISED WHEN SHE FLAT OUT GAVE IT TO HIM A FEW MINUTES LATER!
AND AFTER HE LEFT, I SUPPOSE I DID GO A BIT FAR IN CRITICIZING HER FOR IT.
OH, BE QUIET! IT WAS MY MONEY, WASN'T IT?
WHICH WAS TRUE ENOUGH, AND I SHOULD HAVE LET IT GO AT THAT.
INSTEAD I MADE A CATTY REMARK ABOUT HOW CHUMMY SHE AND RON WERE GETTING.
LOOK, KIM, IF YOU'RE ACCUSING ME OF LIKING RON, YES, I DO.
DO I THINK HE'S A BIT WEIRD? YES AGAIN. I'M NOT ALL THAT FINICKY ABOUT WEIRD BEHAVIOR! I MARRIED YOU, DIDN'T I?
SHE HAD ME THERE.

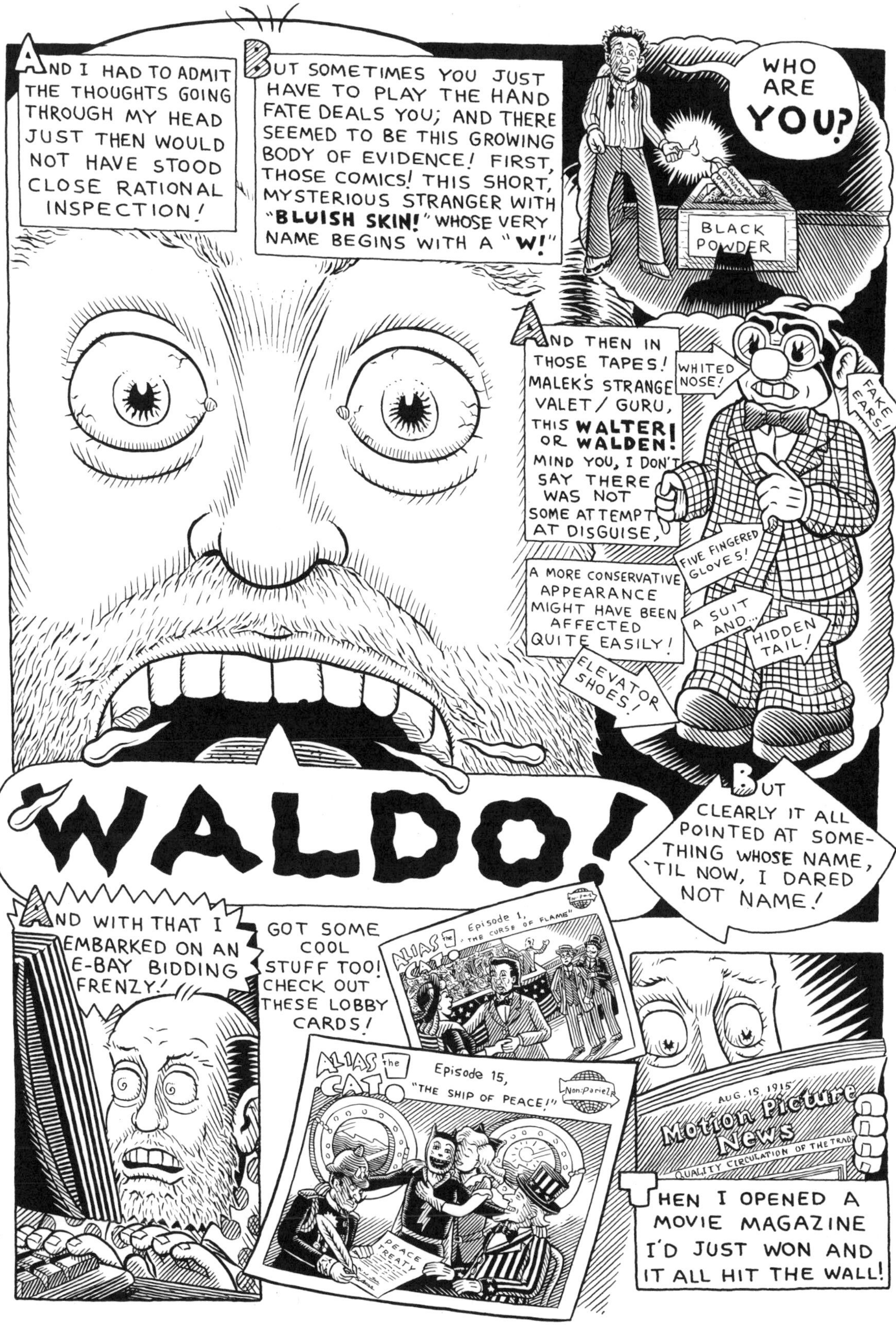
AND I HAD TO ADMIT THE THOUGHTS GOING THROUGH MY HEAD JUST THEN WOULD NOT HAVE STOOD CLOSE RATIONAL INSPECTION!
BUT SOMETIMES YOU JUST HAVE TO PLAY THE HAND FATE DEALS YOU; AND THERE SEEMED TO BE THIS GROWING BODY OF EVIDENCE! FIRST, THOSE COMICS! THIS SHORT, MYSTERIOUS STRANGER WITH "BLUISH SKIN!" WHOSE VERY NAME BEGINS WITH A "W!"
WHO ARE YOU?
BLACK POWDER
AND THEN IN THOSE TAPES! MALEK'S STRANGE VALET / GURU, THIS WALTER! OR WALDEN! MIND YOU, I DON'T SAY THERE WAS NOT SOME ATTEMPT AT DISGUISE,
WHITED NOSE!
FAKE EARS!
FIVE FINGERED GLOVES!
A MORE CONSERVATIVE APPEARANCE MIGHT HAVE BEEN AFFECTED QUITE EASILY!
A SUIT AND...
HIDDEN TAIL!
ELEVATOR SHOES!
WALDO!
BUT CLEARLY IT ALL POINTED AT SOMETHING WHOSE NAME, 'TIL NOW, I DARED NOT NAME!
AND WITH THAT I EMBARKED ON AN E-BAY BIDDING FRENZY!
GOT SOME COOL STUFF TOO! CHECK OUT THESE LOBBY CARDS!
ALIAS the CAT
Episode 1, "THE CURSE OF FLAME"
ALIAS the CAT
Episode 15, "THE SHIP OF PEACE!"
PEACE TREATY
AUG. 15 1915
Motion Picture News
QUALITY CIRCULATION OF THE TRADE
THEN I OPENED A MOVIE MAGAZINE I'D JUST WON AND IT ALL HIT THE WALL!

N IT WAS **THIS** PICTURE OF MALEK JANOCHEK WITH AN EXTREMELY SHORT INDIVIDUAL NAMED ~~WALTER~~ KLEINSCHMIDT! THIS **WALTER** WAS DESCRIBED IN THE ACCOMPANYING ARTICLE AS CHIEF CARPENTER AT MALEK'S STUDIO; BUT HE ALSO SEEMED TO BE A GOOD DEAL MORE!

MOTION PICTURE NEWS

ALIAS THE CAT

Malek Janocheck and Walter Kleinschmidt between scenes on the Alias the Cat s...
MALEK'S LITTLE GIANT
...r recent visit to the
...o willing, ho...
...self, ho...

KLEINSCHMIDT
CARPENTRY
PAINTING
Central 5021

N THE ARTICLE, MALEK IS QUOATED. "In all things **W**alter is my right-hand man, without whom all of my late accomplishments would have been impossible."

DEEPER INTO THE PIECE, IT STATED THAT **WALTER** LIVED IN TOWATA, NEW JERSEY, KNOWN COLLOQUIALLY AS "MIDGETVILLE," BECAUSE OF ITS TINY HOUSES AND MIDGET POPULATION (MOSTLY THEATER AND CARNIVAL PERFORMERS).

ANOTHER PHOTO SHOWED MALEK AND WALTER KLEINSCHMIDT IN FRONT OF WALTER'S "MIDGETVILLE" HOME!

OKAY, ADMITTEDLY THIS SEEMED TO PUT A NEW SLANT ON EVERYTHING. AND I DIDN'T KNOW WHAT TOUGH WAS UNTIL I TRIED TO TRACK DOWN A 1915 TOWATA, NEW JERSEY, PHONE BOOK.

IN FACT, IT WAS IMPOSSIBLE.

BUT, AFTER A LOT OF TROUBLE, I DID FIND THIS 1913 EDITION.

TOWATA N.J. **1913** DIRECTORY AND TELEPHONE EXCHANGE

WALTER KLEINSCHMIDT PAINTING / CARPENTRY CEN... 5021 **NO!** CREDIT

INDIGO SHADES A SPECIALTY

...WOOD ...RRACE
...RDER OF LILIPUTANS ...TRAL 6980
FORMBY...SE... FORBE...

48

AND THERE, IN A DISPLAY AD NO LESS, WAS THIS LISTING FOR **WALTER!**

I WAS IN THE MIDST OF FEVERISH PLANS TO VISIT TOWATA, NEW JERSEY, OR "MIDGETVILLE," WHEN PAM CAME IN, PACKAGE IN HAND.

HI.

WHAT DO YOU MEAN, THERE'S NO DIRECT BUS LINE!

Jazz Records   Jazz Records

TOWATA N.J.

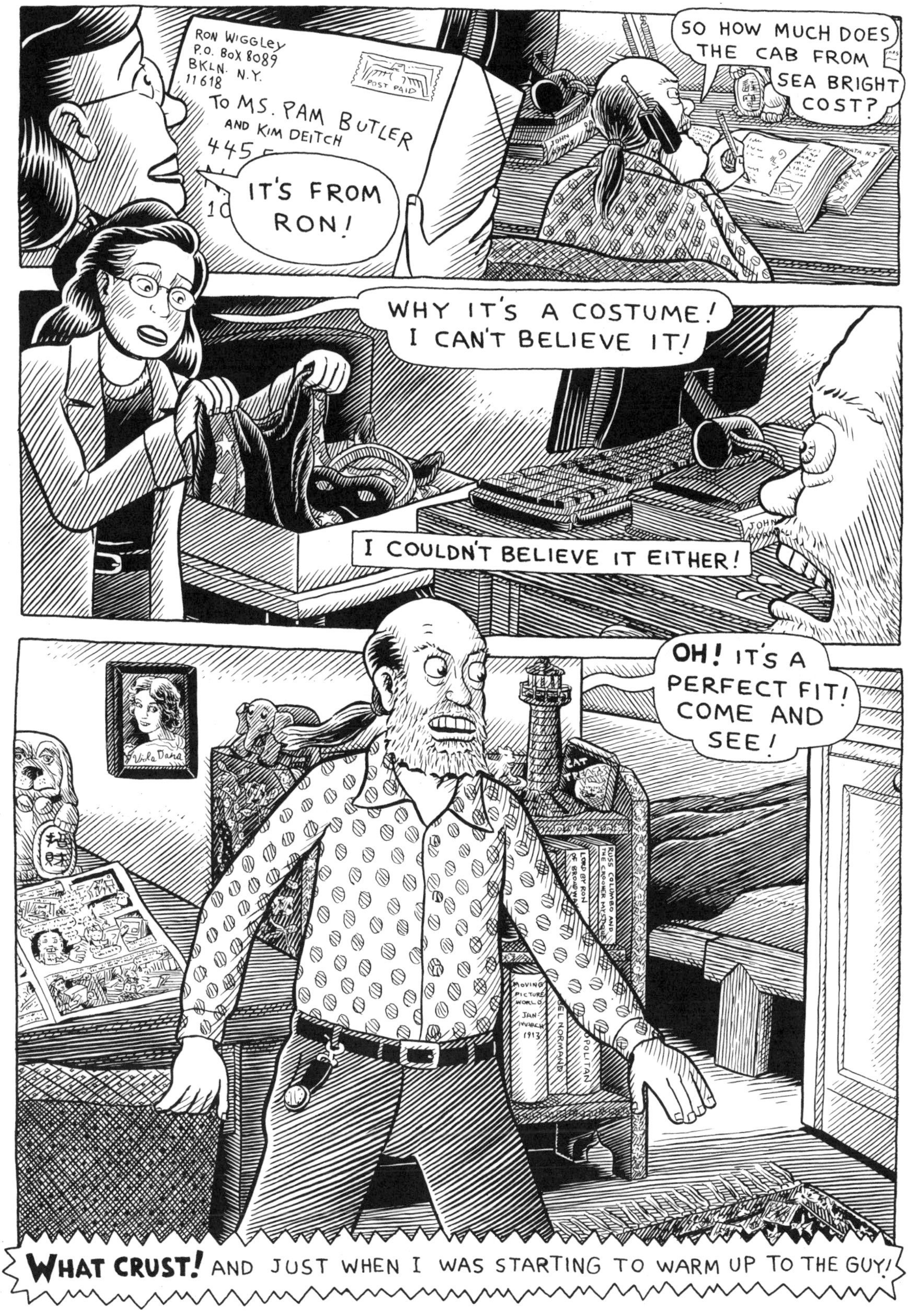
RON WIGGLEY
P.O. BOX 8089
BKLN. N.Y.
11618
TO MS. PAM BUTLER
AND KIM DEITCH
POST PAID
IT'S FROM RON!
SO HOW MUCH DOES THE CAB FROM SEA BRIGHT COST?
WHY IT'S A COSTUME! I CAN'T BELIEVE IT!
I COULDN'T BELIEVE IT EITHER!
OH! IT'S A PERFECT FIT! COME AND SEE!
Viola Dana
CAT TREATS
RUSS COLUMBO AND THE CROONER MYSTERY
LORD BY RON OF BROADWAY
MOVING PICTURE WORLD JAN- MARCH 1913
WHAT CRUST! AND JUST WHEN I WAS STARTING TO WARM UP TO THE GUY!

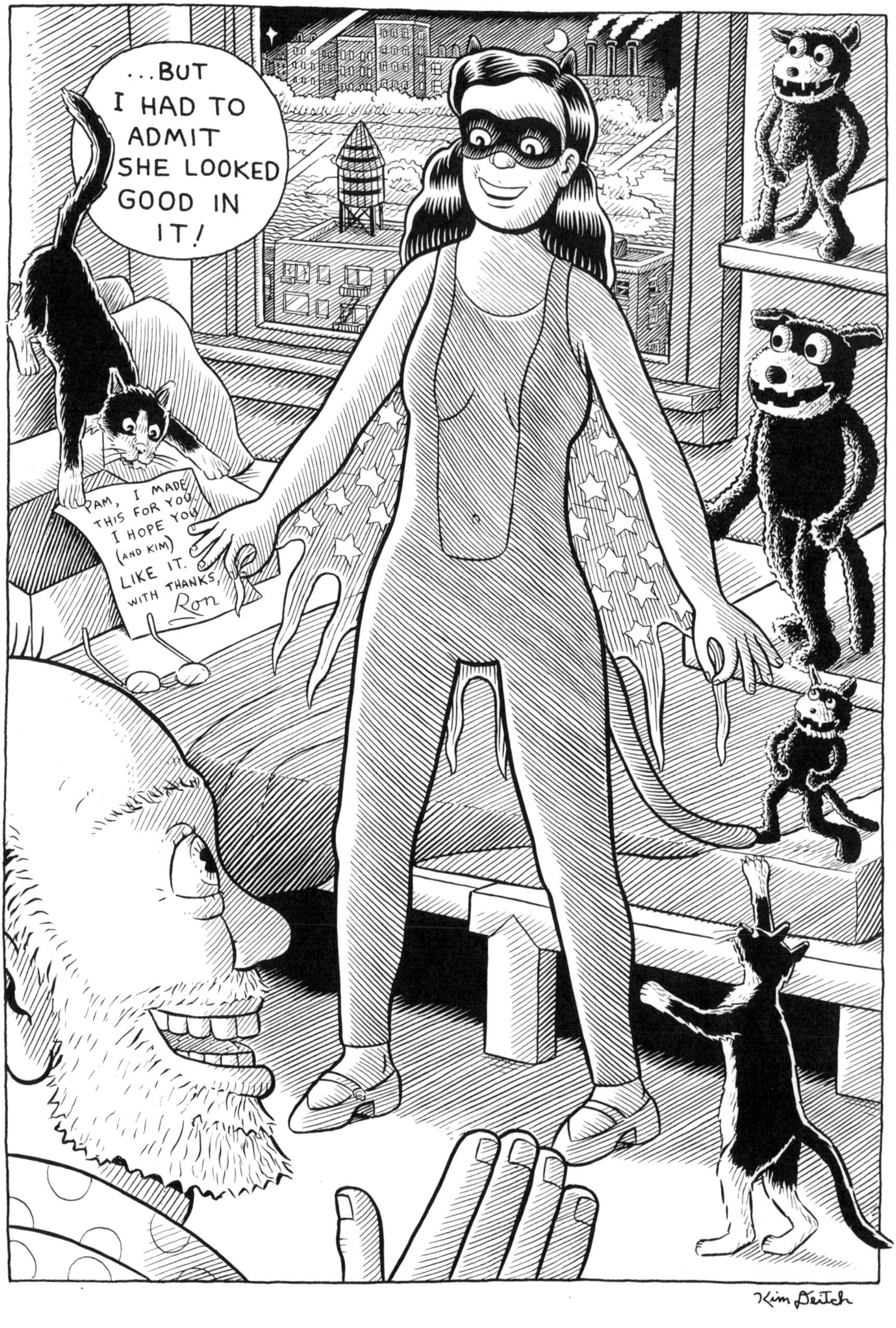
...BUT I HAD TO ADMIT SHE LOOKED GOOD IN IT!
PAM, I MADE THIS FOR YOU I HOPE YOU (AND KIM) LIKE IT. WITH THANKS, Ron

Kim Deitch

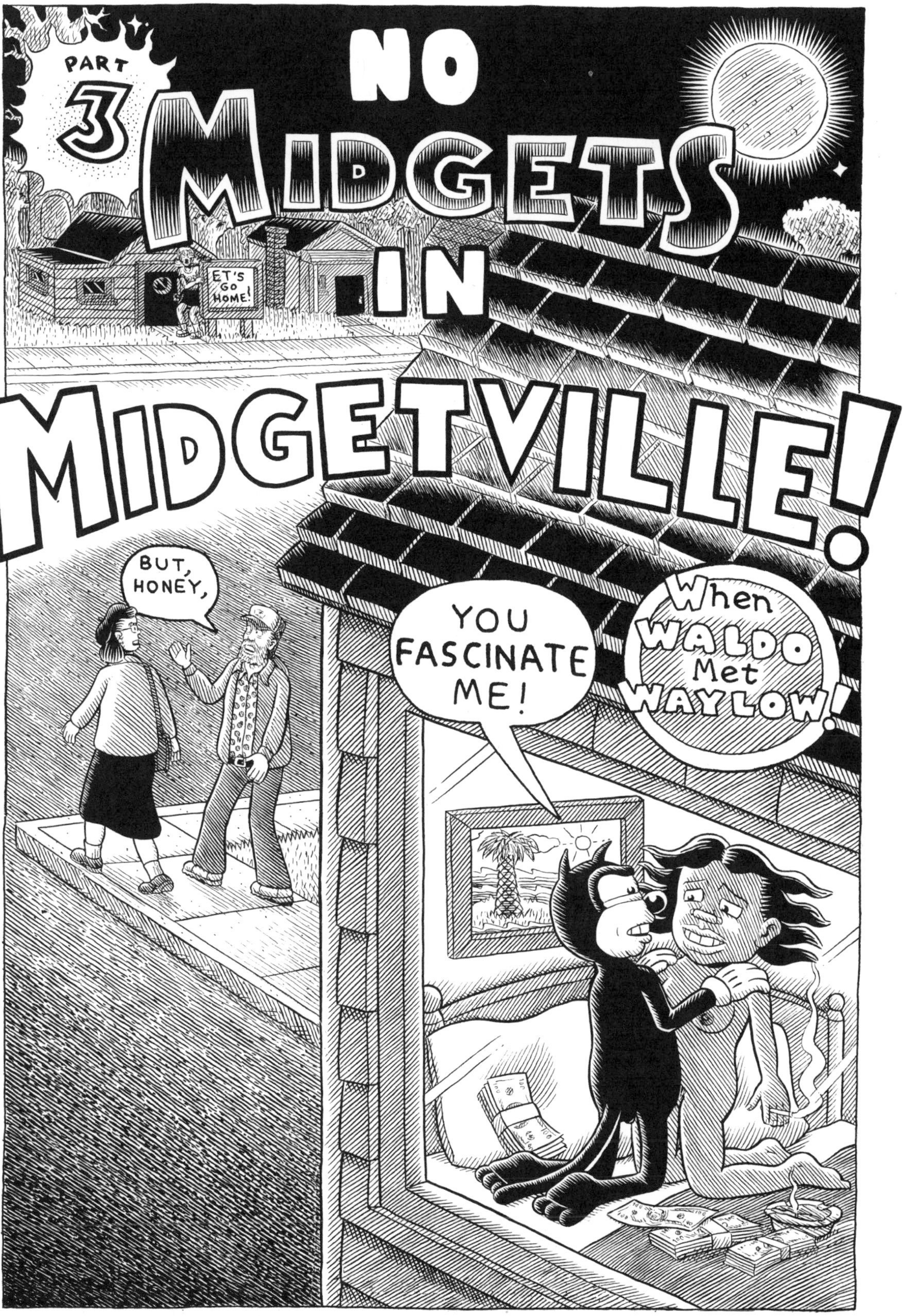
PART 3
NO MIDGETS IN MIDGETVILLE!
ET'S GO HOME!
BUT, HONEY,
YOU FASCINATE ME!
When WALDO Met WAYLOW!

THE MAIL BAG

THIS SHOULD SLOW YOU DOWN!

write to...
Kim Deitch
c/o Pam Butler
445 East 86th St. 16D
New York City, N.Y.
10028
kimpam@earthlink.net

Hey, you crazy fucker! That Alias the Cat was one whacked comic for damn sure! But what's with that bogus Moll Barkeley comic? How come she draws just like you?

Hey, dig this picture I drew for you! David Paleo, Buenos Aires, Argentina

Art by Paleo

Kim, What were you smoking when you tried to palm off that phony Alias the Cat comic strip? Are you Moll Barkeley in drag? Try to get out in the sun every now and then. Dad (Gene Deitch), Czech Republic

Deitch! Don't you mean Alias The Kook? As a historean you're hysterical. As a forger you're pathetic. Maybe you ought to give "Manpower" another shot assuming they'ed even take you back at this late date. B. N. Duncan, Berkeley California

(I DIDN'T DRAW THIS ONE EITHER! K.D.)

Mr. Deitch:
Why haven't you returned for your mandatory third-month evaluation? We cannot be responsible for your continued well-being if you yourself fail to show responsibility by your own active cooperation. We cannot help you if you will not help yourself. Dr. Rhea Santana Bellevue Hospital N.Y.C.

Dear Mr. Deitch, I was so very delighted to hear that, in your last publication, you printed some examples of the early work of my mother, Moll Barkeley-Bakendorf. It may interest you to know that Mother is still alive at the enviable age of one hundred and four years young!

She lives with my son, Morris, and myself here in Rumson, New Jersey. Should you happen to find yourself in our neighborhood, please come by and visit us. Mother still has her good days and would, I'm sure, enjoy a visit from a cartoonist of the younger generation. Warmest regards, Dorothy Bakendorf-Weiss. Rumson, New Jersey

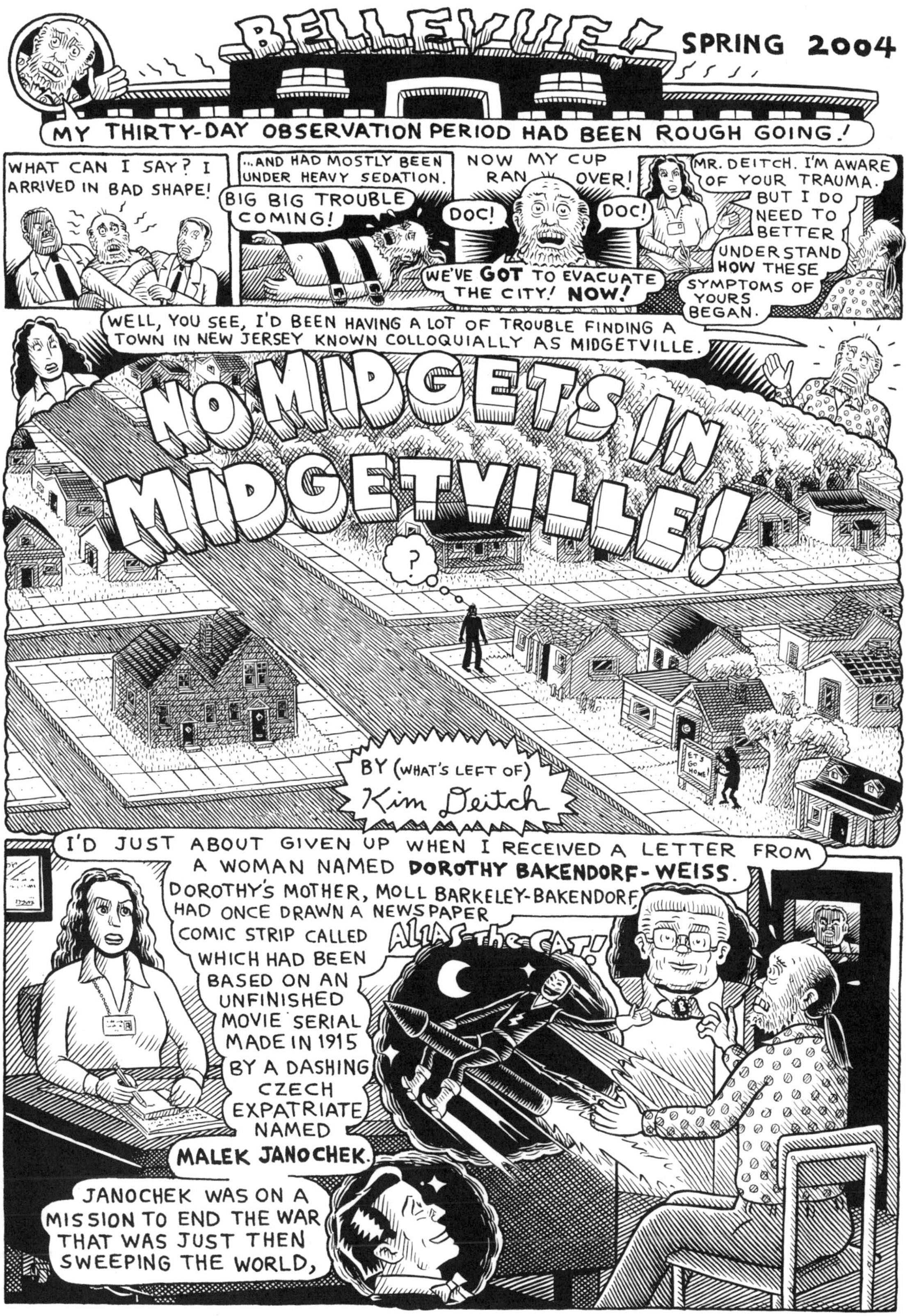
BELLEVUE!
SPRING 2004
MY THIRTY-DAY OBSERVATION PERIOD HAD BEEN ROUGH GOING!
WHAT CAN I SAY? I ARRIVED IN BAD SHAPE!
...AND HAD MOSTLY BEEN UNDER HEAVY SEDATION.
BIG BIG TROUBLE COMING!
NOW MY CUP RAN OVER!
DOC!
DOC!
WE'VE GOT TO EVACUATE THE CITY! NOW!
MR. DEITCH. I'M AWARE OF YOUR TRAUMA. BUT I DO NEED TO BETTER UNDERSTAND HOW THESE SYMPTOMS OF YOURS BEGAN.
WELL, YOU SEE, I'D BEEN HAVING A LOT OF TROUBLE FINDING A TOWN IN NEW JERSEY KNOWN COLLOQUIALLY AS MIDGETVILLE.
NO MIDGETS IN MIDGETVILLE!
?
BY (WHAT'S LEFT OF) Kim Deitch
LET'S GO HOME!
I'D JUST ABOUT GIVEN UP WHEN I RECEIVED A LETTER FROM A WOMAN NAMED DOROTHY BAKENDORF-WEISS.
DOROTHY'S MOTHER, MOLL BARKELEY-BAKENDORF, HAD ONCE DRAWN A NEWSPAPER COMIC STRIP CALLED
ALIAS the CAT!
WHICH HAD BEEN BASED ON AN UNFINISHED MOVIE SERIAL MADE IN 1915 BY A DASHING CZECH EXPATRIATE NAMED MALEK JANOCHEK.
JANOCHEK WAS ON A MISSION TO END THE WAR THAT WAS JUST THEN SWEEPING THE WORLD,

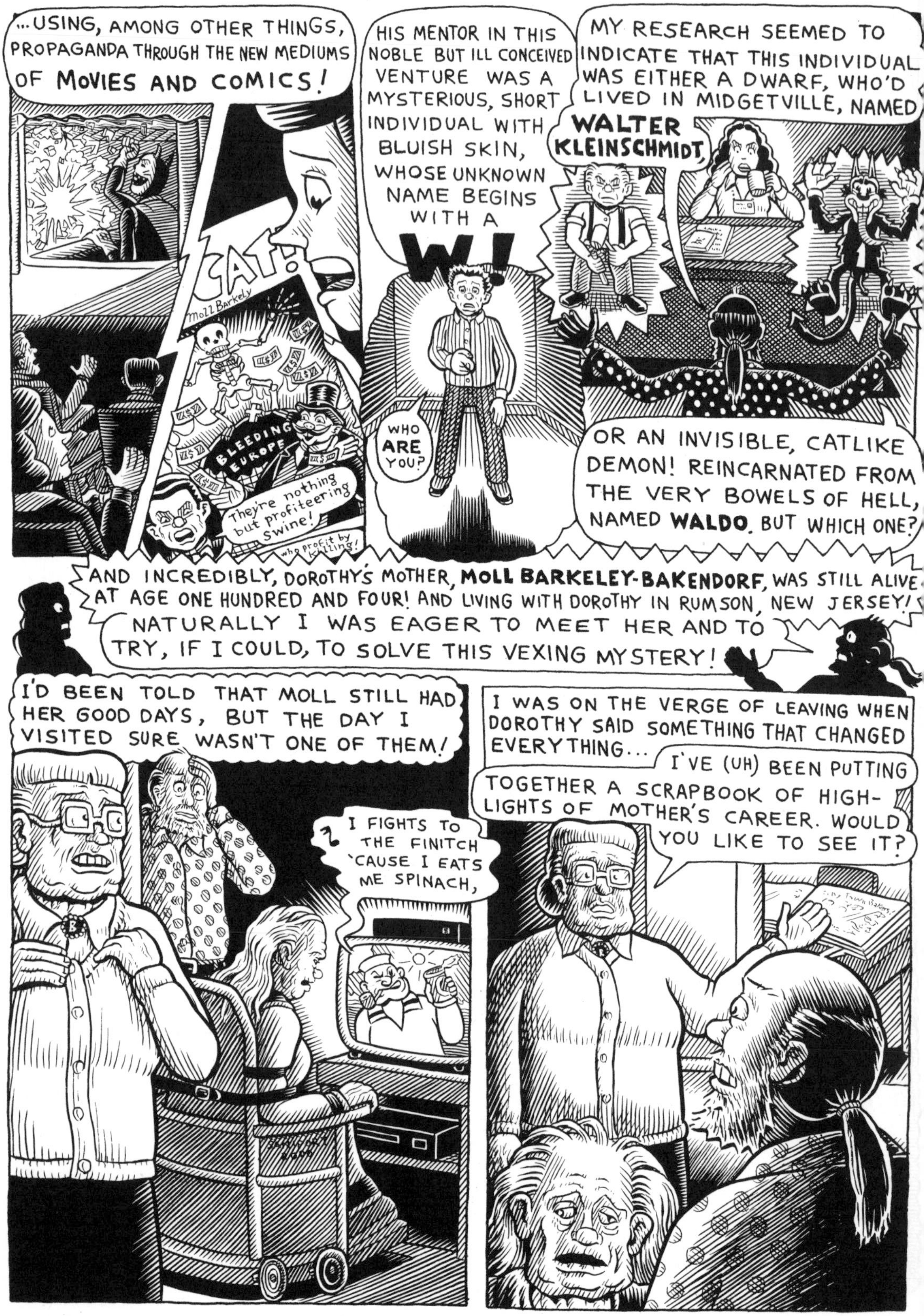
...USING, AMONG OTHER THINGS, PROPAGANDA THROUGH THE NEW MEDIUMS OF MOVIES AND COMICS!
CAT!
moLL Barkely
BLEEDING EUROPE
They're nothing but profiteering Swine!
who profit by killing!
HIS MENTOR IN THIS NOBLE BUT ILL CONCEIVED VENTURE WAS A MYSTERIOUS, SHORT INDIVIDUAL WITH BLUISH SKIN, WHOSE UNKNOWN NAME BEGINS WITH A
W!
WHO ARE YOU?
MY RESEARCH SEEMED TO INDICATE THAT THIS INDIVIDUAL WAS EITHER A DWARF, WHO'D LIVED IN MIDGETVILLE, NAMED
WALTER KLEINSCHMIDT,
OR AN INVISIBLE, CATLIKE DEMON! REINCARNATED FROM THE VERY BOWELS OF HELL, NAMED WALDO. BUT WHICH ONE?
AND INCREDIBLY, DOROTHY'S MOTHER, MOLL BARKELEY-BAKENDORF, WAS STILL ALIVE AT AGE ONE HUNDRED AND FOUR! AND LIVING WITH DOROTHY IN RUMSON, NEW JERSEY!
NATURALLY I WAS EAGER TO MEET HER AND TO TRY, IF I COULD, TO SOLVE THIS VEXING MYSTERY!
I'D BEEN TOLD THAT MOLL STILL HAD HER GOOD DAYS, BUT THE DAY I VISITED SURE WASN'T ONE OF THEM!
Z
I FIGHTS TO THE FINITCH 'CAUSE I EATS ME SPINACH,
I WAS ON THE VERGE OF LEAVING WHEN DOROTHY SAID SOMETHING THAT CHANGED EVERYTHING...
I'VE (UH) BEEN PUTTING TOGETHER A SCRAPBOOK OF HIGHLIGHTS OF MOTHER'S CAREER. WOULD YOU LIKE TO SEE IT?

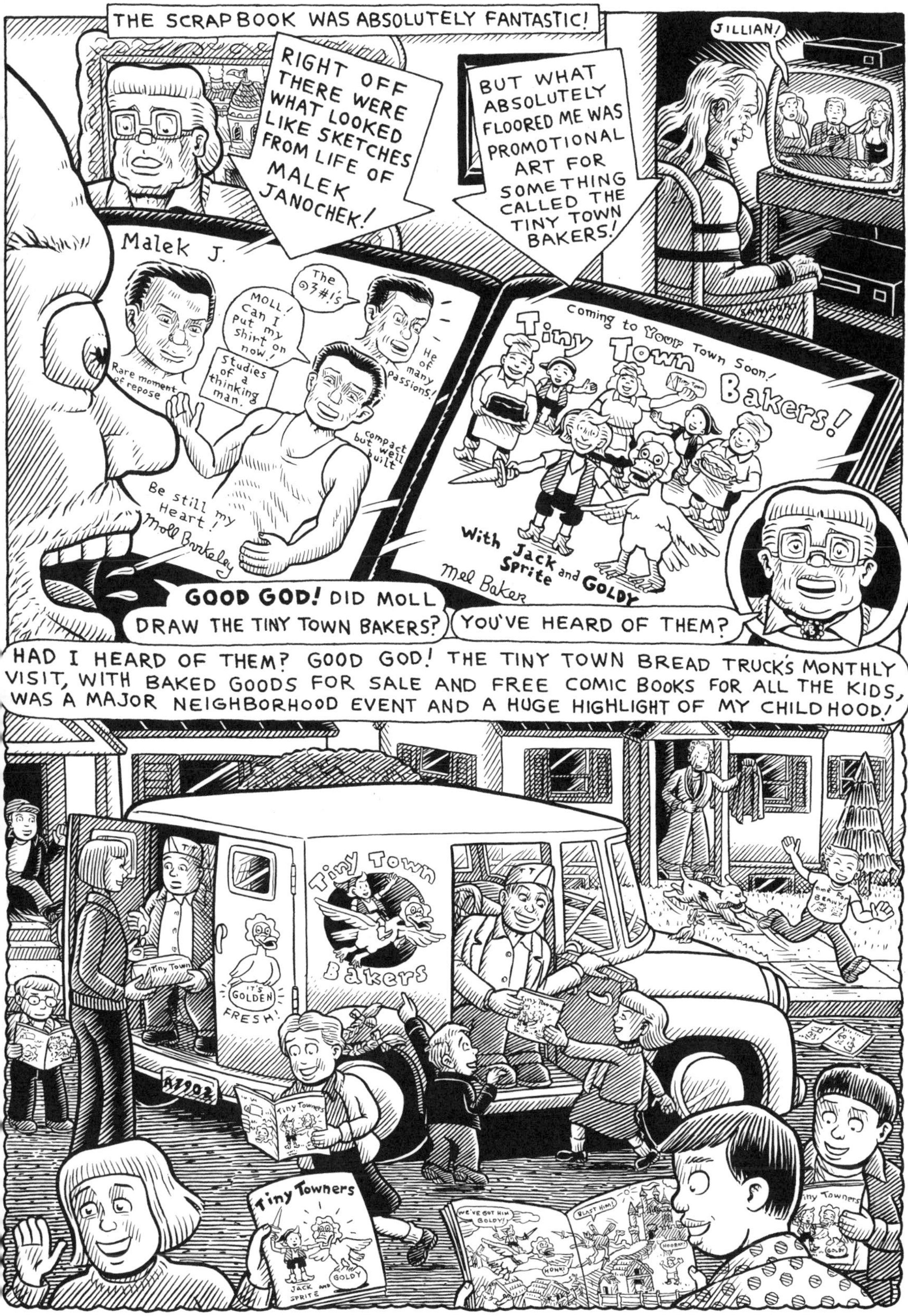
THE SCRAPBOOK WAS ABSOLUTELY FANTASTIC!
RIGHT OFF THERE WERE WHAT LOOKED LIKE SKETCHES FROM LIFE OF MALEK JANOCHEK!
BUT WHAT ABSOLUTELY FLOORED ME WAS PROMOTIONAL ART FOR SOMETHING CALLED THE TINY TOWN BAKERS!
JILLIAN!
Malek J.
Rare moment of repose
MOLL! Can I put my shirt on now!
Studies of a thinking man.
The @?#!'s
He of many passions!
compact but well built
Be still my Heart!
Moll Barkeley
Coming to Your Town Soon!
Tiny Town Bakers!
Tiny Town
With Jack Sprite and Goldy
Mel Baker
GOOD GOD! DID MOLL DRAW THE TINY TOWN BAKERS?
YOU'VE HEARD OF THEM?
HAD I HEARD OF THEM? GOOD GOD! THE TINY TOWN BREAD TRUCK'S MONTHLY VISIT, WITH BAKED GOODS FOR SALE AND FREE COMIC BOOKS FOR ALL THE KIDS, WAS A MAJOR NEIGHBORHOOD EVENT AND A HUGE HIGHLIGHT OF MY CHILDHOOD!
Tiny Town Bakers
IT'S GOLDEN FRESH!
Tiny Town
A7902
Tiny Towners
Tiny Towners
JACK SPRITE AND GOLDY
WE'VE GOT HIM GOLDY!
BLAST HIM!
HONK!
HOORAY!
Tiny Towners

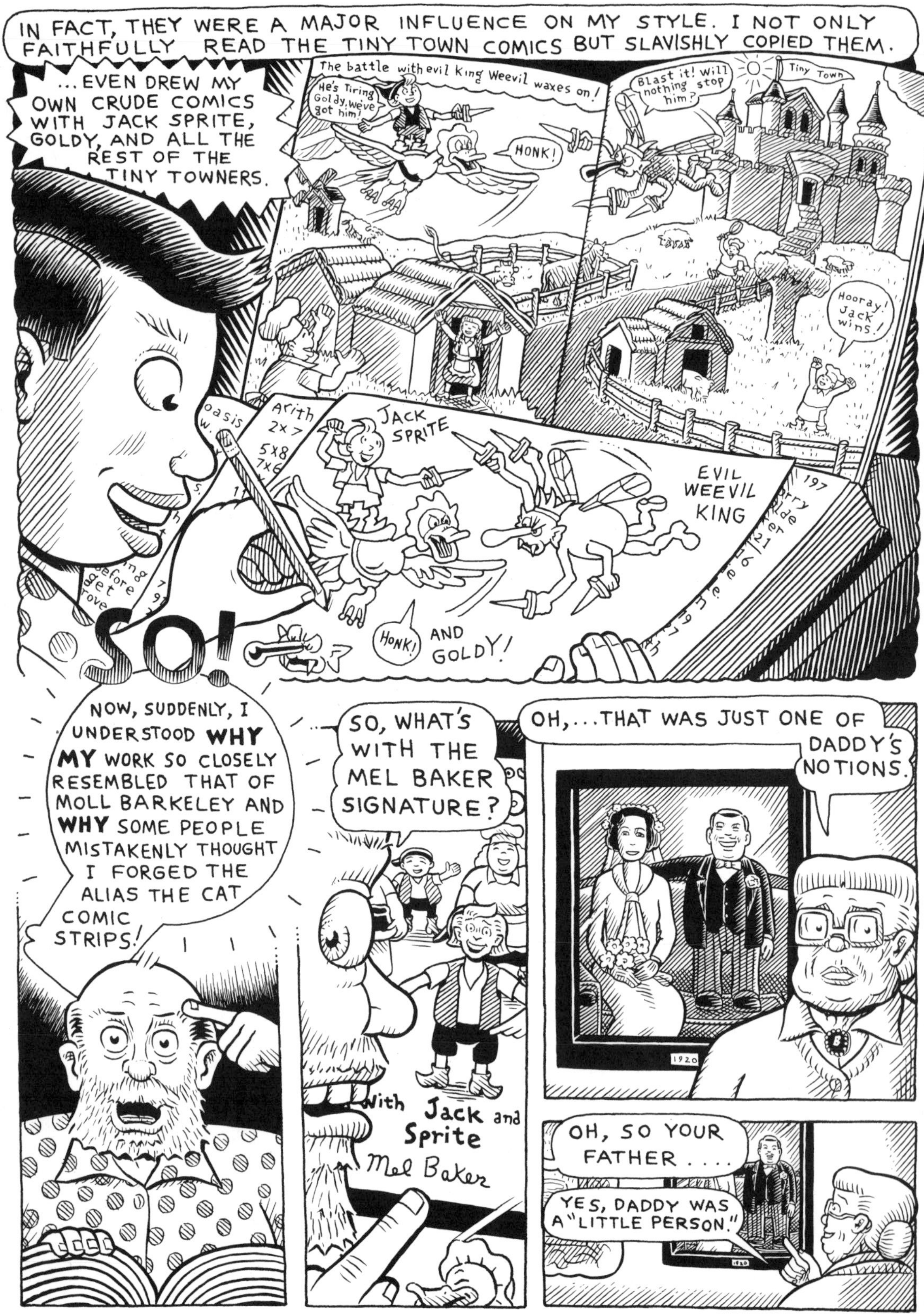
IN FACT, THEY WERE A MAJOR INFLUENCE ON MY STYLE. I NOT ONLY FAITHFULLY READ THE TINY TOWN COMICS BUT SLAVISHLY COPIED THEM.
... EVEN DREW MY OWN CRUDE COMICS WITH JACK SPRITE, GOLDY, AND ALL THE REST OF THE TINY TOWNERS.
The battle with evil King Weevil waxes on!
He's Tiring Goldy, we've got him!
HONK!
Blast it! will nothing stop him?
Tiny Town
Hooray! Jack wins!
JACK SPRITE
EVIL WEEVIL KING
HONK!
AND GOLDY!
SO!
NOW, SUDDENLY, I UNDERSTOOD WHY MY WORK SO CLOSELY RESEMBLED THAT OF MOLL BARKELEY AND WHY SOME PEOPLE MISTAKENLY THOUGHT I FORGED THE ALIAS THE CAT COMIC STRIPS!
SO, WHAT'S WITH THE MEL BAKER SIGNATURE?
With Jack and Sprite
Mel Baker
OH, ...THAT WAS JUST ONE OF DADDY'S NOTIONS.
1920
OH, SO YOUR FATHER ....
YES, DADDY WAS A "LITTLE PERSON."

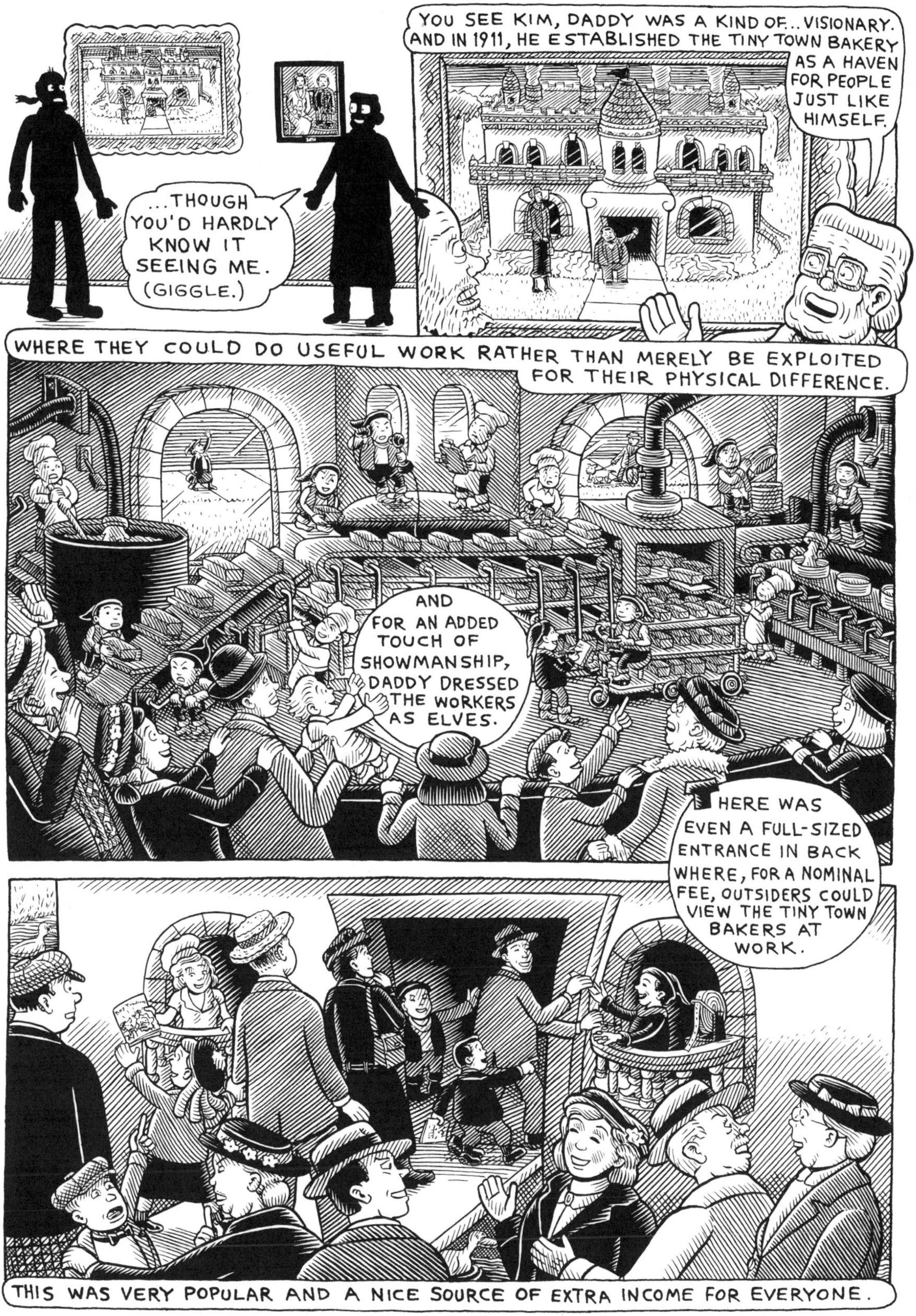
...THOUGH YOU'D HARDLY KNOW IT SEEING ME. (GIGGLE.)
YOU SEE KIM, DADDY WAS A KIND OF... VISIONARY. AND IN 1911, HE ESTABLISHED THE TINY TOWN BAKERY AS A HAVEN FOR PEOPLE JUST LIKE HIMSELF.
WHERE THEY COULD DO USEFUL WORK RATHER THAN MERELY BE EXPLOITED FOR THEIR PHYSICAL DIFFERENCE.
AND FOR AN ADDED TOUCH OF SHOWMANSHIP, DADDY DRESSED THE WORKERS AS ELVES.
THERE WAS EVEN A FULL-SIZED ENTRANCE IN BACK WHERE, FOR A NOMINAL FEE, OUTSIDERS COULD VIEW THE TINY TOWN BAKERS AT WORK.
THIS WAS VERY POPULAR AND A NICE SOURCE OF EXTRA INCOME FOR EVERYONE.

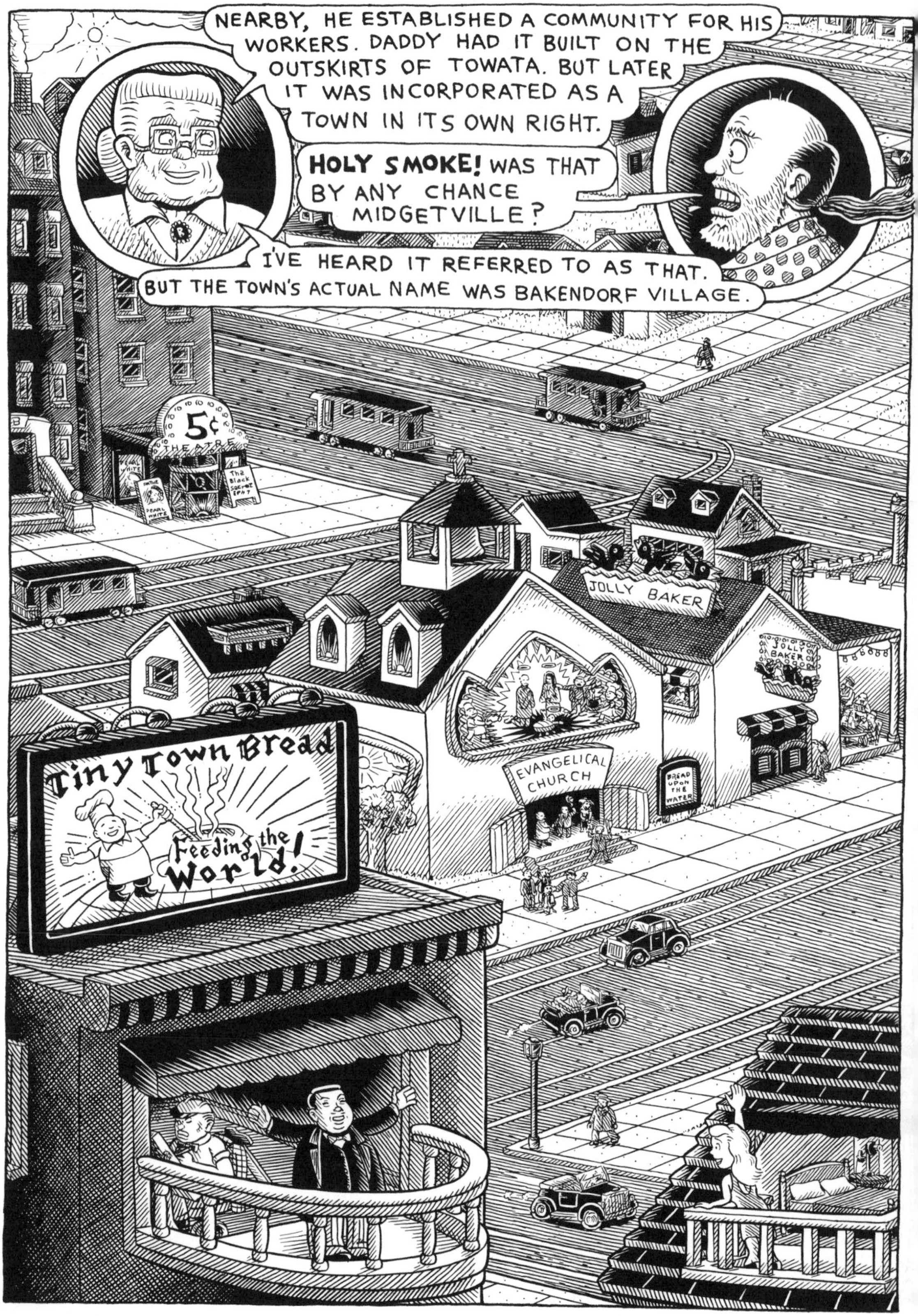
NEARBY, HE ESTABLISHED A COMMUNITY FOR HIS WORKERS. DADDY HAD IT BUILT ON THE OUTSKIRTS OF TOWATA. BUT LATER IT WAS INCORPORATED AS A TOWN IN ITS OWN RIGHT.
HOLY SMOKE! WAS THAT BY ANY CHANCE MIDGETVILLE?
I'VE HEARD IT REFERRED TO AS THAT. BUT THE TOWN'S ACTUAL NAME WAS BAKENDORF VILLAGE.
5¢ THEATRE
JOLLY BAKER
JOLLY BAKER
EVANGELICAL CHURCH
BREAD UPON THE WATER
Tiny Town Bread
Feeding the World!

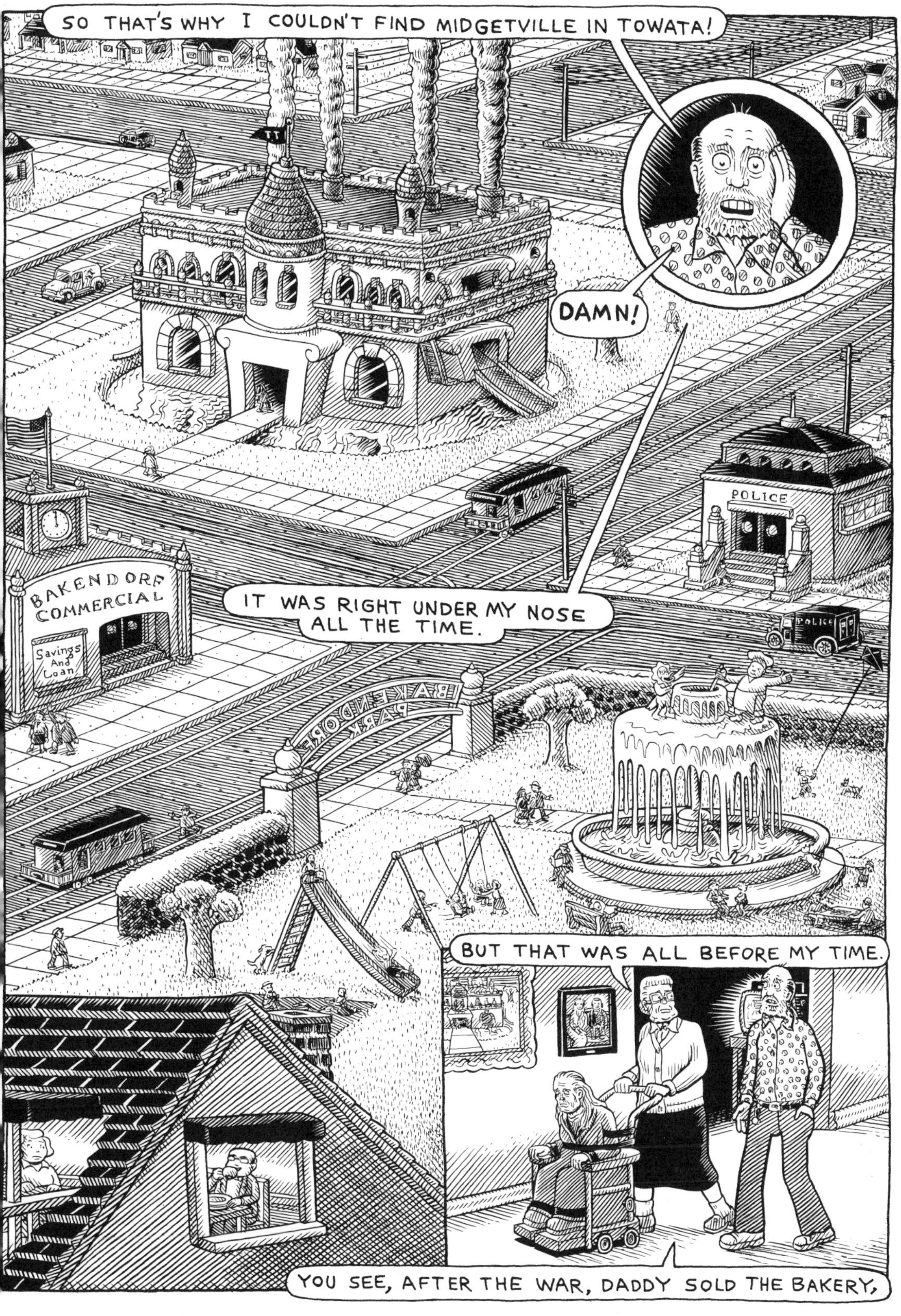
SO THAT'S WHY I COULDN'T FIND MIDGETVILLE IN TOWATA!
DAMN!
POLICE
BAKENDORF COMMERCIAL
Savings And Loan
IT WAS RIGHT UNDER MY NOSE ALL THE TIME.
POLICE
BAKENDORF PARK
BUT THAT WAS ALL BEFORE MY TIME.
YOU SEE, AFTER THE WAR, DADDY SOLD THE BAKERY,

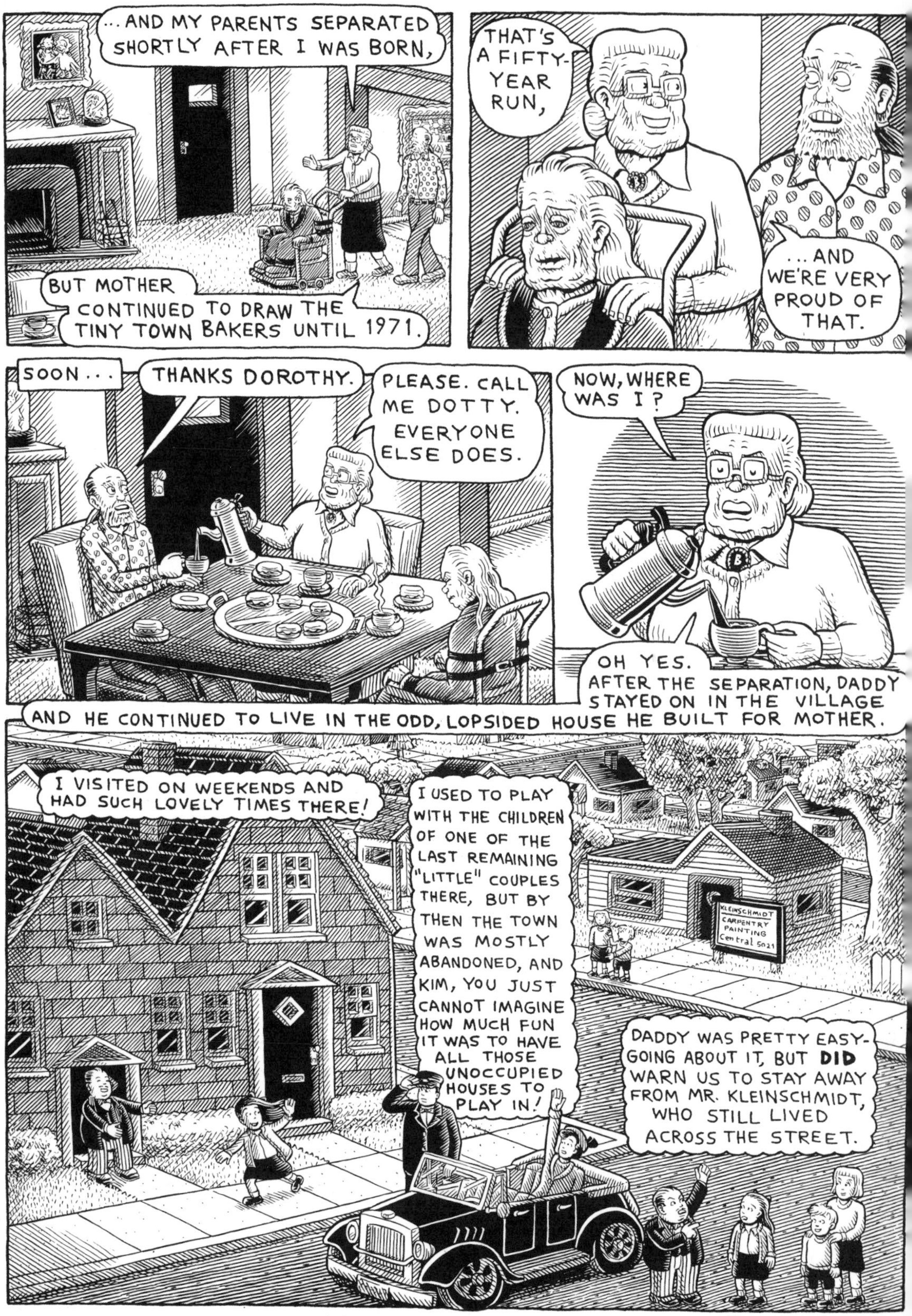
...AND MY PARENTS SEPARATED SHORTLY AFTER I WAS BORN,
BUT MOTHER CONTINUED TO DRAW THE TINY TOWN BAKERS UNTIL 1971.
THAT'S A FIFTY-YEAR RUN,
...AND WE'RE VERY PROUD OF THAT.
SOON...
THANKS DOROTHY.
PLEASE. CALL ME DOTTY. EVERYONE ELSE DOES.
NOW, WHERE WAS I?
OH YES. AFTER THE SEPARATION, DADDY STAYED ON IN THE VILLAGE
AND HE CONTINUED TO LIVE IN THE ODD, LOPSIDED HOUSE HE BUILT FOR MOTHER.
I VISITED ON WEEKENDS AND HAD SUCH LOVELY TIMES THERE!
I USED TO PLAY WITH THE CHILDREN OF ONE OF THE LAST REMAINING "LITTLE" COUPLES THERE, BUT BY THEN THE TOWN WAS MOSTLY ABANDONED, AND KIM, YOU JUST CANNOT IMAGINE HOW MUCH FUN IT WAS TO HAVE ALL THOSE UNOCCUPIED HOUSES TO PLAY IN!
KLEINSCHMIDT CARPENTRY PAINTING Central 5021
DADDY WAS PRETTY EASY-GOING ABOUT IT, BUT **DID** WARN US TO STAY AWAY FROM MR. KLEINSCHMIDT, WHO STILL LIVED ACROSS THE STREET.

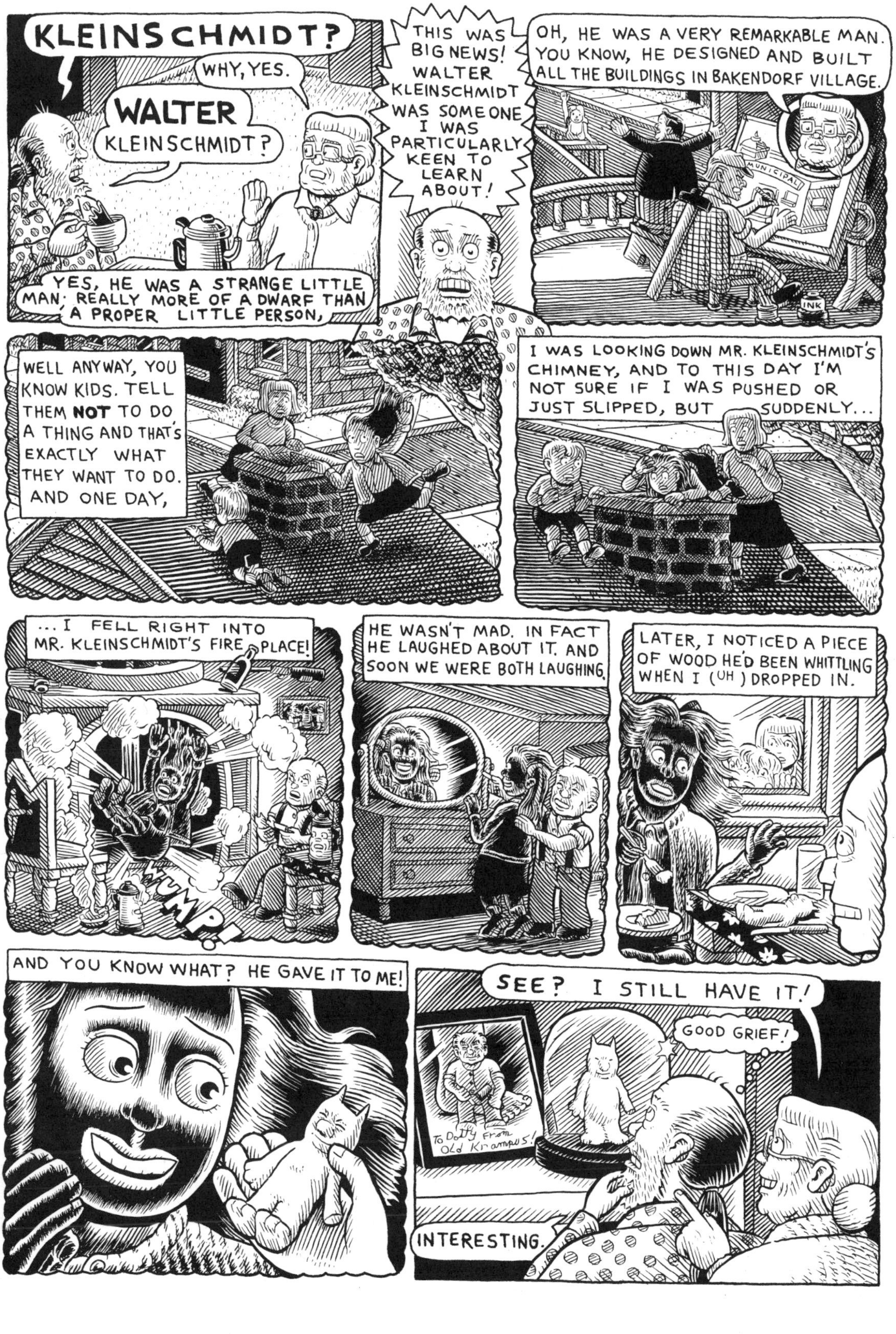
KLEINSCHMIDT?
WHY, YES.
WALTER KLEINSCHMIDT?
YES, HE WAS A STRANGE LITTLE MAN; REALLY MORE OF A DWARF THAN A PROPER LITTLE PERSON,
THIS WAS BIG NEWS! WALTER KLEINSCHMIDT WAS SOMEONE I WAS PARTICULARLY KEEN TO LEARN ABOUT!
OH, HE WAS A VERY REMARKABLE MAN. YOU KNOW, HE DESIGNED AND BUILT ALL THE BUILDINGS IN BAKENDORF VILLAGE.
MUNICIPAL
INK
WELL ANYWAY, YOU KNOW KIDS. TELL THEM NOT TO DO A THING AND THAT'S EXACTLY WHAT THEY WANT TO DO. AND ONE DAY,
I WAS LOOKING DOWN MR. KLEINSCHMIDT'S CHIMNEY, AND TO THIS DAY I'M NOT SURE IF I WAS PUSHED OR JUST SLIPPED, BUT SUDDENLY...
...I FELL RIGHT INTO MR. KLEINSCHMIDT'S FIREPLACE!
WUMP!
HE WASN'T MAD. IN FACT HE LAUGHED ABOUT IT. AND SOON WE WERE BOTH LAUGHING.
LATER, I NOTICED A PIECE OF WOOD HE'D BEEN WHITTLING WHEN I (UH) DROPPED IN.
AND YOU KNOW WHAT? HE GAVE IT TO ME!
SEE? I STILL HAVE IT!
GOOD GRIEF!
To Dotty From Old Krampus!
INTERESTING.

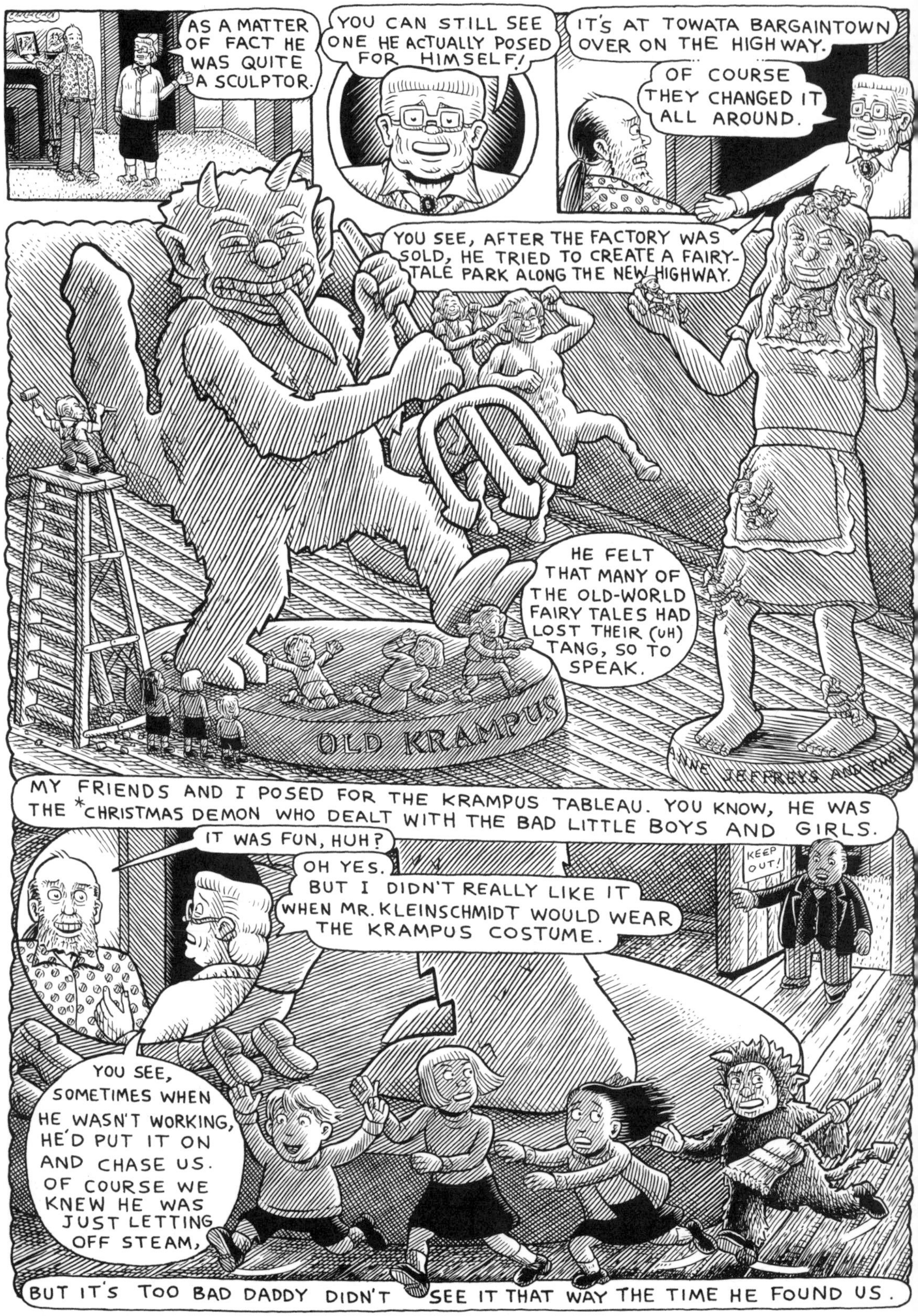
AS A MATTER OF FACT HE WAS QUITE A SCULPTOR.
YOU CAN STILL SEE ONE HE ACTUALLY POSED FOR HIMSELF!
IT'S AT TOWATA BARGAINTOWN OVER ON THE HIGHWAY.
OF COURSE THEY CHANGED IT ALL AROUND.
YOU SEE, AFTER THE FACTORY WAS SOLD, HE TRIED TO CREATE A FAIRY-TALE PARK ALONG THE NEW HIGHWAY.
HE FELT THAT MANY OF THE OLD-WORLD FAIRY TALES HAD LOST THEIR (UH) TANG, SO TO SPEAK.
OLD KRAMPUS
ANNE JEFFREYS AND
MY FRIENDS AND I POSED FOR THE KRAMPUS TABLEAU. YOU KNOW, HE WAS THE *CHRISTMAS DEMON WHO DEALT WITH THE BAD LITTLE BOYS AND GIRLS.
IT WAS FUN, HUH?
OH YES. BUT I DIDN'T REALLY LIKE IT WHEN MR. KLEINSCHMIDT WOULD WEAR THE KRAMPUS COSTUME.
KEEP OUT!
YOU SEE, SOMETIMES WHEN HE WASN'T WORKING, HE'D PUT IT ON AND CHASE US. OF COURSE WE KNEW HE WAS JUST LETTING OFF STEAM,
BUT IT'S TOO BAD DADDY DIDN'T SEE IT THAT WAY THE TIME HE FOUND US.

* OLD GERMAN FOLKLORE

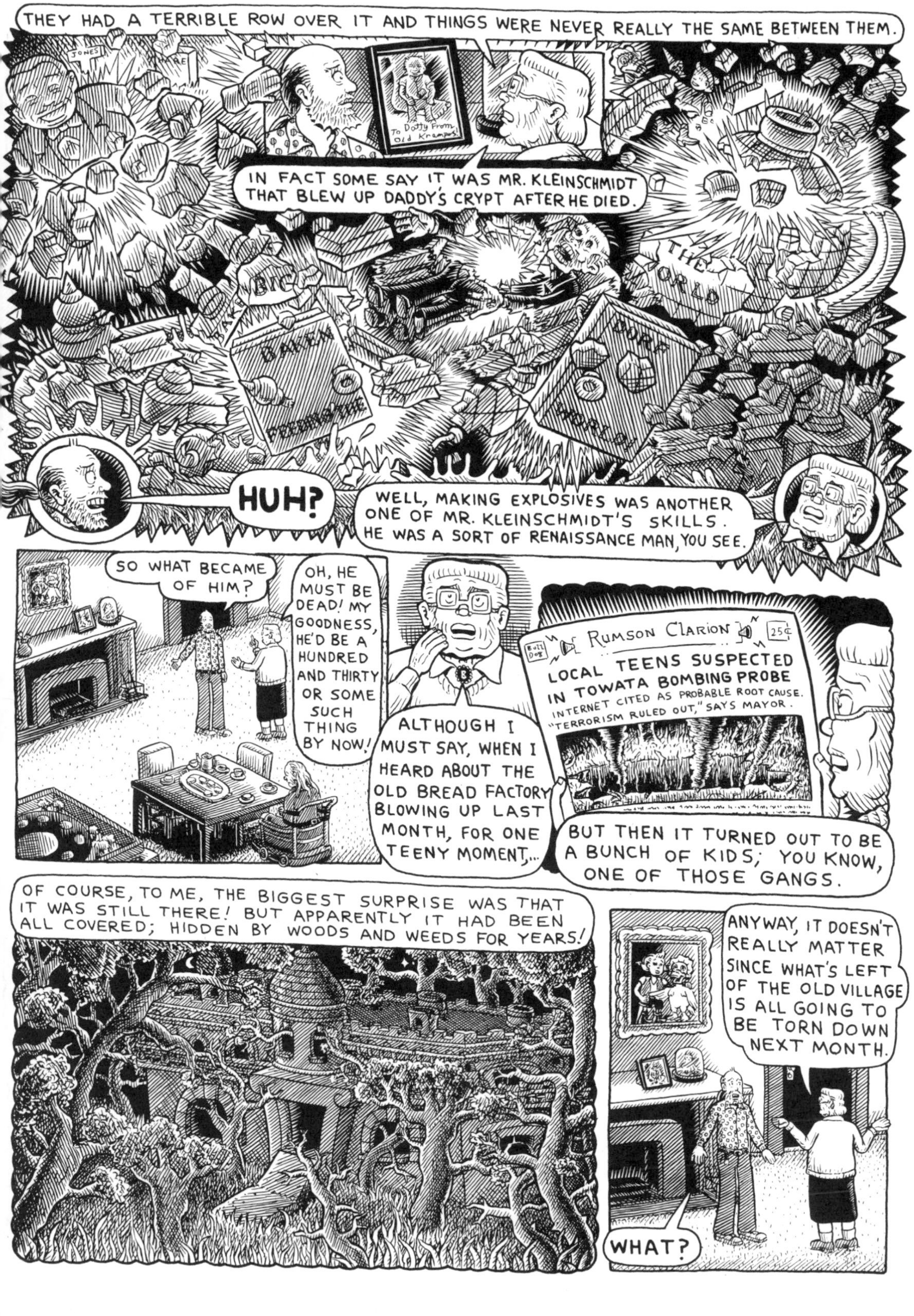
THEY HAD A TERRIBLE ROW OVER IT AND THINGS WERE NEVER REALLY THE SAME BETWEEN THEM.
To Dotty From Old Krampus
IN FACT SOME SAY IT WAS MR. KLEINSCHMIDT THAT BLEW UP DADDY'S CRYPT AFTER HE DIED.
HUH?
WELL, MAKING EXPLOSIVES WAS ANOTHER ONE OF MR. KLEINSCHMIDT'S SKILLS. HE WAS A SORT OF RENAISSANCE MAN, YOU SEE.
SO WHAT BECAME OF HIM?
OH, HE MUST BE DEAD! MY GOODNESS, HE'D BE A HUNDRED AND THIRTY OR SOME SUCH THING BY NOW!
ALTHOUGH I MUST SAY, WHEN I HEARD ABOUT THE OLD BREAD FACTORY BLOWING UP LAST MONTH, FOR ONE TEENY MOMENT,...
RUMSON CLARION
25¢
LOCAL TEENS SUSPECTED IN TOWATA BOMBING PROBE
INTERNET CITED AS PROBABLE ROOT CAUSE.
"TERRORISM RULED OUT," SAYS MAYOR.
BUT THEN IT TURNED OUT TO BE A BUNCH OF KIDS; YOU KNOW, ONE OF THOSE GANGS.
OF COURSE, TO ME, THE BIGGEST SURPRISE WAS THAT IT WAS STILL THERE! BUT APPARENTLY IT HAD BEEN ALL COVERED; HIDDEN BY WOODS AND WEEDS FOR YEARS!
ANYWAY, IT DOESN'T REALLY MATTER SINCE WHAT'S LEFT OF THE OLD VILLAGE IS ALL GOING TO BE TORN DOWN NEXT MONTH.
WHAT?

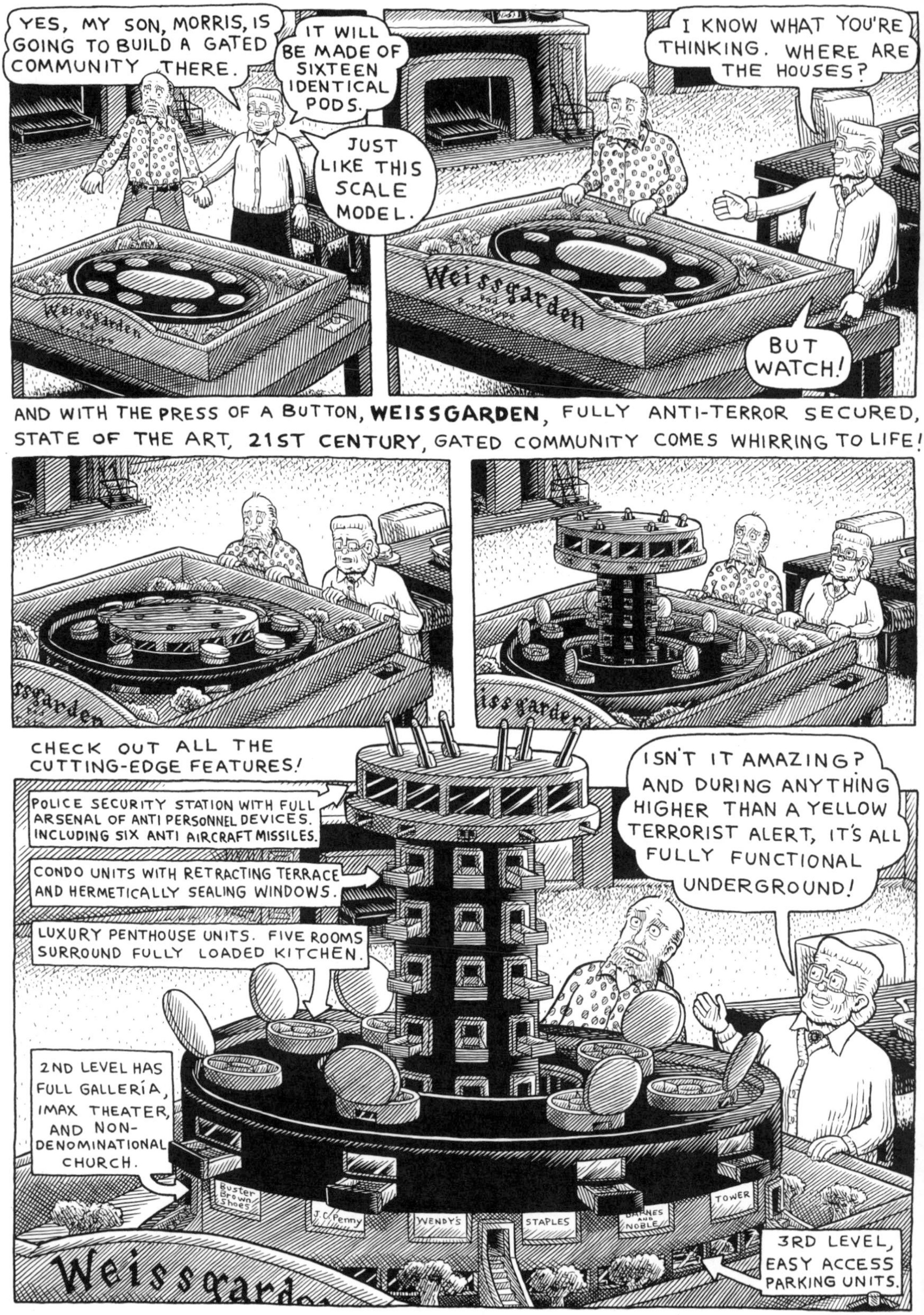

YES, MY SON, MORRIS, IS GOING TO BUILD A GATED COMMUNITY THERE.
IT WILL BE MADE OF SIXTEEN IDENTICAL PODS.
JUST LIKE THIS SCALE MODEL.
Weissgarden
I KNOW WHAT YOU'RE THINKING. WHERE ARE THE HOUSES?
BUT WATCH!
Weissgarden
AND WITH THE PRESS OF A BUTTON, WEISSGARDEN, FULLY ANTI-TERROR SECURED, STATE OF THE ART, 21ST CENTURY, GATED COMMUNITY COMES WHIRRING TO LIFE!
CHECK OUT ALL THE CUTTING-EDGE FEATURES!
POLICE SECURITY STATION WITH FULL ARSENAL OF ANTI PERSONNEL DEVICES. INCLUDING SIX ANTI AIRCRAFT MISSILES.
CONDO UNITS WITH RETRACTING TERRACE AND HERMETICALLY SEALING WINDOWS.
LUXURY PENTHOUSE UNITS. FIVE ROOMS SURROUND FULLY LOADED KITCHEN.
ISN'T IT AMAZING? AND DURING ANYTHING HIGHER THAN A YELLOW TERRORIST ALERT, IT'S ALL FULLY FUNCTIONAL UNDERGROUND!
2ND LEVEL HAS FULL GALLERÍA, IMAX THEATER, AND NON-DENOMINATIONAL CHURCH.
Buster Brown Shoes
J.C. Penny
WENDY'S
STAPLES
BARNES AND NOBLE
TOWER
3RD LEVEL, EASY ACCESS PARKING UNITS.
Weissgarden

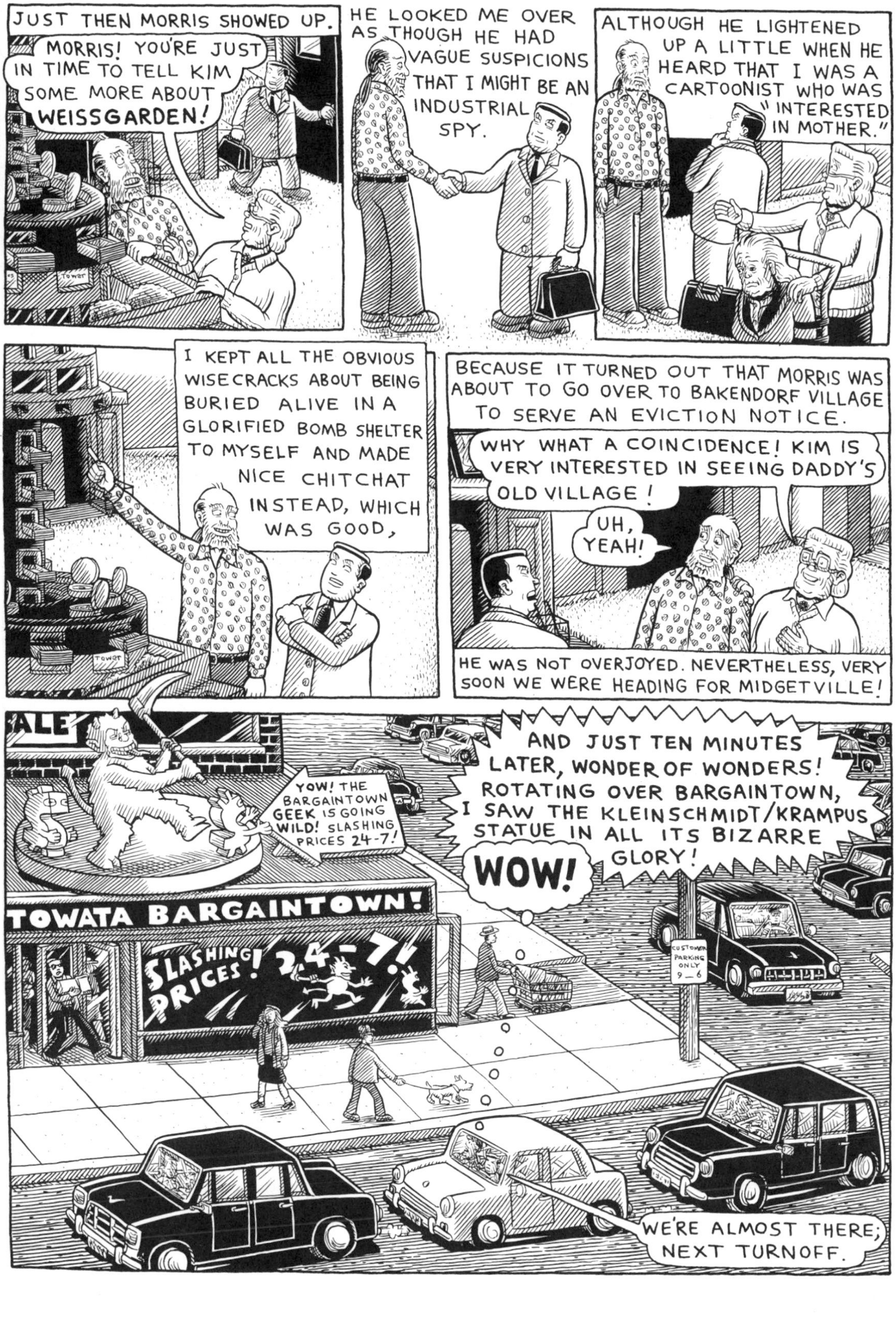

JUST THEN MORRIS SHOWED UP.
MORRIS! YOU'RE JUST IN TIME TO TELL KIM SOME MORE ABOUT WEISSGARDEN!
TOWER
HE LOOKED ME OVER AS THOUGH HE HAD VAGUE SUSPICIONS THAT I MIGHT BE AN INDUSTRIAL SPY.
ALTHOUGH HE LIGHTENED UP A LITTLE WHEN HE HEARD THAT I WAS A CARTOONIST WHO WAS "INTERESTED IN MOTHER."
I KEPT ALL THE OBVIOUS WISECRACKS ABOUT BEING BURIED ALIVE IN A GLORIFIED BOMB SHELTER TO MYSELF AND MADE NICE CHITCHAT INSTEAD, WHICH WAS GOOD,
TOWER
BECAUSE IT TURNED OUT THAT MORRIS WAS ABOUT TO GO OVER TO BAKENDORF VILLAGE TO SERVE AN EVICTION NOTICE.
WHY WHAT A COINCIDENCE! KIM IS VERY INTERESTED IN SEEING DADDY'S OLD VILLAGE!
UH, YEAH!
HE WAS NOT OVERJOYED. NEVERTHELESS, VERY SOON WE WERE HEADING FOR MIDGETVILLE!
SALE
YOW! THE BARGAINTOWN GEEK IS GOING WILD! SLASHING PRICES 24-7!
AND JUST TEN MINUTES LATER, WONDER OF WONDERS! ROTATING OVER BARGAINTOWN, I SAW THE KLEINSCHMIDT/KRAMPUS STATUE IN ALL ITS BIZARRE GLORY!
WOW!
TOWATA BARGAINTOWN!
SLASHING PRICES! 24-7!
CUSTOMER PARKING ONLY 9—6
WE'RE ALMOST THERE; NEXT TURNOFF.

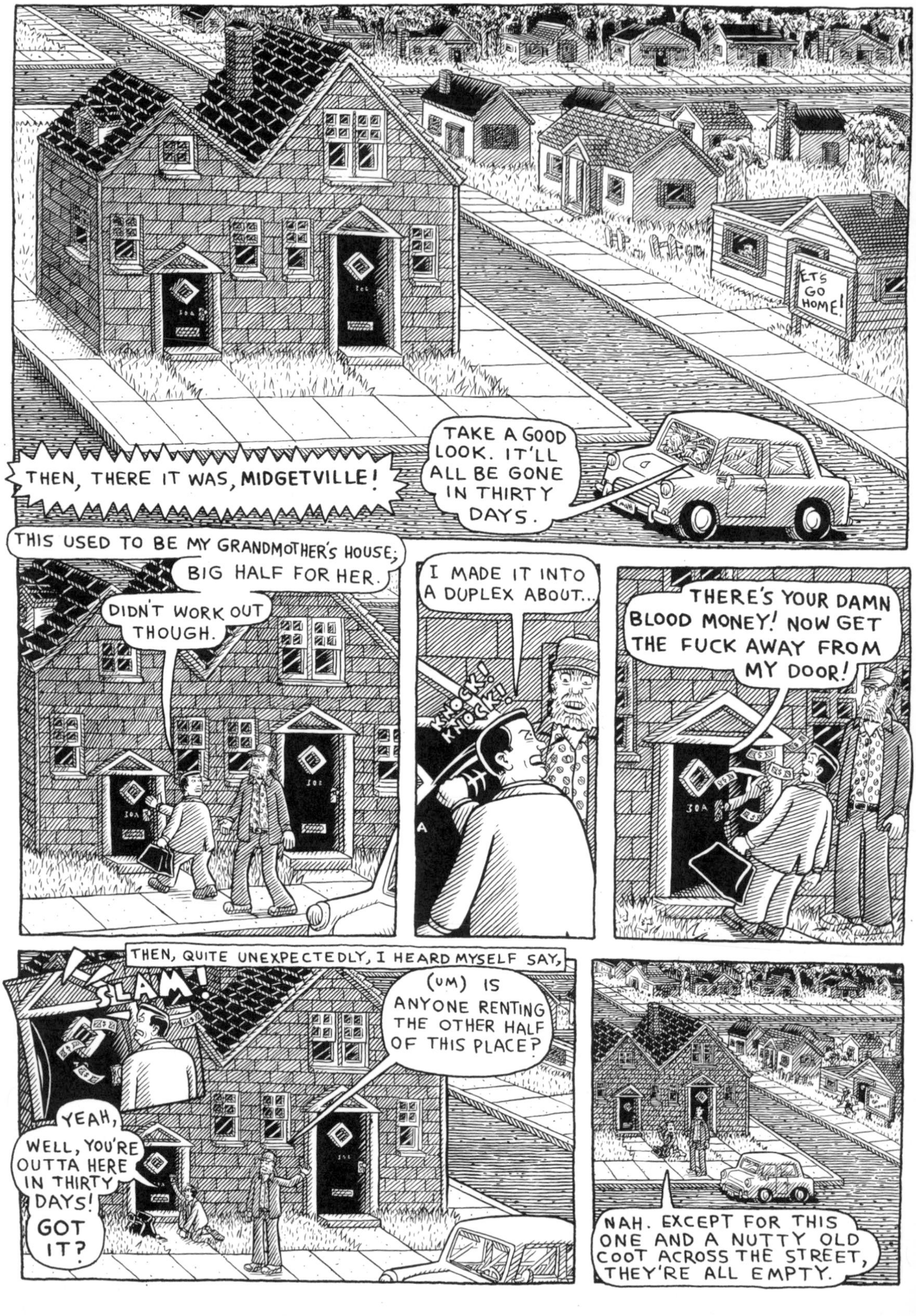
LET'S GO HOME!
THEN, THERE IT WAS, MIDGETVILLE!
TAKE A GOOD LOOK. IT'LL ALL BE GONE IN THIRTY DAYS.
THIS USED TO BE MY GRANDMOTHER'S HOUSE;
BIG HALF FOR HER.
DIDN'T WORK OUT THOUGH.
I MADE IT INTO A DUPLEX ABOUT...
KNOCK! KNOCK!
THERE'S YOUR DAMN BLOOD MONEY! NOW GET THE FUCK AWAY FROM MY DOOR!
SLAM!
THEN, QUITE UNEXPECTEDLY, I HEARD MYSELF SAY,
(UM) IS ANYONE RENTING THE OTHER HALF OF THIS PLACE?
YEAH, WELL, YOU'RE OUTTA HERE IN THIRTY DAYS! GOT IT?
NAH. EXCEPT FOR THIS ONE AND A NUTTY OLD COOT ACROSS THE STREET, THEY'RE ALL EMPTY.

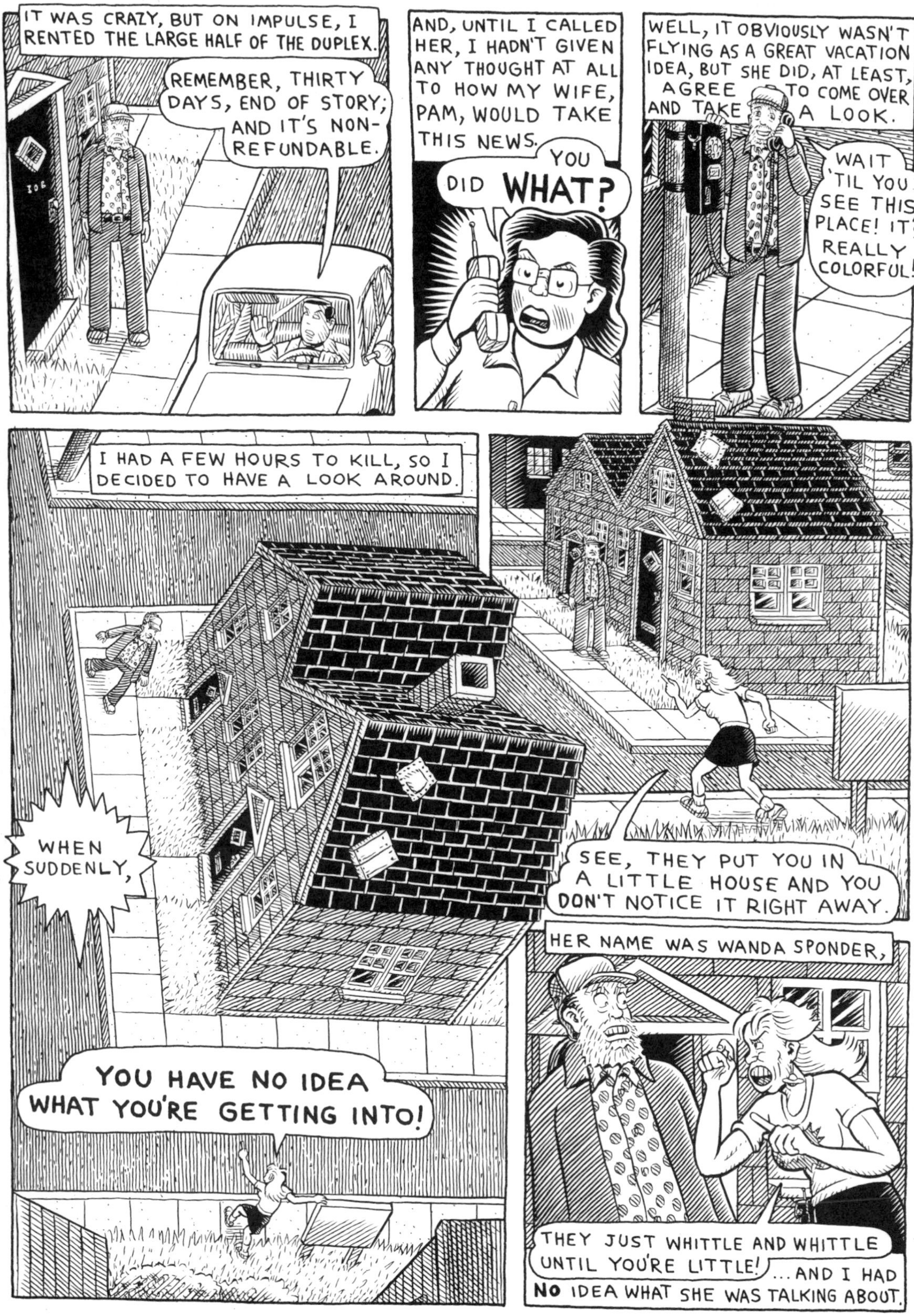
IT WAS CRAZY, BUT ON IMPULSE, I RENTED THE LARGE HALF OF THE DUPLEX.
306
REMEMBER, THIRTY DAYS, END OF STORY; AND IT'S NON-REFUNDABLE.
AND, UNTIL I CALLED HER, I HADN'T GIVEN ANY THOUGHT AT ALL TO HOW MY WIFE, PAM, WOULD TAKE THIS NEWS.
YOU DID WHAT?
WELL, IT OBVIOUSLY WASN'T FLYING AS A GREAT VACATION IDEA, BUT SHE DID, AT LEAST, AGREE TO COME OVER AND TAKE A LOOK.
WAIT 'TIL YOU SEE THIS PLACE! IT'S REALLY COLORFUL!
I HAD A FEW HOURS TO KILL, SO I DECIDED TO HAVE A LOOK AROUND.
WHEN SUDDENLY,
YOU HAVE NO IDEA WHAT YOU'RE GETTING INTO!
SEE, THEY PUT YOU IN A LITTLE HOUSE AND YOU DON'T NOTICE IT RIGHT AWAY.
HER NAME WAS WANDA SPONDER,
THEY JUST WHITTLE AND WHITTLE UNTIL YOU'RE LITTLE!
... AND I HAD NO IDEA WHAT SHE WAS TALKING ABOUT.

YOU WANT PROOF? YOU'LL GET IT. C'MON!

LET'S GO HOME

IN SECONDS, SHE WAS DRAGGING ME TOWARD WHAT I WAS PRETTY SURE (FROM AN OLD PHOTO I'D SEEN) WAS WALTER KLEINSCHMIDT'S OLD HOUSE. AMAZING!

THIS HAPPENED THE OTHER NIGHT.

SOON WE WERE STANDING ON A CHARRED PLATFORM COVERED WITH WHAT SEEMED TO BE FRAGMENTS OF SOME SORT OF LARGE STATUE.

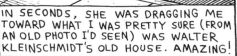

AND SURE ENOUGH, TWO NIGHTS AGO, ONE OF THEIR ATTACK VEHICLES CAME OUT OF THE SKY!

I'D BEEN WATCHING 'EM EVER SINCE THEY BLEW UP THE OLD CASTLE IN THE WOODS OVER THERE. I MISSED THAT ONE, BUT I KNEW THEY'D BE BACK.

...AND ZAPPED THE BIG STATUE, THAT WAS BACK HERE, WITH SOME KIND OF DISINTEGRATOR RAY.

JEFFREYS AND THE LITTL

SEE, THERE USED TO BE TWO OF 'EM BACK HERE.

THIS ONE AND THE ONE THE LANDLORD SOLD TO BARGAINTOWN OVER BY THE HIGHWAY.

I SAW YOU RIDE IN WITH HIM TODAY AND YOU'D BEST WATCH OUT. HE'S IN WITH 'EM.

I'VE BEEN WATCHING HIM FOR A WHILE NOW AND THAT FOOL IS A LITTLE SMALLER EVERY TIME I SEE HIM.

THEN, AFTER STUDYING ME FOR A LONG AND THOUGHTFUL MOMENT,

SHE OPENED AN ENTRANCE TO THE BASEMENT.

HEY! C'MERE!

DOWN BELOW WERE DOZENS OF CLAY MODELS THAT I'M PRETTY SURE WERE CREATED FOR THE FAIRYTALE HIGHWAY ATTRACTION THAT DOTTY TOLD ME ABOUT. WEIRDLY, TO ONE DEGREE OR ANOTHER, THEY ALL BORE THE HATCHET-FACED PHYSIOGNOMY OF WALTER KLEINSCHMIDT!

YEAH, THAT ONE'S A MODEL FOR THE ONE THAT JUST GOT ZAPPED.

LATER, WHILE SITTING WITH WANDA, MY SENSE OF HAPPINESS, TO FINALLY BE IN MIDGETVILLE, WAS SO OVERWHELMING THAT I TOOK IN ONLY MERE SNATCHES OF HER COMPLICATED, CRACKPOT THEORY.

THEIR HIGH CONCEPT IS SHRINK AND CONQUER...

ONE DAY YOU WAKE UP AND YOU'RE A FOUR-FOOT GALACTIC SLAVE.

THEY'VE ALREADY TAKEN FOUR INCHES OFF MY HEIGHT.

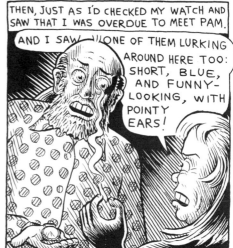

THEN, JUST AS I'D CHECKED MY WATCH AND SAW THAT I WAS OVERDUE TO MEET PAM,

AND I SAW ONE OF THEM LURKING AROUND HERE TOO: SHORT, BLUE, AND FUNNY-LOOKING, WITH POINTY EARS!

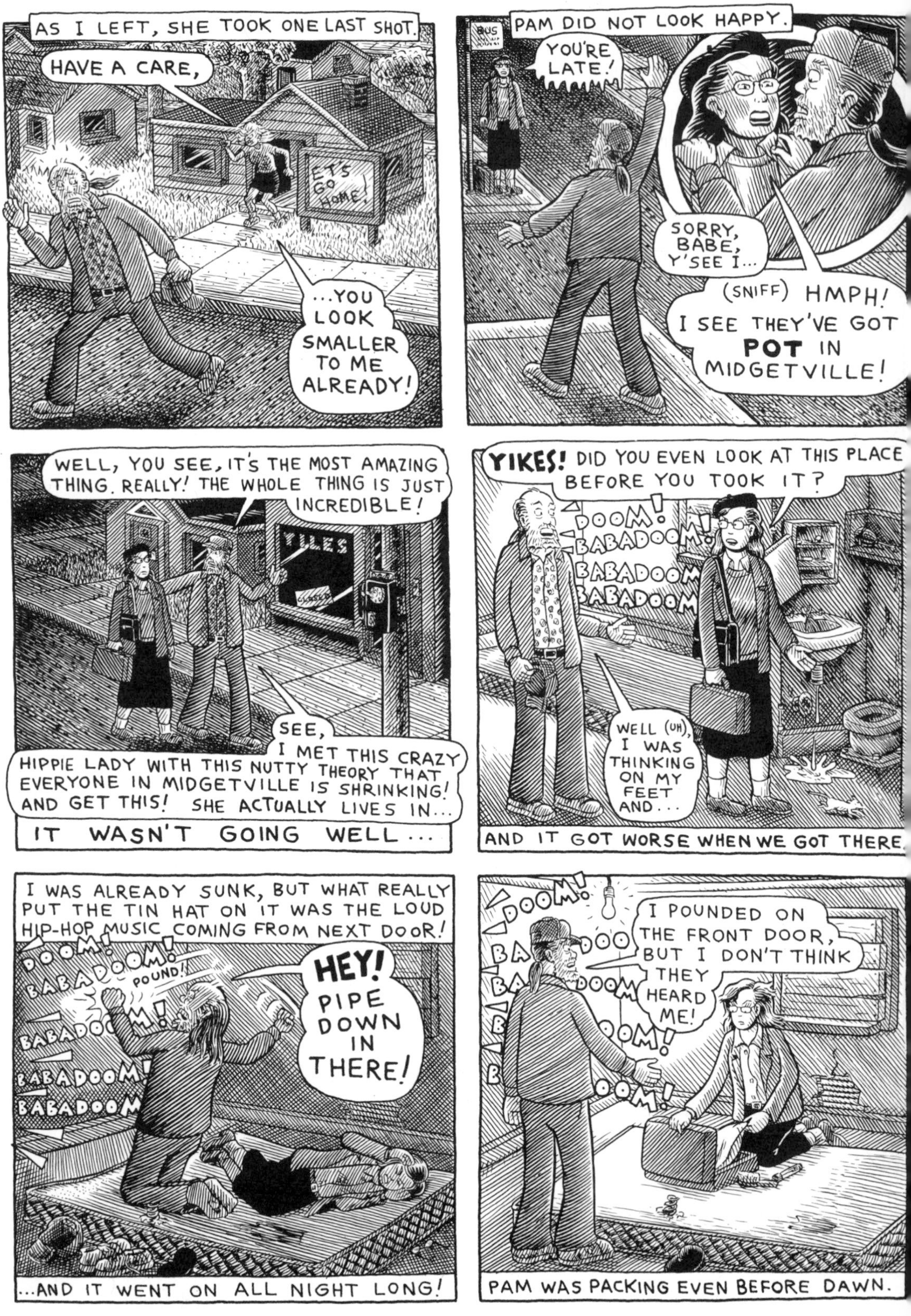
AS I LEFT, SHE TOOK ONE LAST SHOT.
HAVE A CARE,
...YOU LOOK SMALLER TO ME ALREADY!
ET'S GO HOME!
PAM DID NOT LOOK HAPPY.
BUS
YOU'RE LATE!
SORRY, BABE, Y'SEE I...
(SNIFF) HMPH! I SEE THEY'VE GOT **POT** IN MIDGETVILLE!
WELL, YOU SEE, IT'S THE MOST AMAZING THING. REALLY! THE WHOLE THING IS JUST INCREDIBLE!
TILES
SEE, I MET THIS CRAZY HIPPIE LADY WITH THIS NUTTY THEORY THAT EVERYONE IN MIDGETVILLE IS SHRINKING! AND GET THIS! SHE ACTUALLY LIVES IN...
IT WASN'T GOING WELL...
YIKES! DID YOU EVEN LOOK AT THIS PLACE BEFORE YOU TOOK IT?
DOOM! BABADOOM! BABADOOM BABADOOM
WELL (UH), I WAS THINKING ON MY FEET AND...
AND IT GOT WORSE WHEN WE GOT THERE.
I WAS ALREADY SUNK, BUT WHAT REALLY PUT THE TIN HAT ON IT WAS THE LOUD HIP-HOP MUSIC COMING FROM NEXT DOOR!
DOOM! BABADOOM! POUND! BABADOOM! BABADOOM BABADOOM
HEY! PIPE DOWN IN THERE!
...AND IT WENT ON ALL NIGHT LONG!
DOOM! BADOOM BADOOM BOOM! BOOM!
I POUNDED ON THE FRONT DOOR, BUT I DON'T THINK THEY HEARD ME!
PAM WAS PACKING EVEN BEFORE DAWN.

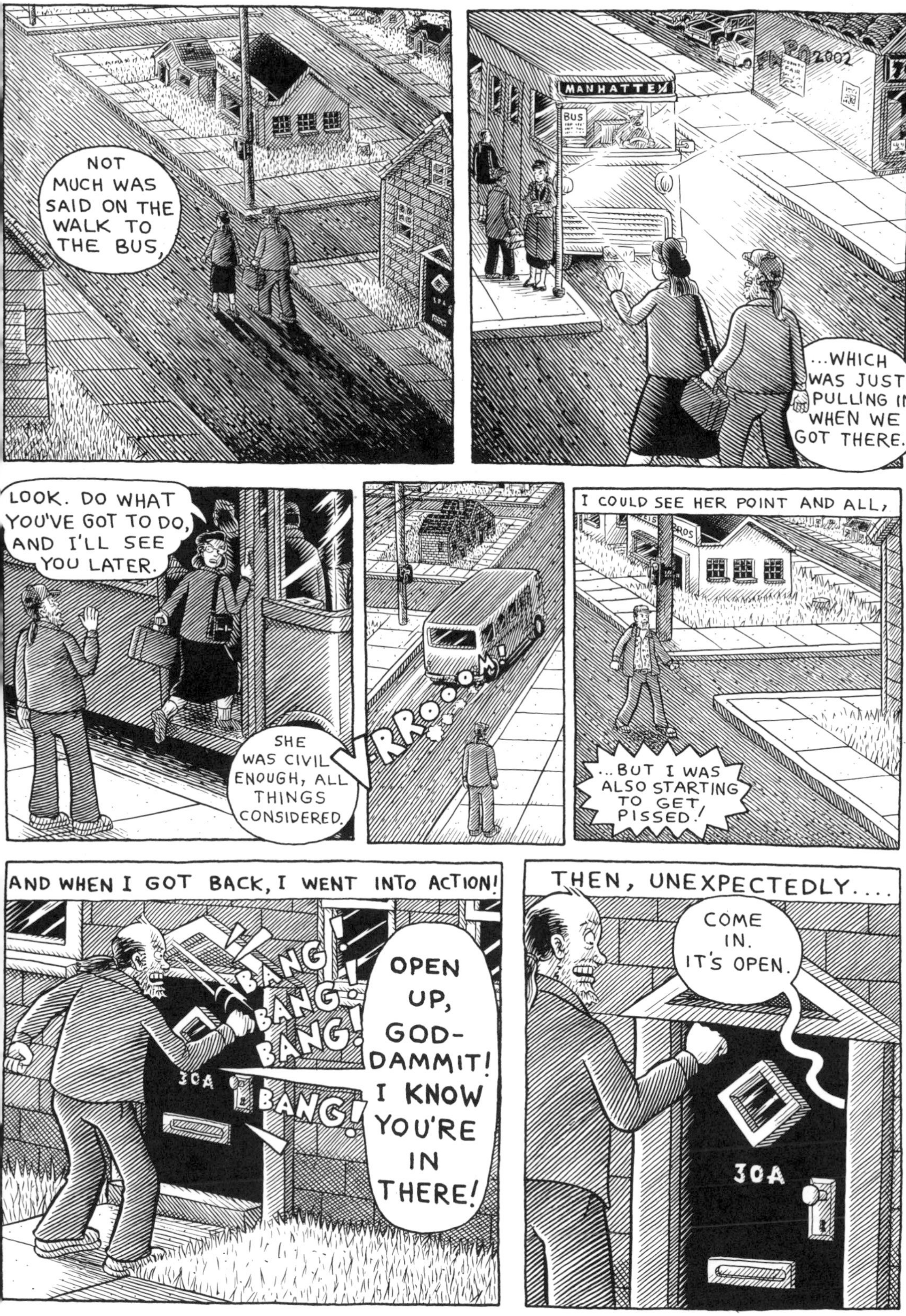
NOT MUCH WAS SAID ON THE WALK TO THE BUS,
...WHICH WAS JUST PULLING IN WHEN WE GOT THERE.
LOOK. DO WHAT YOU'VE GOT TO DO, AND I'LL SEE YOU LATER.
SHE WAS CIVIL ENOUGH, ALL THINGS CONSIDERED.
VRROOOOM!
I COULD SEE HER POINT AND ALL,
...BUT I WAS ALSO STARTING TO GET PISSED!
AND WHEN I GOT BACK, I WENT INTO ACTION!
BANG! BANG! BANG!
OPEN UP, GOD-DAMMIT! I KNOW YOU'RE IN THERE!
30A
BANG!
THEN, UNEXPECTEDLY....
COME IN. IT'S OPEN.
30A

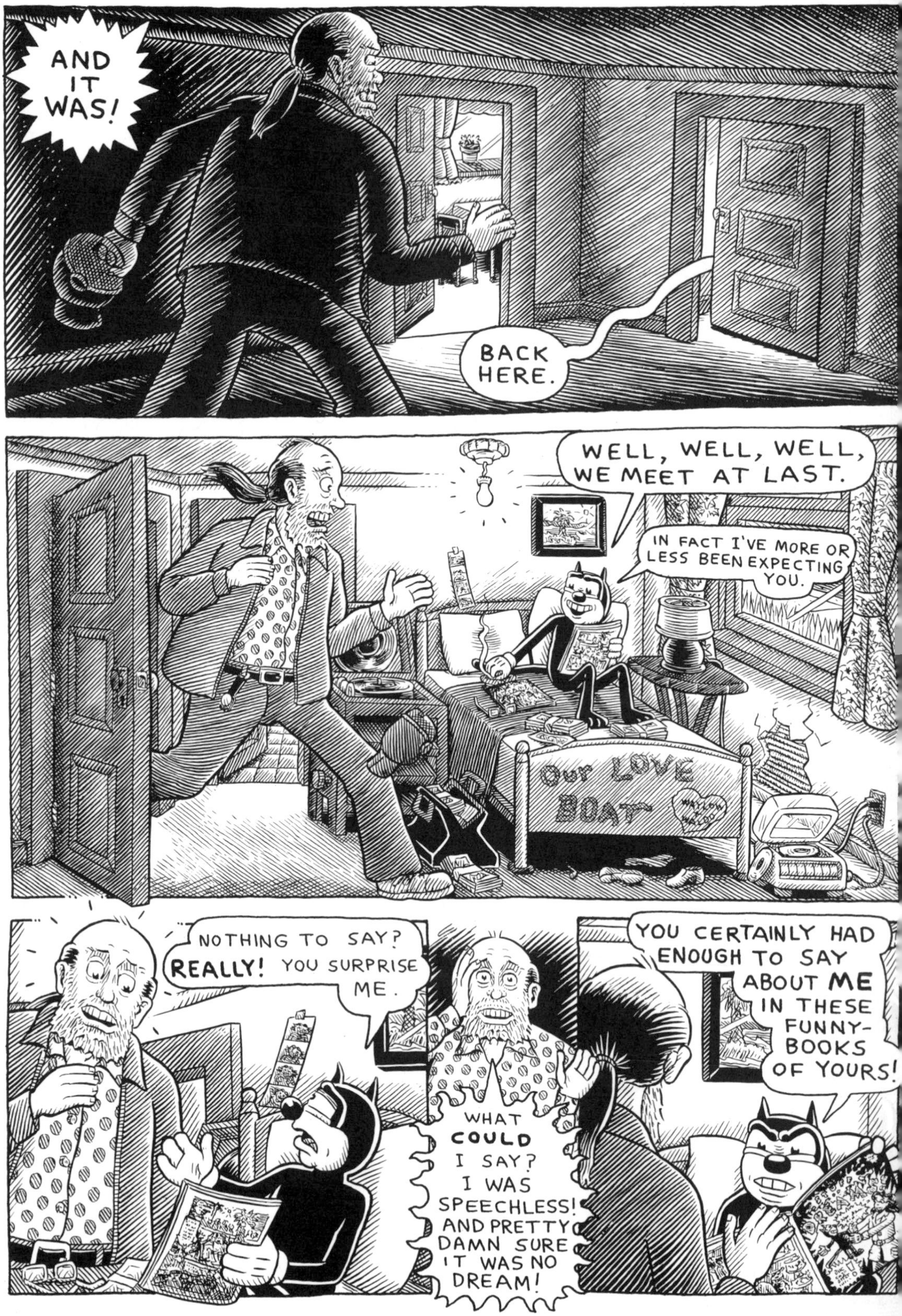
AND IT WAS!
BACK HERE.
WELL, WELL, WELL, WE MEET AT LAST.
IN FACT I'VE MORE OR LESS BEEN EXPECTING YOU.
Our LOVE BOAT
NOTHING TO SAY? REALLY! YOU SURPRISE ME.
WHAT COULD I SAY? I WAS SPEECHLESS! AND PRETTY DAMN SURE IT WAS NO DREAM!
YOU CERTAINLY HAD ENOUGH TO SAY ABOUT ME IN THESE FUNNY-BOOKS OF YOURS!

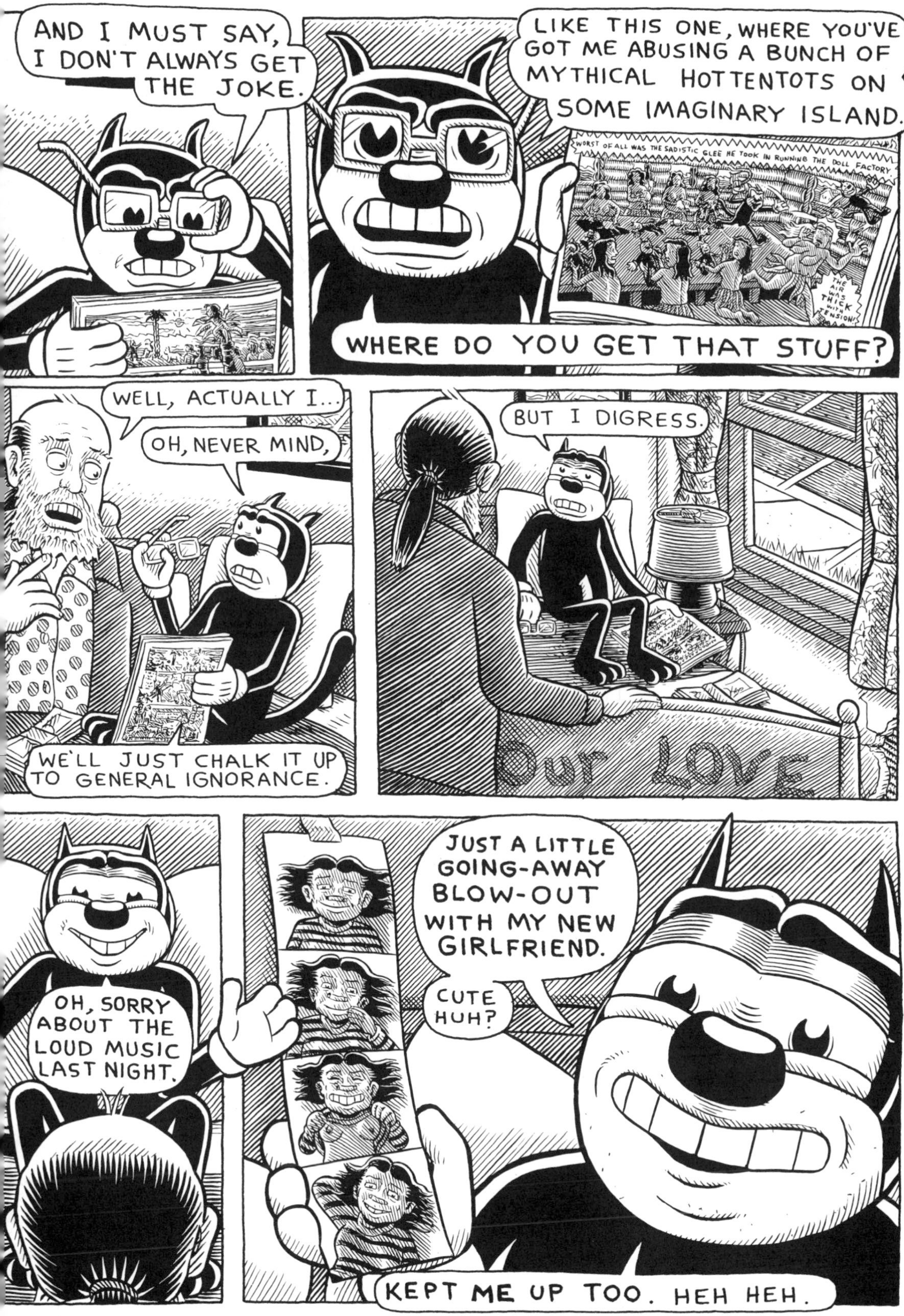
AND I MUST SAY, I DON'T ALWAYS GET THE JOKE.
LIKE THIS ONE, WHERE YOU'VE GOT ME ABUSING A BUNCH OF MYTHICAL HOTTENTOTS ON SOME IMAGINARY ISLAND.
WORST OF ALL WAS THE SADISTIC GLEE HE TOOK IN RUNNING THE DOLL FACTORY.
THE AIR WAS THICK WITH TENSION!
WHERE DO YOU GET THAT STUFF?
WELL, ACTUALLY I...
OH, NEVER MIND,
WE'LL JUST CHALK IT UP TO GENERAL IGNORANCE.
BUT I DIGRESS.
Our LOVE
OH, SORRY ABOUT THE LOUD MUSIC LAST NIGHT.
JUST A LITTLE GOING-AWAY BLOW-OUT WITH MY NEW GIRLFRIEND.
CUTE HUH?
KEPT ME UP TOO. HEH HEH.

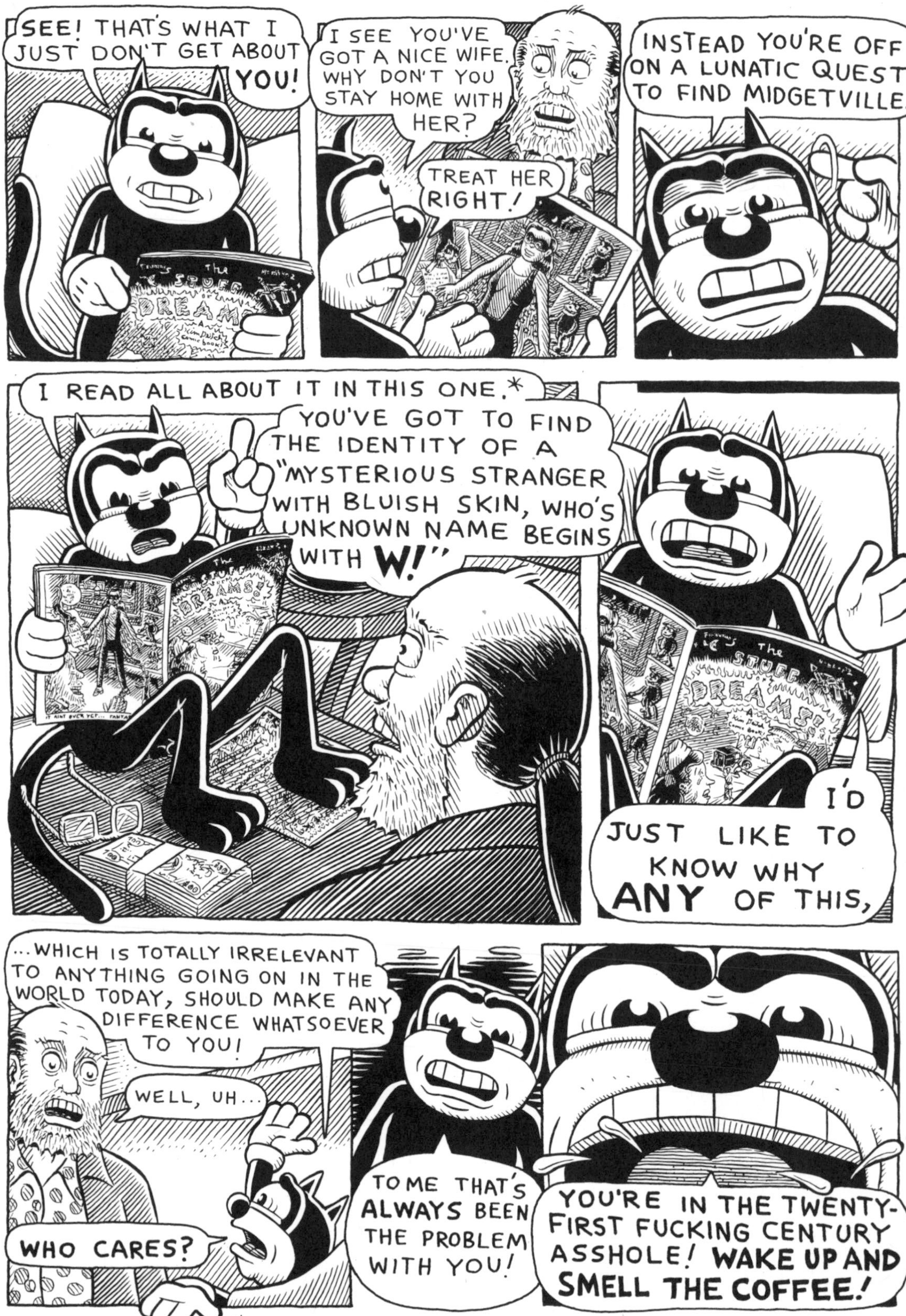
SEE! THAT'S WHAT I JUST DON'T GET ABOUT YOU!
I SEE YOU'VE GOT A NICE WIFE. WHY DON'T YOU STAY HOME WITH HER?
TREAT HER RIGHT!
INSTEAD YOU'RE OFF ON A LUNATIC QUEST TO FIND MIDGETVILLE.
I READ ALL ABOUT IT IN THIS ONE.*
YOU'VE GOT TO FIND THE IDENTITY OF A "MYSTERIOUS STRANGER WITH BLUISH SKIN, WHO'S UNKNOWN NAME BEGINS WITH W!"
I'D JUST LIKE TO KNOW WHY ANY OF THIS,
...WHICH IS TOTALLY IRRELEVANT TO ANYTHING GOING ON IN THE WORLD TODAY, SHOULD MAKE ANY DIFFERENCE WHATSOEVER TO YOU!
WELL, UH...
WHO CARES?
TO ME THAT'S ALWAYS BEEN THE PROBLEM WITH YOU!
YOU'RE IN THE TWENTY-FIRST FUCKING CENTURY ASSHOLE! WAKE UP AND SMELL THE COFFEE!

* THE STUFF OF DREAMS #2

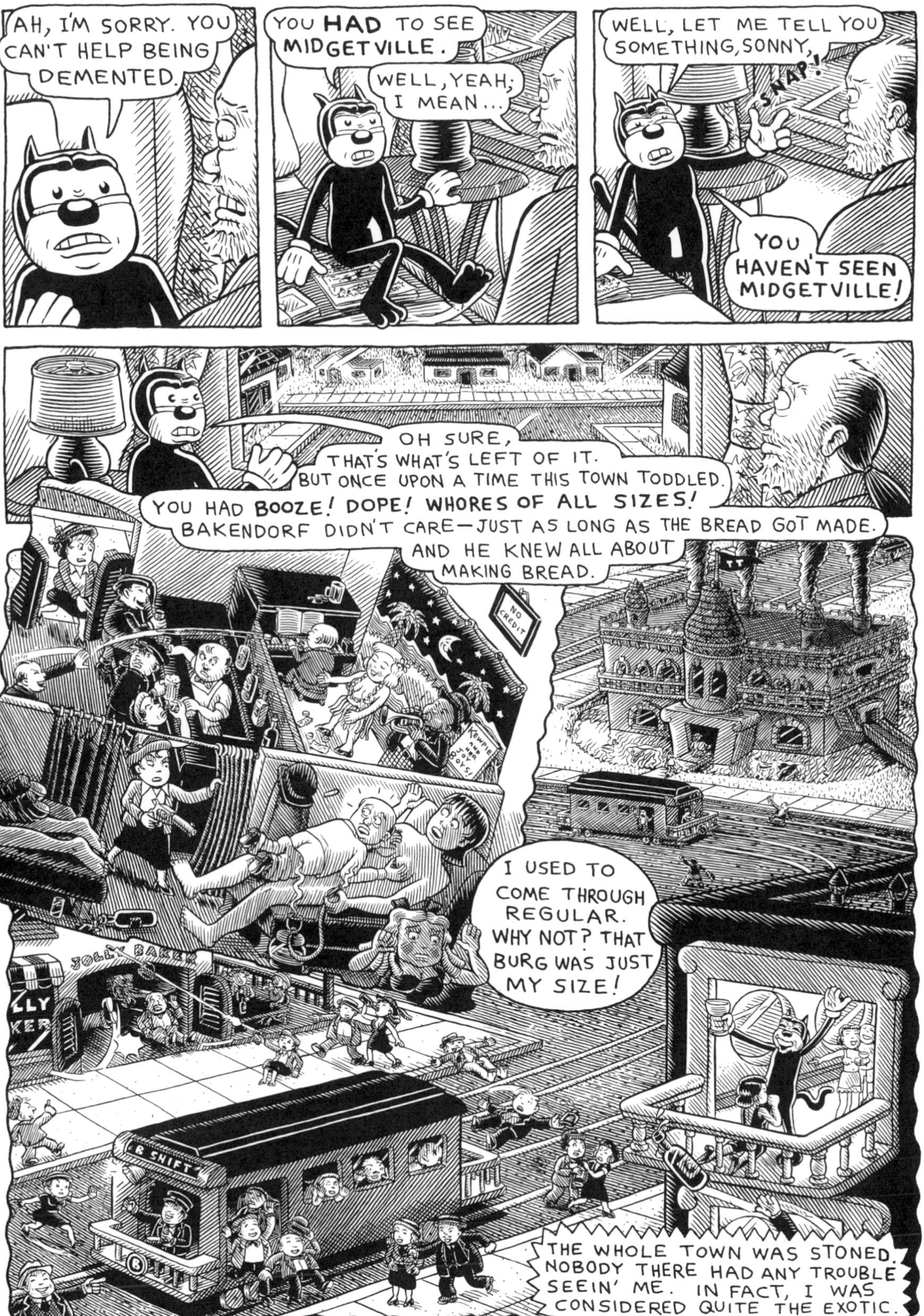
AH, I'M SORRY. YOU CAN'T HELP BEING DEMENTED.
YOU HAD TO SEE MIDGETVILLE.
WELL, YEAH; I MEAN...
WELL, LET ME TELL YOU SOMETHING, SONNY,
SNAP!
YOU HAVEN'T SEEN MIDGETVILLE!
OH SURE, THAT'S WHAT'S LEFT OF IT. BUT ONCE UPON A TIME THIS TOWN TODDLED.
YOU HAD BOOZE! DOPE! WHORES OF ALL SIZES! BAKENDORF DIDN'T CARE—JUST AS LONG AS THE BREAD GOT MADE.
AND HE KNEW ALL ABOUT MAKING BREAD.
NO CREDIT
KEWPIE AND JOBY BOYS!
I USED TO COME THROUGH REGULAR. WHY NOT? THAT BURG WAS JUST MY SIZE!
B SHIFT
THE WHOLE TOWN WAS STONED. NOBODY THERE HAD ANY TROUBLE SEEIN' ME. IN FACT, I WAS CONSIDERED QUITE THE EXOTIC.

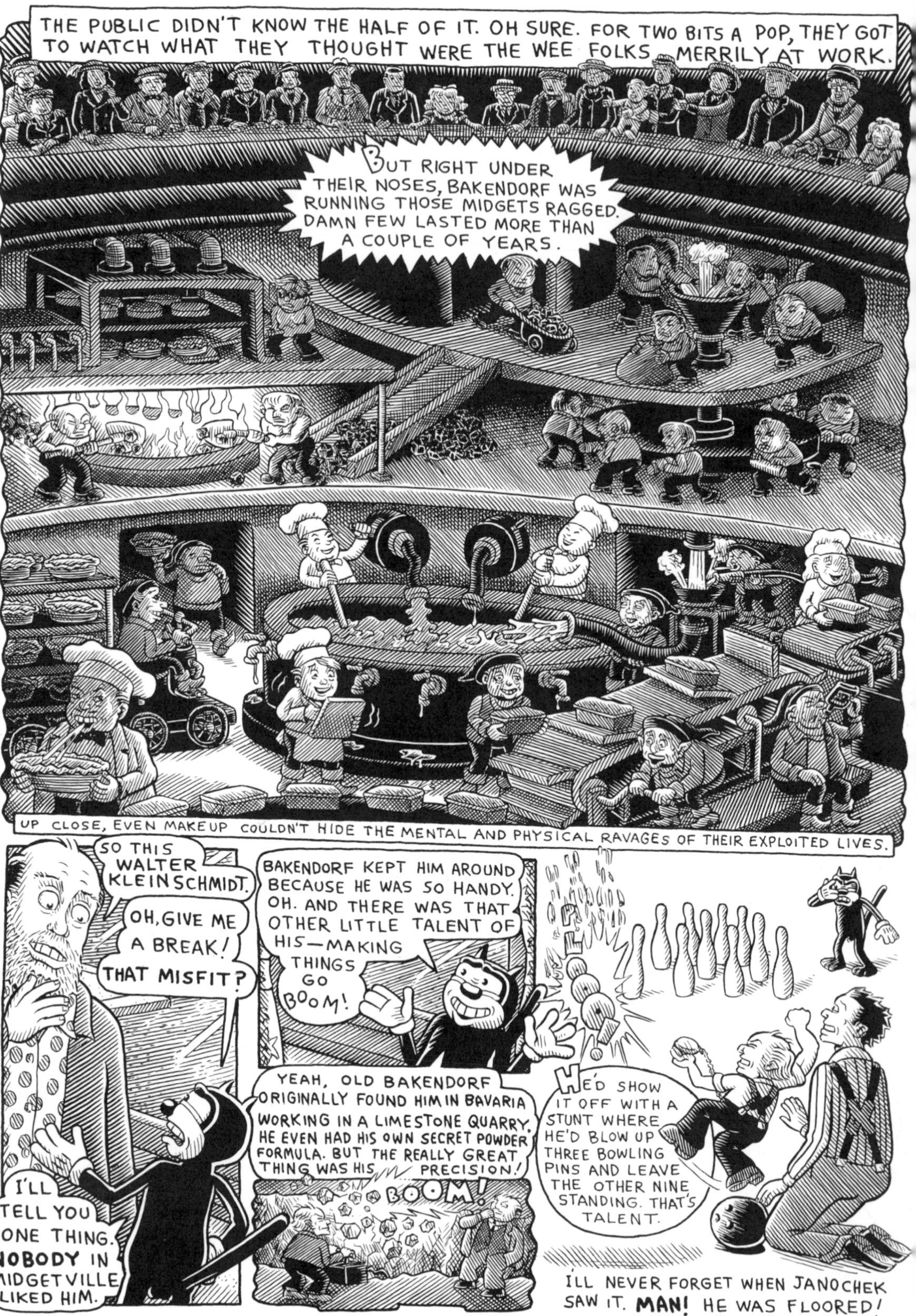
THE PUBLIC DIDN'T KNOW THE HALF OF IT. OH SURE. FOR TWO BITS A POP, THEY GOT TO WATCH WHAT THEY THOUGHT WERE THE WEE FOLKS MERRILY AT WORK.
BUT RIGHT UNDER THEIR NOSES, BAKENDORF WAS RUNNING THOSE MIDGETS RAGGED. DAMN FEW LASTED MORE THAN A COUPLE OF YEARS.
UP CLOSE, EVEN MAKEUP COULDN'T HIDE THE MENTAL AND PHYSICAL RAVAGES OF THEIR EXPLOITED LIVES.
SO THIS WALTER KLEINSCHMIDT.
OH, GIVE ME A BREAK! THAT MISFIT?
I'LL TELL YOU ONE THING. NOBODY IN MIDGETVILLE LIKED HIM.
BAKENDORF KEPT HIM AROUND BECAUSE HE WAS SO HANDY. OH. AND THERE WAS THAT OTHER LITTLE TALENT OF HIS—MAKING THINGS GO BOOM!
YEAH, OLD BAKENDORF ORIGINALLY FOUND HIM IN BAVARIA WORKING IN A LIMESTONE QUARRY. HE EVEN HAD HIS OWN SECRET POWDER FORMULA. BUT THE REALLY GREAT THING WAS HIS PRECISION!
BOOM!
HE'D SHOW IT OFF WITH A STUNT WHERE HE'D BLOW UP THREE BOWLING PINS AND LEAVE THE OTHER NINE STANDING. THAT'S TALENT.
I'LL NEVER FORGET WHEN JANOCHEK SAW IT. MAN! HE WAS FLOORED!

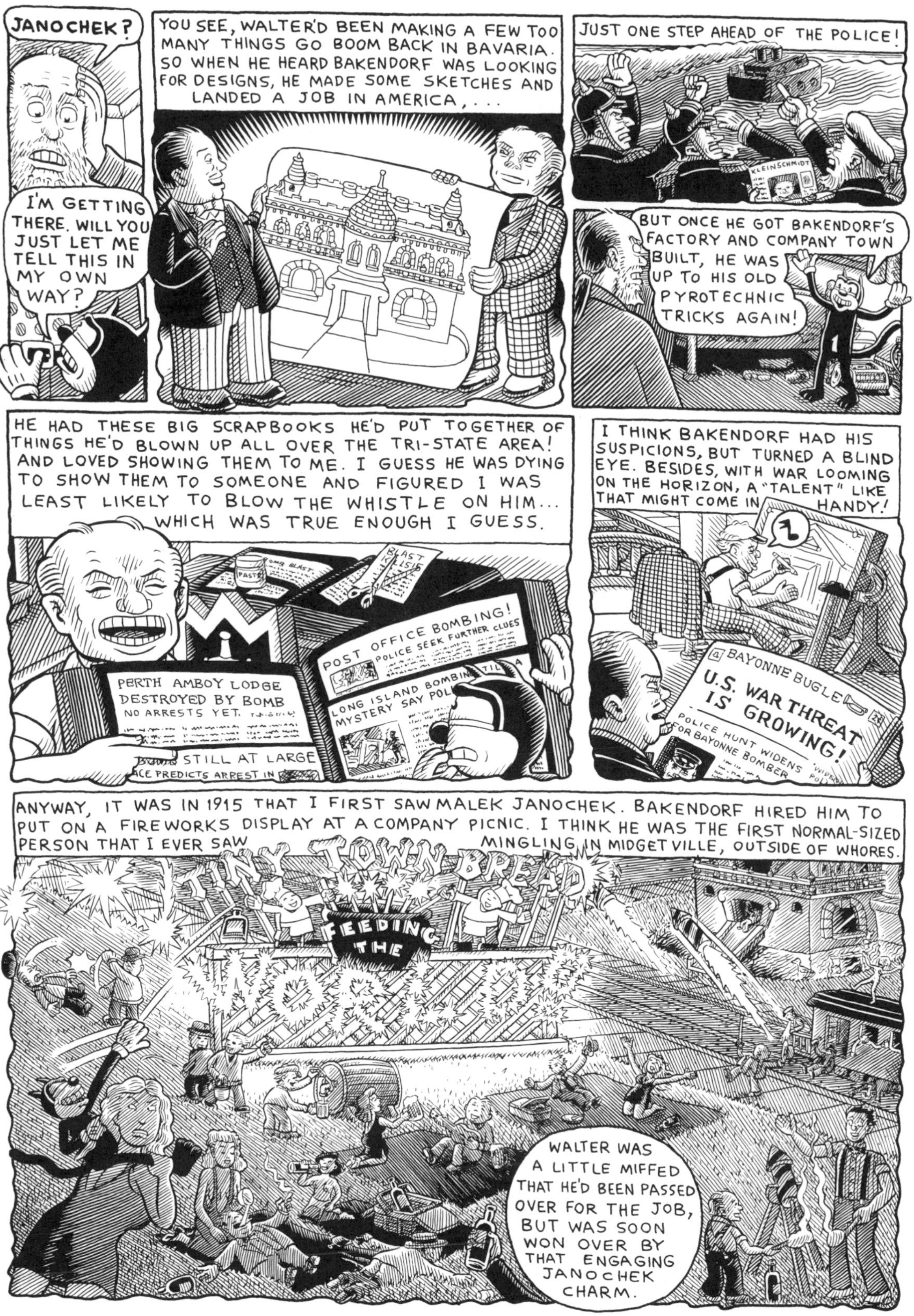

JANOCHEK?
YOU SEE, WALTER'D BEEN MAKING A FEW TOO MANY THINGS GO BOOM BACK IN BAVARIA. SO WHEN HE HEARD BAKENDORF WAS LOOKING FOR DESIGNS, HE MADE SOME SKETCHES AND LANDED A JOB IN AMERICA, . . .
JUST ONE STEP AHEAD OF THE POLICE!
I'M GETTING THERE. WILL YOU JUST LET ME TELL THIS IN MY OWN WAY?
BUT ONCE HE GOT BAKENDORF'S FACTORY AND COMPANY TOWN BUILT, HE WAS UP TO HIS OLD PYROTECHNIC TRICKS AGAIN!
HE HAD THESE BIG SCRAPBOOKS HE'D PUT TOGETHER OF THINGS HE'D BLOWN UP ALL OVER THE TRI-STATE AREA! AND LOVED SHOWING THEM TO ME. I GUESS HE WAS DYING TO SHOW THEM TO SOMEONE AND FIGURED I WAS LEAST LIKELY TO BLOW THE WHISTLE ON HIM... WHICH WAS TRUE ENOUGH I GUESS.
PERTH AMBOY LODGE DESTROYED BY BOMB
NO ARRESTS YET.
STILL AT LARGE
POST OFFICE BOMBING!
POLICE SEEK FURTHER CLUES
I THINK BAKENDORF HAD HIS SUSPICIONS, BUT TURNED A BLIND EYE. BESIDES, WITH WAR LOOMING ON THE HORIZON, A "TALENT" LIKE THAT MIGHT COME IN HANDY!
BAYONNE BUGLE
U.S. WAR THREAT IS GROWING!
POLICE HUNT WIDENS FOR BAYONNE BOMBER
ANYWAY, IT WAS IN 1915 THAT I FIRST SAW MALEK JANOCHEK. BAKENDORF HIRED HIM TO PUT ON A FIREWORKS DISPLAY AT A COMPANY PICNIC. I THINK HE WAS THE FIRST NORMAL-SIZED PERSON THAT I EVER SAW MINGLING IN MIDGETVILLE, OUTSIDE OF WHORES.
TINY TOWN BREAD
FEEDING THE WORLD
WALTER WAS A LITTLE MIFFED THAT HE'D BEEN PASSED OVER FOR THE JOB, BUT WAS SOON WON OVER BY THAT ENGAGING JANOCHEK CHARM.

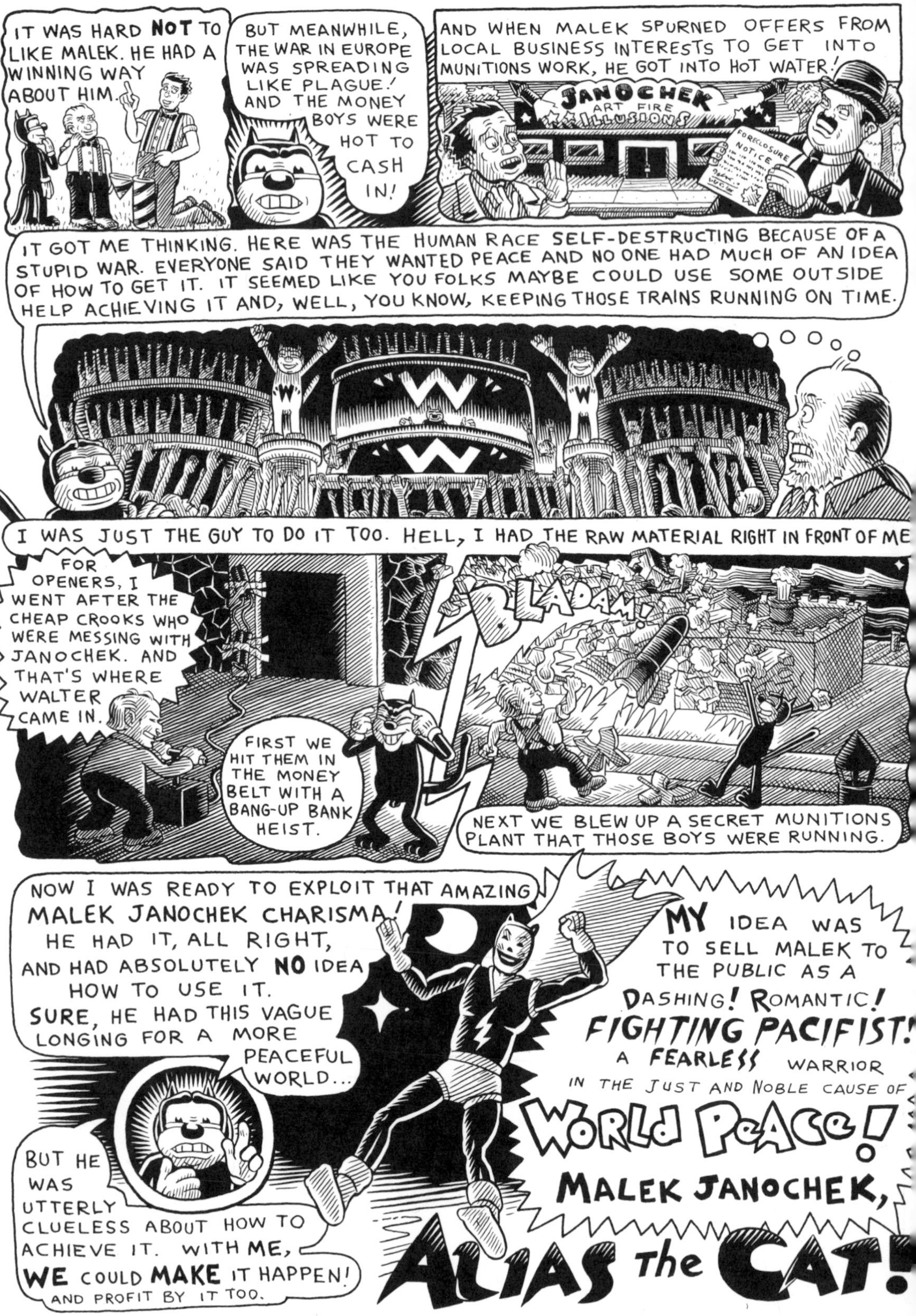
IT WAS HARD NOT TO LIKE MALEK. HE HAD A WINNING WAY ABOUT HIM.
BUT MEANWHILE, THE WAR IN EUROPE WAS SPREADING LIKE PLAGUE! AND THE MONEY BOYS WERE HOT TO CASH IN!
AND WHEN MALEK SPURNED OFFERS FROM LOCAL BUSINESS INTERESTS TO GET INTO MUNITIONS WORK, HE GOT INTO HOT WATER!
JANOCHEK ART FIRE ILLUSIONS
FORECLOSURE NOTICE
IT GOT ME THINKING. HERE WAS THE HUMAN RACE SELF-DESTRUCTING BECAUSE OF A STUPID WAR. EVERYONE SAID THEY WANTED PEACE AND NO ONE HAD MUCH OF AN IDEA OF HOW TO GET IT. IT SEEMED LIKE YOU FOLKS MAYBE COULD USE SOME OUTSIDE HELP ACHIEVING IT AND, WELL, YOU KNOW, KEEPING THOSE TRAINS RUNNING ON TIME.
I WAS JUST THE GUY TO DO IT TOO. HELL, I HAD THE RAW MATERIAL RIGHT IN FRONT OF ME
FOR OPENERS, I WENT AFTER THE CHEAP CROOKS WHO WERE MESSING WITH JANOCHEK. AND THAT'S WHERE WALTER CAME IN.
BLADAM!
FIRST WE HIT THEM IN THE MONEY BELT WITH A BANG-UP BANK HEIST.
NEXT WE BLEW UP A SECRET MUNITIONS PLANT THAT THOSE BOYS WERE RUNNING.
NOW I WAS READY TO EXPLOIT THAT AMAZING MALEK JANOCHEK CHARISMA! HE HAD IT, ALL RIGHT, AND HAD ABSOLUTELY NO IDEA HOW TO USE IT. SURE, HE HAD THIS VAGUE LONGING FOR A MORE PEACEFUL WORLD...
BUT HE WAS UTTERLY CLUELESS ABOUT HOW TO ACHIEVE IT. WITH ME, WE COULD MAKE IT HAPPEN! AND PROFIT BY IT TOO.
MY IDEA WAS TO SELL MALEK TO THE PUBLIC AS A DASHING! ROMANTIC! FIGHTING PACIFIST! A FEARLESS WARRIOR IN THE JUST AND NOBLE CAUSE OF WORLD PEACE!
MALEK JANOCHEK, ALIAS THE CAT!

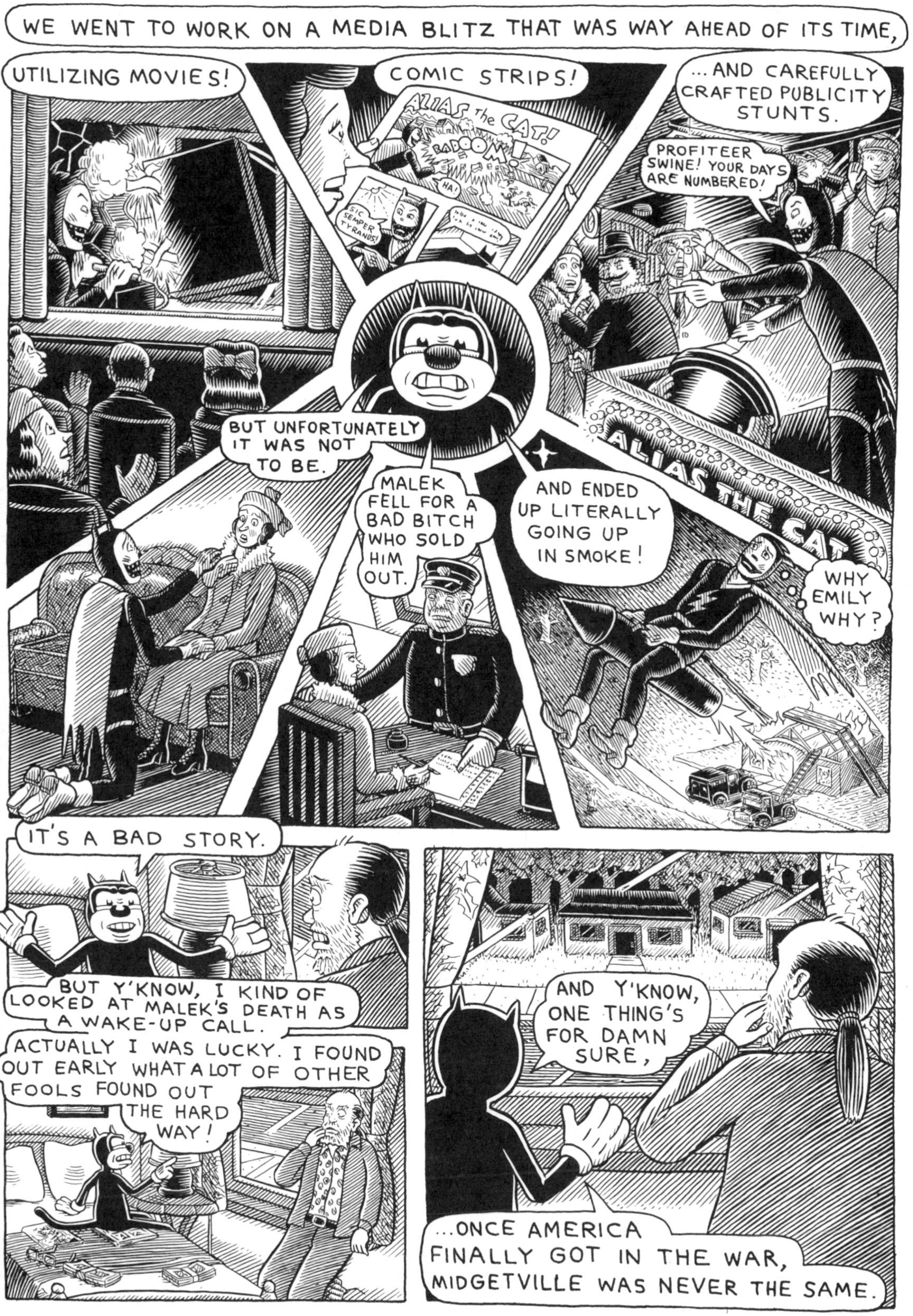
WE WENT TO WORK ON A MEDIA BLITZ THAT WAS WAY AHEAD OF ITS TIME,
UTILIZING MOVIES!
COMIC STRIPS!
ALIAS the CAT!
BADOOM!
HA!
SIC SEMPER TYRANUS!
...AND CAREFULLY CRAFTED PUBLICITY STUNTS.
PROFITEER SWINE! YOUR DAYS ARE NUMBERED!
ALIAS THE CAT
BUT UNFORTUNATELY IT WAS NOT TO BE.
MALEK FELL FOR A BAD BITCH WHO SOLD HIM OUT.
AND ENDED UP LITERALLY GOING UP IN SMOKE!
WHY EMILY WHY?
IT'S A BAD STORY.
BUT Y'KNOW, I KIND OF LOOKED AT MALEK'S DEATH AS A WAKE-UP CALL.
ACTUALLY I WAS LUCKY. I FOUND OUT EARLY WHAT A LOT OF OTHER FOOLS FOUND OUT THE HARD WAY!
AND Y'KNOW, ONE THING'S FOR DAMN SURE,
...ONCE AMERICA FINALLY GOT IN THE WAR, MIDGETVILLE WAS NEVER THE SAME.

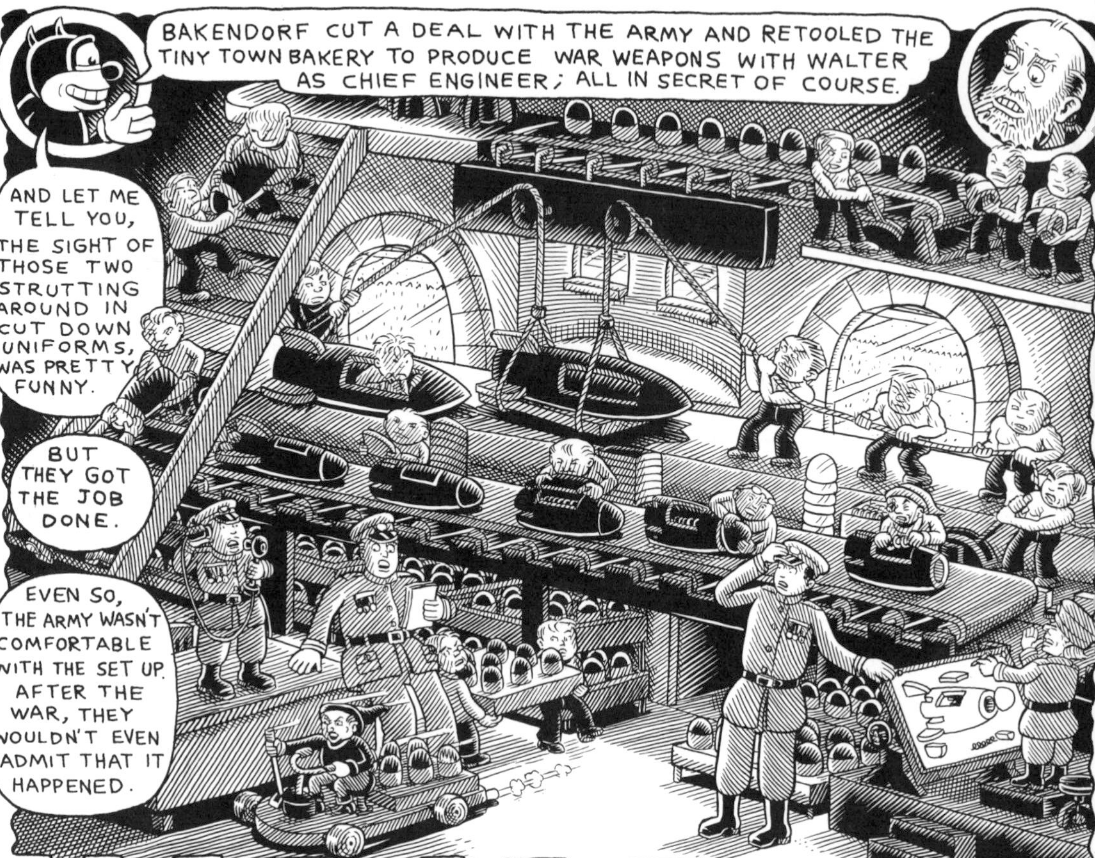
BAKENDORF CUT A DEAL WITH THE ARMY AND RETOOLED THE TINY TOWN BAKERY TO PRODUCE WAR WEAPONS WITH WALTER AS CHIEF ENGINEER; ALL IN SECRET OF COURSE.
AND LET ME TELL YOU, THE SIGHT OF THOSE TWO STRUTTING AROUND IN CUT DOWN UNIFORMS, WAS PRETTY FUNNY.
BUT THEY GOT THE JOB DONE.
EVEN SO, THE ARMY WASN'T COMFORTABLE WITH THE SET UP. AFTER THE WAR, THEY WOULDN'T EVEN ADMIT THAT IT HAPPENED.

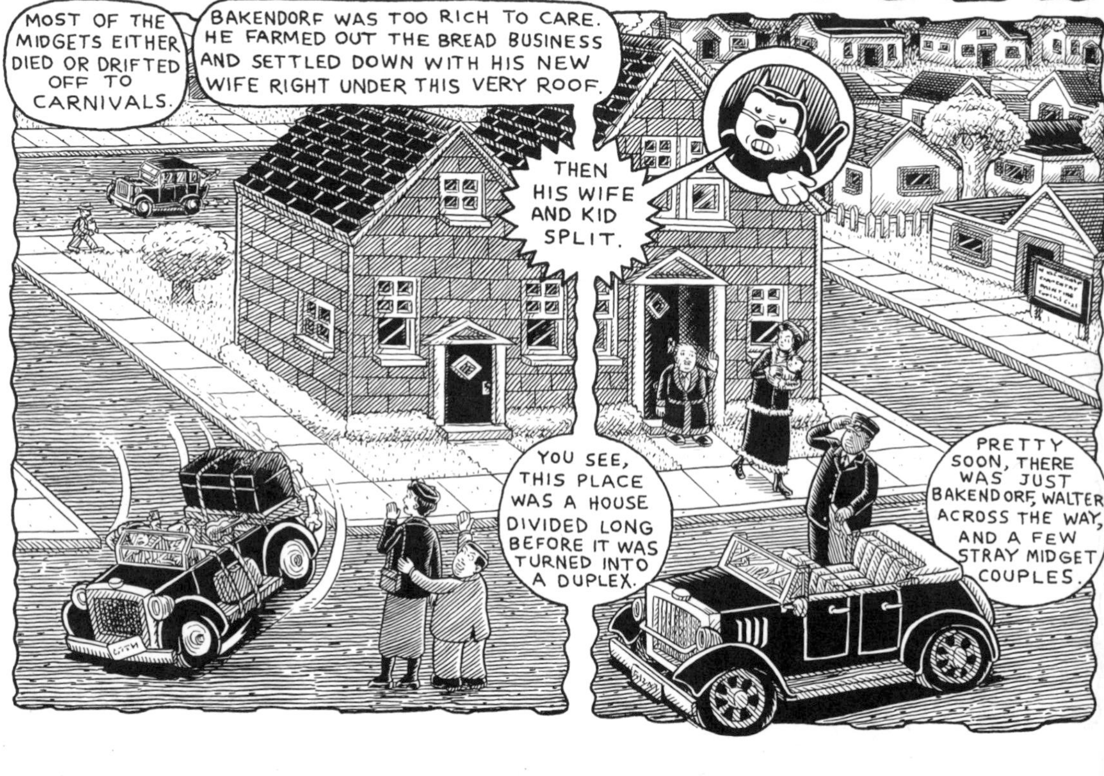
MOST OF THE MIDGETS EITHER DIED OR DRIFTED OFF TO CARNIVALS.
BAKENDORF WAS TOO RICH TO CARE. HE FARMED OUT THE BREAD BUSINESS AND SETTLED DOWN WITH HIS NEW WIFE RIGHT UNDER THIS VERY ROOF.
THEN HIS WIFE AND KID SPLIT.
YOU SEE, THIS PLACE WAS A HOUSE DIVIDED LONG BEFORE IT WAS TURNED INTO A DUPLEX.
PRETTY SOON, THERE WAS JUST BAKENDORF, WALTER ACROSS THE WAY, AND A FEW STRAY MIDGET COUPLES.

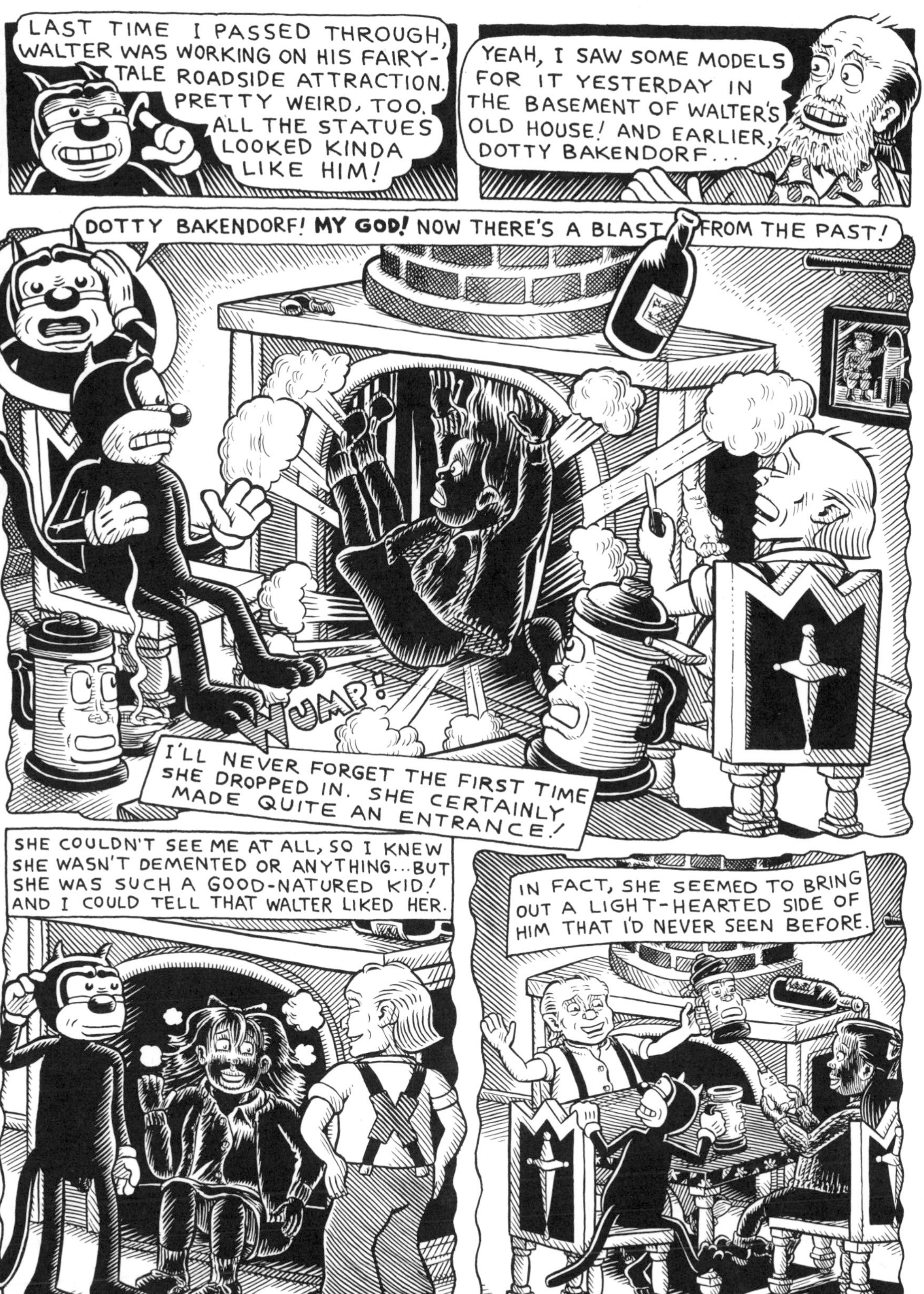
LAST TIME I PASSED THROUGH, WALTER WAS WORKING ON HIS FAIRY-TALE ROADSIDE ATTRACTION. PRETTY WEIRD, TOO. ALL THE STATUES LOOKED KINDA LIKE HIM!
YEAH, I SAW SOME MODELS FOR IT YESTERDAY IN THE BASEMENT OF WALTER'S OLD HOUSE! AND EARLIER, DOTTY BAKENDORF...
DOTTY BAKENDORF! MY GOD! NOW THERE'S A BLAST FROM THE PAST!
WUMP!
I'LL NEVER FORGET THE FIRST TIME SHE DROPPED IN. SHE CERTAINLY MADE QUITE AN ENTRANCE!
SHE COULDN'T SEE ME AT ALL, SO I KNEW SHE WASN'T DEMENTED OR ANYTHING... BUT SHE WAS SUCH A GOOD-NATURED KID! AND I COULD TELL THAT WALTER LIKED HER.
IN FACT, SHE SEEMED TO BRING OUT A LIGHT-HEARTED SIDE OF HIM THAT I'D NEVER SEEN BEFORE.

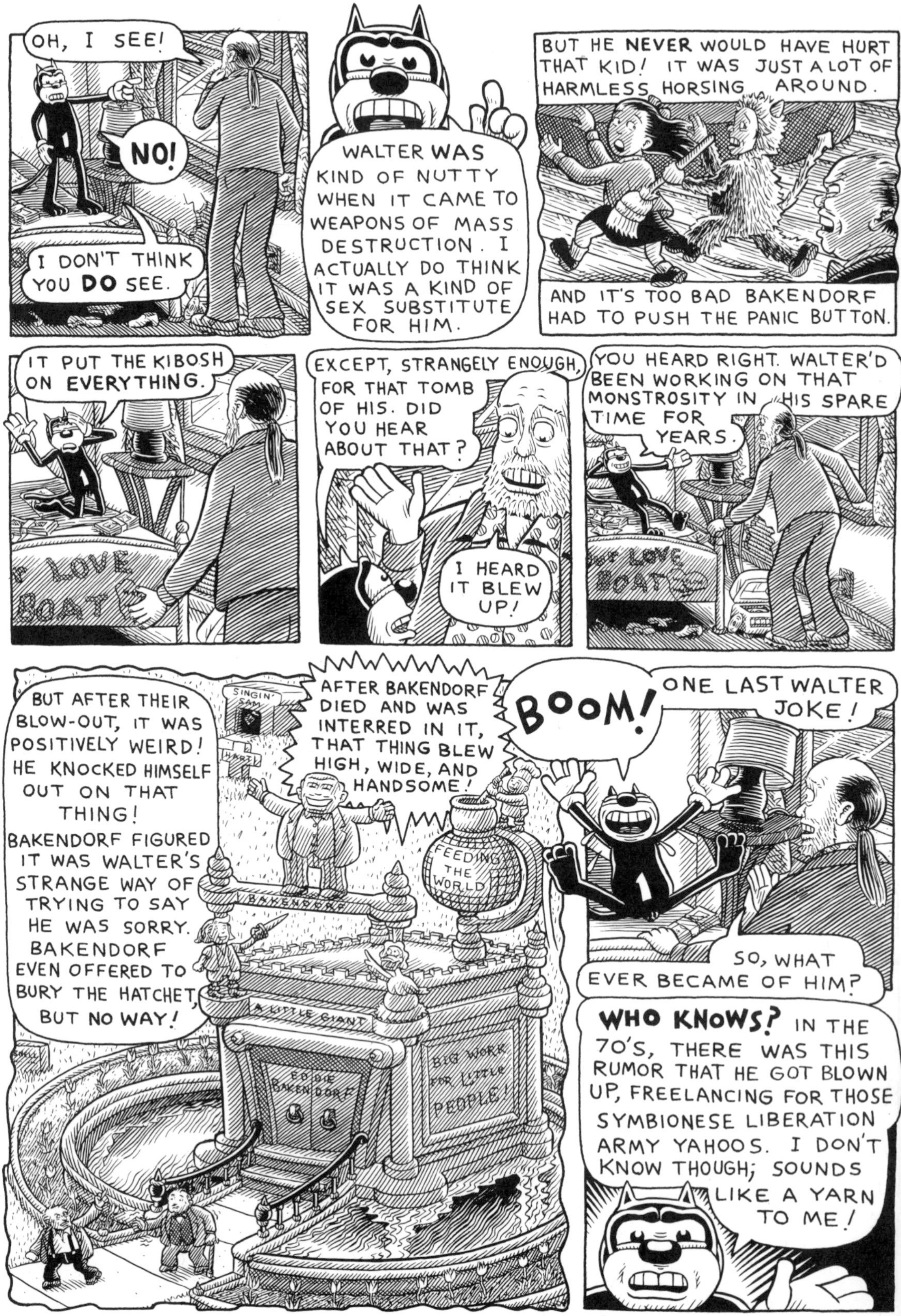
OH, I SEE!
NO!
I DON'T THINK YOU DO SEE.
WALTER WAS KIND OF NUTTY WHEN IT CAME TO WEAPONS OF MASS DESTRUCTION. I ACTUALLY DO THINK IT WAS A KIND OF SEX SUBSTITUTE FOR HIM.
BUT HE NEVER WOULD HAVE HURT THAT KID! IT WAS JUST A LOT OF HARMLESS HORSING AROUND.
AND IT'S TOO BAD BAKENDORF HAD TO PUSH THE PANIC BUTTON.
IT PUT THE KIBOSH ON EVERYTHING.
LOVE BOAT
EXCEPT, STRANGELY ENOUGH, FOR THAT TOMB OF HIS. DID YOU HEAR ABOUT THAT?
I HEARD IT BLEW UP!
YOU HEARD RIGHT. WALTER'D BEEN WORKING ON THAT MONSTROSITY IN HIS SPARE TIME FOR YEARS.
LOVE BOAT
BUT AFTER THEIR BLOW-OUT, IT WAS POSITIVELY WEIRD! HE KNOCKED HIMSELF OUT ON THAT THING! BAKENDORF FIGURED IT WAS WALTER'S STRANGE WAY OF TRYING TO SAY HE WAS SORRY. BAKENDORF EVEN OFFERED TO BURY THE HATCHET, BUT NO WAY!
SINGIN' SAM
HART
AFTER BAKENDORF DIED AND WAS INTERRED IN IT, THAT THING BLEW HIGH, WIDE, AND HANDSOME!
FEEDING THE WORLD
BAKENDORF
A LITTLE GIANT
EDDIE BAKENDORF
BIG WORK FOR LITTLE PEOPLE!
BOOM!
ONE LAST WALTER JOKE!
SO, WHAT EVER BECAME OF HIM?
WHO KNOWS? IN THE 70'S, THERE WAS THIS RUMOR THAT HE GOT BLOWN UP, FREELANCING FOR THOSE SYMBIONESE LIBERATION ARMY YAHOOS. I DON'T KNOW THOUGH; SOUNDS LIKE A YARN TO ME!

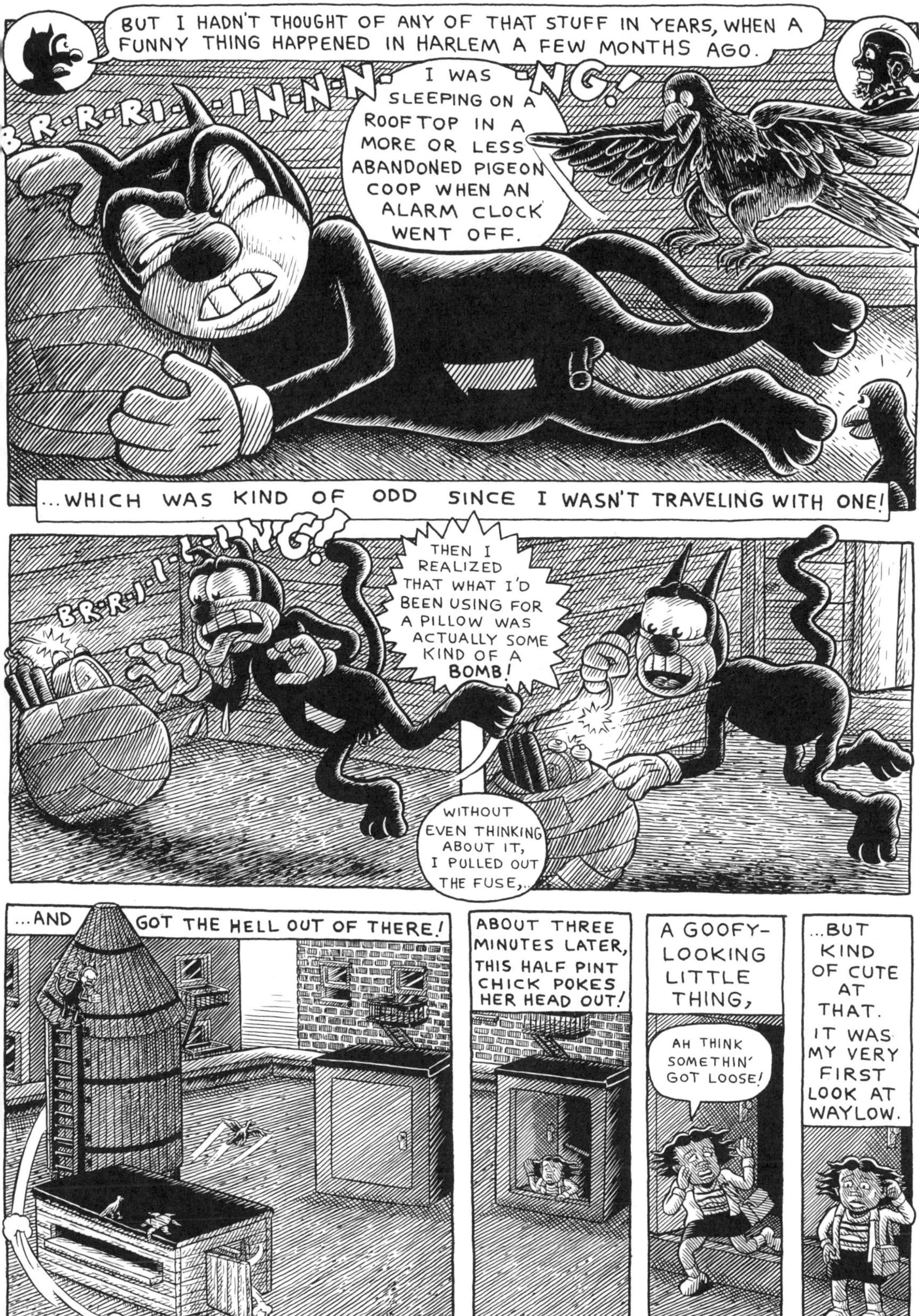
BUT I HADN'T THOUGHT OF ANY OF THAT STUFF IN YEARS, WHEN A FUNNY THING HAPPENED IN HARLEM A FEW MONTHS AGO.
B-R-R-RI-I-INN-N-N-NG!
I WAS SLEEPING ON A ROOFTOP IN A MORE OR LESS ABANDONED PIGEON COOP WHEN AN ALARM CLOCK WENT OFF.
...WHICH WAS KIND OF ODD SINCE I WASN'T TRAVELING WITH ONE!
B-R-R-I-I-I-NG!!
THEN I REALIZED THAT WHAT I'D BEEN USING FOR A PILLOW WAS ACTUALLY SOME KIND OF A BOMB!
WITHOUT EVEN THINKING ABOUT IT, I PULLED OUT THE FUSE,...
...AND GOT THE HELL OUT OF THERE!
ABOUT THREE MINUTES LATER, THIS HALF PINT CHICK POKES HER HEAD OUT!
A GOOFY-LOOKING LITTLE THING,
AH THINK SOMETHIN' GOT LOOSE!
...BUT KIND OF CUTE AT THAT. IT WAS MY VERY FIRST LOOK AT WAYLOW.

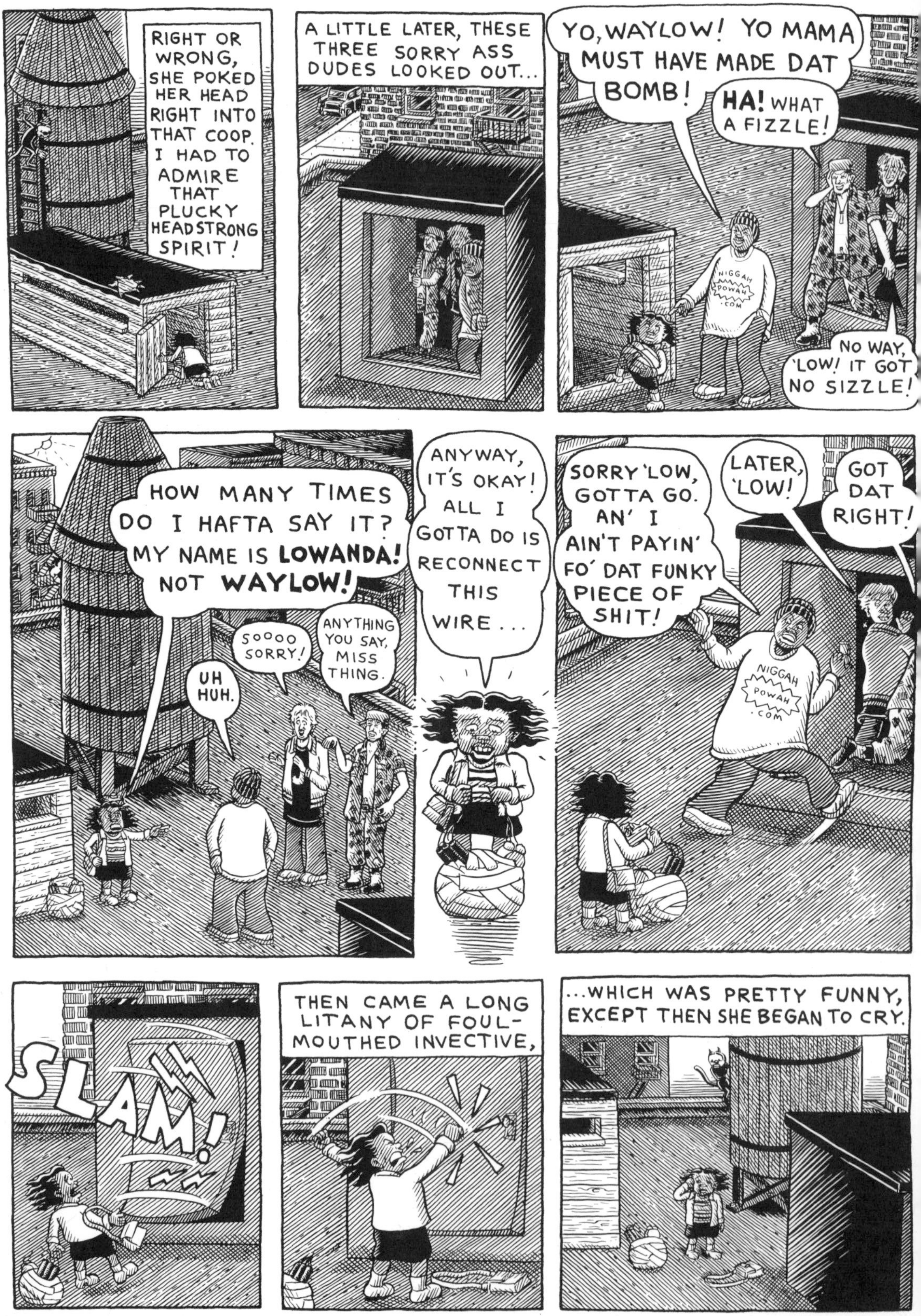
RIGHT OR WRONG, SHE POKED HER HEAD RIGHT INTO THAT COOP. I HAD TO ADMIRE THAT PLUCKY HEADSTRONG SPIRIT!
A LITTLE LATER, THESE THREE SORRY ASS DUDES LOOKED OUT...
YO, WAYLOW! YO MAMA MUST HAVE MADE DAT BOMB!
HA! WHAT A FIZZLE!
NO WAY, 'LOW! IT GOT NO SIZZLE!
HOW MANY TIMES DO I HAFTA SAY IT? MY NAME IS LOWANDA! NOT WAYLOW!
UH HUH.
SOOOO SORRY!
ANYTHING YOU SAY, MISS THING.
ANYWAY, IT'S OKAY! ALL I GOTTA DO IS RECONNECT THIS WIRE...
SORRY 'LOW, GOTTA GO. AN' I AIN'T PAYIN' FO' DAT FUNKY PIECE OF SHIT!
LATER, 'LOW!
GOT DAT RIGHT!
NIGGAH POWAH .COM
SLAM!
THEN CAME A LONG LITANY OF FOUL-MOUTHED INVECTIVE,
...WHICH WAS PRETTY FUNNY, EXCEPT THEN SHE BEGAN TO CRY.

AS I WAS CLIMBING DOWN, I GUESS I STILL HAD THE TRACE OF A SMILE 'CAUSE,

HUH? WHAT YOU LAUGHIN' AT!

...MISTAH BIG NOSE, BLUE-SKIN POINTY EARS!

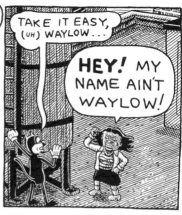

TAKE IT EASY, (UH) WAYLOW...

HEY! MY NAME AIN'T WAYLOW!

THEY JUST CALL ME THAT TO DIS ME 'CAUSE I'M LITTLE.

ALL OF A SUDDEN I HEARD MYSELF SAYING THAT IT WAS TOO BAD, SINCE MY NAME WAS WALDO AND I SORT OF LIKED THE WAY IT SOUNDED WITH WAYLOW.

SHE WAS STILL FROWNING, BUT I HAD THE FEELING THAT I WAS BEGINNING TO INTEREST HER.

AND SHE WAS DEFINITELY GETTING TO ME!

BUT I WAS ALSO A LITTLE WORRIED. I MEAN, WHEN A PERSON CAN SEE ME, IT USUALLY MEANS THEY'RE KIND OF SCREWY!

AND BESIDES, I THOUGHT I WAS BEYOND ALL THAT ROMANCE STUFF.

KNOW WHAT I'M SAYIN'?

Our LOVE BOAT

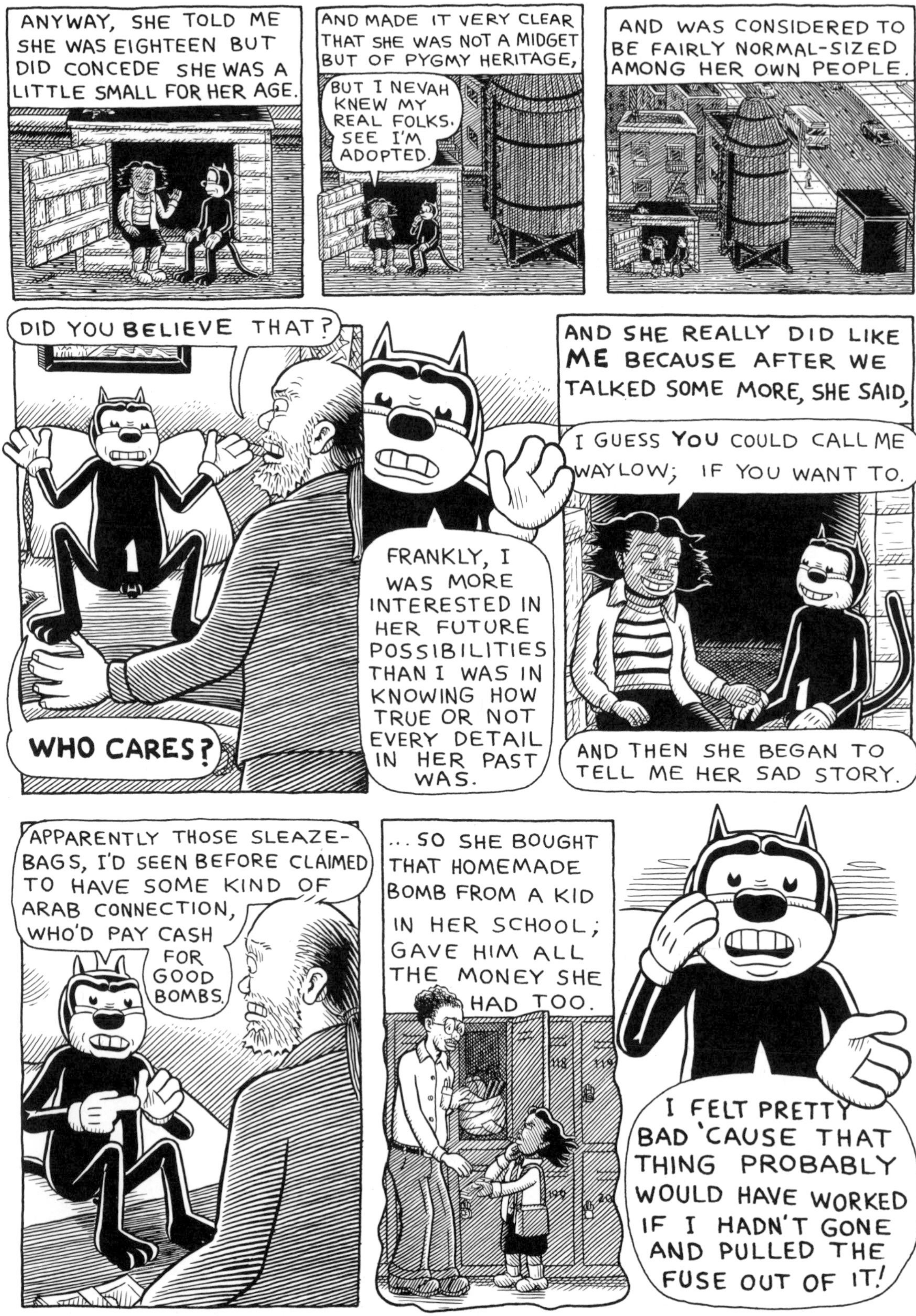
ANYWAY, SHE TOLD ME SHE WAS EIGHTEEN BUT DID CONCEDE SHE WAS A LITTLE SMALL FOR HER AGE.
AND MADE IT VERY CLEAR THAT SHE WAS NOT A MIDGET BUT OF PYGMY HERITAGE,
BUT I NEVAH KNEW MY REAL FOLKS. SEE I'M ADOPTED.
AND WAS CONSIDERED TO BE FAIRLY NORMAL-SIZED AMONG HER OWN PEOPLE.
DID YOU BELIEVE THAT?
WHO CARES?
FRANKLY, I WAS MORE INTERESTED IN HER FUTURE POSSIBILITIES THAN I WAS IN KNOWING HOW TRUE OR NOT EVERY DETAIL IN HER PAST WAS.
AND SHE REALLY DID LIKE ME BECAUSE AFTER WE TALKED SOME MORE, SHE SAID,
I GUESS YOU COULD CALL ME WAYLOW; IF YOU WANT TO.
AND THEN SHE BEGAN TO TELL ME HER SAD STORY.
APPARENTLY THOSE SLEAZE-BAGS, I'D SEEN BEFORE CLAIMED TO HAVE SOME KIND OF ARAB CONNECTION, WHO'D PAY CASH FOR GOOD BOMBS.
...SO SHE BOUGHT THAT HOMEMADE BOMB FROM A KID IN HER SCHOOL; GAVE HIM ALL THE MONEY SHE HAD TOO.
I FELT PRETTY BAD 'CAUSE THAT THING PROBABLY WOULD HAVE WORKED IF I HADN'T GONE AND PULLED THE FUSE OUT OF IT!

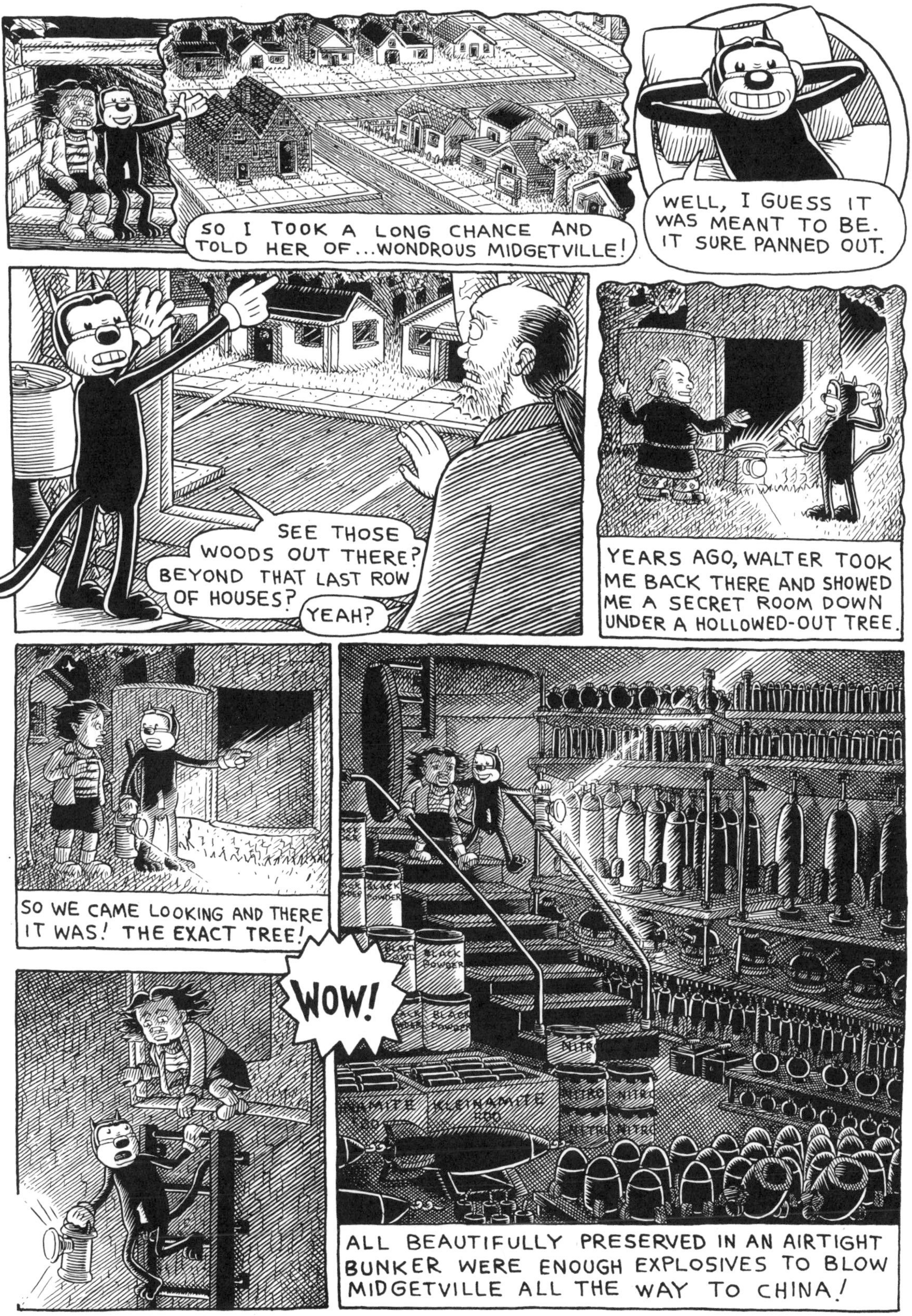
SO I TOOK A LONG CHANCE AND TOLD HER OF...WONDROUS MIDGETVILLE!
WELL, I GUESS IT WAS MEANT TO BE. IT SURE PANNED OUT.
SEE THOSE WOODS OUT THERE? BEYOND THAT LAST ROW OF HOUSES?
YEAH?
YEARS AGO, WALTER TOOK ME BACK THERE AND SHOWED ME A SECRET ROOM DOWN UNDER A HOLLOWED-OUT TREE.
SO WE CAME LOOKING AND THERE IT WAS! THE EXACT TREE!
WOW!
ALL BEAUTIFULLY PRESERVED IN AN AIRTIGHT BUNKER WERE ENOUGH EXPLOSIVES TO BLOW MIDGETVILLE ALL THE WAY TO CHINA!

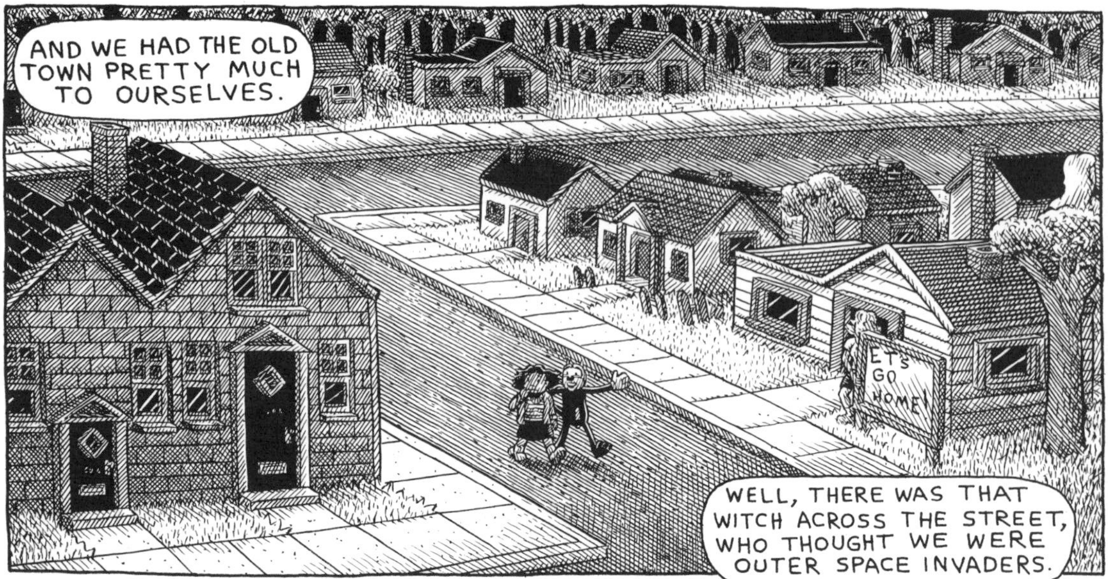
AND WE HAD THE OLD TOWN PRETTY MUCH TO OURSELVES.
ET'S GO HOME!
WELL, THERE WAS THAT WITCH ACROSS THE STREET, WHO THOUGHT WE WERE OUTER SPACE INVADERS.

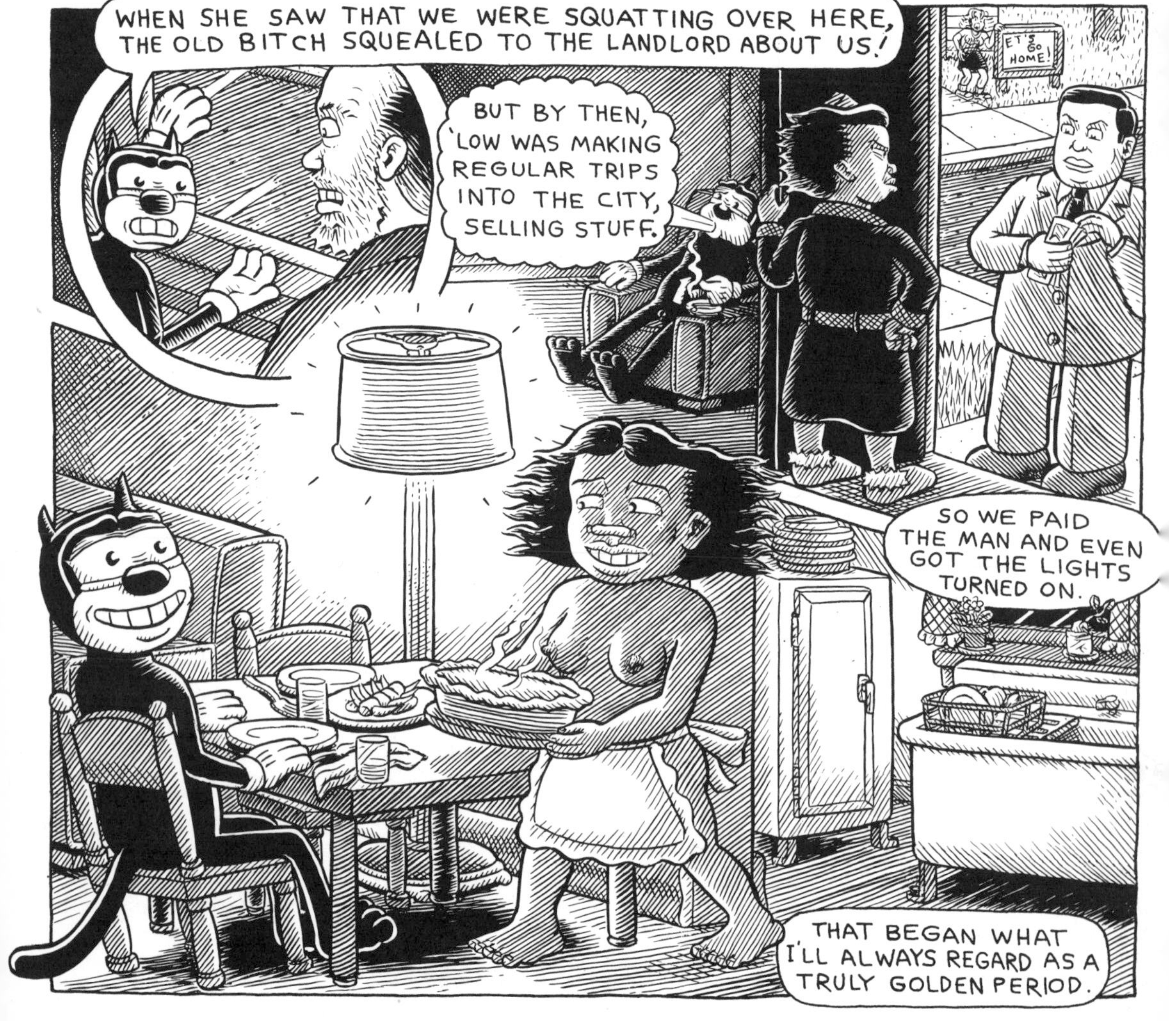
WHEN SHE SAW THAT WE WERE SQUATTING OVER HERE, THE OLD BITCH SQUEALED TO THE LANDLORD ABOUT US!
ET'S GO HOME!
BUT BY THEN, 'LOW WAS MAKING REGULAR TRIPS INTO THE CITY, SELLING STUFF.
SO WE PAID THE MAN AND EVEN GOT THE LIGHTS TURNED ON.
THAT BEGAN WHAT I'LL ALWAYS REGARD AS A TRULY GOLDEN PERIOD.

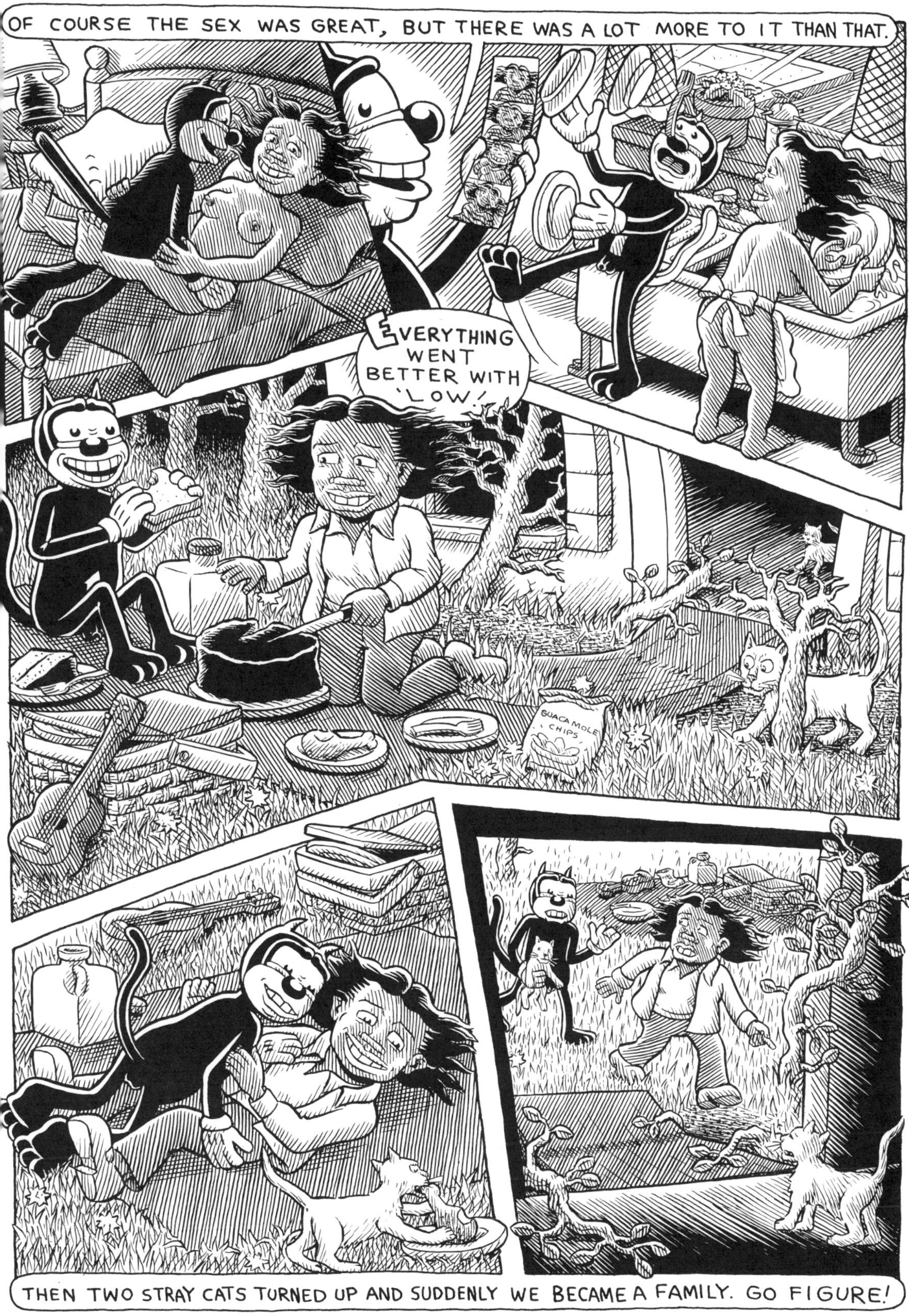
OF COURSE THE SEX WAS GREAT, BUT THERE WAS A LOT MORE TO IT THAN THAT.
EVERYTHING WENT BETTER WITH 'LOW!
GUACAMOLE CHIPS
THEN TWO STRAY CATS TURNED UP AND SUDDENLY WE BECAME A FAMILY. GO FIGURE!

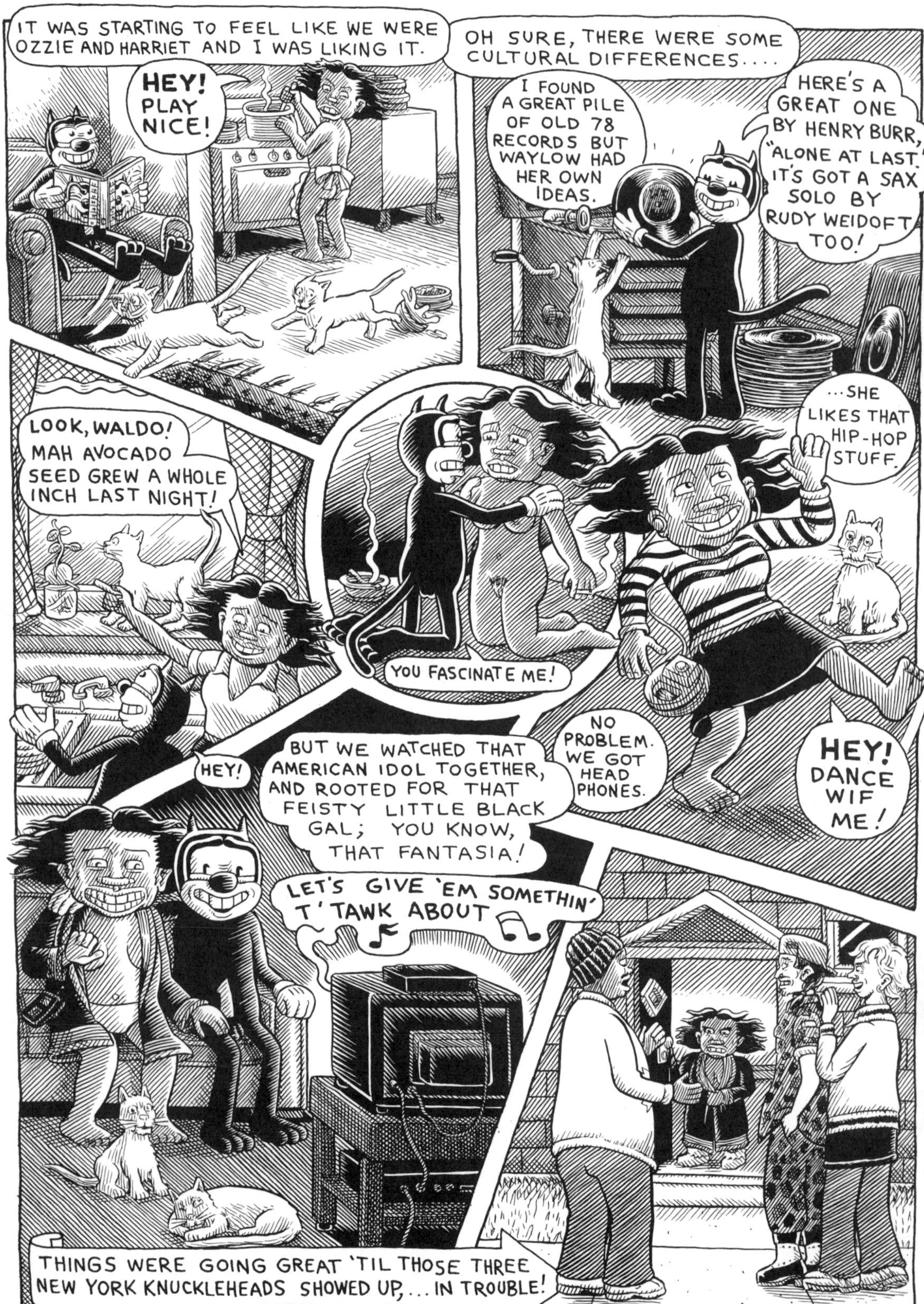
IT WAS STARTING TO FEEL LIKE WE WERE OZZIE AND HARRIET AND I WAS LIKING IT.
HEY! PLAY NICE!
OH SURE, THERE WERE SOME CULTURAL DIFFERENCES....
I FOUND A GREAT PILE OF OLD 78 RECORDS BUT WAYLOW HAD HER OWN IDEAS.
HERE'S A GREAT ONE BY HENRY BURR, "ALONE AT LAST." IT'S GOT A SAX SOLO BY RUDY WEIDOFT TOO!
LOOK, WALDO! MAH AVOCADO SEED GREW A WHOLE INCH LAST NIGHT!
YOU FASCINATE ME!
...SHE LIKES THAT HIP-HOP STUFF.
HEY!
BUT WE WATCHED THAT AMERICAN IDOL TOGETHER, AND ROOTED FOR THAT FEISTY LITTLE BLACK GAL; YOU KNOW, THAT FANTASIA!
NO PROBLEM. WE GOT HEAD PHONES.
HEY! DANCE WIF ME!
LET'S GIVE 'EM SOMETHIN' T' TAWK ABOUT
THINGS WERE GOING GREAT 'TIL THOSE THREE NEW YORK KNUCKLEHEADS SHOWED UP, ... IN TROUBLE!

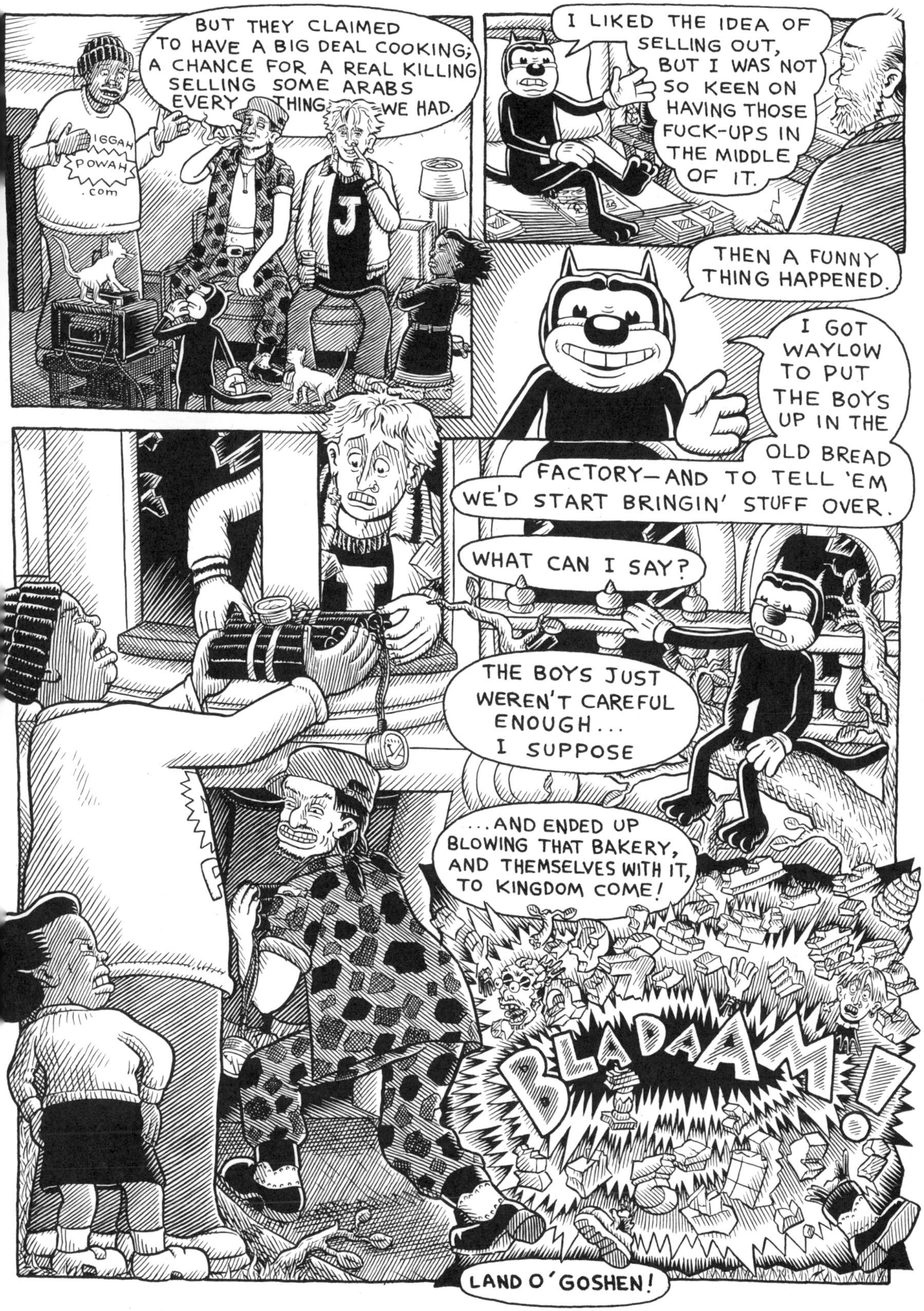
BUT THEY CLAIMED TO HAVE A BIG DEAL COOKING; A CHANCE FOR A REAL KILLING SELLING SOME ARABS EVERYTHING WE HAD.
NIGGAH POWAH .com
J
I LIKED THE IDEA OF SELLING OUT, BUT I WAS NOT SO KEEN ON HAVING THOSE FUCK-UPS IN THE MIDDLE OF IT.
THEN A FUNNY THING HAPPENED.
I GOT WAYLOW TO PUT THE BOYS UP IN THE OLD BREAD FACTORY—AND TO TELL 'EM WE'D START BRINGIN' STUFF OVER.
WHAT CAN I SAY?
THE BOYS JUST WEREN'T CAREFUL ENOUGH... I SUPPOSE
...AND ENDED UP BLOWING THAT BAKERY, AND THEMSELVES WITH IT, TO KINGDOM COME!
BLADAAM!
LAND O'GOSHEN!

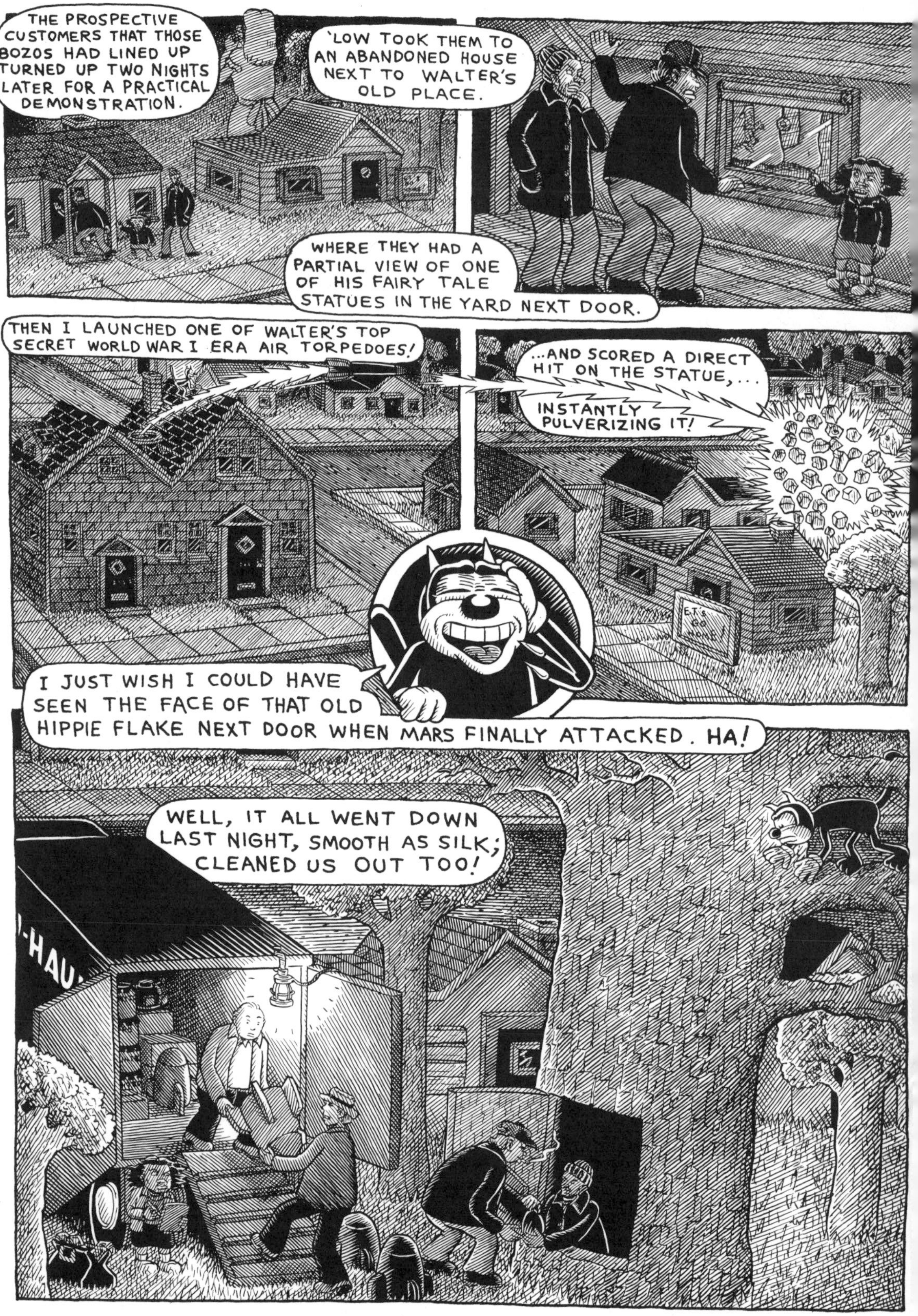
THE PROSPECTIVE CUSTOMERS THAT THOSE BOZOS HAD LINED UP TURNED UP TWO NIGHTS LATER FOR A PRACTICAL DEMONSTRATION.
`LOW TOOK THEM TO AN ABANDONED HOUSE NEXT TO WALTER'S OLD PLACE.
WHERE THEY HAD A PARTIAL VIEW OF ONE OF HIS FAIRY TALE STATUES IN THE YARD NEXT DOOR.
THEN I LAUNCHED ONE OF WALTER'S TOP SECRET WORLD WAR I ERA AIR TORPEDOES!
...AND SCORED A DIRECT HIT ON THE STATUE,...
INSTANTLY PULVERIZING IT!
I JUST WISH I COULD HAVE SEEN THE FACE OF THAT OLD HIPPIE FLAKE NEXT DOOR WHEN MARS FINALLY ATTACKED. HA!
WELL, IT ALL WENT DOWN LAST NIGHT, SMOOTH AS SILK; CLEANED US OUT TOO!

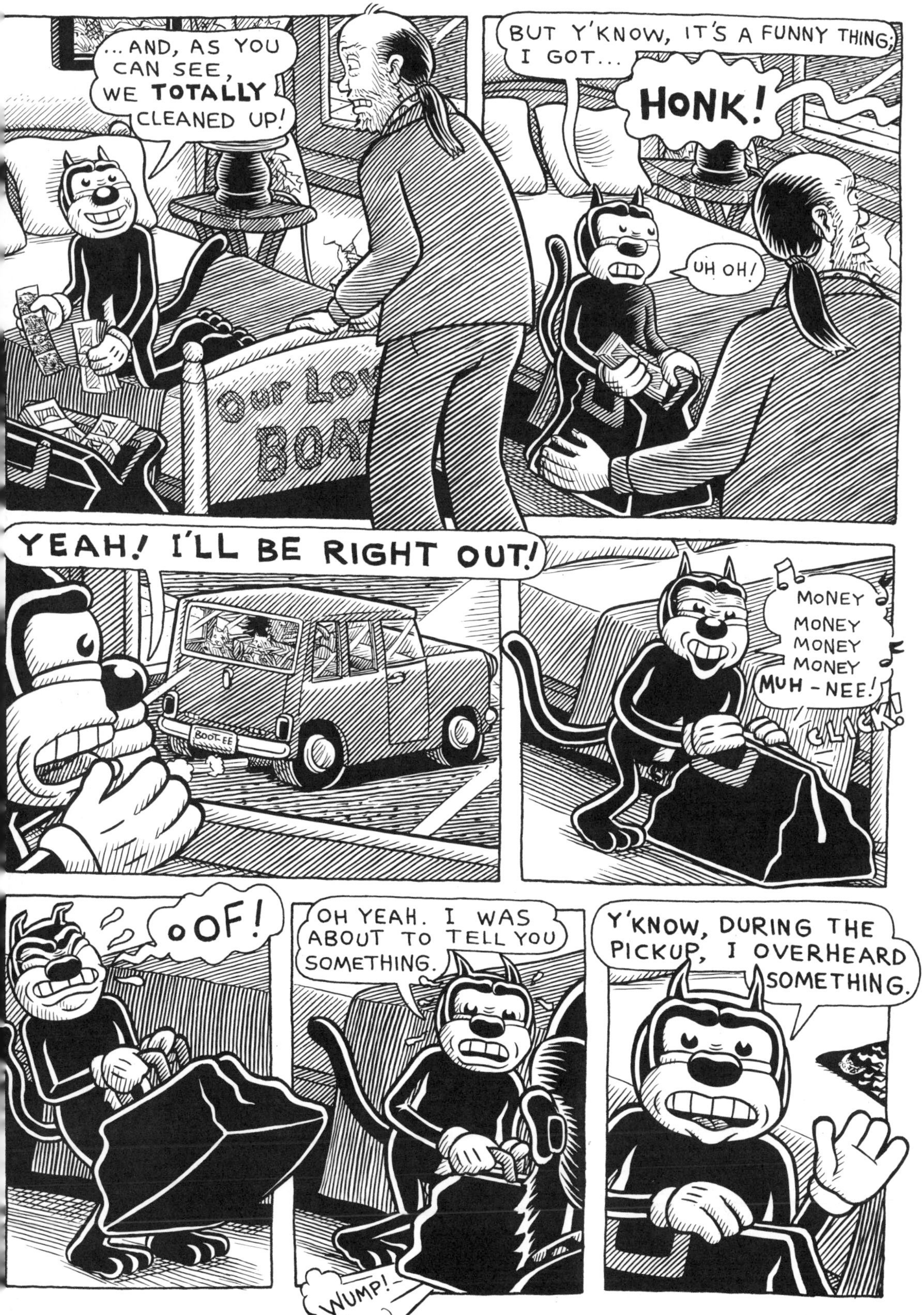
...AND, AS YOU CAN SEE, WE TOTALLY CLEANED UP!
Our Lov BOAT
BUT Y'KNOW, IT'S A FUNNY THING; I GOT...
HONK!
UH OH!
YEAH! I'LL BE RIGHT OUT!
BOOT-EE
MONEY MONEY MONEY MONEY MUH-NEE!
CLICK!
oOF!
OH YEAH. I WAS ABOUT TO TELL YOU SOMETHING.
WUMP!
Y'KNOW, DURING THE PICKUP, I OVERHEARD SOMETHING.

I GUESS WHAT I'M SAYING IS, YOU MIGHT WANT TO GIVE SOME THOUGHT TO CLEARING OUT.

DON'T WORRY, I'VE HAD MY FILL OF MIDGETVILLE!

WELL, THAT'S A GOOD IDEA TOO,

BUT I WAS ACTUALLY THINKING MORE ALONG THE LINES OF NEW YORK CITY.

SEE, AT ONE POINT, WHILE WAYLOW WAS MAKING SURE THAT SCREWBALL IN WALTER'S OLD HOUSE, WAS MINDING HER OWN BEESWAX, I HEARD THOSE BOYS TALKING AMONG THEMSELVES.

I HEARD THEM SAY THEY WERE GONNA BLOW A HOLE, IN NEW YORK SOMEWHERE, A MILE WIDE AND A MILE DEEP, AT TWELVE NOON, IN EXACTLY THIRTY-ONE DAYS! AND HERE'S SOMETHING ELSE TO CHAW ON: THOSE BOYS DIDN'T LOOK LIKE **NO** ARABS!

THEY WERE TALKIN' PLAIN AMERICAN! AND WHAT'S MORE, I'M PRETTY DAMN SURE I RECOGNIZED ONE OF 'EM!

N.Y. POST

BUSH JR NIXES GAY NUPTIALS

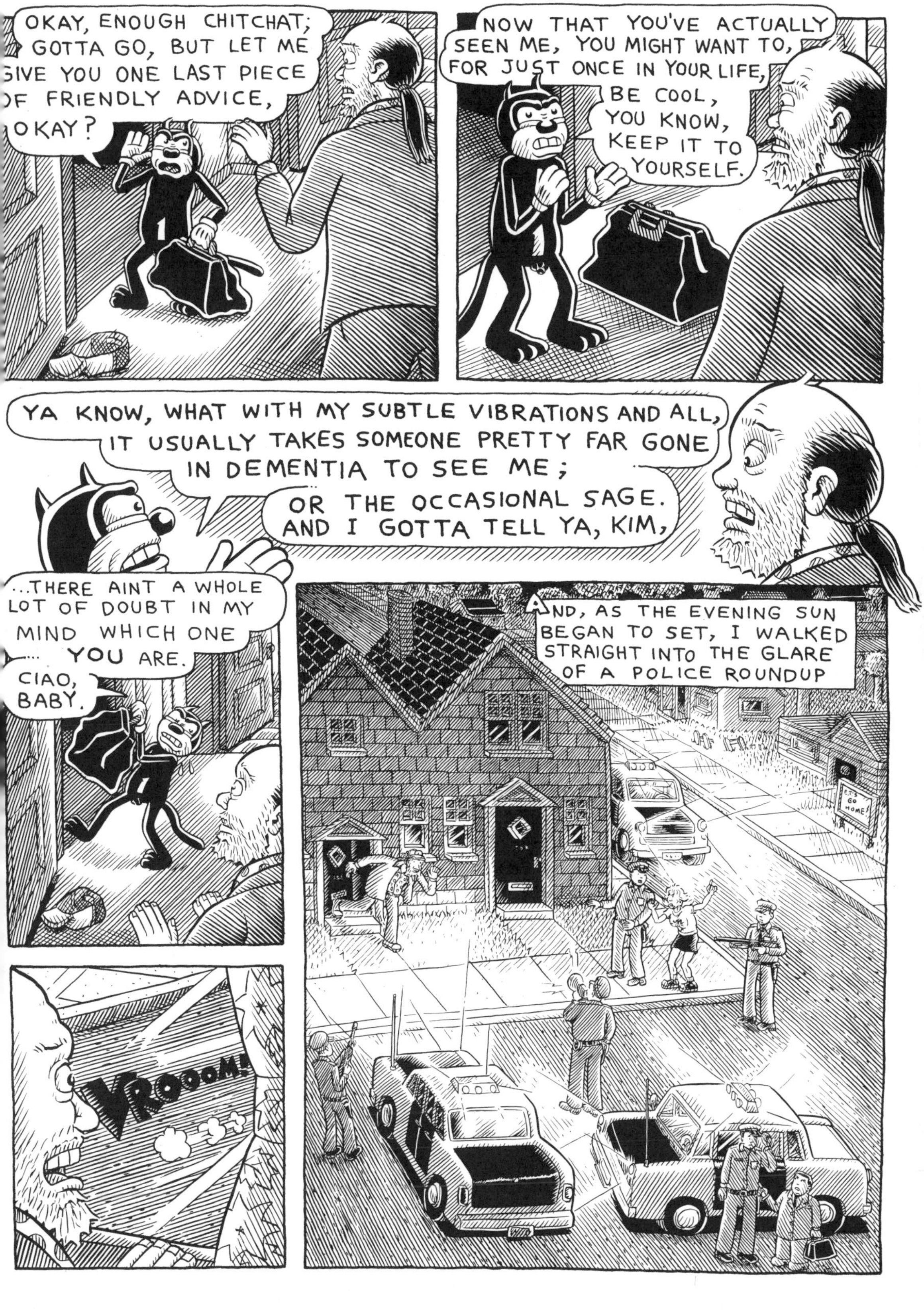
OKAY, ENOUGH CHITCHAT; GOTTA GO, BUT LET ME GIVE YOU ONE LAST PIECE OF FRIENDLY ADVICE, OKAY?
NOW THAT YOU'VE ACTUALLY SEEN ME, YOU MIGHT WANT TO, FOR JUST ONCE IN YOUR LIFE,
BE COOL, YOU KNOW, KEEP IT TO YOURSELF.
YA KNOW, WHAT WITH MY SUBTLE VIBRATIONS AND ALL, IT USUALLY TAKES SOMEONE PRETTY FAR GONE IN DEMENTIA TO SEE ME;
OR THE OCCASIONAL SAGE. AND I GOTTA TELL YA, KIM,
...THERE AINT A WHOLE LOT OF DOUBT IN MY MIND WHICH ONE YOU ARE.
CIAO, BABY.
VROOOM!
AND, AS THE EVENING SUN BEGAN TO SET, I WALKED STRAIGHT INTO THE GLARE OF A POLICE ROUNDUP

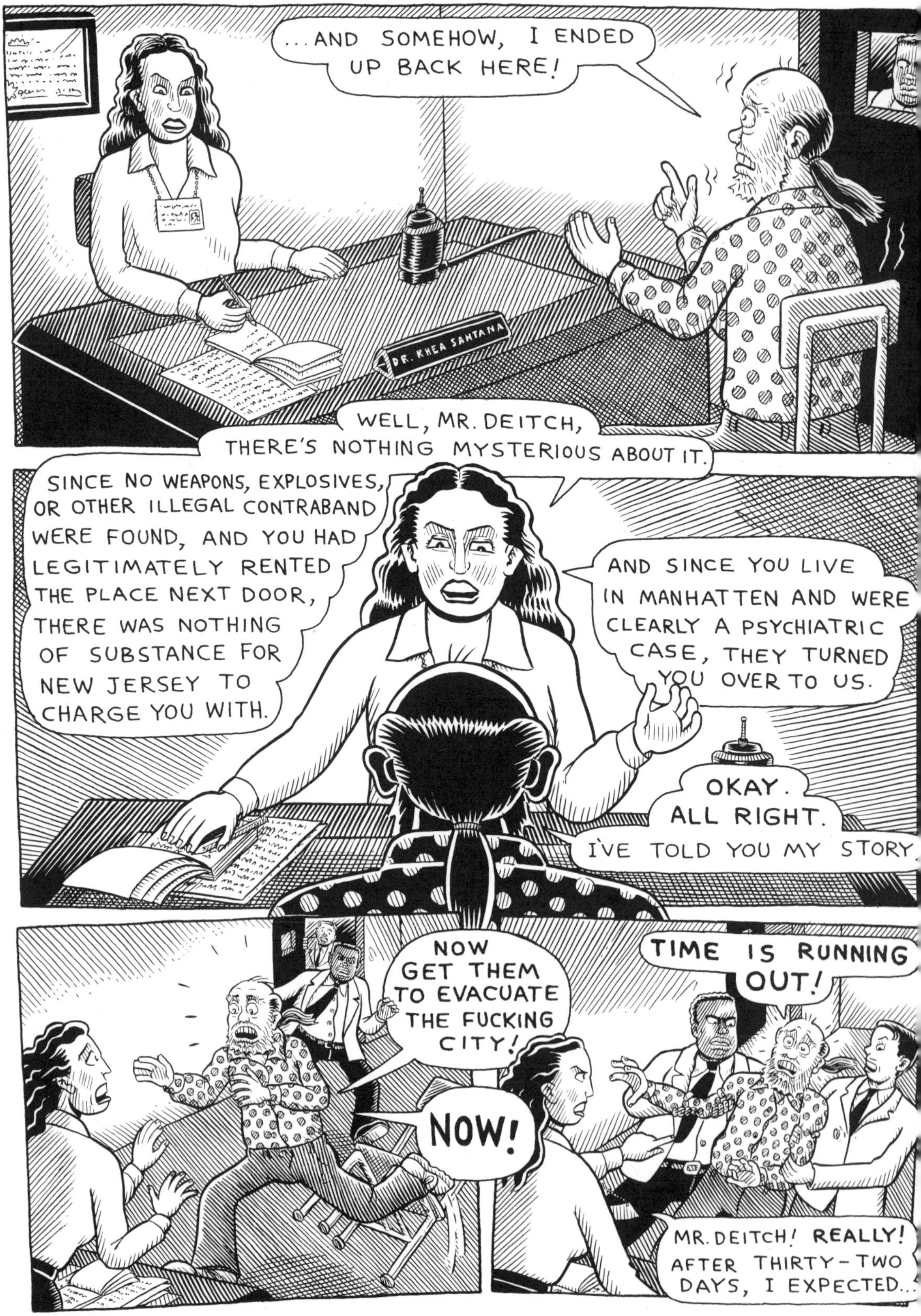

...AND SOMEHOW, I ENDED UP BACK HERE!
DR. RHEA SANTANA
WELL, MR. DEITCH, THERE'S NOTHING MYSTERIOUS ABOUT IT.
SINCE NO WEAPONS, EXPLOSIVES, OR OTHER ILLEGAL CONTRABAND WERE FOUND, AND YOU HAD LEGITIMATELY RENTED THE PLACE NEXT DOOR, THERE WAS NOTHING OF SUBSTANCE FOR NEW JERSEY TO CHARGE YOU WITH.
AND SINCE YOU LIVE IN MANHATTEN AND WERE CLEARLY A PSYCHIATRIC CASE, THEY TURNED YOU OVER TO US.
OKAY. ALL RIGHT. I'VE TOLD YOU MY STORY.
NOW GET THEM TO EVACUATE THE FUCKING CITY!
TIME IS RUNNING OUT!
NOW!
MR. DEITCH! **REALLY!** AFTER THIRTY-TWO DAYS, I EXPECTED...

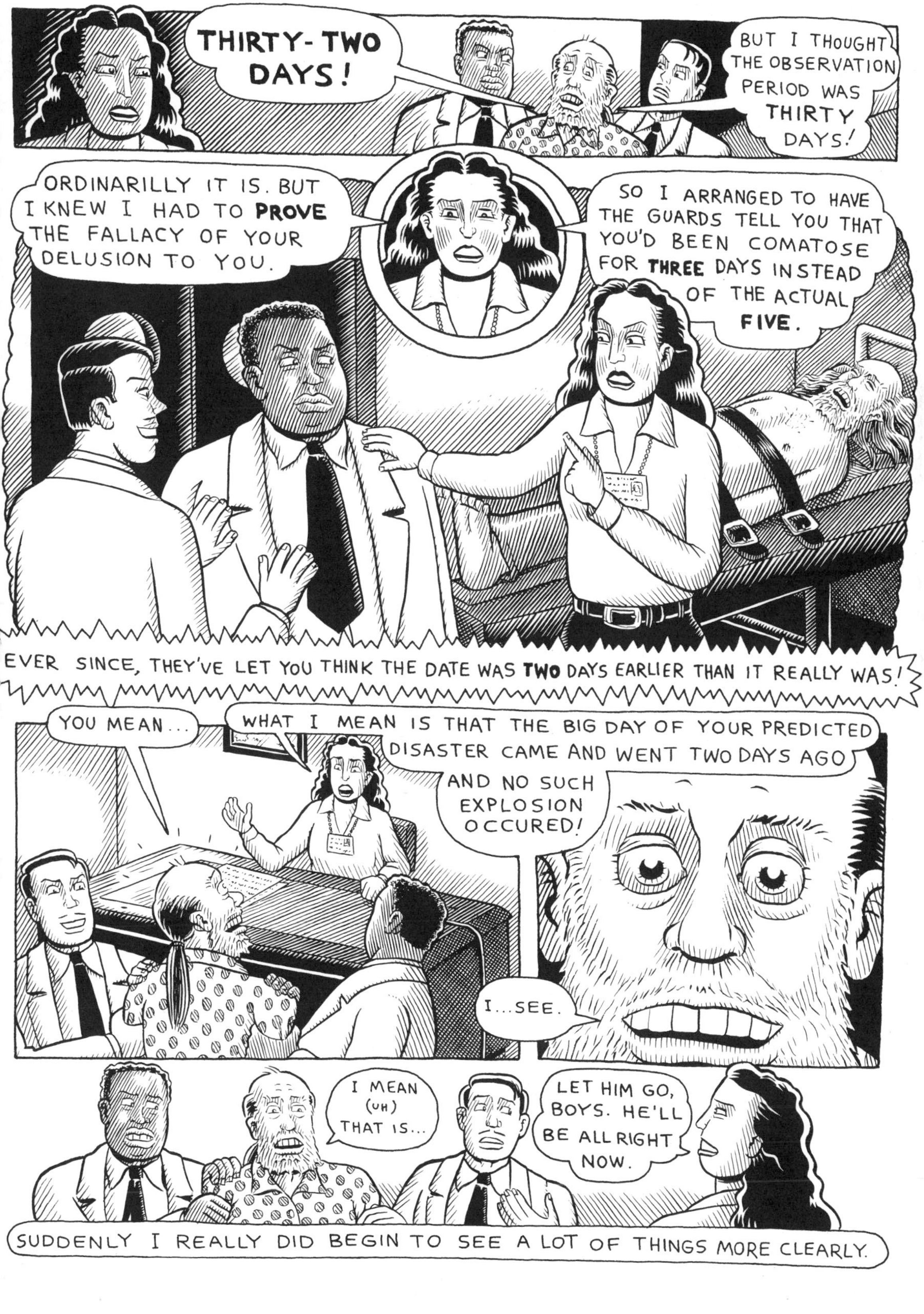
THIRTY-TWO DAYS!
BUT I THOUGHT THE OBSERVATION PERIOD WAS THIRTY DAYS!
ORDINARILLY IT IS. BUT I KNEW I HAD TO PROVE THE FALLACY OF YOUR DELUSION TO YOU.
SO I ARRANGED TO HAVE THE GUARDS TELL YOU THAT YOU'D BEEN COMATOSE FOR THREE DAYS INSTEAD OF THE ACTUAL FIVE.
EVER SINCE, THEY'VE LET YOU THINK THE DATE WAS TWO DAYS EARLIER THAN IT REALLY WAS!
YOU MEAN...
WHAT I MEAN IS THAT THE BIG DAY OF YOUR PREDICTED DISASTER CAME AND WENT TWO DAYS AGO
AND NO SUCH EXPLOSION OCCURED!
I...SEE.
I MEAN (UH) THAT IS...
LET HIM GO, BOYS. HE'LL BE ALL RIGHT NOW.
SUDDENLY I REALLY DID BEGIN TO SEE A LOT OF THINGS MORE CLEARLY.

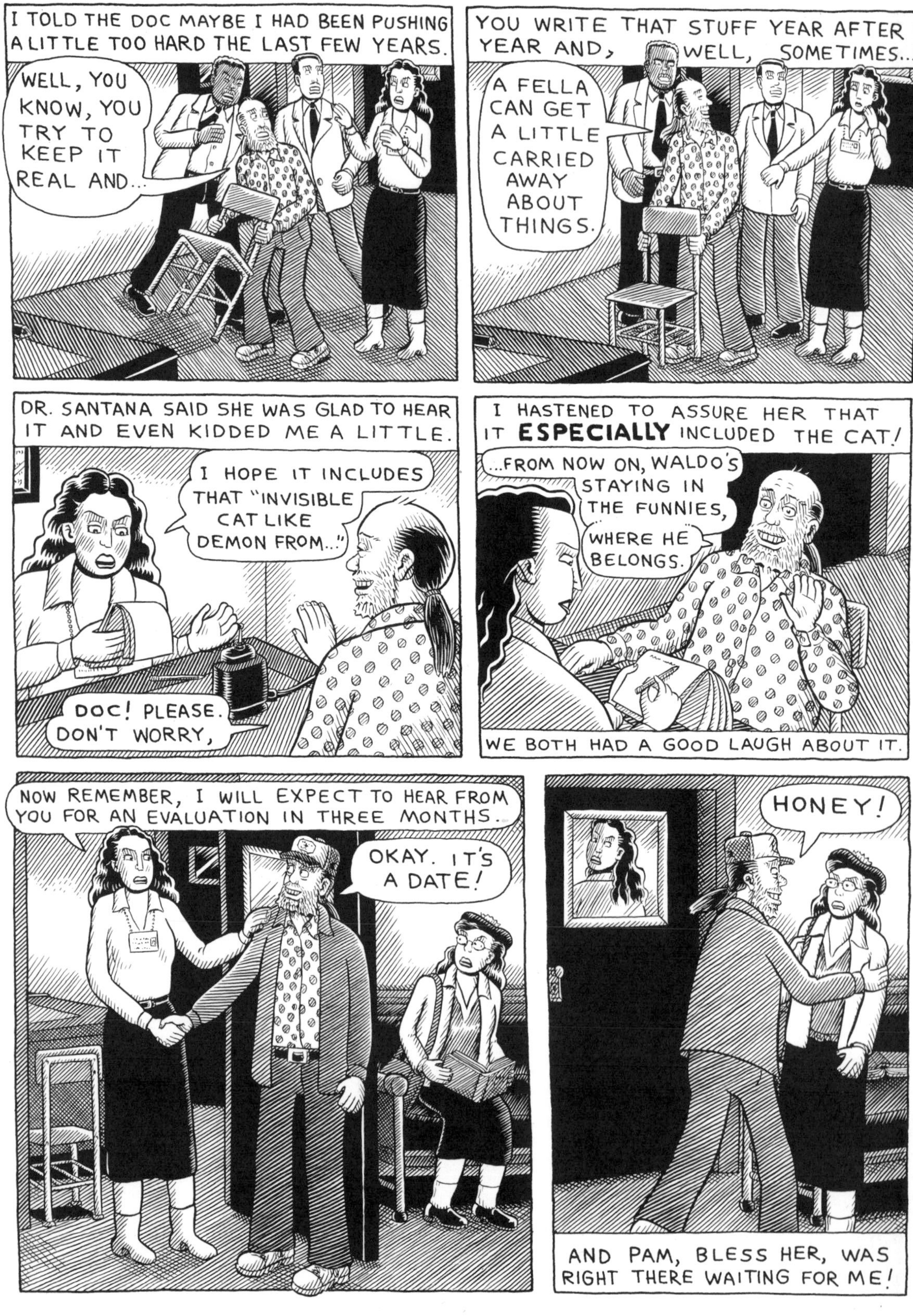
I TOLD THE DOC MAYBE I HAD BEEN PUSHING A LITTLE TOO HARD THE LAST FEW YEARS.
WELL, YOU KNOW, YOU TRY TO KEEP IT REAL AND...
YOU WRITE THAT STUFF YEAR AFTER YEAR AND, WELL, SOMETIMES...
A FELLA CAN GET A LITTLE CARRIED AWAY ABOUT THINGS.
DR. SANTANA SAID SHE WAS GLAD TO HEAR IT AND EVEN KIDDED ME A LITTLE.
I HOPE IT INCLUDES THAT "INVISIBLE CAT LIKE DEMON FROM..."
DOC! PLEASE. DON'T WORRY,
I HASTENED TO ASSURE HER THAT IT **ESPECIALLY** INCLUDED THE CAT!
...FROM NOW ON, WALDO'S STAYING IN THE FUNNIES,
WHERE HE BELONGS.
WE BOTH HAD A GOOD LAUGH ABOUT IT.
NOW REMEMBER, I WILL EXPECT TO HEAR FROM YOU FOR AN EVALUATION IN THREE MONTHS.
OKAY. IT'S A DATE!
HONEY!
AND PAM, BLESS HER, WAS RIGHT THERE WAITING FOR ME!

ON THE WAY HOME, SHE HANDED ME MY THIRTY-TWO-DAY ACCUMULATION OF MAIL,

...MOSTLY BILLS AND ADS, ... NEW COMICS JOURNAL; NO CHECKS.

BUT AT THE BOTTOM OF THE PILE WAS A BEAT-UP MANILA ENVELOPE WITH NO RETURN ADDRESS.

INSIDE WAS A THREE-AND-A-HALF-WEEK-OLD STORY CLIPPED FROM A MONTANA NEWSPAPER!

KIM DIETCH
445 E 86 (16D)
NYC/NY
10027̸8

April 5, 2004 MONTANA DAILY COURIER LATE CITY ED

MASSIVE EXPLOSION CREATES NEW TOXIC LAKE

Butte, April 5 - Butte, Montana's biggest tourist attraction, its famous lake of toxic waste, got some stiff competition yesterday, when Police pursuit of a truck containing an illegal cache of explosives resulted in a massive explosion just beyond Butte city limits.

The mile-wide explosion, which left no trace of the truck, or its pursuing Police vehicle, began quickly filling with toxic liquid residue from several nearby abandoned strip mines.

An I.D. check of the rented truck showed its driver to be Edward Keller, a former merchant seaman who may

Above. Newest lake of toxic waste outside of Butte. Left. Keller.

...AND A NOTE!

have had connection outlaw survivalist active in outlying areas of arab connne toxic guide area expe Polic

I GUESS THOSE FUCK-UPS WON'T BE GETTING TO NEW YORK AFTER ALL. GOOD THING WE GOT ALL THE MONEY UP FRONT! P.S. FORGET ME IF YOU CAN. HA!

1002̸

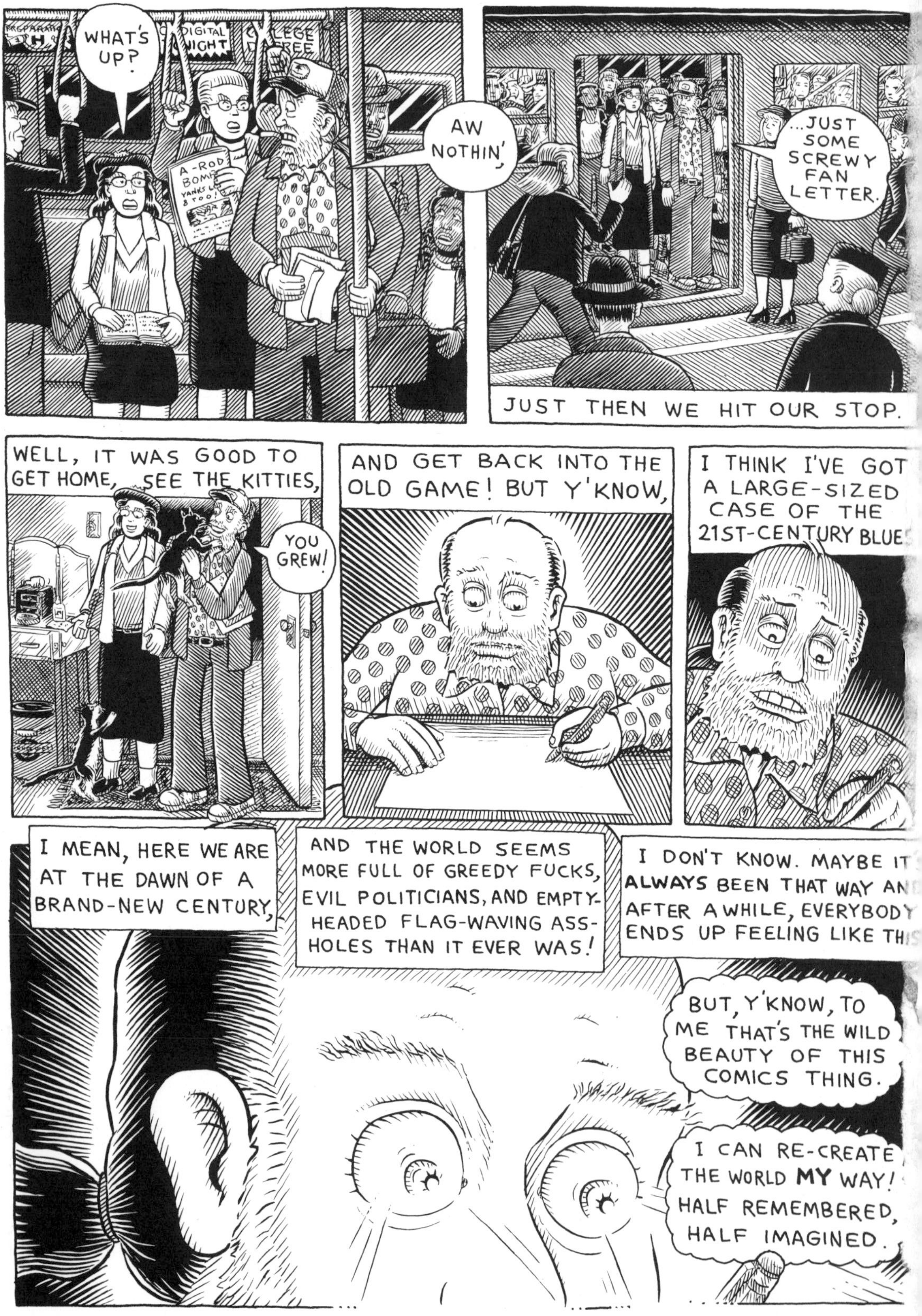
WHAT'S UP?
AW NOTHIN'
...JUST SOME SCREWY FAN LETTER.
JUST THEN WE HIT OUR STOP.
WELL, IT WAS GOOD TO GET HOME, SEE THE KITTIES,
YOU GREW!
AND GET BACK INTO THE OLD GAME! BUT Y'KNOW,
I THINK I'VE GOT A LARGE-SIZED CASE OF THE 21ST-CENTURY BLUES
I MEAN, HERE WE ARE AT THE DAWN OF A BRAND-NEW CENTURY,
AND THE WORLD SEEMS MORE FULL OF GREEDY FUCKS, EVIL POLITICIANS, AND EMPTY-HEADED FLAG-WAVING ASS-HOLES THAN IT EVER WAS!
I DON'T KNOW. MAYBE IT'S ALWAYS BEEN THAT WAY AND AFTER A WHILE, EVERYBODY ENDS UP FEELING LIKE THIS
BUT, Y'KNOW, TO ME THAT'S THE WILD BEAUTY OF THIS COMICS THING.
I CAN RE-CREATE THE WORLD MY WAY! HALF REMEMBERED, HALF IMAGINED.
...

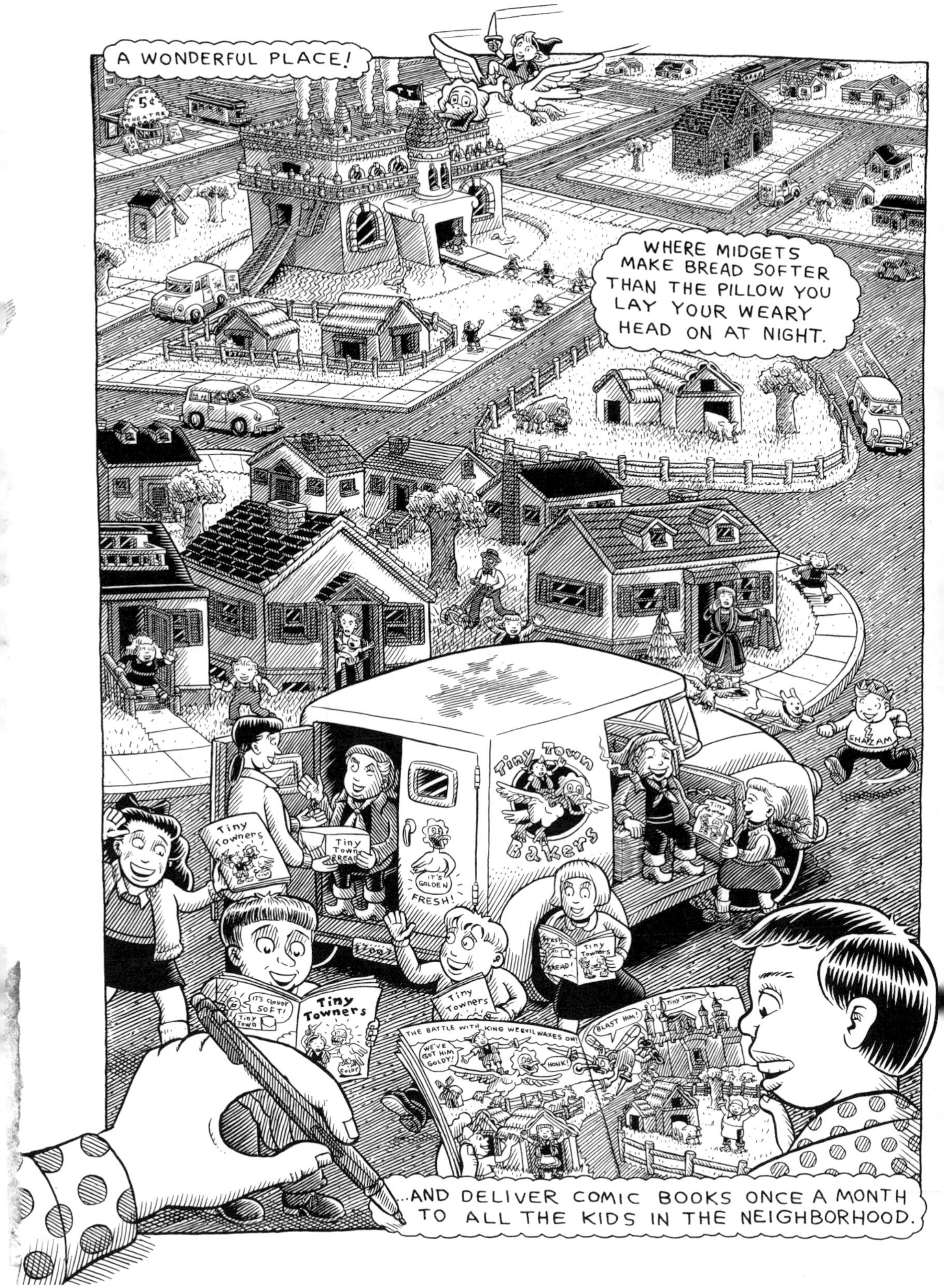
A WONDERFUL PLACE!
5¢ THEATRE
WHERE MIDGETS MAKE BREAD SOFTER THAN THE PILLOW YOU LAY YOUR WEARY HEAD ON AT NIGHT.
Tiny Town Bakers
IT'S GOLDEN FRESH!
SHAZAM
Tiny Towners
Tiny Town BREAD
FRESH BREAD!
IT'S CLOUDY SOFT!
THE BATTLE WITH KING WEEVIL WAXES ON!
WE'VE GOT HIM GOLDY!
HONK!
BLAST HIM!
...AND DELIVER COMIC BOOKS ONCE A MONTH TO ALL THE KIDS IN THE NEIGHBORHOOD.

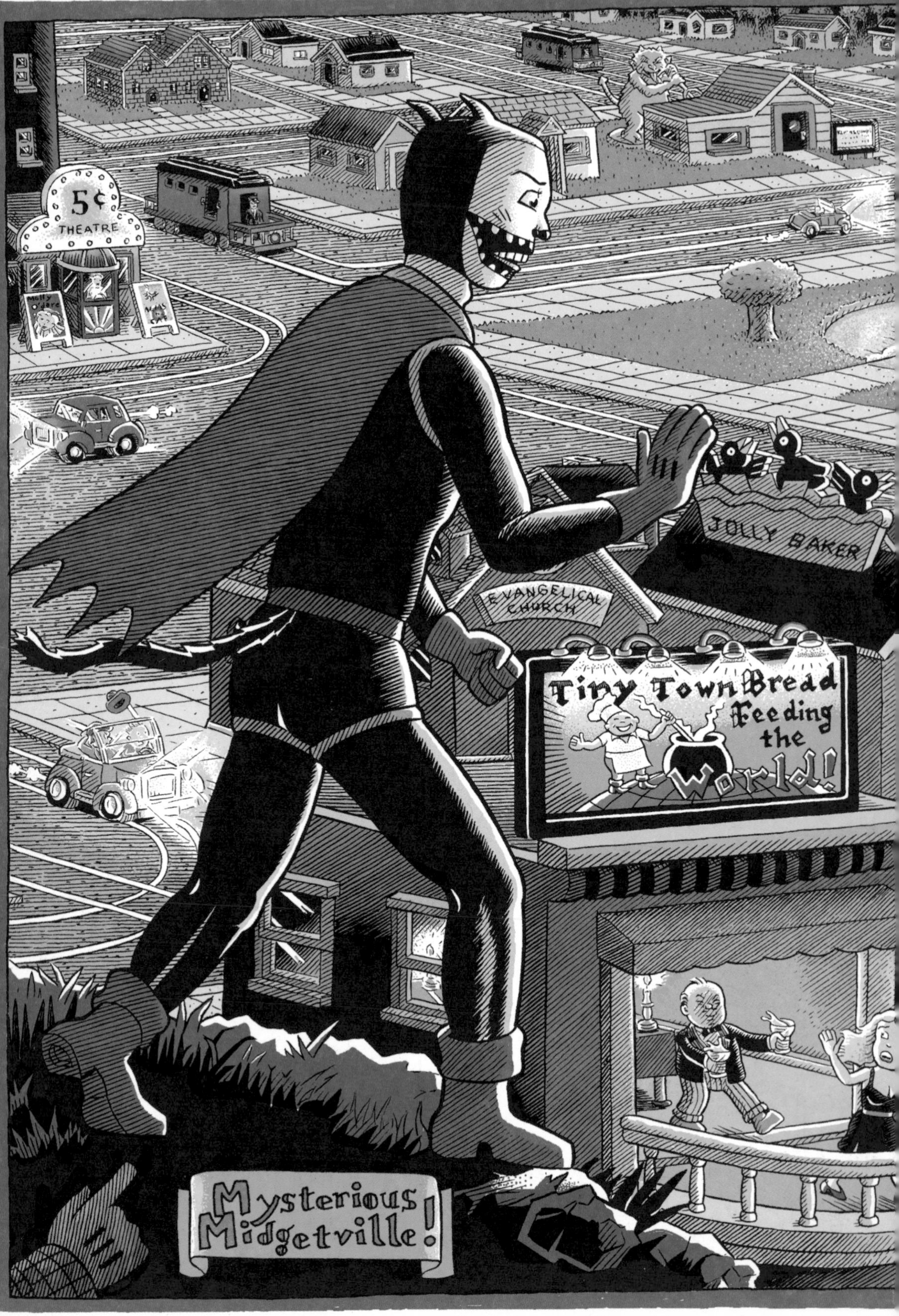
5¢
THEATRE
JOLLY BAKER
EVANGELICAL CHURCH
Tiny Town Bread
Feeding the World!
Mysterious Midgetville!